IN THE MIRROR

LISE GOLD
MADELEINE TAYLOR

Edited by Debbie McGowan

Cover design by Lise Gold Books

Seek to be whole, not perfect.

— Oprah

1

FAITH

Wincing against the morning light, I turn on my side and cover my face with a pillow. It's the intercom, and whoever is at the door just won't give up. A delivery guy, maybe? That's unlikely on New Year's Day. Anything can wait; my head hurts and I feel nauseous. Squeezing my eyes tight shut, I try to ignore the noise, but the buzzer is too loud. Desperate to make it stop, I stumble out of bed and head for the hallway, cursing under my breath as I see a woman on the screen with a smile way too chirpy for this time of the day. She's wearing a beanie and she's carrying a gym bag over her shoulder.

"Who is this? Do you have any idea what time it is? I'm trying to sleep."

"Miss Astor? It's Silva. We have an appointment at eight." The woman frowns when I don't answer, wracking my brain over who she could be. "Personal training?"

"Oh, fuck." It all comes back to me then. The party, the afterparty, champagne, more champagne, dancing, drunk conversations with my friend Roy about how we'd like to get in shape and look fabulous in the new year and booking a

PT at an extortionate last-minute price to kickstart 2022 with a "bang," as it said on the website. They're only vague flashes, but I remember last night's mantra clearly. *Everything will be better next year.* "Sorry, I forgot. It was a mistake." I hesitate, then continue in a croaky voice, "I assume it's too late to cancel?"

Silva shrugs. "Yes, it's too late for a refund. Can I at least come in for a minute? It's kind of cold out here."

"Sorry, of course." In my groggy state, I barely registered it was still snowing hard, so I buzz her in and fetch my robe. I barely have the chance to tie it before she's made it upstairs and knocks on the door.

"Good morning and a happy new year," she says, her beaming smile almost making me laugh. She's the epitome of health, her cheeks rosy and her eyes sparkling with energy. The opposite of me, I suspect, although I haven't looked in the mirror yet, and I have no intention to do so.

"Yes, good morning and the same to you." I clear my throat and take a step back to let her in. "Please call me Faith. Would you like a coffee?"

"Yes, please. And why don't you make yourself one too?" She takes off her beanie and her coat and hangs them on one of the wall hooks by the door.

"I think I'll hold off on the coffee. I intend to go back to bed," I say, hoping she'll get the hint. She's welcome to warm up; it's my fault that she came all the way out here for nothing, but then again, I've already paid her, so if I want to sleep in her time, that's my prerogative.

Silva shakes her head and ruffles a hand through her shaggy, blonde hair. "Hey, let's not start off like this. You wanted to feel good about yourself again, so why not get the ball rolling right now? You've got me for three whole hours, so it's not too late to wake up and kickstart the new year with a fresh and positive mindset."

"Feel good about myself?" I walk to the kitchen, and she follows me and drops her bag on the floor.

"Yes, you filled in the questionnaire on my website. It said you wanted to feel good about yourself." Silva hesitates and arches a brow at me. "Actually, your exact words were that you longed to feel desired again."

"Oh." I chuckle uncomfortably and blush. "That was drunk me talking. Drunk Faith tends to say dumb things sometimes. I feel just fine about myself." Focusing on the coffeemaker, I avoid her gaze. I wonder what she thinks of me. "Milk?"

"No, thank you, I like it black." Silva takes a seat at my kitchen table, and as I fill two cups and add a shot of soy milk to mine, I feel her eyes on me. She's judging me, for sure. *Silly, impulsive woman. No self-control and no respect for her body.* Isn't that what all health freaks think about people who like to have fun? Looking down at the two mugs, I realize I've done exactly the opposite of what I intended. I've made myself a coffee and I'm about to sit down and talk to her.

"So, how much did I pay for your visit?" I ask, reaching for the box of aspirin in the fruit bowl. I pop out two pills and wince as I swallow them with the hot coffee. "And how on earth did I manage to get an appointment on January first?"

"You paid five hundred dollars," Silva says as if it's nothing. "Purely because of the date. I'm normally only a hundred an hour."

"Only..."

"It's a small price to pay for feeling great," she says,

glancing around my modern, open-plan apartment as she sips her coffee, undoubtedly thinking I can easily afford it.

She's not wrong; I can afford it, but whether I want to work out or not is up to me, not her.

"And to answer your second question," she continues, not in the least fazed by my look of offense, "the reason I had a free spot is the same reason you're about to send me away. Someone got drunk and canceled late last night, giving up before they'd even started."

"And that was not refundable either, I assume?"

"No. I have a forty-eight-hour cancellation policy."

"Right." I nod and rub my temple. The throbbing has started now, and it's radiating toward my eye sockets. "So you've just made a thousand dollars? Smart."

Silva sits back and crosses her arms. "Hey, don't insult me. You're making it sound like this is some sort of scam, but I'm actually not doing it for the money. It's not my fault someone canceled, and it's not my fault you booked me while you were drunk."

"I'm sorry, that came out wrong. I don't think you're a scammer." I let out a long sigh and shoot her an apologetic look. "I'm sorry."

"It's fine." She leans in to look me in the eyes. "I like helping people and you need help, so please give it a try. Let's at least talk about what you want to achieve. I see you're in no state to start the heavy work right away, but we can make a plan together."

I'm quiet as I consider this. I'm not awake enough to make a decision, so I leave it with her. What's the worst thing that can happen? It's only three hours, and when she leaves, I'll go back to bed where I'll spend the rest of my day watching Netflix. "Okay."

"Great." Silva points to my robe. "Before we start, take

ten minutes for a shower while I make you a smoothie. I promise it will make you feel a little better. Now, do you have any fruit or vegetables in the house?"

"I may have some," I say, my eyes flicking from the sad selection of wilted fruits in the bowl to the fridge, then to the juicer I've never used, and back. I quickly get up and open it just far enough to check the contents without giving her a view of the vodka bottles. It annoys me that we haven't even had a conversation and I feel judged already. Relieved to find half a bag of spinach and two avocados, I place them on the kitchen counter. At least the kitchen is tidy, apart from the empty champagne bottle Roy and I polished off before we went out last night. The living room, on the other hand, is littered with clothes, as I couldn't decide what to wear, and I cringe as I spot a pile of lingerie on my sofa. "Will this do?" I ask, gesturing to the greens.

"That's perfect." Silva gets up and pats me on the arm. "Leave it with me."

"Okay, I guess I'll go and have a shower." Her bouncy energy is annoying me already, but maybe this isn't such a bad idea after all. I really do want to get in shape, and it's not like I've made plans for today.

2

SILVA

I look away and try not to laugh when Faith hastily clears a bunch of lingerie from the sofa on her way to the bathroom. The apartment is beautiful; spacious, open-plan, and all white with luxurious fittings and furniture. She must pay a fortune on rent, or perhaps she owns it? As I throw the spinach into the juicer and scoop out the flesh from the avocados, I wonder what she does for a living. *Faith Astor.* The name rings a bell, and her face looks familiar. It's a typical rich girl's name, and I can't deny that I was prepared for my morning to go exactly like this. People don't make rash decisions that involve five hundred dollars in the middle of the night unless they're wealthy and can afford to pull off a stunt like that. I've seen this many times, and although it's easy money for me, I don't like it. Still, her answers to the questionnaire seemed brutally honest, and they told me she needs a change in her life. Maybe I can help her.

The juicer still has a sticker on the inside, so I peel it off and throw in the ingredients, then add a shriveled apple and the juice from half an old lemon in the fruit bowl that holds more hangover cures than actual fruits. Aspirin, vitamin C tablets, and Tylenol—I suspect Faith parties a lot. Despite her sorry state this morning, she's very pretty. No older than thirty-five for sure, she looks like the kind of woman who is used to being pampered. Her nails are pristine, her hair—although a little messy—looks well taken care of, and her skin is flawless. She's curvy with a figure most people would be envious of, but I've learned from my years of experience that self-esteem is sadly often linked to weight, especially in New York.

I pour the smoothie into a tall glass I find in her cupboard, then open my bag and take out my iPad. I like to get an idea of people before we start, but her apartment is devoid of any trinkets or personal pictures, at least as far I can see. She does like art; that much is clear. A huge painting of a woman and a baby is hanging on the wall above the fireplace in her seating area, and she has numerous photographs and sculptures on display. *Art dealer, maybe?*

Before I have the chance to contemplate any further, Faith appears dressed in yoga pants and a sweatshirt. Her dark hair is wet and brushed back, the mascara stains are gone from underneath her eyes, and her skin is shimmering from the cream she's just applied. She looks innocent; nothing like the sexy vixen in the red, silk robe who opened the door to me twenty minutes ago.

"Okay, I'm ready." She eyes the big, green smoothie on the table. "As long as it doesn't involve anything too strenuous because my head is seriously killing me."

"Let's talk for now," I say, not wanting to put her off the program on her first day. I gesture to the smoothie, and she picks it up and starts sipping it. "So, your primary goal is to lose weight, it says here." Flicking through her questionnaire on my iPad, I skip past her personal details and get right into the motivational section. "Your secondary goal is to feel des—"

"Forget the desire bullshit," she interrupts me, clearly embarrassed. "As I said, I was drunk. But I wouldn't mind losing weight. I've gained a couple pounds over Christmas, and it's all piled on here." She pats her thighs and behind and sighs. "I want to be back in shape before New York Fashion Week. It's a big deal, and I need to look my best."

"Okay. So how long do we have? Four, five weeks?"

"It starts on February nineteenth."

I nod and make a note of the timeline. "Forty days. That's good. Are you a model?"

Faith throws her head back and laughs as if that's a ridiculous question. "No way. I could never get away with being in front of the camera. I'm a fashion photographer."

"Oh." My first thought is that she'd look beautiful in front of the camera, but it's too early for conversations like that, so I smile and glance at a picture on the kitchen wall instead. It's a photograph of a woman who looks a lot like Faith, except she's younger, taller, and slimmer. She's dressed in black, standing in a desert with a crow perched on her arm. It's dark and a little unsettling but beautiful, nevertheless. "Is that your work?"

"Yes. That's my sister." Faith picks at her fingernails. "She's the pretty one. I'm the creative."

"Well, I have to disagree on the looks," I say, then continue when she doesn't answer, "You must be pretty successful. You have an amazing apartment."

"I do all right, but my mother bought this apartment for me. She's a celebrated artist. Mary Astor-Goldstein—you might have heard of her. I carry her last name. I don't like my stepfather's last name." Faith peels off the tip of her thumbnail and flicks it in the ashtray on top of a dozen or so cigarette butts.

"Yes, I've heard of her. Well, it's a beautiful place. You're lucky." Faith doesn't answer and avoids my gaze. She seems uncomfortable talking about her family, so I change the subject. "Tell me about your lifestyle. If you want fast results, we're going to have to make some changes."

"My lifestyle..." She shrugs and sits back, then finally meets my eyes again. Hers are big and dark, almost feline. The way she bites her lip while in thought is incredibly sensual, but I don't think she knows that. "I ehm..." She pauses. "I go out a lot. I'm what some people might call a socialite, and I get invited to a lot of parties and networking events. And because I go out a lot, I probably drink too much. Too much in your opinion, anyway."

"I don't judge," I say, making a note. "How many drinks would you say a week?"

"I'm not sure. Three to four a day, maybe? I rarely get drunk. It just helps me cope with all the socializing. Well, apart from last night. I was definitely drunk then," she adds with an uncomfortable chuckle. "But it was New Year's Eve, so I'm not going to beat myself up about that."

I laugh along and shake my head. "So, in a normal week, would you say you drink every day?"

Faith is quiet for a long moment before she answers. "Six days a week, probably. I have social commitments most days."

"And you find it hard to be social without drinking?"

"Yes." Faith crosses her arms in a defensive manner, as if she's expecting me to tell her off. "I don't see how anyone can be social without a drink. It's just awkward."

I'm not going to argue with her. If she takes a disliking to me, we'll never get anywhere. "Do you smoke?" I ask, glancing at the ashtray.

"Not much. Only when I'm alone."

"Drugs?"

"Not anymore." She purses her lips and shrugs. "I used to, but I managed to break that habit. It was getting out of hand."

"Well done," I say. "That's something you should be proud of. It's not easy."

"How do you know?" Faith shoots me a skeptical look, and I know she's thinking I can't possibly relate.

"Because I used to have an addiction problem too," I say honestly.

"Oh." Her expression softens. "So you weren't always a shining beacon of health, huh?"

"No, I was quite the opposite." I refocus on the questionnaire because this is not about me. I have no problem being open about my past, but she's paying for my time, and I want to get to know her so I can help her achieve her goals. "Do you exercise? Walking counts too."

"Not really. I've tried the gym, but I wasn't motivated enough to actually go there, even though there's one in the building. It bored me. And no, I don't walk much either. I usually take a taxi." Faith winces as if, again, she's expecting me to tell her off.

"When was the last time you went for a walk by yourself?"

At that, she laughs. "Just a walk for no reason?" She glances at the ceiling like she'll find an answer there, then shakes her head. "Never, I guess. That's terrible, isn't it?"

"Nothing is terrible," I assure her. "The good thing about bad habits is that you can change them. Do you eat healthy, regular meals? What do you eat in a day?"

"Hmm..." Faith picks up her green juice and finishes it. "Nothing like this, that's for sure. I only eat real meals when I'm out for lunch or dinner, which I don't do very often because I don't really care for food. If I'm home alone, I'll get a takeout, and sometimes I'll throw together a salad."

"You never have breakfast?"

"When I'm off work, I rarely get out of bed before midday, and on the days I work, I usually have to leave so early that I'm not hungry, so I bring protein bars with me."

"Okay." I write everything down and notice she's eyeing my notepad. "Would you like to read what I've written? I'm not analyzing you. I'm just jotting down the facts." The latter isn't entirely true; I always analyze my clients, but that process takes place in my head, not on my iPad.

"No, it's fine. You have a lot of questions."

"And I have many more." I look outside to check on the weather. It's not snowing as hard anymore, but I still expect resistance to my next question. "How about we discuss the rest over a walk?"

Faith's eyes widen as she follows my gaze to the window. "A walk?"

"Yes. The act of physically moving from A to B while putting one foot in front of the other," I joke. "Do you have walking shoes and a warm coat?"

"But... it's cold," she protests.

"We'll warm up once we start moving." I get up and wait for her to follow. Miraculously, she agrees and peels herself off her stool. "Come on, and drink a glass of water too. You need to hydrate."

3

FAITH

Walking and talking is an alien concept to me. I always have somewhere to go, somewhere to be, and I never saw the point of walking just for the sake of it. I'd expected to be too hungover to walk, but the fresh air is making me feel better. New York on New Year's Day makes for a surreal experience. It's quiet; even most coffee shops are still closed. Last night's celebrations turned the sidewalks brown and slushy, but now the streets are covered in a beautiful, fresh layer of snow. The city looks so innocent in its virginal white and dormant state, like it's still waiting for the new year to kick off.

"So, you think you can get me in shape by February nineteenth?" I ask, burying my hands deep in my pockets.

"That depends on you, of course," Silva says. "But I think you can do it if you're open and ready for change. You see, this is not just about losing weight or getting fit. That's only a small part of the work I do. My aim is to make you feel good about yourself. And if you feel good about yourself, you're more likely to make healthy choices. It's a vicious circle—a positive one."

"You sound more like a life coach than a personal trainer."

Silva shrugs. "It's the biggest lesson I've learned since I started working as a personal trainer. It may sound cliché, but in the end it's about how you feel inside, not about how you look." She picks up her pace a little, and I'm struggling to keep up as my feet keep sinking into the snow. I found a pair of snow boots I'd never used, and my big, fake-fur coat is keeping me warm.

"What other lessons have you learned?" I try not to sound skeptical because to be honest, everything she's said so far does sound like a total cliché.

"That drastic temporary actions may give direct results, but that small, permanent lifestyle changes have a much bigger effect." She pauses. "And that the process needs to be fun. If you don't enjoy it, you're not going to stick with it."

"Sure. That's what everyone says." *More clichés.*

"That's because it's true." Silva looks over her shoulder when I fall behind. "Are we going too fast?"

"Yes," I say, stopping to catch my breath. "But I have to give it to you. You're smart. I had no intention of leaving my bed before you arrived, and here I am, plowing through the fucking snow at stupid o'clock."

Silva laughs. "It's good to get your heart rate up. You'll feel the difference when you get home, and you'll be thankful we did this." She stops and turns to me. "Are you in a relationship?"

"No," I say and leave it with that. The last thing I want to talk about is the string of useless men I've dated in the past years, or the last one who dumped me just before Christmas.

"Are you recently single?"

I'm not sure why, but the question irritates me. Perhaps

because I've been trying so hard not to think about that. "Why are you so interested in my love life? I don't understand what it has to do with getting in shape."

Silva holds up a hand. "Hey, I'm not hitting on you. I'm just trying to get an idea of your life."

"I know you weren't hitting on me." I frown. "Why would I think that? That's just—" I swallow my words. *Of course. She's gay.* "Oh. Sorry, I didn't mean it like that."

"That's okay. The reason I asked is because all of this has to do with mindset. If you've recently gone through a breakup, your subconscious revenge system may give you an extra kick of motivation. Simultaneously, it's important to remember that you're doing this for you and not for someone else." She beckons me to start walking again. "But you don't have to tell me anything you don't want to."

I nod and look away, embarrassed that I raised my voice at her. We turn into Maddison Square Park and follow the outer path that circles around it. "My last relationship ended ten days ago," I finally say after a long silence.

"I'm sorry to hear that. It's very recent."

"We hadn't been together for very long," I say with a sigh. "It wasn't that serious, so I'm not heartbroken, but I won't deny that yet another breakup has dented my confidence. I can't stop wondering what's wrong with me because I've never been in a long-term relationship. It's New York men, I suppose. They're all the same, always looking out for someone younger, prettier, richer, and more successful."

"You sound like my sister. She always complains about New York men. But there are nice men out there. You're probably just attracted to the wrong kind."

"It must be a lot easier dating women," I say.

"I can assure you that dating women is not much different from dating men. Not that I've ever tried and tested it with men," she jokes. "But I believe in faith. Finding a real connection isn't a given, and it will happen when it happens. I'm not looking or waiting for anything."

"So you're single?" I ask.

"Yes. I've been single for years." She winks. "Doesn't mean I don't have fun."

"Oh." I blush as a vision of Silva kissing another woman flashes before me. She's very attractive, and I imagine she's quite popular with the ladies. "I've never been into one-night stands."

"Well, I don't make a habit of them either, but there's nothing wrong with the occasional fling." She speeds up again, and I rush after her. "Now, let's talk about what you enjoy doing. Because as I said, this has to be fun. Running, yoga, dancing, weightlifting, swimming—it can be anything."

I take my time to think about that, but nothing comes to mind. "I have no idea. I haven't tried much, to be honest. Apart from swimming in the ocean, which I love, but that's kind of challenging in New York."

Silva laughs and shakes her head. "Wild swimming is about the only thing we can't do here, but let's try some different things so you can figure it out as you go along." She locks her eyes with mine and gives me a beaming smile. "How does that sound?"

4

SILVA

"How are you feeling?" I'm pleased when we get back to Faith's apartment. She seems much better already, and she has a healthy blush on her cheeks. After peeling off her coat, she fans her face and takes off her sweatshirt too, leaving her in a skimpy tank top. She's not wearing a bra, and I force my eyes away from her hard nipples, which are poking against the thin, white, stretchy fabric.

"I feel good, actually." Faith stretches and rolls her shoulders. "My headache's gone too."

"Fantastic! Fresh air can work miracles."

"So, what now?" she asks as we sit down again.

"Now I'm going to make you a tailored nutritional plan and then we can talk about how many times a month you'd like to meet."

"Oh." Faith pauses. "I just assumed this would be a daily thing."

I'm surprised by her statement, as I rarely have full-time clients. It's simply too expensive for most people, and I don't fall into the category "trainer to the stars."

"I'm not sure I can make that work. I have other clients too, but if you want, we can meet every other day? Sunday is my day off, and you need a day off too. It's important to have a rest day on which you treat yourself to whatever you feel like."

"Every other day works for me," Faith says. "I'm sorry. I had no idea how this would work."

"Don't apologize, I love your enthusiasm." I point to the stove. "Can you cook?"

"I'm not great, but I'll give it a go." Faith laughs. "I can make an omelet. Does that count?"

"Sure, that counts. And if you're not a big fan of cooking, I'll teach you some quick cheat tricks. Now, you'll need to cut down on the drinking. I'm not saying you can't drink at all, but I promise you'll feel the difference after a few days."

Faith nods, but she doesn't look convinced. "As I said, I find it hard to socialize without a drink, but I could stick to one or two and go home after that. In the end, it's more about showing my face."

"That's a start. And after a while, you might find it gets easier to cut down, and perhaps a couple of times a week you're able to keep your social anxiety at bay without a drink."

"I never said I have social anxiety." Faith frowns. "Why do you think that?"

I'm baffled how little self-insight she has because to me, she's pretty easy to figure out. "Do you get nervous if you go somewhere sober? I mean a party, not the supermarket."

"No." Faith hesitates. "Yes, a little."

"Do you find it hard to start a conversation with a stranger without a drink?"

"Yes."

"Do you feel like you're being watched or judged all the time?"

She sighs. "Yes. I'm always worried what people think of me. Mainly of how I look. And a drink helps with that. It stops me from overthinking everything."

"I'm sorry you feel that way," I say. "Are you comfortable around me?"

"Yes." Faith gives me a small smile. "Yes, I am. And I'm comfortable when I'm with my best friend, Roy. I don't feel like I have to be someone I'm not around him."

I nod. "That's nice. Is this something you could discuss with him? Do you go out together?"

"Usually. But he lives in Brooklyn, so we usually arrive separately, and he tends to bring a date. It's the first fifteen minutes that do me in." She shrugs. "I suppose I could ask him to meet me before we go out next time."

"That could work." I return her smile and place a hand on her arm. "As I said, you don't have to go cold turkey, and I don't expect you to stay at home. You have a life, and networking is important to your job. I get that. It's just that, if you want results, these lifestyle changes are important."

"I know." Faith purses her lips and looks me over. "Do you drink? I bet you don't."

"I'll have a drink when I feel like it, and I love a glass of good red wine."

"Huh." Faith seems surprised that I'm not a saint. "And what about the drugs you mentioned? Or is that too personal?" She shakes her head. "I'm sorry, that was out of line."

"No, it's fine." I haven't talked about it in years. I've been trying to forget about that period in my life, but for some reason, I told her this morning. "I wasn't into recreational drugs or prescription drugs," I say. "I was addicted to slimming pills."

"You?" Faith stares at me, and I see a hint of recognition, of understanding in her eyes. "I find that hard to believe."

"It's true."

She nods and leans in. "I've been there. I used to take them all the time, but they made my anxiety worse, especially when I mixed them with... well, with other stuff."

"I'm not surprised. They can cause anything from restlessness, extreme anxiety, headaches, and dizziness to heart palpitations, fever, and everything in between. Frankly, I've never felt so horrible in my life as when I took them on a daily basis."

"Yeah, that wasn't a nice time for me either." Faith is about to say something else, but she paints on a smile instead. "Good thing we both realized that."

5

FAITH

This is a first. I have no shoots planned, it's not even midday and I'm already showered and dressed. Silva left me with a digital nutritional plan after showing me some basic stretch and yoga poses to do tomorrow, and I've been completely surprised by my own willingness to cooperate. Somehow, in those three hours, she managed to get me excited about the idea of getting fit and healthy on New Year's Day of all days. Taking advantage of my positive state of mind as I have no idea how long I'll be able to maintain it, I tidy the living room and even wash the coffee cups, which is something I would normally leave for my cleaner to do. I only ever shop for groceries online, but Silva suggested I should walk to the store and get them myself from now on to up my step count, so I make a list of things I'll need in the coming days.

As I'm about to head out, the doorbell rings again, and I'm baffled to see my best friend Roy staring into the camera.

"Hey there, princess," he says when he waltzes into my kitchen and plonks a bottle of tomato juice on my counter.

"I didn't expect you to be up and let me in. Just thought I'd try my luck."

"Well, I am up, thanks to that personal trainer who showed up at eight a.m."

Roy slams a hand in front of his mouth and laughs. "That's hilarious. I totally forgot about the trainer. Don't tell me you've been working out? How's your head? How was it?"

"It wasn't so bad, and I feel fine now. We went for a walk, she set up a nutritional plan for me, and then we did some gentle exercises and stretching before she left."

"You and walking?" Roy laughs even harder and removes his red, fake-fur coat. "Let me call the papers, this is a big story." He pulls a bottle of vodka from the fridge and holds it up. "Bloody Mary?"

My initial reaction is to embrace the offer, but remembering I'm supposed to be good, I shake my head. "No, thanks. That's not part of my nutritional plan, but I'll have a virgin one."

Roy stares at me incredulously. "Who are you? Am I supposed to drink alone after that PT brainwashed you?" His eyes widen even more, and he holds up a hand. "Wait a minute, was he hot?"

I roll my eyes and laugh. "It was a woman. Don't you remember?" My gaze travels over Roy's red silk shirt that is unbuttoned all the way down to his navel, the hem tucked into his leather designer pants. "You haven't changed. Have you not been to bed yet?"

"Oh, I've been to bed all right." Roy seasons the tomato juice with tabasco, Worcestershire sauce, celery salt, and black pepper from my cupboard and adds a slug of vodka to his own. "I went home with that hot guy from the afterparty. The German. I think his name is Karl, but it's all a bit of a blur. Anyway, he lives around the corner from you, and I woke up there, so I thought I'd swing by and treat you to a Bloody. Can we watch a movie in your bed? I'm tired."

"Ehm, sure. I need to get groceries, but make yourself at home. I'll join you later."

"Why are you getting groceries?" Roy downs his Bloody Mary and winces.

"Because I finally feel motivated to get healthy, so don't ruin it by offering me takeout or cocktails or whatever. Just pick a movie, okay? I'll be right back."

"Why did we decide on the PT again?" Roy asks as we're lying in bed an hour later. He's had a shower and is wearing my robe that is way too small for him. The fact he's half-naked doesn't bother me because Roy is my best friend. We dated a long time ago, before he realized he preferred men. I should have known from the way he used to stare at some of our mutual male friends and started dressing differently toward the end of our relationship.

"Because I want to look good for Fashion Week."

"And you know you'll see Michael over Fashion Week? Is that it?" Roy makes a gagging gesture and sighs. "You're not trying to win him back, are you? That guy dumped you like a sack of potatoes. He's a total dick."

"No, I'm not trying to win him back. I want to look good to show him what he's missing. It's like revenge, you know?" Of course, I didn't tell Silva any of that. She seems too emotionally stable and wholesome to understand how my twisted mind works. I don't want him back; I just want him to desire me.

"It won't be revenge if you go through all this trouble

and he ends up ignoring you and taking off with some random model like he did last time," Roy says with a hint of anger in his expression. "You're beautiful and kind and talented. You don't need to prove yourself to anyone."

"But I don't feel beautiful." As I say it, a lump forms in my throat and my voice breaks. "I don't feel beautiful, Roy. I've never felt beautiful." The sharp stab of emotion comes out of nowhere. I have no idea why my good mood has suddenly shifted, but I'm pretty sure I'm not crying for Michael. I don't miss him, and I never really liked him all that much anyway. But at thirty-three in New York, there's this pressure to have your shit together, and I can't even manage to hold a relationship for longer than two months. I suspect the breakup has dented me more than I realized. "No one wants me. What's wrong with me?"

"Oh, come here, babe." Roy takes me in his arms. "There's nothing wrong with you, it's them. You have to stop dating bad guys. They've made you feel this way. He inches back and taps the tip of my nose. "Listen, I admire you for wanting to better your life and take care of your body. Just make sure you do it for you and no one else, okay?"

6

SILVA

I'm exhausted by the time I get home. It seems every woman in New York decided she wanted a transformation kickstart on January first, and I've had a twelve-hour day. As I enjoy a long shower, my mind keeps going back to Faith Astor, my first client. Out of everyone, I want to help her the most. Maybe it's because of the twisted view she has of herself. I noticed it in the detached way she talked about her body, as if it didn't belong to her. She's gorgeous, but not being a size zero while working in the fashion industry can make women doubt themselves; although that saddens me deeply, I also understand it. We have things in common, and as weird as it seems, I feel connected to her.

I step out of the shower and wrap a large towel around me. My bathroom is small, like every other room in my apartment, but I love my modest pad situated in a beautiful brownstone in Brooklyn, and I'm proud to call it my own. It's nice to be inside with the heat on full blast while the snow falls in the streets below. The view from the fifth floor is great, and I don't mind all the stair climbing, as it keeps me in shape even on days when I'm not training people or working out myself.

After drying off, I put on my robe and head for the kitchen, where I heat up last night's stir-fry leftovers and make a cup of fresh mint tea with honey. I spent New Year's Eve with my sister and went to a friend's birthday party the night before, so falling back on the couch in my tired but content state is heavenly. Covering my bare legs with a blanket, I scroll through my phone while I eat, and look up Faith Astor.

The work on her website is contemporary and stylish, and the amount of fashion magazine covers she's shot is impressive. I'm no expert on fashion or anything artistic for that matter, but all her pictures have a certain darkness to them, like the one of her sister in her kitchen. They're sad, and even a little sinister, no matter how bright the background or how colorful the models are styled. There's some older, personal work in her online portfolio too. Black-and-white portraits, mainly. They're hauntingly beautiful and feel a lot more personal, the way the subjects look at her. Unable to stop myself, I look her up on Instagram and scroll through the many pictures of her with various friends, posing in fabulous outfits. Daughter to a successful artist and half-sister to a famous model, this talented photographer and It-girl seems to have it all, yet I keep remembering the sadness behind her smile. Zooming in on one of the pictures in which she's drinking champagne at a club opening, I see that same look I saw this morning.

From what I gather, Faith is quite the deal, at least, to those who work in the fashion industry. Gallery openings, brand launches, fashion shows and afterparties, club openings, celebrity birthday parties, and movie premieres seem to take up most of her time, but there are also occasional shots of a vacation, or snaps from pretty sets. I'm surprised she's not showing any of her own work on here, but I suppose the people who need to know her work know it already and she needs to sell herself on a personal level too. One of the pictures farther down is of her and her sister, and I click on her sister's name to check out her profile. I have no idea why I'm doing this, as I don't make a habit of scrolling through people's social media channels, but my curiosity has gotten the better of me.

Frankie, her sister, is an avid traveler. She's friends with the rich and famous and records every detail of her life: her morning routine, her breakfast, her cab rides and flights to shoots or meetings, the collaboration with an online retailer she's working on, her photoshoots, her friends, the exotic locations she visits, her spectacular hotel rooms, her outfits, which she changes at least twice a day; there are also some pictures with her parents, Mary Astor-Goldstein, and Andrew Goldstein. Faith is in very few of them, which leads me to believe they don't see much of each other.

Not everyone follows through with my program, but the majority of my clients do. People like Faith, though, who book in the spur of the moment, are a different story. Changing one's lifestyle isn't easy; it takes determination and willpower, and I'm not sure if she'll even last a week.

I put my empty plate on the coffee table, and as always, the devil whispers in my ear. *Nine-hundred and twenty calories. Nine-fifty including the honey in your tea. It's not too late, you can still leave the tea.* He never goes away, but I've learned to shrug him off by focusing on everything good in my life. My health, my strength, my job, my family. There was a time when I was about to lose it all, and I never want to go back to that.

It's true. I'm able to calculate the number of calories in just about anything, and even though I'm better now, stronger and way more confident, the disease will always linger in the background, enticing me to return to the toxic vicious circle of false beliefs and self-destruction. I've learned that as long as I maintain my healthy weight, which has been stable for over five years, I'll be okay. I won't relapse. My life is a string of carefully weighed decisions: what to eat, how much to exercise, and when not to exercise. That keeps me sane and balanced, and I'm proud of how I managed to get my life back on track, of how I've bounced back after hitting the ultimate low point. I have a wonderful home, a job I love, and nothing will take that away from me. Not the devil inside me, and certainly not the honey.

"I won't let you beat me," I say out loud, then reach for my tea and take a sip, savoring the warm sweetness that glides down my throat. *I win.*

7

FAITH

It's funny how I've been looking forward to Silva coming today, but maybe that's just because I haven't spoken to anyone since New Year's Day. It's day three of my new, healthy lifestyle, and miraculously, I haven't strayed too far from my regime. Eight a.m. and I'm showered and dressed in yoga wear, which isn't too much of a chore, as I didn't go out last night. Admittedly, it was strange sitting here with nothing but my own company, and honestly, I'm not sure how long I'll be able to sustain it. I had no idea what to do with myself, so I rearranged my wardrobe and looked up a stir-fry recipe online. The meal I attempted to cook looked disastrous and unappetizing, but it tasted okay.

My FOMO was playing up, though. Canceling the party I was supposed to attend last night made me restless, so I spent the rest of the evening scanning people's Instagram accounts to see what I'd been missing. It would have been easier if I had more jobs lined up, but January is always a quiet time and I only have nine shoots booked in for this month.

After our warm-up, Silva rolls out two yoga mats in the

living area and pulls weights from her bag. She's wearing gray tracksuit pants and a tight, blue tank top that shows off her broad shoulders and toned arms. She's sculpted in a way that makes me want to squeeze her arms to feel her strength. I've never seen a woman who is so fit and muscular close-up, and it fascinates me. Her face is striking and equally sculpted too, with high cheekbones and a strong jawline, like those female superheroes in video games.

"Did you drag those all the way here?" I ask.

"It's only six pounds, not a big deal." Silva gestures to one of the mats. "You can borrow this mat and the weights until you've ordered your own. They're not expensive. I'll send you a link."

"Sure. I'll order them today." Again, I'm staring at her arms, then at her hands. *Why does it feel wrong to look?* Silva catches me staring, and the corners of her mouth pull into a small smile, letting me know I'm busted. *Fuck.* I should compliment her or say something, anything, but instead, I look away and feel totally awkward.

She sits down cross-legged on one mat and pats the other. "Lie on your back and bend your knees."

I do so and focus on the ceiling, trying not to think about what just happened.

"Are you okay?" she asks.

"Yes, I'm fine." *Why do I feel so self-conscious? Stop overthinking.* I force myself to look at her. "Let's do this."

"Let's do this," she repeats, and her smile widens. "We're going to work on your core today." She places a hand on my belly and pushes down. "These are the muscles you want to engage. Do a simple crunch for me, will you? Yes, right there. Can you feel that? One more, keep breathing."

I nod and let out my breath. Suddenly I'm hyperaware of everything. Her hand on my stomach, the silence in the room, my breathing that is slightly faster than usual, and my heartrate that's already shot up without even doing much. It's silly, and it makes no sense, yet I can't help but think it's got something to do with her.

"Okay, let's focus on form now. Heels hip distance apart," she says. "You should be able to touch your heels with your hands. Yes, that's good." Her hand is still on my belly, and I'm holding it in so much I can barely breathe. "Now keep your elbows open, your head in a neutral position, and your lower back on the mat as you lift your upper body."

I do another crunch; it's much harder this time.

"That's great, but don't forget to breathe. Let's do ten of these." Silva counts down from ten, and all I can think of as I fall back into a rest position for ten seconds is how I look. *Are my cheeks flushed? What about my skin? I'm not wearing makeup and she's so close. Does my belly look flabby in this top?*

"Don't let your mind wander." Silva finally retracts her hand. "Stay present in the movement and in the moment. Another ten."

This time, I try to focus on my core, on my body, on how it feels, but it's hard to concentrate when I'm so aware of her presence. I didn't feel like this the first time she was here. *Why is that?*

"Perfect." Silva places her hand back on my stomach, just underneath my ribs. "Now raise yourself again but hold it this time." Her other hand slides under my neck to correct my posture, and when she brushes my skin, I feel the hairs on my arms rise. "Hold it, hold it..." She chuckles when I groan in agony. "Hold it. No pain, no gain. You can do this—your real strength is in your mind."

Somehow, my ridiculously out-of-shape body manages to hold the position for ten seconds, and when I fall back, she catches my head in the palm of her hand.

"Fuck, that was hard."

"That was nothing," she says, getting up. "But you did well. Just remember to never collapse after you've done a routine. It can cause injuries. Always move back into rest position slowly, no matter how tired you are."

"I can't get up," I say, panting as I hold on to my stomach.

"Yes, you can. You'd be surprised at what you can do." Silva takes my hand and helps me up. "You, Faith, can do anything you want, as long as you stay focused."

8

SILVA

Faith surprised me today. She was ready and willing to give it her all, and we had a great workout. I'm walking with a stride in my step and can't quite grasp why I'm feeling exceptionally upbeat as I head for the restaurant where I'm meeting my sister for lunch. Trinny works and lives in Manhattan, so having a client here presents me with a convenient opportunity to catch up with her without having to travel back and forth.

"Hey, Sis. Am I late?"

"No, was early," she says, getting up from the table to give me a hug. "I couldn't wait to get out of the office, it's been a crazy morning. How was work?"

"It was great, actually. I saw a new client for the second time today. She lives just a block from here, hence my message this morning. Glad you could make it for lunch."

Trinny sits back, her attention spiked. "A client around here, huh? She must be wealthy."

"It seems so. She asked for full-time training. I couldn't give her six days a week because I already have my current client base, but she's happy with four. Anyway, how was your morning?"

Trinny lets out a dramatic sigh. "I made it through a tough four-hour meeting, let's just leave it at that." She holds up a menu. "I'm starving, so I already ordered for us. Hope you don't mind."

"Not at all. You're kind of hard to be around when you're hangry," I joke. "What did you order?"

"Two Caesar salads with a side of sweet potato fries and a bottle of sparkling water." She smiles at the waiter, who pours us water.

"You know me so well."

"I do." Trinny blows me a kiss and reaches for a bread-stick. "How's the new year been so far?" she asks through a mouthful.

"Busy, being January and all. But that's good. I can't complain about too much work."

"Well, I don't know about that." Trinny points to her satchel. "I still have four files to re-read before court tomor-row, but I really needed a break and a good gossip with my big sis." She leans in and grins. "So, any cute new clients this year? Or did you sign up for that dating site I told you about?"

I laugh and shake my head. "No, no dates lined up, and you know I don't date clients."

"That's a lie. You dated that woman. What was her name again? Bettina?" Trinny shoots me a sarcastic look.

"Yes, well she was the first and the last, and it only lasted two months," I say, realizing I haven't thought of Bettina in a long time. She and I were never a great match, but back then, I couldn't resist when she started flirting with me. Although she wasn't really my type, she was attractive and the idea of having a gay personal trainer was a serious turn-on for her. Before I knew it, one thing led to another, and suddenly we were in one of those rushed relationships that made little sense. "The client I just came from is interesting."

"Oh?" Trinny takes a sip of her wine. "Do tell."

"Have you heard of Faith Astor? She's a fashion photographer."

Trinny gasps and almost chokes on her water. "Faith Astor is your client?" She holds up her hands in a dramatic gesture. "Of course I know who she is. She's quite the socialite. I saw a feature about her in *Style Today*."

"I didn't know you read that crap," I say, bemused that my intelligent lawyer sister who I totally look up to is engaged with such nonsense.

"Hey, I'm only human." Trinny shrugs. "I didn't know she worked for a living, though. I assumed she lived off her mother's wealth. Her mother is a famous artist but I'm sure you know that by now." She continues when I nod. "Faith must be hard work. Is she?"

"No, she's really nice, actually. I don't know how long she'll stick with me. Maybe she'll give up, or maybe she'll start enjoying working out. If she pushes through, it's likely someone will recommend her a more high-profile trainer, but as long as she's willing, I'm happy to train her."

Trinny reaches for another breadstick and nibbles on it. She eats them the way a rabbit or a guinea pig would chomp on a carrot; small, quick bites, like she's in a rush but her mouth isn't big enough. I always pay attention to the way people eat; it's something that will never go away. Our mother eats like a sloth; slow and... well, slow. Chewing every bite in slow motion. She even swallows slowly, to the point I worry she might choke.

Comparing people's eating habits to animals has become this thing, and I let these thoughts in because it's easier than fighting them. One of my friends eats like a Labrador: he practically inhales his food within seconds. Bettina ate like a bird. She picked at her food, taking tiny bites until only the bits she didn't like were left on her plate. And one of my male friends eats like a chimp, which is close to the way humans eat, minus the cutlery. He prefers finger food and eats with his hands whenever he gets the chance.

"Regardless, you're lucky to have her. She might put in a good word for you with her famous friends," Trinny says, pulling me out of my thoughts. "That aside, how are you finding training her?" She grins. "I mean, come on. You can't deny she's super-hot."

"You're right, she's beautiful," I say, my mind going back to that split second this morning when Faith looked at me in a way that stirred something inside me.

"And single?" Trinny asks.

"Yes, she's single and also very straight, so don't you get any ideas."

"But I never meet anyone exciting, so I have to live my life vicariously through you." Trinny makes space on the table when our lunch arrives. "Surely you must look at her in a certain way, since you're into women and all. And she's a brunette. That's your type, right?"

I roll my eyes and laugh at her absurd comment. "I'm not a predator. Do you undress all attractive men with your eyes?"

"Yes," Trinny says matter-of-factly, and I laugh along with her. She does have a point, though. If I'm honest, Faith is exactly my type, at least in the physical sense. I didn't feel it the first day I saw her, but perhaps the time I've spent thinking about her over the past two days fueled my curiosity. Whatever it was, I should focus on other things than her because as my sister just established, I'm a sucker for brunettes, and Faith has already taken up more of my thoughts than a client should.

9

FAITH

"Was that your personal trainer leaving the building?" Roy drops a half dozen shopping bags from exclusive designer stores on my floor and walks over to the window to watch Silva disappear down the street.

"Yes, and she totally butchered me." I roll my shoulders and take a sip from my water bottle.

"Huh." Roy grins as he turns back to me. "Is she gay? I got that vibe when I saw her coming out of the elevator."

"Yes, she is. Does it matter?"

Roy grins. "Well, she's kind of sexy, don't you think? I mean, not that I'm into lesbian women or any women for that matter," he hastily adds. "But it could be interesting."

"I have no idea what you're talking about," I say, heading for the kitchen to make us coffee. He's not wrong; the session was certainly interesting, mainly because my body seemed to react to her in strange ways. I felt nothing in our first session, but I won't deny I thought of her a lot yesterday. It was probably boredom, or perhaps it's admiration. She seems so self-assured and put together, which is everything I aspire to be.

"Oh, come on, you know what I mean," Roy says. "A bit of girl-on-girl action with your PT? Nothing wrong with that."

I burst out in laughter and stare at him incredulously. "Seriously, Roy? When have I ever shown interest in a woman?"

"Never. But there's a first time for everything. I didn't know I was gay until my early twenties."

"You knew very well you were gay. You were in denial," I say, handing him his coffee. "And besides, she's a PT, not an escort."

"She's cute, though." Roy shoots me a wink. "Just saying."

I roll my eyes and point at his shopping bags, changing the subject. "Have you been splurging again? I thought you were cutting down on your spending. Most of your cards are maxed out."

"I know, but there's sales on everywhere, and I couldn't resist. Most of it was fifty percent off, so technically I saved a lot of money."

"Technically, that means you've bought a lot of stuff you don't need," I shoot back at him.

"I do need it, actually." Roy pulls out a navy velvet blazer. "I've got a date tonight, and this will go perfectly with that pashmina I bought in Marrakesh."

"A date?" I chuckle. "I'm surprised you managed to find someone in New York you haven't dated yet. Or is it an old flame?"

"Nuh-uh. New flame." As we take our coffees through to the living area, Roy pulls his phone out of his back pocket and shows me a picture of a half-naked man.

"Megadick?" I throw my head back and laugh at the man's profile name. "I sure hope for you he'll live up to his reputation. What happened to meeting The One?"

"Megadick is The One," Roy says in all seriousness. "I can feel it."

"You're sure to feel something, but I doubt it'll be love." I fall back on the couch; Roy sits next to me and pulls my feet onto his lap.

"We'll see about that." His expression turns sincere as he pats my leg. "Are you feeling better, honey? You were all over the place on New Year's Day."

"A little. The exercise helps." I give him a small smile and check my phone when it lights up. "Damn it. My shoot next week has been canceled."

"Oh. Any reason?" Roy asks.

"They're not giving a reason. You know what that means?"

"No." Roy frowns. "But you clearly do."

"It means I was a backup, and that their number one choice has confirmed availability," I say with a sigh. "I've never been canceled before, but I knew it was only a matter of time. There are so many new, talented photographers out there, and they all have their own unique and eclectic style. What if I'm not fresh enough to compete with them anymore?"

"Don't be silly. This is just a one-off."

"I'm not so sure about that. Two years ago, I was *the* fashion photographer in New York. Now I have to share that status with at least seven others."

"Lots of new kids on the block, huh?"

"Yeah. I'm under no illusions. I know how this world works, and I'm grateful for every job I get, but if it's starting to go downhill now, what's going to happen next year, or the year after? I'll be old news." I groan. "All my boyfriends cheat on me, the world is forgetting about me, and I haven't heard from Mom or Frankie in weeks."

"You're still successful, babe." Roy juts out his bottom lip. "You're right. The New York fashion scene is a shit-show. It's unforgiving and fickle, and yes, maybe you're not getting as much work as you used to, but you can come back from this." He pauses. "And as far as your sister's concerned, she's living the life right now, enjoying her number one position, so she's super busy. I'm sure you'll see her soon enough. Your mother is a different story. She's highly unstable and probably going through one of her phases."

I chuckle. "That she is, and I'm happy to stay away from her when she's like that, but I miss Frankie. We used to speak weekly and now all I get is a short reply when I message her. Don't get me wrong. I want this for her, and I'm glad her modeling career has taken off, but I feel like she's forgotten all about me." I realize I'm being a brat. "I'm sorry, that's selfish."

"It's not." Roy rubs my legs. "How about some distraction? Are you going to that perfume launch tomorrow?"

"I guess I'll have to." I curse myself for my lack of enthusiasm because I'm starting to sound really whiney. "Do you ever feel like this life we're living is empty?" Roy looks at me as if he has no idea what I'm talking about, so I continue. "Maybe it's a January thing. I always feel down during and after Christmas because there's less work, so I have too much time on my hands to think. But sometimes all I do is worry about how I look and how I come across to others. There must be more to life than this."

Roy nods and turns to me, propping his arm on the sofa's backrest. "Maybe you need a break."

"What I need is the opposite from a break. I need to work more."

"I meant a mental break." Roy smiles. "Maybe this health regime you've embarked on is exactly what you need. Use it as a time to reflect and work out a plan for yourself. It's not like you have to worry about money, so you can afford to focus on yourself for a while."

"That's another thing that bothers me," I say. "I'm thirty-three and what have I accomplished? My mother bought this place for me. I've been a photographer for five years and my breakthrough was purely because my mother got me my first job through her contacts. I've spent all the money I earned on designer clothes and luxury vacations, and I've got nothing to show for it. I have nothing to be proud of."

"Hey, don't be so hard on yourself." Roy clucks his tongue. "It wasn't your mother who got you all the gigs after your first one. You're very good at what you do."

He looks like he wants to shake me, and I don't blame him. I rarely voice my insecurities, but the winter months have really gotten me down. At work, I cover it up with a nice outfit and a beaming smile. I rock up at events looking the part, and being a socialite, I'm often the center of attention. It's all show, though, because deep down, I've always felt insecure. Never good enough to compete with my beautiful, and smart half-sister, whom our mother loves more than me, and never good enough for anyone else either.

"Come on, what happened to my sassy friend? Just focus on your health journey and see where it takes you. It's day three already. You're doing so well. That's more than you've ever managed."

I laugh at his joke but only half-heartedly. "Will you do something for me, Roy?"

"Anything, babe."

"Will you support me in this? I'm trying to drink less, but I don't like going places on my own sober. Will you be my plus-one, just for the coming weeks, until I can face nightlife alone?" Roy seems shocked at my proposal, as if he hadn't expected me to be in quite such a bad state. "I just... I can't do this alone."

"Oh, Faith, come here." He pulls me in for a hug and holds me tight. "Anything you need, babe. I'm here for you."

10

SILVA

Just two more minutes. Come on, now. Don't give up. I run until my legs burn and my chest hurts from the cold air I'm breathing in. By the time I reach my front door, I'm shaking with fatigue, but at least some of my anxiety has faded. Upstairs, I undress and fall down on the couch, too tired to jump under the shower right away. I check my smart watch to make sure my effort was enough. *Fifty minutes of running: 816 calories. Fuck. That's not enough.* Last night was fun, but panic hit me as soon as I woke up this morning. My friend Ava, who's a captain for an Emirati airline and often in New York when she has a layover, suggested we go for dinner, but I hadn't anticipated the Persian feast she ordered for us to share. The whole table was filled with dishes, and not wanting to be rude, I ate way more than I normally would. She doesn't drink, so that saved me calories on wine, but despite that, I have to burn off at least 1,300 calories today, even after the twenty-minute run late last night. The idea of skipping breakfast and lunch is tempting, but I know that will be my downfall. Once I start, I won't be able to stop; the feeling of emptiness is calming and addictive to me. Groaning in pain, I get up and go into the kitchen where I put two eggs in a pan of water and slice up half an avocado.

Sitting at the kitchen table, I move the food around on my plate in an attempt to make it look more appetizing, but it makes no difference. The trash can is in my line of sight, and I want to dump it in there, including the plate that is smothered in yolk after I sliced the eggs in half. Throwing it away would make me feel gloriously hollow inside, but it would ruin so much more.

No, devil. I've learned to love food over the years, to appreciate the nutritional value that fuels my body. To savor flavor and texture. But on days that my scale is in the plus, all of that hard work goes out of the window and food becomes my enemy. It's impossible to describe the sensation forcing down a meal evokes, even when I'm hungry. Mostly, it feels like a sin, but I know that's just in my head. The eggs taste like rubber, the yolks look like daunting blobs of dripping fat, and the avocado feels disgustingly slippery on my tongue. *You need to eat.* When my input-output scale is off, nothing tastes good, and swallowing is a challenge. Because once I've swallowed, it's inside of me and there's nothing I can do. It will cling onto my body wherever it wants with total disregard for my sanity. But on days like this, doing the right thing is essential because any loss of control will result in one bad decision after another.

Four more bites. Do it. Staring at my plate, I hesitate as every nerve and muscle protests. Even my hand tenses like a claw, causing me to drop my fork. It's been a while since it's been so bad, but it's also been a while since I had a five-course meal with baklava and lavender cheesecake for dessert. Taking a couple of deep breaths, I pick up my fork again and brace to finish it before I can change my mind.

Chewing each bite way longer than necessary, I shut my eyes tight as I swallow. Clearing my plate is essentially a victory, but it doesn't feel that way. I feel dirty and full. Too full.

Pull yourself together. It's just breakfast. It's not the end of the world. I hate it when I can't stop overthinking. It rarely happens anymore, and when it does, it's hard to imagine I used to be like this all the time. I'll have to join my clients in their workouts today. It's the only way I'll be able to burn off yesterday's excess. They won't mind; I think they appreciate it when they're not the only ones doing the hard work. If they saw me now, they'd label me a total fraud. I promote healthy living and teach people to love their bodies, yet I'm unable to practice what I preach.

Becoming a personal trainer was the only way for me, just like becoming an airline captain was the only way for my friend Ava, who's a recovering alcoholic. The enormous responsibility, long hours, extensive drug and alcohol testing and the amount of time she spends in the Middle East means she won't be tempted to drink at any time. For me, working out for a living means I can control how many calories I burn in a day, so I won't have to worry about what I eat all the time. So I can live a normal life. Apart from today. I should have told Ava that I'm a recovering anorexic and I couldn't possibly have dessert, especially since she confided in me years ago. But it's not something I openly talk about, and I had no idea how to bring it up. I'm ashamed, and I want people to see *me*, not this horrible disease of the mind.

Jabbing with my fork, I separate the egg and the avocado because eating it together is just too disgusting, then scoop up a bite and swallow it without chewing. My gagging reflex kicks in, but I try to think of something else and persevere.

Three more bites. It doesn't get easier, and I feel like I'm attempting to swallow a whole pig in one go. I wonder if I should spread the last bite over my plate so it looks like I'm done, but that would be cheating, and I promised myself I wouldn't. I need water before I finish, so I pour a tall glass and drink all of it, then refill it and down the second glass. My stomach churns as I eat the rest, but I manage to swallow.

Exhausted both physically and mentally, I push my plate aside and sit back, allowing the toxic anxiety to climb to an almost unbearable peak and then slowly subside. Minutes pass until my mind clears enough for me to think straight again, and I get up and head for the bathroom. I undress and make a point of avoiding the mirror because what I'll see in my current state will not be a true reflection of me. The shameful monster staring back at me will fill my thoughts with poison and seduce me to hate myself even more. *No, devil. Not a chance. I win.*

11

FAITH

"A little to the left, please." I point to the life-sized high-gloss, black horse statue next to the model. "Drape your arm over its back. Yes, that's good. Hold it there." I shoot three series of twenty from different angles. "And you—Dasha, was it?"

"Yes."

"A little more to the back so you're looking over her shoulder. Perfect." I take another couple of shots and lower my camera. "Thanks, guys, this one's a wrap. You can go and get changed into the next outfit."

While the models head for the dressing area, I hand my camera to Shahari, my assistant, who is sitting behind a desk in the corner of the studio. He connects it to his laptop, and we scroll through the pictures together to check we have enough quality shots to choose from.

"Looks good," he says, zooming in on one where both models are sitting on the horse.

"Yeah, I like that one too," I say, picking up my tall, skinny latte. Shooting in a studio is practical and time efficient, as we're not dependent on weather or light, but it's also very manufactured and not my preference. Most shoots are done in front of a green screen nowadays, and after I hand over the photos, the editor of the magazine I'm shooting for will select her favorites and pass them on to her graphic designer, who superimposes the background. Even the super-lean models will be photoshopped, their minor imperfections, as the editors like to call them, smoothed or removed. It's a twisted business and nothing is real, but they pay me well, and as I'm not the most popular photographer on the block anymore, I embrace any opportunity I'm given and don't complain.

"Do you need to take a break?" Shahari asks me. "The girls told me they'd rather keep shooting as they have a party to attend later."

"No problem, I'm fine to continue," I say, sipping my coffee. I've noticed I have more energy than normal, and I wonder if it's because of the workouts, but I'm also super hungry as I didn't have breakfast or lunch today.

The stylist changes the props in front of the screen for the next set, and I head for the dressing room to check how long the models need. The makeup artist is in there with them, and the door is open, but hearing my name, I instinctively step back into the dark corridor.

"It must be so frustrating for her," Oksana says. "Being Frankie Astor-Goldstein's sister. I mean, she doesn't look terrible or anything, but imagine being second best to one of the most beautiful women in the world."

"They have different fathers, though," Dasha says. "That's probably why Frankie is so much skinnier. Faith's ass is..." She lowers her voice. "Well, she wouldn't fit into these shorts, that's for sure."

The comment hits me like a dagger, and I steady myself against the wall. Closing my eyes, I try to breathe as I feel anxiety balling in the pit of my stomach, radiating out like a cancer. *They're just girls. They don't know any better than the industry they've worked in since they grew breasts.*

"She's not that bad," the makeup artist adds. "But let's face it, we would all die for Frankie's figure. She's so much fun too. I worked with her a couple of times."

I walk away from the gasps and comments that follow and return to the studio. My hands are trembling, and I need something to help me calm down or I won't be able to continue shooting.

"Are you okay?" Shahari asks me.

I ignore his question and hand him some cash from my purse. "Could you get me a bottle of vodka, please? There's a liquor store opposite the entrance downstairs." I know I'm crossing a line. Buying alcohol for me is not his job, but I can't think of anything else to keep my anxiety at bay.

Shahari hesitantly looks at the cash before he takes it. "Are you sure?"

"Yes. And please hurry. They're almost ready."

I slump down in his chair and feel ashamed as I watch him leave. He's not my PA; he's my talented technical assistant, and he shouldn't be doing menial chores for me. I don't need much, but I do need a little because I'm in charge today, and my confidence has just shattered into a million pieces. It's not the first time this has happened, and it won't be the last. It sucks being compared to my perfect sister when even our mother has a clear favorite.

"Is everyone ready?" Dasha asks as she appears in a sheer, leopard printed kimono and a huge, black hat.

"Five minutes," I say, forcing a smile. I don't want her to know she's brought me down. No one on set will ever see my insecurities; I leave those for Roy and our occasional drunken conversations. I want to shout at her. I want to tell her that she'll never get anywhere in life with her attitude. That if she thinks it's all about looks, she's in for a serious wake-up call by the time she's thirty and without work. That she has no fucking idea what happens to women in fashion after that magical number. That she may be one of the sought-after models today, but it won't last forever. At the same time, deep down, I worry that she may be right and I truly am unattractive, perhaps even repulsive to some.

"Sure," she says. "Do you have any codeine on you? I have a headache."

"No, but I have Tylenol." I take a box from my purse and hand it to her.

Dasha shakes her head. "Never mind. That stuff stopped working for me a long time ago."

I stare at her for a moment, and I recognize myself in her, at that age. "You shouldn't take heavy painkillers just to keep going. That stuff will kill you."

"Mind your own business." Dasha rolls her eyes and walks off. She can't be older than eighteen. From her accent, I gather that like so many others she's far from home and, in my opinion, too young to be on her own in this industry.

12

SILVA

"You did well today, Yvonne." I roll up the yoga mat I've brought along and secure it to the strap on my backpack. "Keep up the good work. I'll see you next week."

"Thanks." Yvonne, my fifty-five-year-old client who has recently been through a divorce, has made amazing progress since we started, and she loves heavy workouts and endurance challenges. Seeing her self-esteem grow makes my job worth it; she's gone from an insecure, broken being to a woman with clear goals and new hopes and dreams. She's even started online dating and couldn't wait to tell me all about the man she's meeting tonight.

"Enjoy tonight and be careful," I add as I turn at the door.

"Sure, Mom," she jokes and shoots me a wink.

Heading out, I note that I feel more like me again. The reason I don't always join in with the workouts is because I don't want to turn up sweaty for my next client. Sometimes needs must, though, and Yvonne's grilling workout has burned off the last of my excess calories and more, which means I can have a quick bite to eat before I see my last client.

My phone rings as I'm on my way to the train station, and when I see it's my mom, I look for a quiet corner to take the call. "Hey, Mom."

"Hi, sweetie. How are you doing?" she asks in a chirpy voice.

"Great. Just on my way to my last client of the day. How's retirement in the sunshine?"

"It's a little overcast today, but we haven't had rain in a while so that's a good thing. The plants will be happy. How's the weather in New York?"

"Nothing like Hawaii. It's dark and freezing—I bet you've forgotten what that's like since you haven't been here in over a year."

"Oh, we'll be back to visit you and Trinny soon, honey. But I know you both prefer to come here, so how about we arrange that first? Your dad has finally finished the guest room. It has two single beds so you can share, like in the old days on Staten Island."

"Sweet." I smile as I imagine them bickering over the color scheme. "Trinny's really busy with work right now, but I'll check if she's able to take some time out this summer. I can certainly make it work."

"Good. Don't forget to ask her when you see her. She's always busy, that girl. Can't even get on the phone for longer than five minutes."

I don't have the heart to tell her that I should get going too, so instead I say, "I know. There's this big case she's working on, and she's under a lot of pressure."

"Yes, well, never mind. "Now what about you? Are you dating?"

I laugh and shake my head. "You always ask me that. And no, I'm not. Not at the moment."

"That's a shame. We would love to see you bring a girlfriend home."

By "home," she means Hawaii, and although I was dating a little last year, I haven't exactly been serious enough with someone to tell my parents about them, let alone bring them on vacation with me.

"I thought now that you're better..." She pauses. "Are you still keeping healthy and eating?"

"Yes," I say. "I'm taking care of myself." Even if I wasn't, I wouldn't tell her. They've been through hell and back with me, and I don't want to be the source of any more stress. "And if I meet someone, you'll be the first to know," I assure her. "But I'm busy with work too, and with all the exercise I'm getting during the day, I'm generally too tired to meet women at night, so I'm going to leave the dating for a while."

"Sure, sweetie, but don't wait too long. You're not getting any younger."

"Hey, I'm only thirty-six." I suppress a sigh. With my parents being so happily married, I can't blame her for wanting the same for me, but a relationship just isn't my priority. They're high school sweethearts and still together, which is rare nowadays. After retiring from their busy jobs and finding their dream home in the sun, their life is complete and now they need something else to focus on, which is where their daughters' love life comes in. However, they mean well, and if that's the worst thing about them, I count myself very lucky.

"Exactly. Your father and I were married by eighteen and look at us now. Still living in marital bliss with a beautiful family. Perhaps you could consider a matchmaker? That's how Aunt Tina found Uncle Boris."

"I think I'll pass on the matchmaker, Mom. I don't even think that's a thing anymore." Sometimes I want to quiz her to make sure she knows what year she lives in, because some of her ideas stem from decades back. "Look, I'm really sorry but can I call you back? I need to take the train to Manhattan and eat something before my next session. I can see the foot traffic is picking up and I don't want to be squashed like a sardine. It gets bad at the end of the day."

"Oh, I'm sorry. Of course. You go and eat. I'm very glad you're eating."

"Great. "I'll call later." Even though I'm not lying, I'm aware the eating comment is cruel ammunition. But she tends to go on and on and I only use it when I really don't have the time to talk. "Love you, Mom. Say hi to Dad."

13

FAITH

The pizza place under my apartment is the vein of my existence. The smell of food each time I come home reminds me of everything I shouldn't have. Carbs, fat, sugar—everything that brings me a moment of comfort when I feel low and shitty. I'm exhausted from the shoot. Not just physically, but the comment about my looks and my ass have made me feel so small I want to curl up in a dark corner and sleep. The bottle of vodka is in my purse and my only consolation is that I just had two sips, which might not be a sign of self-restraint to some, but it is to me. *At least I'm not drunk.*

Glancing at the pictures of big, cheesy pizzas, I head for my door, already knowing I'm about to do the thing again that I've been doing more frequently lately, and slipping my key back into my pocket, I take a deep breath before I enter the pizzeria. The last time I did this was a week ago, the day before New Year's Eve. In the past couple of years, I've managed to restrain myself a little and not succumb to this sick ritual more than once a month, but today is a bad day and I don't know what else to do. *It's fine. As long as you don't do it every day. A daily thing is a problem. This is just incidental.*

"One triple cheese, extra-large," I say to the man behind the counter. "And a large Coke." I hesitate as I scan the menu above him. "And a tub of chocolate chip ice cream."

My stomach grumbling, I impatiently wait for my order while I scroll through Instagram. Immediately, a picture of Frankie pops up. She's standing on a yacht somewhere in the Caribbean, surrounded by glamorous people. The first shot is a frontal, and she's posing with two friends. The next is a shot from behind, where she stands on the bow of the boat, her perky behind sparsely covered by a pair of tiny bikini bottoms as she's about to dive in, or pretending to dive in, as Frankie isn't exactly a daredevil.

I haven't been on a beach vacation in years. The idea of being in a bikini in public terrifies me. I have cellulite and yes, my behind is indeed generous. After the last time a newspaper published a shot taken while I was on vacation with my mother and sister, I haven't even tried one on. Anyway, we don't go away together anymore. My sister is too busy with her career and my mother is too busy with the man she's just married for the second time, my sister's father and my stepfather. My mother claims the self-absorbed, cruel asshole is the love of her life and she's gone through great lengths to win him back.

"Your order, ma'am." The guy's voice pulls me out of my thoughts, and I quickly grab the food and rush upstairs, afraid someone will spot me going inside with a giant pizza box and more.

Finally back in the safety of my apartment, I burst into tears. I've felt the urge all day, but I kept my composure. Now, I let it all out. I want to feel miserable on my own with my self-destructive behavior. Sitting on the couch with the food next to me, I cry and cry until I have no more tears left to shed, then open the pizza box and start to eat.

As I'm doing this, I know I'm doing something very wrong. Not because of the calories. They don't matter because I don't intend to keep the food down. I never digest junk food, at least, not if I can help it. This has been my downfall since I was sixteen. Since my stepfather's words started hurting me the most. Moving here two years later to live on my own only made it worse, as I had no social control anymore.

I made friends through my mother's contacts; rich and connected kids whose parents worked in fashion, the arts, and the music industry. Most were beautiful as well as smart, and I envied them for their looks. They were striking, while I was average looking and bigger than them. After my mother bought this apartment for me, she provided me with generous funds on a monthly basis, perhaps to make up for her guilt at wanting to be rid of me. My stepfather and I never got along, as he always treated me like an outsider, and I guess she wanted some peace in the household, a chance to live a happy family life with her husband and their young daughter before she grew up too.

"How would you like to be independent?" Mom asked me one day, and who was I to say no?

I had money and no one looking over my shoulder; I was invited to parties and clubs. A little overwhelmed with my newfound freedom, I literally used the only ammunition I had to feel like I had a place in society: my camera. Taking pictures on nights out was my way to feel validated, and my friends loved their glamour shots, which I shared on my blog or social media. It was never me in the pictures. I hated seeing myself in a shot, but my social accounts featuring my friends became very popular and I rapidly gained followers.

That was how I made my very first paycheck, on the back of other people's beauty. I still do it to this day.

I never felt part of that scene, though; I was always on the outside, never as perfect as my friends were, and I hated my body—especially my behind—and whenever I was home alone, I turned to food for comfort. Not much has changed there either.

The food numbs my senses and the warm gooey cheese calms me down. No people, no judgment. Just me and my food. Of course, I judge *myself*. I always do. I know this is no solution, filling a hole inside of me that is not physical. But it's better than nothing. Better than drugs or tranquilizers, I suppose.

The doorbell rings. I suspect it's Roy, but I leave it ringing again and again. My lights are still out, and he'll leave once he concludes I'm not home. I can't have him here right now. I don't want him to see the pizza, and besides, I need twenty-two minutes to let the food settle in my stomach. It's all a question of timing, and if the timing is right, I can get away with it. Everything that went in will come out.

My phone starts ringing, and I sigh when I see that it is indeed Roy. If only I'd called him on my way home from the shoot. If only I'd told him what had happened today, he would have come right away, and I wouldn't be doing this now.

When I can't possibly eat anymore, I glance at the ice cream. It's not that I love ice cream; I don't actually care much for it. I only bought it for one reason. The cold, creamy texture makes it easier to throw up the entire contents of my stomach.

14

SILVA

"Rough night?" I ask as I enter Faith's apartment. My eyes briefly flick to the vodka bottle on the kitchen counter, but I pretend I don't see it. "You look tired."

"Yeah." She sighs deeply. "Work was a bitch yesterday."

"Well, kudos for getting up. I see you're dressed and ready to go." My eyes meet hers, and there's a deep sadness in them that makes me want to put my arms around her. Again, I refrain from acting on my instincts. It's not my job to tell her off or console her. "Are you up for working out outside?"

Faith hesitates. She looks like she has no energy for anything, but she nods anyway. "Sure. Is it still freezing?"

"It's a little colder than yesterday but you'll warm up soon enough." I wait for Faith to layer up, and she flinches when she, too, spots the vodka bottle.

"About that," she says. "I screwed up."

"There's no such thing as screwing up, as long as you try again. Today is a new day, and we're going to make you feel better."

"I'll take better." Faith puts on her third sweatshirt and gives me a small smile.

"Have you had breakfast?"

"Yes," she says hesitantly.

"Are you sure?" Faith is a bad liar; I know she hasn't eaten.

"Actually, no. I don't feel like eating."

"You're going to have to eat something before the workout." I point to the fruit bowl. "Take a banana with you."

The morning is cold and crisp with lovely blue skies. The roofs of the cars parked in front of Faith's block are still covered in snow, and so are the trees and the small patches of green we pass on our way to Central Park.

"Do you want to tell me about yesterday?" I ask, walking briskly beside her.

"It was nothing. Just a couple of silly, young models talking about me. I don't know why it upset me so much, but it made me..." Her voice trails away, and she pulls her beanie farther over her head, avoiding my gaze.

"What did they say?"

Faith shrugs. "They were commenting on how my sister is so much prettier than me, and about my ass being big. I overheard them talking in the dressing room."

"Your ass?" I frown and can't help but stare at her because that seems crazy. "Your ass is perfect," I say, studying her for any signs of a joke. "Seriously, take it from someone who is attracted to women." I hold up a hand when I see her blush. "Sorry, was that overstepping? I'm being honest here. There's nothing wrong with your beautiful behind. Your curves are amazing."

Finally, Faith breaks out into a chuckle. "Thank you, I guess, but that's not how I feel. And working with size-zero models doesn't help."

"You don't know how beautiful you are." I turn to look at her, but she stares straight ahead. "It's not about how big or small your ass is or what size you are. It's about how you feel about yourself. And I'm going to help you change that mindset."

Faith doesn't look convinced, but she nods and starts jogging when I do, following me into the park. Even in her rough state, she's doing better than the first day already, and we've only had three sessions together. I like working with her. She's one of those people who, once she gets started, seems incredibly driven and even when she's in pain or exhausted, she still won't give up. She's not a quitter; I have to give her that. Panting heavily behind me, she sighs and steadies herself on her knees, relieved that we've reached the spot where we'll train. The equipment in the outdoor gym here is not great, but the benches are useful for weight exercises, and I can attach my resistance bands to the parallel pull-up rails.

"Let's warm up first," I say, and laugh when she looks at me incredulously.

"Are you telling me jogging for ten minutes isn't a warm-up? Because that's the most I've ever managed to run in my life."

"We're going to push ourselves today." I hand her a pair of elastic resistance bands to go around her ankles. "Star jumps on the move for two minutes. I want to see all the snow trodden down before you go into three sets of ten squats."

With no makeup, layers of clothing, red cheeks, and the beanie pulled low over her forehead, she looks nothing like the woman on Instagram. She looks like the girl next door, albeit a very attractive girl next door. She's panting heavily but doesn't give up, and I join her in the routine, helping her to tread down the snow.

"Are you joining me in the squats too?" she asks as she goes through her knees.

"I will today. I'm with you." Counting down from ten together, I don't struggle as much as she does, but it's not easy. Knowing how many calories we're burning, I make a mental note to have a big lunch. After the past two days, I can't afford to stray from my regime again because experience has taught me that it will mess me up more than I can handle. The feeling of hunger can be addictive, and although I know this is hard to imagine for most, I still long for it every single day. When I see Faith bend over to catch her breath, I realize we've done twenty squats instead of ten.

"I'm so sorry," I say. "My mind wandered for a second. Let's take a short rest."

15

FAITH

I'm starting to feel like me again, and I must admit, I've enjoyed every moment of my workout with Silva. For whatever reason, she makes me want to push harder, and I haven't looked at my watch once. Maybe I want to impress her; to prove I'm worthy of her time and effort. Or maybe I like her because she's one of the few people I can be myself around.

"You did really well today," she says as we exit the park.

"Thank you." I feel a sense of achievement and pride because I really did give it my all. My limbs are shaky, and everything hurts, but my energy is up and I feel clear-headed. "Are you seeing your next client now?"

"Not until after lunch." Silva hesitates as we approach the subway, and she glances at a café on the other side of the road. "Do you want to grab a bite to eat?"

"Oh." I'm obviously not aware that I'm staring at her because she chuckles and shakes her head.

"Hey, don't feel obliged. It was just an idea. You haven't had a proper breakfast and I need to eat too so—"

"No, I… I'd like that," I say, interrupting her a little faster and louder than I meant to. "Do you want to go there?" The restaurant looks warm and cozy, and their Christmas decorations are still adorning the windows. Admittedly, I'm feeling very hungry, and having something healthy with her now will stop me from repeating yesterday's actions.

Silva smiles as she holds the door open for me and the warmth welcomes us. "This is nice, right? After ninety minutes in the freezing cold." She asks for a table in the back by the fireplace, and as we follow the waiter, a curious feeling creeps up on me. If I'm not mistaken, I'm excited, which is strange as very few things excite me in life, especially not restaurants. There's also a hint of nervousness, and that makes even less sense. I'm Faith Astor; people tend to get nervous around *me*, not the other way around. When she pulls out a chair for me, my core flutters and for a moment, I don't know how to sit, what to do with my hands or what to say.

"Are you going to take that off?" she asks, pointing to my scarf and beanie.

I laugh and roll my eyes. "Of course. I guess my brain is exhausted too."

I take them off and put them on my lap, then realize I'm still sweltering with my three sweatshirts on, so I remove my top layer too. My hair becomes static, and I can hear it crackling as I run my hand over my ponytail to smoothen it. I wish I could go home and get dressed before sitting here opposite Silva, with nothing to focus on but each other. She, on the other hand, is probably in her comfort zone, as I can't see her wearing anything but sportswear.

"I can't say I've ever been out for lunch looking like this before."

"Don't stress it, you look great. I like the whole natural thing. It suits you."

I give her a small smile and focus on the menu, so she won't see how much that comment affects me. It never means anything coming from others. Although I always accept compliments gracefully, I don't tend to believe them. Then why do I believe *her*? And why is my heart rate suddenly up? "I don't think you've seen me any other way."

"I looked you up," Silva admits with a goofy shrug, then sits back and regards me. "You have a dazzling camera smile, but I prefer the real you."

"Nothing you see online or in the gutter press is real," I say, stunned that I'm admitting this to her. "It's all carefully orchestrated. The clothes, the hair, the makeup, the location —even the company. Being seen means everything when you work in fashion. If I didn't hang out with the 'right' people," I make quote marks in the air, "I'd be long forgotten and out of work."

"That's sad."

"Yes, it is."

Silva nods. "Can I ask you a personal question?"

"Haven't you been doing that since day one?" As Silva has only seen me stripped of all glitz and glamour, I already feel like she knows me better than most people, so I'm not uncomfortable having private conversations with her. Besides, it's always easier opening up to a stranger, and I can always cancel my training sessions if I feel she's getting too close.

"I suppose so." She pauses while she pours us sparkling water from the bottle on the table. "Do you have any close friends? People you can really talk to?"

The question is personal indeed, and not what I expected. "Yes, I have a good friend. His name is Roy. I told you about him."

"Good." She nods. "That's good."

"Why do you ask?"

Silva bites her lip as she meets my eyes. "Because you have a certain sadness about you, and I hope that you feel you can share whatever makes you feel that way with someone."

I swallow hard and look away. Silva's observant: it's like she sees right through me. I trust Roy, and I have a couple of other fairly close friends, but I would never tell any of them what I did last night, including Roy. How sometimes I loathe myself so much that I can't even look in the mirror. How sometimes the sick ritual of stuffing myself and throwing my guts up is the only way to feel better for a little while. "Don't worry about me. I'm fine. I'm always fine."

"I'm sorry, I know it's none of my business." Silva winces as if she's realized she's crossed her professional boundaries. She opens her menu and scans the first page. "Let's talk food instead. What do you feel like?"

16

SILVA

"Hey, there. Sorry I had to reschedule." Thankfully, Faith was flexible when I asked her if we could do our training tonight instead of this morning, as I had to deal with a leak in my apartment. When I take off my coat and look at her, I immediately know something is wrong. She looks like she's just woken up; confused and bewildered.

"Fuck," she says. "I took a nap after I came home and fell asleep." Looking over her shoulder, her face goes pale as she spots the empty food packaging on the coffee table. "Let me just clear that up." She rushes off and manically starts clearing chocolate wrappers, an ice cream tub and leftovers of a burger.

"You seem upset. What's the matter?" I ask.

"I fell asleep," she says again, this time through sniffs. "And this..."

"What about it? I'm not going to judge you, I already told you that."

"You weren't supposed to see this, and I wasn't supposed to fall asleep." She heads to the kitchen, and I hear the lid of her trash can slam hard before she returns. "I've ruined everything. All the hard work. The healthy eating, the exercise... I poisoned my body with all this crap over two hours ago, and then I fell into a fucking food coma."

At first, none of this makes any sense to me. Why get so upset over a few extra calories? It finally clicks when I see the panic in her eyes. It's a look I recognize all too well from my time in recovery. She never intended to keep that junk food down. "Hey, come here," I say, and pull her into a tight hug. Holding her, I wait until she's calmed down a little before I inch back and cup her face. "You haven't ruined anything, okay? Nothing bad is going to happen. That burger is not going to attach itself to your thighs, and even if it does, it's not the end of the world. It's just food."

"Then why does it feel like the end of the world?"

I take her hand. "Faith... will you please be honest with me so I can help you?" I pause as I wait for her to nod, but she simply stares at me, wide-eyed. I have to address this. I can't let her suffer alone. "Are you bulimic?"

The look on her face says it all. I've invaded her deepest, darkest, most private depths, and it must feel like I've opened her diary and read it out loud in front of an audience.

"It's okay, you can talk to me, Faith. How often do you do this?"

Faith bursts out in tears and covers her face with her hands. "How do you know?" She sits on the sofa, and I sit next to her and put an arm around her. "Fuck. I'm so embarrassed."

"You don't need to be embarrassed around me."

"Yes, I should be. You're the only one who knows what a vile, weird, and twisted creature I am."

"You're none of those things." I hesitate. "Did something trigger you today? Or is this a part of your daily life?"

Faith takes a couple of deep breaths before she dries her tears. "I thought I had it under control, but I've done it more frequently since Christmas," she says through sniffs. "And no, there was no trigger today. I've been feeling low a lot lately. Well, those comments from the shoot the other day still bother me, I suppose." She stares right ahead, avoiding my gaze.

I'm quiet while I give her time to process that I know. I'm aware this is a big deal for her; I've been through something similar.

"Never in the morning," she finally says after a long silence. "I only ever do it at night. That's another reason why I go out so much. It distracts me from those thoughts. But then I tend to drink a lot, and that's not great either."

"Listen," I say, running a hand through her hair. "The next time you feel that urge, you call me, okay? I'll come over and we'll go for a run together, or we could go and see a movie or something if you don't feel like exercising. There are healthier distractions than drinking."

"Come on, I'm not going to do that. You have a life. I'm sure you wouldn't normally do such a thing for your clients."

"No, not for clients. But I'd do it for a friend."

"Friends," Faith repeats. "Do you see me as your friend?"

"Yes. I've told you things about me very few people know, and I know very private things about you. I trust you, and I hope you trust me too."

"I do," she says, and the corners of her mouth pull into a sad smile.

I smile back at her and squeeze her hand. "Come on, Faith. You can fight this. Just call me and I'll help you fight it." She leans in farther and locks her eyes with mine. They're so intense I can barely handle it.

"Okay." She swallows hard and nods. "But if you're busy, you—"

"Yes, if I'm doing something really important, I'll tell you."

"Okay," she says again. "Like a date, or a—"

"I'm not dating all that much, babe, so don't worry about that." I shoot her a wink, and she chuckles. "There you go, I love that smile."

"Why is that?" she asks.

"What? Why do I love your smile?"

Faith laughs. "No, why don't you date much. I imagine women are lining up for you."

"I'm not all that. There's no reason they'd be lining up for me."

"Well, I happen to think you *are* all that, hence the question." For a split second, her gaze lowers to my mouth and it makes me feel funny inside.

"You do, huh?" I narrow my eyes at her, desperate to know what she's thinking.

"Yeah. Why are you single?"

"No particular reason. I haven't met the right person, and I'm bored with online dating." I tilt my head. "Are you one of those women who always go for the bad guys?"

"I guess so." Faith sighs. "But that phase of my life ended over the holidays. I think I've gone off men."

"That's a big statement."

Faith nods, and she looks like she has more to say, but she doesn't.

"Do you want to work out?" I ask, noting she's turning back into herself again. It's probably best if we end this conversation and continue as normal so she can move on instead of harboring regrets.

"Yes, please. Let's work out. I have thousands of calories to burn off."

"It's not about the calories, it's about how you'll feel after," I say, shamefully aware I have trouble living by my own mantra.

17

SILVA

Snow is still falling, and although it makes New York look pretty, it's also disruptive. Traffic jams line every street, and the train is crammed as the bus services are heavily delayed. When I finally escape Prospect Park subway station and breathe in fresh air, I can't wait to get home. Heading down Maple Street, I walk slowly as the sidewalk is slippery. My mind is consumed with Faith and the shocking but not totally surprising discovery I made tonight. I'm honored that she opened up to me and knowing how hard it is to be in such a place, I'm determined to support her in whatever way I can. Over the past two weeks, Faith has become more than a client to me. We've talked a lot, we've had lunch together a couple of times, and I usually stay for a coffee after training, so yes, I suppose we are friends.

Remembering how upset she looked when I arrived, I stop and close my eyes for a moment because it reminds me of my own struggles. Despite the silence in the streets tonight, I only vaguely register a noise behind me, and I freeze, knowing it's coming my way faster than it should. A car or a motorcycle? I hear the sound of tires screeching and then a car horn beeps, but before I've even had the chance to turn around or move aside, something slams into me and I'm lifted off the ground. Everything happens in a haze, and although I technically know I can't be spinning in the air that slowly, it feels that way. There's no pain when I land with a thud, and for a moment, I don't even know if I'm lying on my front or my back. Everything goes fuzzy, and then, nothing. When I open my eyes, there are two people kneeled next to me, shouting and patting my face.

"Miss, can you hear me? Miss? Miss?"

"What?" is all I can say because I feel nauseous and dizzy.

"Could you tell me your name, please? An ambulance is on its way, it won't be long. What's your name?"

"Silva," I mumble. My lashes flutter. I want to close my eyes again, but they won't let me.

"Okay, Silva, stay with us now, come on." There's an eerie silence while I open them again, then sighs of relief. "That's good. Stay with us." More words are exchanged, but I have trouble understanding what is said. Something about a slippery road and losing control over the wheel. They sound worried. Should I be worried?

I hear the ambulance and slowly return to reality. I'm on the sidewalk on Maple Street and in front of me is a parked car, its engine still running. I've been hit, I'm on my back, and the moment I realize that, the agonizing pain in my ankle sets in. It's instant and sharp, and I know something is wrong.

"Fuck!" I shout as I try to move my leg, then rub my sore head. I think the damage is at the back of my head, but the banging thud moves through my entire skull, my ears, and even my eye sockets. The blinding, flashing lights of the ambulance are close to unbearable when it comes to a halt next to me. Paramedics rush out and examine me while they ask a ton of questions I don't want to answer because everything hurts when I speak.

"You're going to be okay," one of them tells me, so I let my eyes close.

~

"Hey, sis." When I wake up, Trinny is beside me, holding a huge bunch of flowers. "They told me you were hit by a car. We've been so worried about you. Mom and Dad called me like a hundred times. They wanted to fly over, but the doctor said you'd be okay, so I told them not to panic."

"Trinny." I give her a smile and manage to turn my head her way. It's not that my neck hurts, but my whole body feels heavy and limp, so it's hard to move. "Yeah, I had an accident." I'm slurring my words like a drunk person, and it annoys me. "What's the damage? And why do I feel so weird?"

"That's probably the anesthetic they gave you before they set your leg." She puts the flowers on my nightstand, pulls in a chair and takes my hand as she sits. "You were lucky. You have a concussion and a broken ankle, but it could have been way worse. They've already set it, but it's still swelling, so they have to wait before they can put the cast on."

"My ankle?"

"Yeah. They want to keep you overnight because of the concussion, but if you're okay, I can take you home with me tomorrow."

"Fuck. Not my ankle..." I let out a long sigh of frustration.

"Hey, as I said, you've been lucky. Your ankle will heal soon enough, and you'll be back to normal in two months."

I know I should be grateful that it's not worse, but right now, there's only one thing on my mind. "I won't be able to work out."

"True." Trinny shrugs. "I suppose you could give online classes if your clients are interested in that, and you're insured for injuries, aren't you?"

"Yeah."

She's right; this doesn't have to affect my income drastically unless my current clients decide to take on another trainer as I won't be able to come to their homes. I can make it work, and even if they do leave me, I'll find new clients. What really bothers me, and what I meant to say, is I won't be able to exercise *myself*. Clients or no clients, the thought of not being able to run or do heavy workouts that burn calories to keep my weight stable terrifies me, but I can't tell Trinny that. She's been worried about me for years and still keeps a close eye on me to make sure I don't fall back into old habits.

"You're right," I say, putting on a brave face. "I've been lucky, and I'll be fine." I point to the flowers and smile. "Those are beautiful. Thank you."

18

FAITH

I'm afraid I have to cancel our sessions for the coming two months, as I had an accident and broke my ankle. I'll call you to see if we can do them online if you want. Big discount, of course. I totally understand if you prefer to find someone to replace me. Really sorry about this. Silva.

My stomach tightens, and I'm about to type a reply when I change my mind and call her instead. I'm worried, and I need to know that she's okay. "Silva?"

"Hey, Faith. Did you get my message?" Considering the situation, she seems surprisingly cheerful, but her speech is a bit slow, and she sounds tired. It's strange to hear her voice over the phone; it's so intense in my ear.

"Yes, I did. How are you? What happened?"

"I was hit by a car on my way home after our training," she says. "I was lucky it was just my ankle. I hit my head pretty hard too, and I have a concussion."

"Oh, God." I pause. "Are you in pain?"

"No, not really. They gave me medication at the hospital, and I have enough for five days. They're making me feel a bit foggy, though. I don't like it."

"Poor thing... you won't be able to move around or do your job or anything."

"Yeah, that sucks," she says. "Not for a while anyway."

"Is someone taking care of you? You're not there by yourself, are you?" Remembering not everyone has the luxury of living in Manhattan like I do, I imagine it might be hard for her to get groceries delivered last minute.

"I'm fine. My sister wanted me to stay at her place, but I'd rather be at home. Her apartment is tiny, and we'd constantly be in each other's space. She's coming over later with some groceries as I can't get down the stairs with my cast and crutches, but it should be fine after tomorrow, as I've signed up for online delivery."

"Ouch. So you don't have an elevator in your building?"

"No, it's one of those old redbricks. They're lovely as long as you don't break anything," she jokes.

I chuckle and desperately search for something to keep the conversation going. "How long will you be in a cast?"

"Six to eight weeks. And then I'll need a bit of time to recover. But as I said, if you want to continue our training online, we can do that. I just need a full week's rest first because of the concussion."

"Okay, I'm happy to continue online when you feel better. Do you need help with anything? Can I cook for you or get you a wheelchair?"

Now it's Silva's turn to laugh. "I wouldn't dare ask Faith Astor, my one and only celebrity client, to cook for me. Come on."

"Hey, don't be like that. I'm not a celebrity, and besides, we're friends, so let me help you." Then another idea strikes me. A very, very appealing idea. It's crazy, but it makes sense. "Why don't you come and stay with me while you recover?"

"What?" Silva sounds astounded. "That's very sweet of you, but I'm fine, honestly."

"There's an elevator in my building, and I have a big guest room and a cleaner. Surely it would make life a lot easier for you? You'll have your own bedroom, and you can do online workouts from my office. I never use it anyway."

"Faith... as sweet as it is, I can't take you up on that offer. It's too much."

Not one to take no for an answer, I let out a long sigh. "But it would help me too. You can get me in shape from the comfort of my big couch, and you wouldn't be alone in your apartment while you're confined to crutches. There are numerous cafés crutch-distance away from here, and I could cook for you and help you out."

"So you want a live-in personal trainer?"

"It's not just that," I say. "I wouldn't mind the company either. It's kind of boring on my own now that I'm trying not to drink and not going out as much. And it would also help me with my..."

"With your bulimic tendencies?"

I wince at her words. *Bulimia.* I've never said it out loud, and hearing it from her again makes reality hit home hard. For years I've told myself that it's just a thing I do. I've refused to give it a name, but I really do have a problem.

"Yes, I suppose it would help with that too. It's..." My voice trails off, and I need a moment. "It's easier when I'm not alone."

"Of course, I get that." Silva is silent while she thinks it over. "I might drive you mad."

"I might annoy you too," I say. "But then again, it might work really well, and if you don't like living here you can always move back home. There's no harm in trying, right?"

"Okay," she finally says. "It's super sweet of you and I'll

think about it, but only if you're sure it would benefit both of us. I don't like accepting favors from people."

"Everyone needs help now and then. We'll work on that." My heart is racing at the thought of having Silva here. "Oh, and by the way, happy Valentine's Day." Rolling my eyes, I curse myself for being so cliché.

"Happy Valentine's Day to you too," she says with a chuckle. "I hope Cupid is good to you."

"No cards so far. Not that I was expecting any. What about you?"

"Nothing. And no dates lined up for the obvious reasons, so I'm just going to lie here and space out with the Hallmark channel."

I chuckle and imagine her on my couch instead. "You do that, and please think about my offer. I'd love to help you out."

19

SILVA

As I hang up, I'm still trying to figure out what just happened. Faith Astor wants me to move in with her. Recovering in her beautiful Manhattan apartment is a crazy thought but I can't say I mind the idea. I can't say I mind being around *her* twenty-four seven either. Between the last time we saw each other and the accident, I've barely had time to process what she told me. Eating disorders are serious; it's not something I'm qualified to deal with, but at least I can relate, and for that reason, I may be able to help her, so perhaps she's right. I let out a long sigh and shift on the couch, but it's hard to get comfortable with the thick cast around my lower leg. For someone who's used to constantly being on the move, this is seriously boring, and already, I have no idea what to do. Relieved when the door opens, I smile when Trinny lets herself in.

"I finally have a reason to use your spare key without worrying I'll find you in bed with someone. It's safe now you're wearing that cast," she says with a chuckle. "Two years later and I'm still traumatized."

"Hey, your trauma is entirely self-inflicted. That was just

once, and you should have messaged me or at least knocked."

"You're right, I should have." Trinny laughs. "Trust me, for a straight person, seeing your sister wearing one of those—"

"Okay, enough," I say playfully, cutting her off, because I've already heard that story more times than I can handle. "What's with all the stuff? You've brought enough food for a family of six." I point to the three big grocery bags she drops on the floor.

"Yeah, I went a bit overboard. God, those stairs are killing me." Trinny wipes her forehead dramatically.

"I told you I'd order groceries online. I only need the bare necessities."

"I know. But your situation sucks, and I wanted to do something nice for you. Since I can't fix your leg, I thought I might as well cook you a couple of meals for the coming days. You know, food prep. It's all the rage nowadays." She perches on the edge of the sofa. "How about my famous dirty noodles? I know you love them."

"Thank you, that's very sweet." I manage to return her smile, already dreading Trinny's signature dish. I'm usually honest with my sister, but the first time she cooked "dirty noodles" for me was when she'd just moved into her new apartment. The table was beautifully laid out and she'd made such a fuss that I didn't have the heart to tell her the instant noodles with queso tasted awful.

"No problem." She winks and rubs my shoulder. "Now, first things first. Are you in pain?"

"No, I'm on meds. And before you ask, yes, they're strong and no, I'm not going to share them with you," I joke. "But there's white wine in the fridge if you want."

Trinny throws her head back and laughs. "Don't make

assumptions, Miss Perfect. I haven't swallowed anything naughty since the late nineties, but I will have a glass of wine. What do you want?"

"I'll have a tea."

"Tea coming up." Trinny pours herself a large glass of white wine and makes my tea as she talks. "So, next question. What about work? Have any clients come back to you yet?"

"Yes, surprisingly. More than half have already confirmed they're fine with online classes, so I think I'm going to carry on working from home."

"Okay. That's good," she says, handing me my tea. "What about Faith Astor? I bet she's dumping you for someone who can actually walk."

"No. Faith is staying. She asked if I wanted to move in with her while I recover."

"Sure, she did. Did she also say she'd nurse you back to health and tend to your every need?"

"No. It's more of a two-way situation. Me being there will help her too."

Trinny holds up both hands and frowns. "Wait... you're serious?"

"Yeah. And I might take her up on her offer. She has an elevator in her building so I can go outside on my crutches, and I think she's lonely."

"She can't possibly be lonely," Trinny says. "I started following her on social media since you told me she was your client, and that woman is always surrounded by people."

"That's what her followers see. What I see is just a down-to-earth, sweet woman who struggles like everyone else."

"Wow." Trinny arches a brow and points a finger at me. "You have that look when you talk about her."

"What look?"

"The look that says you like her."

My eyes widen as I gasp. "Will you stop it with the whole 'digging my client' thing? I already told you she's straight."

"And if she wasn't?"

"Seriously, Trinny," I warn her. "It's a practical arrangement. I can train her while I live there, she has an elevator so I can go outside, and her apartment is big, so we wouldn't be in each other's way all the time.

"Hmm." Trinny shoots me a skeptical look. "I bet her apartment's stunning. Want me to move you in there? I'd love to see it."

"If you wouldn't mind, that would be really great. She said she could send someone over, but I don't want to be any trouble. I'll probably be okay to pack some stuff and head over there in a week or so, but for now I need to stay horizontal and rest."

"Yeah, you do that." Trinny continues to stare at me while she takes the bags over to the kitchen. If I'm not mistaken, she still thinks I'm joking. "Well, I'd better start cooking you those dirty noodles because I doubt you'll be getting that from Miss Astor."

20

FAITH

"Shoot me. Your sexy trainer is moving in with you?" Roy laughs so hard that the popcorn he's eating shoots straight up his nose.

"Only while her leg recovers," I say, patting his back as he sits up. "She's coming on the weekend. Her sister is moving her in." I shrug and pretend it's nothing, but in truth I've been in turmoil for days.

"And why exactly did you offer your swanky sanctuary? It's not like you need a discount on your training."

"I do actually," I say with a chuckle. "I'm not getting all the covers anymore, so I have to tighten my belt a little."

"Sure, honey." Roy's voice is dripping with sarcasm. "I think you're into her. You should see yourself."

"I'm so not into her. You know I'm not into women. I like her the same way I like you, that's all." I tug at the bedsheets, claiming back my share.

"But where am I going to fall asleep to Netflix on a weeknight when I have nothing better to do? You know I hate being alone." Roy falls back into the pillows, turns to me, and juts out his bottom lip, his expression comically dramatic.

"She'll be in the guest room. You can still come over for Netflix and a cuddle."

"Uh-huh." He laughs. "We'll see about that. I think you're about to be sexually adventurous and you need it, girl. Have I ever told you why sex with people of the same gender is so good?"

Suppressing an eye roll, I let out a long sigh. "Yeah, you've told me like a million times. Because they know how your body works and what feels good and then there's the connection on an emotional level that's unique to same-sex couples, blah, blah, blah."

"Hmm... so you do listen sometimes."

"Sure," I say, wishing he would stop talking about Silva because now I'm picturing her in my bed. On top of me. Naked. *Fuck. How am I going to be around her if these fantasies don't stop?* "Can we please get back to the series?"

"No. You literally just told me you thought it was boring and I'm having too much fun winding you up," Roy shoots back. "So be honest for once because I know that although I'm your best friend, you always hold back with me. Are you the slightest bit attracted to her?" He takes my hand when I don't answer. "I'm your best friend, Faith. I'm on your side."

I nod and meet his kind eyes. "I know you're on my side." Pursing my lips, I contemplate how honest to be with him. "I suppose I find her attractive," I finally say.

"There you go. Good girl." Roy smiles, and for once, he's not joking or being sarcastic. "Now, that wasn't so hard, was it?" He tilts his head and regards me. "What is it that you like about her?"

Feeling my cheeks burn up, I scoot farther under the covers and look up at the ceiling. "Silva has great energy.

And she's... I don't know. So grounded and refreshingly normal. I don't know anyone like her."

"That's because you only hang out with people who work in fashion. And me," he adds with a wink. "I'm normal, though, aren't I?" He laughs when I point to his sequined pink pajamas.

"You call that normal?" I laugh. "You're kind, outgoing, and funny, and I love you, but I wouldn't describe you as normal. Your pajamas give my cleaner headaches. She finds the sequins everywhere."

"Whatever. Back to Silva."

My heart races when I picture Silva bent over me, her face close to mine as she takes my weights after my shoulder presses. "She's just..." I groan at my inability to express myself. "She makes me feel good, and I don't have to be perfect around her. Trying my best is enough, and she makes me feel happy and weird, but in a good way."

"Cute." Roy chuckles. "I don't think I've ever heard you say that before."

"No," I say, failing to remember when I last felt like this. "Do you think it's a bad idea that she's moving in here?"

"No." Roy waves a hand. "I think it's the most sense you've ever made. When you told me you wanted to hire a PT and become healthy, I never thought you'd follow through with it. But here you are, two and a half weeks later and you haven't even had a drink or a cigarette tonight. She's good for you, Faith."

"I haven't exactly been perfect, though."

"But isn't that the whole point? You're trying your best instead of aiming for perfect, and that's good enough."

"Yes." Failing to keep a straight face, I smile widely.

"Well, then." Roy gestures to my phone on the nightstand. "Also, you're not showing any signs of FOMO. You're usually scanning Instagram for anything you're missing out on, but you haven't been on your phone once since I walked in."

"I've actually been on it an awful lot today." I pick up my phone and scroll to Silva's account. "But instead of my friends' and my sister's account, I've been looking at Silva's." I know he's going to tease me for this, but now I've started, I don't want the conversation to end, and I love saying her name out loud.

"Let me see that." Roy snatches it away from me and gasps at a picture of Silva in a skimpy crop top and loose sweatpants that hang low on her hips. "You dirty, dirty girl." He shoots me a mischievous grin as he zooms in on her. "So this is the kind of porn lesbians look at, huh?"

"I'm not a lesbian."

"Not yet." Roy narrows his eyes and whistles through his teeth. "Look at those abs."

"Sounds to me like she's about to turn *you* instead," I joke, but I still feel a jolt of arousal when my eyes settle on her gorgeous face as she smiles into the camera.

21

SILVA

"Nice pad." Trinny stares up at the high-rise Manhattan building in awe before we enter.

"Wait till you see inside," I say, greeting the security guard. Expecting us, he calls the elevator, and I struggle my way in, followed by Trinny, who is dragging two large suitcases behind her.

"Hey. Come here, let me help you." As soon as the doors open, Faith rushes toward me, looks at my crutches and laughs when she realizes there's nothing she can do. Then she smiles at Trinny and introduces herself. "Hi, I'm Faith."

Trinny greets her back with great excitement, and I feel like kicking her for staring. She's a grown woman, for God's sake, a very serious lawyer. And Faith isn't a movie star; she's not even that famous.

"I love, love, love your outfit," Trinny says, eyeing Faith's pristine, white pantsuit. I have to admit, although I'm not much of a fashion connoisseur, I love it too. She looks so elegant and angelic that I have trouble taking my eyes off her.

"Thank you. It's vintage." Faith is holding up a front, but

I can tell she's a little nervous as she focuses on the luggage and takes one of the suitcases from Trinny. "I asked my cleaner to prepare your bedroom, but I haven't had time to check it before she left. I hope everything's okay," she says, turning to me.

"Anything is okay. I'm just happy I'll be able to go outside. It's been a long week." I meet her eyes, and a flutter runs through me. Being confined to my apartment wasn't the only reason the week crept by at a snail's pace. It was waiting so long to see Faith again that got me antsy. "This is very kind of you."

Her apartment is tidier than normal, and flowers in big, crystal vases are scattered throughout the living room and the kitchen. It's strange, being here in this capacity, and although I'm usually confident and in charge when I'm training someone, right now, I feel at least as nervous as Faith. I'll be living here for the coming six to eight weeks—at least if we get along—and that thought is daunting as well as exciting.

"Sit down and make yourself comfortable." Faith pats the sofa, takes my crutches from me, and lifts my casted leg onto a pile of pillows she's already placed there.

"You really don't have to do this. I didn't hurt my knee. I can still bend my leg." I laugh when she fusses over the huge, wooden coffee table that is out of reach and drags the heavy piece of furniture my way. "I feel bad already, and I haven't even been here for a minute."

"Don't feel bad. I'm so happy you're here. I read it's best to keep your leg up in the beginning, so that's what you'll do." Her smile is genuine, and it puts me at ease. "You stay here. Trinny and I will take your luggage to your bedroom. I've also cleared my office, so it's ready for you to work from."

I'm about to thank her again and tell her she really needn't go to all this trouble for me, but she's already heading into the corridor with Trinny. They're laughing, and I frown when they lower their voices before more laughter echoes through the apartment. "Hey, just because I'm not able to follow you around doesn't give you the right to talk about me," I yell playfully.

Trinny chuckles when they reappear moments later. "I was warning Faith about your sleepwalking, and then we realized you won't be able to." She laughs even harder now as she points to my cast. "I'm sure that won't stop you, so she might have to pick you up from the floor when you decide to go on wandering."

"Is it really that bad?" Faith asks humorously.

"Yes. It started when she was around twelve, and when we shared an apartment a few years back, she was still up regularly, so I doubt that's changed." I shoot Trinny a warning look, but she continues. "One time, I woke up to find her standing over me, and she handed me a skipping rope and told me to get my ass up and start moving. She was totally serious."

Faith looks highly amused as she meets my eyes. "So, sleepwalking, huh?" she asks, burying her hands in her pockets. "Anything else I should know about?"

"Trinny's exaggerating," I lie. "And no, I don't think there's anything else." Although I'm glad the ice is broken and Trinny and Faith are getting along, I hadn't expected them to gang up on me, even if it is in the nicest way possible.

"Sure there is," Trinny says, making me cringe as I already know what's coming. "Silva's got total fridge OCD. She'll probably find a way to rearrange yours even if she has to break the other leg in the process."

Faith finds this hilarious, and she happily points in the direction of the kitchen. "Please knock yourself out. I just did a big grocery shop, so you'll find plenty of food to rearrange. All healthy stuff."

"I wasn't planning on intruding in your system," I say sheepishly. "I'll keep out of your hair. I'll help as much as I can, and of course I'll order groceries and takeout for us, as I might have trouble standing up and cooking."

"Not a chance," Faith insists. "You're here to recover, so don't worry about a thing. You can train me from the couch, but other than that, I'll take care of things. I've been practicing my cooking skills, so I might even be able to impress you." She shrugs and looks more relaxed now. "Anyway, where are my manners? Would you like a drink? I have coffee, tea, wine, vodka, and coconut water. Have you eaten yet?"

Trinny, who promised she'd leave once she'd move me in, nods enthusiastically and plonks down in a chair. "Thank you, I won't say no to a glass of wine. And no, we haven't eaten. Shall we get a takeout? My treat."

"Excellent. Wine for us then, and for the patient..." Faith arches a brow at me. "Chamomile tea?"

I try to keep a straight face as I exchange a brief glance with Trinny. Not only is she sitting snuggled up in Faith's designer chair as if she's about to watch a movie with a bucket of popcorn on her lap, she's also practically invited herself over for dinner. "I'm not taking my pills anymore, so I'll have a glass of wine too, please." I'm glad I can drink, because having my sister and Faith in one room is a lot, and Trinny's not one to hold back.

Faith claps her hands together in delight. "Perfect. I'll open a bottle while you two order whatever you want. But please, it's on me. It's your first night here and I want to give you a warm welcome."

The moment she disappears around the corner, I catch Trinny's gaze again and mouth, "What the fuck?"

Trinny shrugs and rolls her eyes at me. "What?" she says in a hushed tone. "Faith Astor wants to have dinner with me. I'm not going to say no to that."

22

FAITH

Silva's sister is lovely, and I feel like I'm a part of their sacred sisterhood tonight. I've missed hanging out with just women; there are usually an awful lot of men circling me when I'm at parties, and most of them are ruthless lotharios, trying their luck. My sister and I never had nights like this, with wine and food and good conversation. She's a lot younger than me, and once she turned eighteen, she rose to fame. She's been jet-setting ever since, flying from one photoshoot to another. The times we see each other are few and far between and never more than a quick lunch or a hello at a premiere or a club opening.

I've never had close female friends; women in fashion tend to be either competitive or jealous, so I simply don't trust them, and my nights with Roy are fun, but they're not the same. He mainly talks about his conquests and himself, while Silva, Trinny, and I talk about everything and anything from favorite artists and movies to the impossible dating scene in New York and the complexity of family structures. The conversation is flowing so pleasantly that I don't want it to end. Trinny doesn't hold back with her questions, and she wants to know all about my dating history.

"So what about that last guy you dated? The art director —Michael something? He's like a billionaire's son, right?"

"Yeah. He's a piece of scum. He cheated on me with a model and that seems to be the story of my life." I shrug it off with a chuckle, because now that Silva is here, Michael has become a distant memory and I couldn't care less about him. "Even Roy, my ex and best friend, cheated on me, only he did it with a man."

Trinny cracks up in roaring laughter. "Maybe you should try dating women," she says with a wink, her gaze shifting to Silva for a split second. "You have a real lesbian living under your roof now. Maybe Silva can fill you in on how that works?"

"Trinny!" Silva hisses. "That's enough wine for you, I think."

"It's okay, she's only joking." I don't mind Trinny's directness; it's refreshing and real.

Trinny ignores her sister, leans in closer and lowers her voice to a whisper. "I did some experimenting in college and I can tell you, it was great. Not for me long term, but still great. She did this—"

"Trinny, we don't need details," Silva interrupts her, "and besides, it's getting late."

Trinny glances at her almost empty glass and tilts her head from side to side. "You may be right, sis. I'm feeling a little light-headed." She smiles at me. "Well, this has been a lot of fun. We should definitely do it again."

"Feel free to drop by anytime you want," I say. "This is Silva's home too now, and I've had a really great time tonight." I note that I'm not even remotely tipsy. I've talked so much that I hardly drank. It's liberating to be around people who don't make me feel self-conscious or anxious. People who simply want to have a good time and talk for the sake of getting to know each other. No networking and no pressure to impress.

"Thank you, you know I will." She gets up and puts on her coat. "Take care of my little sis, will you? She's not as tough as she makes out."

The comment intrigues me, especially because she seems completely sincere, but with Silva here, I let it slide. "She's in good hands," I assure Trinny, and walk her to the door. "I hope to see you soon."

When I close the door, Silva lets out an exasperated sigh. "I apologize," she says. "I told her not to stick around, but as usual, she ignored me."

"Please, it's okay. She's great company." I smile. "Seriously, I meant it when I said she's welcome anytime."

"That's very sweet of you, but I don't want to disrupt your life in any way while I'm here."

"You won't. I like having you here. Now, can I get you anything? Don't feel like you need to stay up for me, but don't feel like you need to avoid me either. Do you want to watch a movie with me? There's a TV in your room too if you'd rather be alone."

Silva stares at the TV as if she's never seen one before, and I wonder what's going through her mind. "Okay, I'll watch a movie with you. What were you thinking?"

"How about something scary?"

At this, she laughs. "I didn't take you for a horror fan." She shifts farther back against the armrest. "Come and sit with me. I don't want to take up all the space on your comfortable couch, and there's really no need for my leg to be up."

It's a simple comment and it doesn't mean anything, but

I'm still shaken and flustered at the thought. Sitting next to her on the sofa is something I've pictured many times before she arrived, and now the moment is here.

My voice sounds strangled as I lift her leg, sit next to her, and place her casted foot on my lap. "Is this comfortable?" Hoping it's not too much, I study her, but she simply smiles her beautiful, wide smile, making me feel even more heated inside. "This medical website says it helps with the swelling."

"It's definitely comfortable. I'll try not to crush you if I get a fright."

"And I'll try not to break your cast if I suddenly jump up," I joke and reach over her leg for the remotes on the coffee table. Using the first one, I close the electric curtain rail and dim the lights, then switch to the other one to turn on the TV. "I haven't gone Alexa yet, I'm afraid. I'm not the brightest when it comes to technology."

"Well, I still make do with a simple light switch," she says and reaches for the blanket that's hanging over the couch's backrest. "Can I use this?"

"Of course. Are you cold? I can turn up the heat."

"No," she says, shaking her head with a chuckle. "But I might need something to hide behind."

23

SILVA

Watching a movie has never felt so intense. It's not the movie; the movie is scary, but I can handle it. It's the dimmed lights and the intimacy of watching it with Faith while sharing a blanket, and the fact that my leg is resting in her lap that makes me incredibly self-aware. I find it hard to relax when she's sitting so close, and occasionally, I wonder if she feels the same as she doesn't seem to know what to do with her hands. She rested them on my cast for a while, then clumsily dropped them to her sides after staring down at them as if she had no idea how they ended up there. It's not a natural position to sit in; no one watches a movie with their hands along their sides. It's like she's having trouble acting natural, and I feel the same. I didn't anticipate this before coming here. I thought we'd simply coexist in this spacious apartment, apart from during our workouts and maybe dinner. She's not pressuring me into anything, and I appreciate that she wants me to feel at home, but this synergy is already a recipe for trouble because I feel things when I'm with her that I haven't felt in a long time. I want her.

"Are you okay?" she asks sweetly, pausing the movie and turning to me. "Do you want anything? Water? Tea? Something stronger?"

"No, I'm good. I wish I could get you a drink, but I can't carry anything while I'm using my crutches."

Faith shakes her head. "Don't be silly. That's why you're here. So I can help you."

"I just hope I can help you in return," I say, aware that I'm already a nuisance.

"You *are* helping me." Faith looks vulnerable, and I'm honored that she's being so open with me. "I felt entirely comfortable sharing your company tonight—and your sister's. Apart from with my friend Roy, that rarely happens."

"And now?" I hesitate. "You seem nervous."

Faith flinches, and her eyes dart back to the TV. She's about to say something when she shakes her head. "No, I'm fine. Are you nervous around me?"

"Not nervous. Apprehensive, I suppose," I admit, hoping she'll speak her mind if I do.

"Why is that?" Faith's gaze darkens, and she meets my eyes.

"Because I've moved in with a beautiful, kind woman, and I feel bad that she's taking care of me." *Fuck. Why did I say that?* It must be the wine; I had more than Faith, and I don't normally drink more than one glass.

Swallowing hard, Faith continues to stare at me. "You really think I'm beautiful?"

"Of course. You *are* beautiful. Don't you know that?"

"No." Faith looks confused, and it finally clicks. She really has no idea how attractive she is. What she sees in the mirror is far from reality, and I wonder who made her feel this way.

How someone like Faith can have such low self-esteem may be a mystery to others, but I've lived through it and can relate like no other. I'm not a therapist and it's not up to me to take on that role, but I want her to know how *I* see her, because there's nothing wrong with plain and simple honesty.

"Faith, I think you're absolutely stunning and talented and great company. That's partly why I'm not entirely myself right now. I happen to be into women and I'm sitting here with you under a blanket, watching a movie. It's kind of hard to concentrate."

"Oh." Faith glances down at my leg and remains silent. Her hands start trembling and she bites her lip.

A knot forms in my stomach and I'm worried I've said too much. *The first night and I've already screwed up.* "Sorry. I shouldn't have said that." I let out a long sigh. "You must think I'm preying on you, but I promise I'm not." Suddenly, I have no idea how we went from watching a horror movie to this heavy conversation. It's way too much on the first night, and I wouldn't be surprised if I've put her off having me around.

"I know you're not." She pauses. "And I appreciate the compliment, but I've never felt beautiful. You're probably going to tell me I need therapy, but trust me, I've had lots of therapy over the years, and I'm sick of being analyzed. I know exactly why I am the way I am. Understanding it doesn't change the way I feel. I've never been able to flip that switch."

I nod, relieved that she hasn't freaked out after my confession. "Do you want to tell me about it? You don't have to..."

"I don't mind." Faith turns to me and drapes her arm over the backrest. "My half-sister was always the favorite child. I know it sounds silly and petty, but that's what it comes down to. I was always second best."

"It's not silly. Why did you feel like you were second best?"

"I didn't *feel* that way. It was a fact," Faith says. "Andrew, my sister's father and my stepfather, is my mother's one big love. They've been on and off for years, divorcing and remarrying, torturing each other in a turbulent relationship. The one thing that always brought them back together is Frankie."

"What about your dad?" I ask.

"My father was some random guy my mom slept with when she was eighteen. She doesn't even remember his name. She was pretty wild back in the day."

"And you grew up with Andrew?"

"He came into my life when I was eleven and never treated me like his own. Three miscarriages and seven years later, they had my sister, and he always put her first. He showered her with presents, bragged about her all the time, but when it came to me... well, he was kind of a bully when no one was watching."

"I'm so sorry. That must have been terribly hard for you."

Faith shrugs. "When you're a kid, you just accept your situation. I was never any trouble and did well in school, yet I always sensed I wasn't enough, even when it came to my mother. It was like I was in the way of her perfect family life —an intruder who didn't share the blood between her and the love of her life, the man who inspired her to create her best work."

I want to hug Faith, but I'm unable to shift from this position without being clumsy, so I lean in and take her hand instead. "Have you ever talked to your mother about this?"

"I tried to talk to her when I was younger. I asked her if I was adopted because I couldn't think of a reason why she might love me less than my sister. She denied treating me differently, and she didn't want to hear a bad word about Andrew." Faith talks about her life story in a distanced manner; devoid of emotion as if it's about someone else entirely. "I went through a chubby phase when I was between twelve and sixteen, and Andrew bullied me about it. He put me down, made snarky comments about my physique, and sometimes he called me a pig when he'd had a drink. One time, he even told me I should be ashamed for letting myself go like that, and that he couldn't take me anywhere looking the way I did."

"Faith... that's awful. And your mother never put a stop to this?" I squeeze her hand, and Faith gives me a sad smile.

"I never told her about the bullying. She always got angry if I said anything negative about Andrew. Even if I'd told her, I'm not sure she would have stepped in. She must've sensed something was wrong, though, because she bought me this apartment the day I turned eighteen. It was like she knew there was a problem, and this was the easiest way to deal with it without having to face the storm."

"She got rid of you."

Faith tilts her head from side to side. "Well, she asked me if I wanted to live on my own, and considering the situation, I was delighted to move out. It wasn't like she kicked me out."

"But she might as well have."

"Yeah." Faith swallows hard and nods. "It did feel like that."

24

FAITH

Why did I tell her all that personal stuff? Lying in bed, I'm tossing and turning, unable to sleep and unable to stop my mind from going back over our conversation. Why did I tell her intimate things I've only ever discussed with my therapist?

It's not just that I poured my heart out on the very first night she's here that's keeping me awake. It's also her comment about me being beautiful. She said it so sincerely, so convincingly, I almost believed her, and I can't stop replaying the moment. The way she looked at me, almost like she wanted to kiss me, is making me doubt everything I know about myself. Or maybe she didn't want to kiss me. Maybe it's all in my head.

My hand slides down my naked body, tracing my curves as I imagine her lips on mine. My skin has never felt so sensitive, and I'm charged with electric arousal that erupts everywhere my fingers go. Memories of tonight tantalize my senses and send me to higher places. Her face keeps appearing before me. Her cheeky smile, her messy, blonde hair, her handsome face, and those intense, gray eyes.

Men never make me feel this way. I thought I was attracted to my exes, but now I'm starting to suspect it wasn't attraction at all, just a desire to be seen with someone successful and good-looking. Admiration, perhaps? How shallow and how sad. Sex wasn't high on my list either. I slept with them to keep them happy and faked most of my orgasms. Now I can't stop wondering what it would be like to be intimate with Silva because if she can make me feel like this just by being in the same space, I can't begin to imagine how it must be to kiss her, to touch her, and to be touched by her.

My nipples are rock hard, and as I slide lower and spread my legs, I discover I'm soaking wet and so sensitive that my hips shoot up the moment I start stroking myself. What is she wearing in bed? Does she sleep naked? Is she touching herself too on the other side of that wall? What does she fantasize about? What's her type?

I slide a finger inside and moan as I add another, imagining it's Silva filling me up. It's been months since I've done this, and the sensation is overwhelming. My breath catches as I move my hips, bringing myself to the edge in record time. I needed this so much it didn't even occur to me to use a vibrator, and stifling a moan, my whole body shakes when I climax. It's intense, long, and it sends me into a state of total relaxation. I can still see her face when my eyes flutter closed.

I'm startled when my bedroom door suddenly opens in the middle of the night, and my heart races when a silhouette appears in the door opening. My first thought is that it's a burglar, and it takes me a while to remember there's someone else in the apartment. As my eyes adjust to the dark, I can make out Silva's amazing silhouette and the crutches she's leaning on. *What is she doing here? Am I dreaming?* I fantasized about her coming into my bedroom last night, so perhaps it's my vivid imagination. If this is a dream, I'm happy for it to continue and see where it takes me.

"Hey. Are you okay?" I whisper. Silva doesn't answer. She just stands there, so I turn on my bedside lamp. Flinching against the bright light, I see she is wearing little else than a pair of Calvin Klein briefs and a white tank top. *This must be a dream.* She looks vividly real, though, and when I pinch my arm hard, it stings. She's not wearing a bra, her top has crept up, and a sliver of her toned belly is bared, making it hard for me to keep my eyes off her because her beauty slays me. "Silva?"

"I'm going for a run," she says in a strange voice. "Would you like to come?"

"What?" I sit up and stare at her. "No. It's the middle of the night, and you can't run. You're walking with crutches."

She nods as if she's perfectly aware of that. "Calories," she says with a brief nod.

"Calories?" I realize then that she must be sleepwalking because none of this makes any sense. Trinny did say it happened regularly, but I didn't think it would happen so soon.

I get up and put on a robe, then walk toward her, slowly so as not to scare her. If she wakes up, she may lose her balance and fall, and that's not an option with her fragile ankle. "Come on, let's get you back to bed," I say, placing a hand on her lower back while I turn her around. I expect her to protest, but she doesn't, so I lead her to her bedroom. Despite the fact that she's sleepwalking, Silva has no problem crossing the hallway on her crutches, and if Trinny hadn't warned me about this, I'd believe she was wide awake.

"Calories," she mumbles again before sliding under the covers.

"Just go to sleep. You can run when your ankle has healed." I'm dying to know what she means, but inquiring would be wrong as she's not lucid, so I tuck her in instead. She closes her eyes and turns on her side; she looks so vulnerable it brings a lump to my throat.

"You can sleep here if you want," she says with a smile.

My reaction to her request is astounding. My heart is pounding hard at the thought of lying next to her, and it's hard to say no. My whole body is yearning to be close to her, but I have to be sensible. She's sleeping, and this isn't real.

"Maybe some other time," I whisper and, unable to resist, lean in and place a soft kiss on her temple. When her smile widens, I melt. This is not going to be easy.

25

SILVA

"Good morning." I'm up later than usual. Faith's guest bed was so comfortable that I kept turning off my alarm, and it took me forever to wash and put on clothes. I settled for jersey shorts, as those are the easiest to get on and off with the cast. My head is a little sore from the wine I drank last night, and I'm worried I may have said things I shouldn't, but I'm also glad we did talk because I understand her so much better now.

Faith smiles at me from the kitchen table. "Good morning. Did you sleep okay?"

"Like a baby. That mattress is amazing. Did you sleep well?"

"Yeah." She stretches and sips her coffee. "I feel good today."

"That's great. You look refreshed." It's hard to keep my eyes off her cleavage in the tight tank top she's wearing, and knowing how good her behind looks in her leggings, I'm already worried about our workout. I hop toward the table and stop her when she's about to get up. "Please. I need to learn how to do this myself," I insist, resting one crutch against the counter. I grab the mug that is waiting for me and place it under the coffee maker. Balancing on one leg, I wait for the beans to grind and the delicious fresh coffee to fill my mug.

Smug that I've managed, I shake my head and laugh when I realize there's no way I can hop to the table without spilling the coffee everywhere. Frankly, I have no idea how I thought I could live on my own in my apartment for six weeks, and I'm grateful when Faith gets up and takes it from me.

"You poor thing. I have a shoot this afternoon. How will you cope?" She scans the kitchen before her eyes dart to her office door down the hall. "Wait, I have an idea." Heading in there, she comes back with an office chair on wheels. "Try this—it might make it easier to move around."

"That is actually not a bad idea," I say, lowering myself into the chair while she holds it. Rolling toward the table, I laugh at how silly I must look, but at least I'm less dependent. "Thank you." My eyes meet Faith's, and she holds my gaze in a way that makes me question if perhaps she's having similar thoughts about me. It's unlikely; she's not even into women, but my intuition is rarely wrong. "Are you ready for our workout?"

"Yes. I'm looking forward to it. Are you hungry? Want me to make you breakfast?"

"That's very sweet, but I'll just have one of those protein bars I brought. I've stocked up for convenience."

Faith waves a finger in front of me. "No way. I'm not letting you live on those after your lecture about eating fresh. I'll make us an omelet after the workout." She sits back and sips her coffee. "It's nice having you here. You know—someone to talk to in the morning."

"I'm glad you're not sick of me yet."

"No chance," she says. "By the way, you were sleepwalking last night."

"You're joking, right?" I laugh, then stop when I realize she's serious. "Did I?" Burying my face in my hands, I groan. "That's so embarrassing. I can't believe I sleepwalked on my first night here."

"Don't be embarrassed." She shoots me an amused look. "You came into my room and asked me if I wanted to go for a run."

"Seriously? And was I walking on my crutches?" When Faith nods, I feel my cheeks flush as I laugh. I wasn't wearing much in bed and make a mental note to order pajamas.

"Yeah. I put you back in bed and then you quite happily slept through the night. At least, I didn't hear you after that."

"I'm so sorry I woke you up. It might be safer if you lock me in at night," I joke.

"No, it's fine. You didn't make much sense, though. You kept repeating the word 'calories.'"

"Did I? I don't remember anything, I'm afraid." I feign ignorance, but I have a very good idea what I meant by that. It was probably an anxiety dream because of the food and wine I consumed last night. This morning, I don't feel so anxious about it, though. Talking to Faith is distracting me from obsessing, and I'm in a calm mood. "I hope it won't be a regular thing."

"Don't worry about it," Faith says. "Have you ever lived with someone? Apart from your sister?"

I can't help but wonder if this is her way of asking me if I've lived with someone I dated. "Yes. I lived with my ex. But it was a long time ago."

"How was that?"

Taking a sip of my coffee, I buy some time to answer the

question and feel a sting as I think back to my time with Bea. "It was... it was difficult," I say honestly. "But that was mainly because of me. I was difficult to be around at the time."

"Oh." Faith looks desperate to ask me why, but she doesn't, and I'm grateful for that. It's too early for a serious conversation.

"I've never lived with anyone, apart from with my family when I was younger," she says.

"Have none of your exes moved in with you? Not even for a short period of time?"

"No, they never stuck around long enough for it to become that serious. You're my first." Faith shakes her head and laughs. "I mean—"

"It's okay, I know what you mean." I laugh too and point to her cup. "Do you want a refill?"

"Yeah, but I'll do it." Faith is about to get up, but I grab the cup and roll the chair to the counter with a smirk, making her laugh harder. I love her laugh; it's so lyrical, and the way her whole face lights up is beautiful. "Anything I should know about you in regard to mornings? Do you like silence? Do you like to be left alone? Tell me if you do or I might drive you crazy," I say as I wait for the coffee.

"I actually don't know. I'm usually on my own in the mornings so I never talk, and I certainly don't laugh. That must mean I like company first thing." She shoots me a grin when I roll back and hand her the coffee. "Are you one of those super-active morning types?"

"I'm afraid so. But the good thing is, I'm very calm at night. Well, apart from when I'm sleepwalking," I add. "Maybe that's because I've exhausted myself during the day."

"You will exhaust yourself the way you're moving around

like a bullet on that chair." She pulls at the armrest to roll me closer, and I'm probably imagining things, but it feels flirty.

Meeting her eyes, I shoot her a wink. "I might as well. It's the only workout I'll be getting for a while."

26

FAITH

"Where do you want me to set up?" I grab the yoga mat, the resistance bands, and the weights from my office, where Silva keeps her workout gear.

"Let's do it in my bedroom," she says, following me in the office chair.

"What?" I stall and cast her a startled glance over my shoulder. "Are you serious?"

She laughs at my baffled expression and shakes her head. "Don't worry. It won't be that kind of workout. I thought we could work on form today, and the floor-to-ceiling mirrored wardrobes are perfect for that."

"Oh..." I laugh along and force back a thought of us on her bed as I open the door for her and drop the workout gear on the floor. My guest bed suddenly looks a lot more appealing than my own, knowing she slept in it. I rarely come into this room, simply because I have no reason to, and last night felt like I was intruding on her privacy by being here. I forgot all about the mirrored wardrobe, and remembering this is the reason I chose the other bedroom when I moved in, I cringe at my reflection. I hate my body in workout gear with all the lumps and bumps on show; it's too confronting. As long as I can't see it, I can cope with tight clothing, but this is intense and uncomfortable.

"What's wrong?" Silva asks as she shifts from the chair to the edge of the bed.

"Nothing. I just don't like..." I sigh as my gaze lowers to my hips, and I turn to the side to study my behind. It looks so big, so out of place, like it's been taken from someone else and stuck onto my body.

Silva looks at me pensively and beckons me to come closer. "This?' she says, tracing my back down to my behind. "Is this the problem? Because a lot of women would kill for these curves."

I shiver at her touch and turn to her so I don't have to look at myself. "I wish I could see that, but I can't."

Silva nods and takes both my hands. "You, Faith, are beautiful, and you're going to learn to love yourself. Someone planted a false belief in your head when you were at a very vulnerable age, but you're not that kid anymore. You are formed now, your own person, and you can choose to stop believing whatever you were told many years ago because it's not true. Everyone is beautiful in their own way, and you're perfect. You always were, then and now."

I swallow hard and look at our hands. Silva's are strong and covering mine, stroking them. She continues when I don't answer. "It won't happen overnight, but you'll get there. Do you feel better in general on the days you've been working out?"

"Yes," I say. "I like my body more after we've worked out. I feel like it belongs to me."

"Then let's work out every morning. You'll be amazed at the difference it will make to your state of mind. We don't have to do heavy stuff all the time. Even a bit of light yoga will do the trick."

I nod and try not to focus on the long list of things I don't like about myself. The first time Silva was here, I didn't care what I looked like because I didn't care what she thought of me. Now that I've started seeing her in a different light, my insecurities have taken over.

"Today won't be easy, though," she says. "We're going to do squats and shoulder lifts with the weights. Three times twelve. Try not to think about anything but form. Back straight, don't bend forward."

I take a stance with my feet hip-width apart and go through my knees as far as I can while holding the weights. Silva corrects my posture by placing her hands on my hips, and as always when she touches me, my stomach does a flip. My stomach that I'm desperately trying to hold in.

"That's good, keep going. Nine, eight, seven..."

My reaction to her is getting worse by the minute, and I have trouble hiding it now. If she would pull me onto the bed and kiss me, I wouldn't mind that at all. As I check my posture in the mirror, the view is much better with her behind me, and seeing her hands on my body is making me squirm. I watch her as I keep doing squats, then realize she's stopped counting out loud. Normally, I'd be tired by now, so perhaps she was right when she said strength is in the mind.

"Continue if you can," she says, then claps her hands after I do five more. "Fantastic. We might have to use the heavier weights. Can you feel it's easier than when you first started?"

"Yeah. It does seem easier." I'm puzzled by my newfound strength, but if looking at her makes a difference, I'm not complaining. When we start the next set, she rests her hands in her lap and I miss them already.

"Are you up for five-pound weights?" she asks.

"I can try."

"Great. Could you get them from the office, please? We'll do the third set with those."

As I head out to grab the weights, I know her eyes are on my behind. Normally when people look at me like that, I assume they're judging the size of it, but I don't feel that way with her. From what I saw in the mirror, and from what she told me last night, I gather it's more of an appreciative look. As soon as I turn the corner, I let out the breath I've been holding and only then feel how badly my legs are burning.

27

SILVA

Even after a week, it's strange to be alone in Faith's space. She left early this morning for a photoshoot in the Hamptons, and she won't be back until late. As frustrating as it is not being able to walk, I get around fine on the chair, and when the buzzer goes, I push off on the wall and zoom across the room to let Trinny in.

"I think I got everything," she says, dropping two shopping bags on the kitchen table.

"Thank you so much, I really appreciate it. I was trying to order groceries last minute, but they couldn't deliver until later tonight."

"That's okay, sis." Trinny peeks into the living room. "Is Faith not here?"

"No, she has a shoot, and I want to surprise her with dinner when she comes home."

"Bummer, I was hoping to see her. I really like her." Trinny shrugs. "So, you're cooking for her? That's very domestic of you. I didn't take you for the housewife type," she jokes. "Want me to help? I can make dirty noodles. I'm sure she'll love them."

"Thank you for the offer, but that's not necessary," I'm quick to say, rolling toward the table to check the ingredients.

"I can see that. You're quicker than the speed of light on that chair." She pours herself a glass of wine from a bottle she brought and sits at the table like she owns the place. "So, how has it been here? Any arguments?"

"No, it's been great, actually. I'd kill for a shower, though, and I really miss going for a run. I've got so much pent-up energy, I don't know how to relieve myself of it, so I thought cooking might be a good distraction." I take the rice noodles out of the packaging and put them in a bowl of water to soak. "But otherwise, it's great. Faith and I get along well, and I like being around her."

"I think you'd prefer to be on top of her," Trinny says with a mischievous grin. "You can't fool me, Sil. I saw how you looked at her last week, and if I'm not mistaken, the attraction was mutual."

"Shut up." I nudge her as I swivel past on my way to the end of the counter where Faith keeps her oil. "It's all in your head." Truth be told, I lay awake for hours last night, thinking about Faith in the bedroom next door, and I touched myself as I pictured her face before me and imagined kissing her and much, much more.

"Sure, babe. Whatever you say." Trinny tilts her head and regards me. "You two can't possibly have much in common, though. What do you talk about all day when she's not at work? I mean, we had a great night when you moved in here, and she's very chatty, but at some point, you must run out of topics, right?"

Faith and I have more in common than Trinny knows, but I'm not going to discuss Faith's struggles with her. Being my sister, Trinny knows about my history with my eating disorder. I never told her about it; I never told anyone, but she figured it out a long time ago, and she was my rock when I wanted to give up on everything. "It's not like we're both here all the time. I work too," I say. "I'm in her office most of the day for my online classes because it's quiet in there." I shrug. "But when we're together, we're never short of things to talk about."

"Oh, well that's good." Trinny narrows her eyes at me. "Any flirting going on?"

"No." I shoot her a glare. "Nothing at all. Now let's talk about you. How was your day? I didn't expect you so early."

"Oh, my day isn't over yet. This is just a welcome break." She grins when I point to her wine. "Oh, come on. Don't be such a mommy. I've got tons of stuff to read through, so I'm going to do that at home. I've got trial tomorrow."

"I'm sorry, I didn't know," I say. "I'm probably keeping you from things way more important than groceries."

Trinny laughs it off. "No. As I said, it's a welcome break. Although I must admit, I was more enthusiastic because I thought Faith would be home."

"Oh, am I not enough for you now?" I move the chopping block over to the table, because it's easier than working on the high counter, and start chopping chili, ginger, and garlic.

"Nah." Trinny chuckles. "She's way more exciting than you." When I look up, she follows my gaze and points to the higher kitchen cupboards. "Anything you need from up there?"

"Do you mind?" I know I'm going to get butchered for what I'm about to ask, but there are things I'll never be able to reach. "I need fresh candles and napkins. They're in the top-right cupboard."

"Candles?" As expected, Trinny's voice is teasing, and

her face pulls into a comical smirk as she gets up and stands on her tiptoes to reach them. "And you're saying there's nothing romantic going on?"

"It's winter and it's dark. Everyone burns candles in winter. It's hardly romantic," I shoot back at her.

"Sure. Whatever you say." Trinny opens the box and pulls out five candles to go in the modern candelabra on the table. "Want me to go get you some red roses too?" she asks, pushing them in.

"How about you go get yourself home instead?" I suggest, slapping her behind with a ladle. Of course I want to impress Faith, and I want to put a smile on her face. But Trinny doesn't need to know that.

28

FAITH

The smell of food welcomes me even before I've opened the door, and when I walk in, I'm surprised to see that Silva's cooking dinner. The table is laid, and she's lit candles. I almost choke up because no one has done this for me before. Not with so much care and attention to detail. She's even moved flowers from the living area onto the table, and with an old ballad playing in the background, there's a romantic vibe in the kitchen.

"Hey," she says, looking up from the counter. The chair is too low for her to cook from, and the way she's lifting her arms while she's stirring is making me laugh. "I know, it looks weird. But I figured if I only use the front two burners and low pans, I can just about see what's going on in there."

"You shouldn't have. I told you I'd help you when I got home."

"Come on. I've got nothing better to do and you've been working all day. I want to be useful. My last online class finished at two, and I need to move around, or I'll bust out of my skin." She garnishes two bowls of steaming-hot noodle soup with chopped scallion and grins. "Would you mind moving these to the table?"

"Of course not. It smells great." I inhale over the bowls before I take them.

"It's super healthy. Fresh kimchi broth, buckwheat noodles, beansprouts, pak choi, tofu, and a soft-boiled egg. You need energy after a long day on your feet."

"You're so sweet." I'm aware of her intention. If I eat super healthy, I'll be comfortable keeping my food down. This is true in a way, but since Silva has been here, I haven't seriously considered purging once. Most nights we drink tea, so I don't feel hungover in the morning, and in the past week I've consumed more healthy food than I have in years. We've been cooking together, and I've started to enjoy it as a relaxing activity. It's nice to have something to do at night other than go out and engage in meaningless conversations filled with false compliments and promises.

"Sorry if the candles are a bit much..."

"No, it's lovely," I say as I sit, aware that I can't stop smiling.

Silva rolls over to the table and joins me. "How was your day, honey?" she jokes.

"Not bad. The photos look great—one of them might even make the cover even though it wasn't a cover shoot, but it was a long drive, and the traffic was terrible."

"Sore?" Silva asks when I roll my shoulders.

"A little. I'm not used to driving long distances, and I've got another shoot tomorrow. It's going to hurt holding my camera again all day." I pour us sparkling water and down my glass in one go, only now aware of how thirsty I was.

Silva hesitates as her eyes linger on my shoulders. "I can give you a massage after dinner if you like."

She might as well have offered to fuck me because my

body is certainly reacting that way. Heat spreads between my thighs, and my heart feels like it's trying to punch through my ribcage. *A massage. Jesus, what a turn-on.* I'm startled back to reality when the piece of tofu I'd been holding between my chopsticks falls back into my bowl and splashes hot soup onto my face.

"I'm a qualified sports masseuse," she hastily adds. "I used to do it for a living, but I prefer being on the move, so I switched careers."

"Oh." Afraid she'll see how this conversation is making me feel, I wipe my chin and concentrate on my food. "I wouldn't say no to a massage." *Did I just agree to having her hands all over my back? Over my naked skin? Can I even handle that?*

"Great." She smiles. "We can clear the coffee table, as it's big enough and it's a good height for me to sit on."

"Thank you." Retrieving the piece of tofu, I try not to sound too excited. "Do you still give massages? I mean, to your clients when they're injured or sore?"

"I used to do it occasionally, but I haven't done it since a woman came on to me a couple of years ago. I suppose she read more into it than there was, and our training sessions got awkward after that." Silva frowns as if she's just said something she regrets. "It wouldn't be awkward with you, though, because..."

"Because I'm straight?" I regard her, but she shakes her head without answering the question. "Have you ever dated one of your clients?"

Silva chuckles and her cheeks flush. "Honestly, I know this won't make me look good, but yes, I have. Only once."

"I don't see how it would reflect badly on you," I say. "It's not like you're in a position of power, and you work for yourself, so who cares?"

"True. But people are often vulnerable around me. They open up about their insecurities, and don't get me wrong—that's important to the process. But it's not a fair place to start a relationship."

I nod. "I can see how things happen. Training people is pretty intimate." I'm not sure if I regret telling her so much about myself now. Not that I expected anything to happen between us. Even if she does find me attractive, she's way too professional to come on to me, but I can't deny that I've fantasized about the workouts turning more sensual than they're supposed to be.

"Yes, it can feel intimate at times." Silva bites her lip while she stirs her soup. If I'm not mistaken, she's as flustered as I am because I've rarely seen her like this.

"I'm still surprised you don't have a girlfriend," I say. "You have everything going for you. You seem perfect to me."

"You think so?" Silva chuckles. "Trust me, I'm not perfect. Everyone has baggage and issues, including me. Not that it would stop me from having a relationship." She hesitates. "I've only really been in love once. I don't easily fall for people."

"And that relationship ended badly? Was that your ex you used to live with?" Perhaps I'm pushing it with the questions, but I feel like it's her turn to talk now.

"Yes," she says, and a hint of sadness crosses her features. "I'll tell you about it sometime."

29

SILVA

We've cleared the large, robust coffee table, and Faith is lying on top of the towels I've covered it with. Thankfully, her head is facing down over the edge so she can't see my hungry eyes as I lower the towel draped over her back. I'm sitting on the table, and although it's not the ideal position, as I can't put weight on my casted leg, I can reach over her entire back.

"Are you comfortable?"

"Yes." She shivers when I unclip her bra and pull it over her shoulders. I dribble some orange-scented massage oil over her back and watch it run down her spine. The fact that she had the half-empty bottle in her bedroom must mean she's used it before, and I try not to think about her previous massage experiences. *Did she do it to them or the other way around?* It causes a pang of jealousy, which is ridiculous: we're just friends, and Faith is straight. We may have chemistry and she may be giving off signs that she's a little attracted to me, but that doesn't mean she'd act on it or that anything would ever happen between us. Simultaneously, I'm aware that this isn't something friends do, and she was totally up for it. When there's attraction—even a little bit—a massage is never just a massage. It's an excuse to touch someone you're not supposed to touch, and as I slide my hands over her skin to distribute the oil, I feel a tightness grow in my core.

"Mmm... That feels great." Faith takes in a quick breath, and it's clear she finds it hard to relax. It's not because of my skills; I know I'm good at this. *I'm turning her on.*

I pull her long hair to the side, and it falls over her face. Staring at the spot just under her hairline, I imagine my lips there, and resist the urge to lean in and kiss her neck. "Harder?" I ask, kneading her neck to release tension.

"No, that's perfect. You're good at this."

Turning my attention to her shoulder blades, I explore the landscape of her upper body. I never thought shoulder blades to be particularly sexy or elegant, but hers are. Everything about Faith is elegant, and she doesn't even know it. "You're tense."

"I am, but this is helping." She shivers when I run my fingers up and down her spine, and after a couple of minutes, I release the pressure in my movements. She moans, telling me she likes this. She likes the softer strokes that border on caresses. It will do nothing for her muscles, but if she's happy, I won't stop touching her in a way I'd want to be touched. Moving my hands toward her behind that is still covered by the towel, I apply more pressure to her lower back. She wiggles a little, and it drives me wild. *I'm only human*. They're just thoughts; I'm not overstepping here. I'm living with a beautiful woman to whom I'm incredibly attracted, and it's okay to have these feelings as long as I don't act on them.

I run my hands up along her sides and try not to get too close to her breasts, but she moans again, so I repeat the action, expanding my reach a little. She tenses when I skim the sensitive skin at chest height, and I curse myself for taking it too far despite my resolve. "I'm sorry."

"No," she says in a whisper. "Please don't stop, this is great."

Tension builds between my thighs, and I bite my lip when I realize the soft moans are coming from both of us. Wanting to touch all of her at once, I splay my fingers wide as I slide my hands down her back and move the towel a little, enough to expose a glimpse of the curve of her behind and a sliver of black lace from her panties. I want to kiss her there. I want to run my tongue over those curves and taste her skin. I want to turn her around, suck her nipples into my mouth, and fuck her right here on the coffee table, slow and deep, while I cover her body with my own. *Jesus. Does she have similar fantasies?*

"You know, this kind of massage is not the best for relieving tension." I note there's a tremble to my voice.

"I know," Faith says and leaves it with that. The short sentence carries a loaded message. She knows this isn't a normal massage. I'm doing this for her pleasure as much as my own, and she likes that. My arousal grows, and I'm not sure how much longer I can continue. The ache between my legs is becoming unbearable, and I'm throbbing for release.

"Maybe it's better if I stop," I say after a few more minutes. "Not that I don't want to continue, but..."

"But?" Faith covers her breasts with the towel and turns around. When our eyes meet, I see the same desire reflected in her expression, the same need to act on impulse. "Okay." She nods as if she understands the boundaries we're about to cross if we don't put an end to this now. "You're right." She wraps the towel around her and gets up, leaving me with the enticing sight of her bare legs.

As she heads to her bedroom to get changed, there's a seductive wiggle in her hips, and I immediately regret interrupting the moment because she clearly wants me too, and why shouldn't we act on our desires? Deep down, I know why. What's holding me back is that I live here, in her home, and Faith has never been with a woman. I don't want it to become weird between us because it might.

The living room smells of orange blossom, and I take a couple of deep breaths, savoring the recent memory before I remove the towels from the table. I'm aware it's only a matter of time, that we're gravitating toward the inevitable, but I want to give her time to think it through. Faith isn't the most stable person at the moment, and something this big can work for the better or for the worse. I want to make sure it's not the latter.

30

FAITH

"Faith!" Roy waves me over from one of the VIP boxes, where he's sitting with twin young women who look like models, a few mutual friends who work in the fashion industry, one of Roy's friends with benefits, and a designer I shot a look book for last year.

"Hey, guys. It's so great to see you all." I greet everyone individually and introduce myself to the new girls. I'm not delighted they're here. Aside from their perfect bodies and fresh faces that make me feel old and out of shape, the age difference means we'll have very little to talk about. Not that there tends to be a lot of intellectual conversation on nights like these; it's mainly just superficial chitchat and networking.

Anthony, the designer, ushers the party to scoot over so I can join them, and he grabs the ice-cold magnum bottle of Grey Goose from the bucket. "Vodka?" It's the drink of choice for most of us. Contrary to what everyone thinks, we don't drink champagne because drinking champagne or cocktails five nights a week would be way too heavy on the calories.

I contemplate declining because I've got training tomorrow morning, but this place is full of new faces, and I wasn't prepared for that. Facing the night sober fills me with dread, so I nod and grab one of the extra glasses from the table. "Sure, thanks."

"So, what do you think of Meike and Suze?" Anthony asks, referring to the two women beside him. "They're twins —my new muses. They're going to be the faces for my next campaign." He winks. "Or maybe I should say 'face,' as they're identical."

"I think you're fabulous," I say to them as I hate talking about people in front of them. "Unique and very current. Alienesque with a cat-like quality." Their fiery-red hair, strong bone structure, and light-hazel, wide-apart eyes certainly make them look interesting, and I can see why he's selected them to be the lucky ones who will soon rise to fame on billboards and in magazine ads worldwide.

"Right?" Anthony raises his hands in a dramatic manner. "I knew you'd get it. So, can you fit me in for the shoot?"

"I'm sure we can make that work. Give me a call tomorrow when I'm sober," I joke. "As long as it's not during Fashion Week, it won't be a problem." Glad this event led to a job, so I didn't come here for nothing, I take a sip of my vodka and sit back, mentally preparing for a long night of bonding with the twins and reconnecting with Anthony, as we haven't worked together in a while.

"Excellent." Anthony raises his glass again and the others follow. "Let's toast to a spectacular shoot and to..." He glances around. "And to Donna, our hostess. Where is that fabulous birthday girl anyway?"

Donna, New York's latest It-girl, is nowhere to be seen. I suspect she's doing a line in the toilets or maybe she snuck out early after her pictures were taken. Because really, publicity is all that matters. Without the fashion bloggers and media photographers, the night would be pointless, and proof is everything. Proof of who you were with, what you were wearing, and how much fun you were. Even though Donna's not here, the conversation turns into a competition of who knows her best and who has the most history with her.

"We were stuck at Amsterdam airport together after our flight got canceled," Roy's toy boy, who does the PR for Donna, says. "We spent twelve hours there and drank the first-class lounge dry."

"Oh my God," Meike chips in. "Airport lounges are *so* tacky. At least you were in good company."

She's talking nonsense, for sure. Unless her parents are rich, I doubt she's ever even been in a first-class lounge before. Her designer purse is a fake, and I can tell from the fabric that her dress is off-the-rack. Not everyone here has money, especially not the models, unless they're in the current top twenty of most booked girls globally, and these two are new to the scene. Models are put on economy flights for shoots abroad, but they do get a nice hotel room to promote the designer they're shooting for on social media.

In the theater of fashion, we all have a role to play. The role of the models is that of beautiful jetsetters. Their Instagram profiles show exotic locations and healthy tans. What they leave out are their small, shared apartments, their near-empty bank accounts after spending all their income on appearances, and the fatigue that comes with the combination of traveling, long days, and battling their weight.

Anthony's role is that of a fashion mogul, a forward thinker, a creative eccentric. He dresses extravagantly to make sure no one misses his presence. He attends every party in New York, splashing his cash so competitors can see how well he's doing. But reality is, he works his ass off to keep his brand afloat because brick-and-mortar retail is simply not as popular as it used to be. The leases on his premium-location flagship stores must be extortionate, and so far, he hasn't streamlined his business model to win online.

Roy's role is a funny one because he doesn't really do anything. I suppose he portrays himself as an It-boy, a party animal who puts people in touch with one another. He's built a wide network of designers, artists, models, photographers, and other creatives who all want to know him because he knows everyone. And so, he gets invited to every single party as the best-dressed, best-looking gay man, who attracts creatives from the fashion industry. Roy's truth is far less glamorous, and I'm the only one who knows his bling is a façade.

After inheriting money from his father, who committed suicide when Roy was nineteen, he has enough to get by for the next twenty years if he lives frugally. He keeps announcing he's going to find a job or start a business but never takes that step because he doesn't really believe in himself. His mother is not in the picture, he has no other family that he's aware of, he lives in a tiny apartment in Brooklyn, and gets his clothes free from up-and-coming designers in return for promoting their brand. He can't afford vacations unless one of his sugar daddies takes him, and when they do, he feels shitty and used afterward.

None of this affects the rainbow aura of his outward persona, though: what people see is bottomless Roy. Never tired, never without a drink in his hand, and never without interesting people surrounding him. In life, Roy gets most things for free, but there's a price to pay. His whole life, he's been searching for "his thing," the one thing he can do to secure his future and make a living while also doing what he loves. Roy doesn't know what he loves or wants, he never has, and the fact that he cheated on me with a man while we were engaged is a testament to that. But he's my best friend and a good man, and out of all people here tonight, our friendship may be the only one that's real. In a fake world, anything close to a real connection is a blessing.

Roy blows me a kiss and I give him a warm smile. "In lack of a better offer in the form of a hot man, can I come home with you tonight?" he yells over the music that's suddenly gotten louder.

I frown and look at the man by his side, who shakes his head and laughs. "I'm getting on a flight in a couple of hours. Antigua."

"Oh, nice," I say. "Vacation or...?"

"No, I'm checking out some properties for Donna." He turns to Roy. "Wish I could take you with me, honey, but it's a quick back-and-forth, I'm afraid. I'm only staying for a night."

"Still, you'll have more sunshine tomorrow than we will in the coming months," I say, then turn back to Roy. "You can stay at my place as long as you're quiet. Silva will be sleeping."

"Silva's her personal trainer," Roy says, filling everyone in with a mischievous look. "And she's a hot lesbian." He grins when our friends break out in laughter, then turns his attention back to me. "Have you gone there yet?"

"Roy! Boundaries, please. No, I haven't. We're just friends," I say with a chuckle, my temperature rising when I think of yesterday's massage and how it set me on fire. Reaching for my glass, I down the vodka and pour myself another one, cursing myself for feeling so out of control.

31

SILVA

The door opens, and I hear Faith urging someone to be quiet. A man's voice echoes through the apartment; he's saying he's hungry. I hear the fridge door open, more whispering follows, and then some gasps of delight when they discover what I assume to be the stir-fry I left for her. I remind myself that I'm just crashing here, and that Faith and I are not together, yet it still stings to hear her giggle as they head for her bedroom. *She's brought a man home.* Maybe I just imagined our flirtations and the chemistry between us. Maybe she's met someone special tonight. Either way, it's none of my business, and I must let go of my possessiveness; it's not healthy. She closes her bedroom door, and once again I'm left in silence.

Staring at the ceiling, I try not to think about what's happening in there. It's hard because the problem is, I'm jealous, and I'm not proud of that. Two weeks here and I'm already falling for her. I'm crushing on a straight woman and there's nothing more confronting than her bringing a man home to make me realize that. It's not like Trinny didn't warn me I'd be attracted to her; she called it way before I started thinking about Faith in this way.

Knowing I won't be able to fall back asleep anytime soon, I quietly get up and head for the kitchen to make myself a chamomile tea. Carefully moving through the dark on my crutches, I curse when I hit the side of the fridge by accident. *Fuck.* I don't want them to know they woke me up; they might think I'm listening in or something. Not that there's much noise coming from Faith's bedroom. I hear the TV, but other than that, it's quiet.

I lean on the counter and one-handedly grab a mug and a tea bag from the selection Faith put there as I couldn't reach the high cupboard. While I make my tea, I consider my options. The office chair will make too much noise, and I'm not sure if I can even get it over the threshold in my bedroom without spilling, so I hobble across to the kitchen table and settle there. A door opens, and I hear footsteps coming my way; I sincerely hope it's not Faith's new flame.

"Hey, did we wake you up?" Faith turns on the lamp, and I wince against the bright light.

"No," I lie. "I had trouble sleeping. How was your night?"

"It was okay, not an entire waste," Faith says and makes tea for herself. "I apologize. I'm a tiny bit tipsy. Do you mind if I join you?" She looks at the chair opposite me, then chooses the one next to me instead.

"Of course not. Wide awake?" I ask.

"Yes." She lets out a long sigh. "And Roy's already snoring like a trooper, so that's not helping." She rolls her eyes. "He totally denies that he snores, but trust me, he could wake up the entire block once he gets going."

I manage a smile, then remember she's mentioned Roy before in one of our many conversations. Roy, who cheated on her with a man. Perhaps he's bisexual? "Roy, your ex?"

"Yeah."

"You must be very close if he still stays over."

"Very." Faith suddenly slams a hand in front of her mouth and giggles. "Oh, no, not like that. Roy is only with men these days, and we're besties, that's all. Sometimes he stays here after we've been out, so he doesn't have to take a cab home."

"Oh." I'm unable to hide my relief, and Faith must have noticed it because she laughs even harder now.

"Roy and I have sleepovers on a regular basis actually. We watch movies together, and sometimes we even accompany each other on family gatherings, but there's nothing sexual between us." Faith leans in and shoots me a teasing look. She's more outgoing tonight, and I suspect that may be down to alcohol. "Did it bother you? Be honest. Did you think we were... you know..." She winks.

"No." I shake my head. "I mean, yes, I thought you'd brought a man home for sex, but it's none of my business what you get up to."

"So, it didn't bother you?"

There's almost a hopeful hint to her voice as she asks the question, so I take my time before I answer. "Whatever you do is your choice, Faith. I don't judge, and anyway, it doesn't matter what I think."

Faith nods. She looks disappointed. "It does matter," she says, and this time I do hear a slight slur in her words. The night and the alcohol are definitely catching up with her.

"Why?"

"Because I like you. I..." She swallows hard and looks down at her tea. "Never mind. I don't really know what I'm trying to say. I'd better go back to bed."

"Back to your snoring bestie?" I joke before I say something that surprises us both. “You can sleep in my bed. I don’t snore. Not that I know of, anyway.”

The look Faith gives me causes shivers to run down my spine, and her mouth pulls into a small smile. “Are you sure?”

“Yeah. If you help me with my tea.” I chuckle and point to my crutches. “I didn’t really want to sit here.”

32

FAITH

Silva's bed is still warm, and it smells of her body lotion. I've noticed the rose scent before, and I wish I could smother myself with it. I get in under the covers and make sure I lie as close to the edge as I can as I don't want to intrude in her space. Well, that's not true. I kind of do, but I couldn't say what I really wanted to say earlier in the kitchen. That she makes me weak in the knees, that I'm insanely attracted to her, and that I want her to kiss me so badly I fantasize about it all the time. And now, I'm here in her bed and she's wearing skimpy shorts and a T-shirt and I'm not wearing much more.

"I love this bed," she says, turning on her side to face me. Her casted leg is on top of the covers, and I find it hard to keep my eyes off her smooth, muscular thigh.

"This is only the guest bed. Wait till you try mine." I wince. "Okay, that came out wrong."

Silva chuckles and I love the sound of it. "I'd be delighted to test your bed." Her eyes meet mine, and I feel like I'm going insane. Clammy and turned on beyond belief, I bite my lip and tell myself to be brave.

"Maybe tomorrow? It's kind of lonely, sleeping in there all by myself." I meant it to sound like a flirty joke, but instead it sounds desperate.

"So you miss falling asleep with someone?" Silva beckons me to come closer, and trembling with anticipation, I do so.

"Sometimes." I hesitate. "Who doesn't like a warm body in bed?"

"Then turn around," she says with a sweet smile. When I turn on my side, she scoots closer, wraps her arm around me and spoons me. "Is this okay?" Our conversation sounds like one of two teenagers, testing their boundaries for the first time.

"Uh-huh." I'm sure she can feel my heart banging. Her arm around me is more than okay, but I know I won't be able to sleep like this, as I'm so aroused now that I have trouble lying still.

Silva takes me in a tight hold and nuzzles her face in my neck. I can hear her inhaling against my hair, and it brings me shivers. Half expecting and wanting her to make a move, I wait in anticipation, but her body relaxes, and soon her breathing becomes slow and heavy. She's sleeping.

A big, empty space painted white. A full-length mirrored wall and a yoga mat. I have no idea where I am, but it's pretty and it smells like Silva's body lotion.

"Hip lifts," Silva whispers in my ear as she steadies herself over me. She appeared out of nowhere. "Three times ten." Her eyes are dark and full of desire as she licks her lips and looks at my mouth. Her voice is husky, and teasing echoes bounce through the empty space.

Turning my head to face the mirror, I see that I'm naked, and so is she. "Where are my gym clothes?" I ask, both confused and aroused as I admire her beautiful body. The arch of her back, her perky behind, her muscular arms and legs, and her small breasts.

"You won't need clothes for this workout." Silva lowers herself on top of me and wedges a thigh between my legs. The contact sends a rush of delicious heat to my center, and it spreads out, pulsing through my body. I think I'm about to have an orgasm and I don't care because nothing has ever felt so good. "Lift your hips." She shoots me a flirty smile and lingers there forever before she finally brings her lips close to mine. I've been waiting for this for weeks, but now that she's about to kiss me, it's almost too much to handle. I'm a ticking time bomb and about to explode. And then it happens. She grinds into me with her full weight and claims my mouth.

The kiss is fiery and sensual, and as I lift my hips, Silva moans against my mouth. She moves faster and I wrap my legs around her while my hands explore her back and her behind. Her tongue meets mine and she deepens the kiss. It sends me over the edge, shattering me into a million pieces, and from the strangled cry that escapes her, I know she's climaxing too.

"Faith. Hey, Faith, wake up."

I open my eyes and blink in confusion when I see the outline of Silva's face in the dark. My body is on fire and my clit throbbing. *Fuck. I just came in my sleep.* "Fuck," I say, this time out loud.

"You were having a nightmare. Are you okay?"

"Yeah, I think so." I'm relieved she doesn't know what just happened and equally disappointed my dream is over. As I slowly return to reality, I realize something is not right.

My hand is resting on warm skin. When I move it to explore the surface, I gasp and quickly withdraw it from underneath her shirt. I've shifted in my sleep and God knows how long it's been on her breast. "I'm so sorry. I didn't mean to—"

"It's okay," she says, laughing it off. "It's fine, really."

I let out a long sigh and bury my face in my hands. "I'm so embarrassed."

"Don't be." She gestures for me to turn back around, and we return to our spooning position. Her firm grip isn't helping with the twitches that continue to shoot between my thighs, and I'm wet and so ready to be touched. Silva has no idea about my inner turmoil, and she moans quietly as she nestles herself close. "It was just a dream. You're okay."

Once again, I try to relax, but now I crave her even more. It may have been a dream, but the way my body reacts to her is very, very real.

33

FAITH

"Morning, ladies." We're in the middle of our training session when Roy comes out of the bedroom. "Hello, hello. You must be the famous Silva." He chuckles. "I'm glad someone got lucky last night because it sure as hell wasn't me."

"Roy," I hiss, out of breath as I'm on my twenty-fifth crunch. "We're busy right now, and last night was not what you think, so stop speculating." I'm a little on edge this morning, remembering the dream, and on top of that I'm still embarrassed about groping her breast in my sleep.

"Hi, Roy. It's nice to meet you." Silva shakes Roy's hand and studies him with interest. She must assume I was mad to think he was ever straight, but Roy didn't always look as flamboyant as he does now. He used to wear suits and boring sweaters to please his conservative father when he was still alive. Following his death, Roy realized nothing was holding him back from being himself any longer and he started to change. Growing into himself might be a better way to put it, as it was a journey for both of us. All the signs were there then, and yes, I should have known he was gay.

He's wrapped himself in my red, silk kimono and traces of eyeliner are smudged in the corners of his eyes.

"Likewise. I've heard a lot about you." He winks. "Only good things, babe. Only good things."

"I'm glad to hear that." Silva gives him a wide smile. "But Faith is right. It's not what you think. She slept in my bed, is all."

I groan as I reach crunch number thirty, drop the weights next to me and sit up, panting. "You were snoring again," I say through heavy breaths. "Like, so loud it would have given me a migraine if I'd stayed."

"Nonsense, I don't snore." Roy rolls his eyes and waves it off. "That's a bad excuse, Faith. Why don't you stop beating around the 'proverbial bush,'" he says, making quote marks in the air. "Just tell her you think she's hot and then you can go from there. Seriously, it's not that complicated."

I stare at Roy, wide-eyed, and I want to kill him. I want to kick him out of my apartment and tell him to mind his own business because he's just embarrassed me even more. He's already turned the corner, though, and I can hear the coffee bean grinder working its magic. Silva doesn't seem fazed by his comment, but she does have a flirtatious twinkle in her eyes when she beckons me to turn on my front.

"Push-ups," she says, shifting on the floor. "Three times five." As I'm into my fourth, she leans over me and murmurs in my ear, "So, you think I'm hot?" The question causes me to drop to the floor, but she shakes her head and shoots me a playful smile. "Nuh-uh. You're only on three. Come on, keep going."

"Roy's stirring. He loves drama." I'm unable to concentrate on my breathing, and I pant as I say it. Having Roy and Silva in the same room and no idea what else he's about to announce makes me shifty and anxious. Silva's teasing isn't helping either, and my brain isn't geared up enough to think of a witty reply. Her words and her voice in my ear do turn me on, though. More than she could ever imagine. "Okay, I may have told him I find you attractive," I admit after my last push-up, moving back into child's pose so she can't see my flustered face.

"Is that so?" Silva lowers her voice to a whisper in case Roy is listening in. "Well, I happen to think you're pretty damn hot too."

As I stay in the pose, my head bent between my knees and my arms stretched out on the floor in front of me, my heart is beating violently. "You do?"

"Yeah." Silva puts her hand on my back to correct my pose but holds it there for longer than necessary.

So this is where our sessions start to get interesting. I want to stay in this position, with her warm hand on my back. Remembering the massage and how it felt on my bare skin is fantasy overload, and when she slides her hand farther down my spine and finally withdraws, I shiver.

"That was great. Good work," she says casually, as if our mutual confessions were nothing out of the ordinary on a Sunday morning. "Want to do some deep stretches?"

"Sure." I never say no to deep stretches as I love it when she uses her weight on me. I turn on my back and let her lift my left leg before she pushes my knee against my chest and leans on me to further the stretch. I wish my knee wasn't in between us; I wish she were right there on top of me, kissing me wildly.

"So, is this what you would call a typical lesbian work-out?" Roy jokes as he comes back with a coffee in hand. He sips it while he stares at us in a bemused manner, one hand casually resting in the pocket of my robe.

I shoot him a warning look, but Silva bursts out in

laughter and swaps position, lifting my other leg and bending it against my chest. "This is what I call a typical after-workout stretch," she says, leaning on me again. "Want to try it?"

"No. Thanks for the offer but I don't want to make Faith jealous.

"Asshole," I say. "Can you just go home?"

"I will, in a minute." He makes himself comfortable on the couch and pulls his legs up underneath him. "I'm having way too much fun watching you blush like a bride."

34

SILVA

"You've slept together?" Trinny asks with a gasp after I've filled her in on the past week. She takes a bite from her carrot cake and sits back in the brown leather lounge chair, staring at me. The coffee house close to Faith's apartment has become my new favorite hangout spot since it's only a three-minute walk and their coffee is fantastic.

"We've only slept," I say. "Nothing happened."

"But you've slept in the same bed three nights in a row. That's pretty intimate."

"I agree." I shrug. "It only started because her friend who stayed over snored, so she couldn't sleep. And then the following day, there was this joke between us about testing her bed next, so we slept together again. It's become a thing, I suppose. A nice thing."

Trinny looks at me as if I've lost my mind. "And is there any touching involved in this sleeping arrangement?"

"We cuddle..." I pause. "Although I woke up when she had a nightmare the other night and her hand was under my T-shirt and on my breast. I can tell you it wasn't easy to fall back asleep after that."

"So you *do* like her," she says in a teasing tone. "Are you sure it was a nightmare?"

I grin and let out a chuckle. "I suppose it could have been a sex dream. I've wondered about that too."

Trinny throws her head back and laughs. "Well, straight or not, if she's having sex dreams about you, it's only a matter of time before you go there."

"It could have been about someone else," I say. "It could have been about anyone." Remembering Faith's flustered and embarrassed state when she woke up, I do have a strong feeling it might have something to do with me, but I don't want to make assumptions. "Her friend Roy said something the next day, though," I continue. "He said something like, 'just get it over with and tell her you think she's hot.'"

"Wooow..." Trinny draws out the word before her jaw drops. "She's got a crush on you." She throws in a dramatic pause. "And you've got a crush on her too. How convenient."

I'm about to deny it, but she's right. Who am I fooling apart from myself? "I do," I admit. "And as long as I live with Faith and see her every day, that's not going to change."

"And sleeping in the same bed is certainly not going to change your attraction to each other," she adds.

"No..." I let out a long sigh and blow out my cheeks. "Look, I have no idea where this is going. And I know it makes little sense. She's a socialite and a famous photographer and I'm—"

"A sweet, intelligent, kind, and super-sexy personal trainer," Trinny says, interrupting me. "You're a catch, Sil. What are you going to do?"

"What am *I* going to do?" I frown. "Nothing. If she wants more, she'll let me know."

"Maybe she's waiting for you to make the first move." She blows on her latte and takes a careful sip. "I can't believe it. Faith Astor and my little sister."

"You're acting like we're in a relationship or something. We're not."

"We'll talk again in a couple of weeks," Trinny says matter-of-factly. "Anyway, how's your leg? Is it healing well?"

"I think so. Four more weeks to go. Funnily enough, I don't mind my cast so much anymore. Living with Faith has been great, and it's more than made up for the pain and inconvenience." I hesitate. "But between you and me, I do panic about my weight now and then. I exercise on the floor to the best of my abilities, but it's not the same as cardio. I worry about calorie control and... you know."

"I know." Trinny takes my hand. "But you've been doing so well for so long now. I'm aware how important routine and control is to you, but don't let this broken ankle ruin everything you worked so hard for. You can get through this, Sil. Don't fall back into bad habits. Please." She smiles. "I'm glad you told me you're struggling. Thank you for trusting me."

I nod and return her smile. "I haven't dared weigh myself recently, as I'm worried it will cause a relapse. I know I've gained weight because I'm not as active as I normally am, and seeing the actual number is sure to alarm me to the point where I get totally obsessive again."

"It's good you realize that, and you're right. Don't go anywhere near the scale. Not that you look any different. You know as well as I do that it's all in your head." Trinny pauses. "I've been worried about you since your accident. That's why I wanted you to come and live with me so I could keep an eye on you. I get that you don't want to sleep on my sofa bed for such a long stretch of time, and I'm really happy you're living with Faith because I think she's good for you. But call me if your anxiety gets the better of you, okay? Do you promise?"

"I promise," I say, meeting her eyes. I don't like telling Trinny about my struggles because I don't want her to worry about me. At the same time, she's the only person in the world apart from my parents who knows how bad I've been in the past, and right now, I need an anchor. "Thank you. I'll get through this." Stirring my coffee, I look Trinny over. "Enough about me now. How about you? Anything interesting going on in your life?"

35

FAITH

Today's shoot is in an old warehouse in the Meatpacking District. *Zero* magazine's styling team has transformed it into a scene from a fairy tale, with fake flowers, grass, and vines covering the ceiling and the walls. It's an early summer shoot, and the ten heaters that are supposed to keep the models warm in their skimpy outfits aren't doing much good in this vast space. I almost feel guilty about wearing my coat and my scarf, as one of the women wraps herself in a thick robe while waiting for the technicians to adjust the lighting.

"Everyone ready?" the assistant editor, who has been running around like a headless chicken all morning, asks. She looks stressed, even a little panicky. "Valerie will be here any minute to sign off on the set."

The crew mumble they need a few more minutes and start rushing now. Valerie, the head editor of *Zero*, is the most influential person in fashion and a total control freak. I've worked with her a handful of occasions, and although these jobs pay very well, I'm always on edge when she's around. She's a cold woman with very few human qualities.

Always immaculately dressed, always in a hurry, and always confidently opinionated and difficult, she never holds back. And she looks like a vampire. There's that.

When the room falls silent, I know she's here even before I've turned to see her parade in wearing her signature black cape and top hat. Ignoring everyone apart from me, her lips pull into a cold smile.

"Faith, I'm so glad you were available. You always have a certain flair when it comes to weird and whimsical." Without waiting for a reply, she struts past me and points to the ceiling. "Those vines need to hang much lower," she barks at the stylist. "I want the girls to be immersed in the green, not stand underneath like it's some cheap wedding canopy. We're *Zero*, not *Bridal Today*, for Christ's sake."

The stylist looks beat, but she nods and heads for the box of greenery. "These vines aren't long enough, but we can attach them to each other," she says with a tremble in her voice. "We might need an hour."

"I don't have an hour, make it thirty minutes." Valerie turns to the models. "Let me see what you're wearing. Are we starting with swimwear?" The five young women take off their robes to show the swimsuits and bikinis they're wearing, and Valerie inspects them. "You. That color is not good for you." She grabs another swimsuit off the rails and hands it to one of the dressers. "She'll wear this instead." Finally, her eyes rest on the last of the five, and her face pulls into a grimace. "What's going on here?"

The girl frowns and glances down at the bikini she's wearing. "What do you mean? Is it the wrong one?"

"No, not the bikini. Your thighs. When was the last time your agency measured you?"

I look around to see if anyone else is baffled by her comment, but the crew is too busy getting the set right and the stylist is changing the other model's outfit behind the dressing screens. Even if they heard it, I doubt they'd even blink an eye. It's the third time I've heard someone comment on a model's weight. Shamefully, I suppose I found it normal before, but something has changed in me. I don't know if it's Silva who has caused my sense of self-worth to grow, but Valerie's words make my stomach drop, and I can't tolerate what's happening here. By telling this girl, who can't be older than seventeen, that she isn't good enough, Valerie is screwing her up for life.

"Oh..." The poor girl glances at her feet. She's lean like the others; she just has a little bit more curve to her. In fact, she looks healthier, better actually. "Five weeks ago, I think."

"Well, we can't work with this. There's way too much blubber to photoshop. You should be ashamed of yourself for even turning up like this. We have standards, for God's sake."

"Hey," I say, stepping forward. "Don't talk to her like that."

Valerie looks startled, not because she's intimidated by me, but I suspect no one ever talks back to her. She walks up to me but keeps a respectable distance and gives me a cold stare. "Excuse me?"

"I said, don't talk to her like that." My raised voice causes the whole room to fall silent again, and everyone stops what they're doing. It looks like someone's pressed a pause button; no one dares move and it's eerily quiet. I'm fully aware I'm risking my career by calling her out, but I'm too angry to consider the consequences. Telling Silva about my eating disorder, has reopened old wounds, and as I stare back at Valerie, it's not just her but also Andrew I see. If Silva were in my shoes, she would do the right thing, and I need to do the right thing too.

"How dare you," Valerie says dryly. She's all composure, but I can see a nervous twitch at the corner of her mouth.

"You have no idea of the damage you're doing. You should be ashamed of yourself, not her."

"*You*, Faith, have no idea what damage you're doing to your career," she shoots back at me, inching closer. "So stop causing trouble and do the fucking shoot."

I smile because I know I've got her right where I want her. She needs me to do this; it's an expensive shoot, and even though she desperately wants to fire me, she won't get another photographer in on time. The models, the set, the stylist, not to mention the rest of the technical crew, have been booked, and we're on a deadline. She needs me.

"I don't want to be a part of this." I remove the crew lanyard from around my neck, throw it in the trash, and grab my camera bag before I brush past her.

"I'll make sure you never work again," Valerie hisses in a last attempt to win the standoff.

"I'd rather not work at all than work for people like you," I say, and as I turn my back on the best paid job of the season, I've never felt so good about myself.

36

SILVA

"I'm so proud of you," I say, pulling Faith into a hug after she's told me about her morning. I was surprised when she came back early from what she'd said was an important shoot. "You made a difference today. Young women need to know they don't deserve to be treated like that, and the industry needs to learn it's not okay to let it happen."

"It's not going to change anything. It will still happen again and again." Faith inches back and pulls her legs up underneath her on the couch. "But I don't regret it." She chuckles and shakes her head. "Well, I might regret it once I'm out of work."

"She can't actually make that happen, can she? Stop clients from booking you?"

"Valerie?" Faith arches a brow. "Oh, yes, she can. Designers need her support. They need her to showcase their collections in her magazine, and she could boycott them if they continue to work with me."

"But what about other magazines?" Her statement baffles me; I'm clearly not clued up on the world of fashion.

"Even her direct competitors run on fifty percent freelancers, and those freelancers work for Valerie too. That includes stylists, bookers, and art directors. Everyone needs Valerie on their side, not to mention a lot of the other fashion magazines are owned by the same mother company. Everything's connected like a spider's web, and Valerie is the black widow who sits in the middle."

"That's crazy."

"That's not all," she says. "This private club launch I've been invited to tonight, for example. It's going to be the main hub for New York Fashion Week, and it will be packed with designers and people from the industry. Once word gets around, which I suspect will only be a matter of hours, people will be uncomfortable to be seen with me. If I'm Valerie's nemesis, they'll feel like they need to pick sides, and trust me, no one is prepared to throw away their career."

"Except for you." I cup her cheek and run my thumb over her soft skin. Faith closes her eyes and leans into my touch. Everything we do has been highly intimate lately. Everything but a kiss, and right now, I want to kiss her like never before.

"I should have done something sooner," she whispers. "By doing nothing, I've been part of this problem too, and I'm ashamed of myself for that. For years, I've been shooting girls who are unhealthy and allowed them to be sent away if they weren't perfect."

"Don't think like that. You did something today, and that's what counts."

Faith's phone lights up, and she sighs when she reads the message. "It's Roy," she says. "He's already heard what happened."

"Seriously?"

"I told you word travels fast." She frowns as she opens an attachment, then slams a hand in front of her mouth.

"What? What is it?"

"Someone filmed it," she says, turning her phone so we can watch the exchange between her and Valerie together. "It's been forwarded by an anonymous source."

Pulling her phone closer toward me, I watch the video that starts with Valerie uttering the words, "What did you say?" and ends with Faith throwing her lanyard in the trash and walking out on the shoot. *"Bravo to Faith Astor for standing up to body-shaming,"* the caption says.

"This is great." I take the phone from her and watch it again. "Faith, this is fantastic. It's proof."

"Proof that I'm now officially Valerie's number one enemy." She huffs sarcastically. "Like I told you, it's not going to change anything. The only thing that will change is that people will avoid me like the plague, but I'm prepared for that, and I can't even say I mind it so much. I was getting sick of everyone anyway."

"You don't know that."

"I do. I meant it when I said I don't regret it, but I'll have to think about how I'm going to generate income from now on. My apartment is paid for, so at least I won't have a mortgage issue, but long term..." Faith shrugs. "I don't know. I need to work, or I'll go crazy."

I can see her mind is spinning with worries concerning the aftermath of her run-in with Valerie, and I want to turn today into a good day for her, because soon she'll think back with pride to this significant point in her life, even though she doesn't realize that now. "How about you start worrying about work tomorrow and do something fun with me today? Something to take your mind off this?"

As if my words are somehow soothing to her, Faith

visibly relaxes. "I'd like that," she says with a sweet smile. "But don't you have to work?"

"I have two online classes tonight, but my afternoon is free. We could go and see a movie? Take a cab? At least that doesn't require me hopping around like a bunny or tackling pedestrians with my crutches." When Faith bursts out in laughter, I know I've cheered her up already, and that makes me insanely happy.

37

FAITH

The theater is near-empty, which I suspect is not unusual for an afternoon showing. Instead of a movie, we've gone for a documentary about penguins in the Antarctic. Their cute and funny antics made us laugh for the first hour, and now I'm in floods of tears at the emotional sight of a baby's reunion with its mother after being lost in the penguin crowd for hours. It's not just the documentary that's taken my mind off this morning. It's sitting here in the dark, so close to Silva. I can smell her body lotion and her thigh is leaning against mine, causing a rush of arousal every time she shifts.

"I'm sorry," I sniff. "I'm being ridiculous."

Silva turns to me, and when I see tears in her eyes too, we both burst out in laughter, causing the dozen or so other patrons to turn around and glare at us.

"Apologies," Silva yells, holding up a hand. She lowers her voice and turns to me. "Don't worry, I'm a sucker for these things too." We're sitting right at the back in the middle row. Her excuse was that she didn't want to go down the steps with her crutches. After spotting the wheelchair ramp at the side, I'm not so sure how valid that excuse was, but I'm not complaining about the privacy.

She puts an arm around me and pulls me in against her. I've been waiting for her to do this; it's how I envisioned us on our way here. Village East Cinema is spectacular and worth the cab drive. With it's beautiful 1920s décor, deep, comfortable red, velvet seats, and gold-painted, ornamental ceiling, I feel like we've gone back in time, and I can't believe I've never been here before. The cool, eclectic area, where I've attended many parties but never explored during the day, is Silva's old neighborhood, where she used to live with her sister, and she suggested we came here.

As I sink into her embrace and rest my head on her shoulder, I'm aware this is no ordinary friendship. We sleep in the same bed; we live like a couple, and we're tactile and cuddly at every chance we get. I'm crushing on her hard, I fantasize about her all the time, and she literally told me she's attracted to me too. So why is nothing happening?

I turn to look at her, to study the profile of her handsome face that I've been dying to eternalize. My fight with Valerie has not put me off photography. On the contrary, I feel a need to produce my best work yet, to prove to Valerie I don't need her. Feeling my gaze on her, Silva turns and looks at me. Our eyes linger on each other for long moments, and she rubs my shoulder up to my neck, caressing the sensitive spot behind my ear. My eyelids flutter closed, and I shiver at the caress. There's no way she hasn't noticed my reaction.

"Will you let me take your picture?" I whisper, opening my eyes again and taking her in.

Her beautiful lips pull into a smile. "Why do you want to take my picture?"

"I just do." *Damn it. Why can't I just get it over with? Tell her she's the object of all my desires and more?*

Silva tilts her head and regards me with a mischievous look. "And what would a photoshoot with you look like?"

"I want to shoot you in your purest form. Old school, analog, black and white. No frills, no filters, and naked. You can keep your cast on," I add with a wink.

A subtle flinch passes Silva's expression. She leans in close and bites her lip. "Naked?" Her breathy voice slays me, and I swallow hard before I answer.

"Yes."

"And where do you envision this naked shoot takes place?" Her eyes darken, and she tightens her hold on me, making me squirm in my seat.

"In bed," I whisper after a long pause because it's the only place I can picture her right now. "I'll need to get my stuff back first. I left my case with my lights and other cameras behind today, but I've asked to have them sent by courier. Hopefully, I'll have them back tomorrow." Shifting so I can drape my leg over hers, I feel brave and bold. "So, are you up for it?"

"Only if you undress too," she says, never taking her eyes off mine. "Fair is fair."

I give her a subtle nod. "Fair is fair. Tomorrow, then." Tormented by a jumble of raging desire and emotions I can't even identify, I ball my hands into fists so she won't see they're trembling.

Silva's gaze lowers to my mouth and she brings her face closer to mine. She doesn't kiss me, but I can feel her heavy breaths against my lips. This is crazy. She's not doing anything, yet I'm close to combusting. Having her so close and feeling her need is enough to set me on fire. I wait for her to make a move, but nothing happens. *Breathe. Just be in the moment.* This feels more intimate than anything I've ever done. Two people simply staring into each other's eyes, so close to kissing. So close to more.

"You're beautiful," she says, and the breath that comes with her words hits my lips like a tornado. Only a hint of oxygen escapes her, but it feels like she's blowing life into me. Then, suddenly, she turns back to the screen as if nothing has happened. As if she didn't just turn me inside out and teased me until my body screamed with need.

I vaguely register something funny is happening as people are laughing, but with my mind consumed by anticipation, I have no idea what's going on. As I stare into nothing, pretending to watch the documentary, Silva rests her hand on my thigh, and it causes an intense flash of arousal in my center. *I wish I was wearing a skirt.* Sensing I like this, she squeezes my leg and starts stroking me slowly and deliberately while she too, pretends to focus on the screen. She hesitates for a moment before her hand slides farther up and inward, dangerously close to where I need her to touch me most. Her strokes, now firmer, make me throb, and a moan escapes me. I'm not sure she heard it and don't dare look at her.

Who are we fooling? Our chemistry is orgasmic; it radiates between us like an electric storm. My body feels like my own when I'm with her. I sense every nerve, every part of me so intensely, and in those moments, I don't think about my insecurities. I just appreciate and embrace everything that is me, because she wants me as I am.

Murmurs sound through the screening hall, and when people get up and put on their coats, I realize the documentary has ended. When the lights are turned on, Silva retracts her hand and blinks as if waking up from a trance.

"That was fun," she says in a husky voice, leaving me hanging with a delicious, torturous ache for her.

38

SILVA

We're sitting on the couch in our usual positions, talking after dinner. The TV is off, my legs are resting on her lap, and we've lit candles. It's started snowing again, but in here, it's warm and cozy, and Faith has scooted closer to me than she usually does. She keeps glancing at the bedroom door, and I know what she's thinking because I'm thinking the same. I want to go to bed. I love having her against me, but it's ridiculously early, and if we do that, we really need to discuss what's going on: after the documentary today, there's no way we can deny our mutual attraction.

"You must be so sick of that cast," she says, tapping it with her fingers. "Three weeks in—at least you're halfway."

"Yeah, I can't wait till it comes off." I imagine her hand on my leg instead of on my cast, then try to push back the thought. My fantasies have become more intense lately, and they're no longer confined to the privacy of my bedroom. "It's got stains on it and it's starting to look gross."

Faith raises a brow and shoots me a mischievous grin. "Hmm... We should do something about that." She gets up, heads into her office, and comes back with a pack of sharpies. "I'm not an artist, but I went to art college, so I'm slightly better than the average bear at drawing."

I laugh and reach out to stroke her cheek because right now, she couldn't possibly be any cuter. "You want to doodle on my cast?"

"Yeah." Faith scans the selection of colors and picks a red sharpie. "Let's see if I've still got what it takes. I never do this anymore." She starts off by drawing a woman with her leg in a cast, and I must admit, it does resemble me. With a few simple lines, she's managed to capture things about me that stand out: my hair, my jawline, my signature shorts I've been wearing inside since I broke my ankle, and my favorite T-shirt that I bought from a dive bar in Brooklyn.

"You're very observant," I say, amused at her excitement when she swaps the red sharpie for a blue one.

"It's not hard. You practically wear the same stuff every day, and your face..." She pauses and gives me a smile that's bordering on flirty. "Well, it's hard to forget."

Definitely flirty. I stare at her for a long moment, but she's concentrating on her next drawing now. "What's that?"

"This," Faith says, "is a road. It represents everything you're going to do once your cast comes off. If you're feeling fed up and low, all you need to do is look at it and remember what you have to look forward to." She draws a winding path. "Now, what's the first thing you'll do when you have your leg back?"

"I want to go for a long walk," I say, glancing outside.

"That might be a bit of a stretch. You'll need a couple of weeks of rehabilitation, but a short walk should be doable. Where are we going?"

"We?" I try to keep a serious face.

"Yes, we. I'm coming with you."

"Okay. Well, I guess we could walk to my favorite local bar, and I'll buy you a drink. It's called the—"

"Let me guess, Portland Street Pride?" she interrupts me, pointing at my T-shirt. "Okay, I like that," she says when I nod. A blush creeps onto her cheeks as she starts drawing a building. "I didn't take you for the bar type."

"There are a lot of things you don't know about me."

"I'm starting to realize that." Faith writes the name on the bar and draws two cocktails next to it. "But what am I going to do in a bar full of lesbians?"

"Don't worry, I'll protect you." I shoot her a wink, and going on her grin, she likes my comment.

"If you say so." Faith adds slices of lemon to the rims of the martini glasses and looks up, licking her lips as her gaze lowers to my mouth. "What else do you want to do when the cast comes off?"

Was that a hint? What does she want me to say? Although it's pretty clear she's flirting with me, I still don't bite because I'm not sure if she's sincere or simply playing with me. "I want to have a bath," I say. "I'm dreaming of finally having a bath again. Washing at the sink doesn't do it for me."

"A bath, of course." Faith draws a bathtub on my cast, and I laugh when she then draws me in it, naked.

"Hey, no X-rated stuff, you devil. I still have to go outside with this thing. Also, my breasts are not that big."

"Well, I don't know that, do I?" She glances at my chest, then covers her face in her hands as she laughs out loud.

"That's right. You don't," I say, arching a brow at her. "But I guess you'll find out when we're doing that naked photoshoot."

"Mmm. Yes, I guess so." Faith blushes profusely. "You don't have to wait until your cast comes off to have a bath, though." She gestures to her bedroom. "You've seen my tub. It's big and deep, built for the perfect soak."

"That would be messy. My cast would get wet."

"Not if you sit down carefully and don't splash around. You can have your leg on the edge of the tub or on a chair next to it and I can wrap it up for you. A trash bag and some duct tape would do the job." She shrugs and puts the top back on the sharpie. "Want me to run you a bath?"

39

FAITH

"Are you decent?" I ask, raising my voice as I knock on the bathroom door.

"Yes, come in." Silva is subgmerged in the bath, covered by heaps of foam. Her neatly wrapped leg is resting on the edge of the tub, and I lift it and put a nonslip rubber mat underneath it.

"That should be a little better." I try not to stare too much, but it's hard because she looks mesmerizing in the candlelight. Even though I can't see her body under the foam, her neck, collarbones, and shoulders are beautiful and so feminine. "Are you comfortable?"

"God, yes. This feels so incredibly good, I just want to soak for hours," she says with a wide grin.

"Good. My housekeeper washed your robe, and here's a towel." I place the biggest, fluffiest towel I could find on the edge of the sink. "Want me to wash your hair? I mean, not that it's greasy or anything," I hastily add. "I just thought you might want the full experience, and I don't think you'll be able to do it yourself without splashing too much."

Silva's eyes darken, and there's a long, loaded silence

between us before her voice softly echoes off the walls. "Would you mind?"

"No. I'd love to." My hands are trembling as I gather my shampoo and conditioner and pull the showerhead down. I finally have a legitimate reason to touch her hair. For weeks, I've been wanting to run my fingers through it, and when I finally stroke her thick, blonde locks, I get so aroused that I can feel it everywhere. "Too warm?"

"Perfect," she whispers, closing her eyes.

I wet her hair and try not to use my hands in any other way than necessary but it's hard. Massaging in the shampoo, I watch her take in a subtle gasp. *She's enjoying this.* I never thought washing someone's hair could be so erotic, but there's no doubt she can feel it too. This week we've been different around each other. The dinner, the massage, the sleepovers, our heated conversations, and now this. Everyday life, even the mundane things, has turned into an improvised dance of seduction, and neither of us know where it will lead. I'm scared, but my desire took over from my fear days ago, and I'm not going to stop flirting unless she asks me to.

"Mmm..." Her moan makes me quiver, and I picture her making the same noise in bed. Taking way longer than necessary, I flush out the shampoo and move on to the conditioner. By the time I'm done, the bathroom's not the only thing that's hot and steamy.

How on earth did I go from having my heart broken by a man to lusting after my female personal trainer in the span of only five weeks? I was never heartbroken, I realize then. It was just my ego that was crushed. Because if I'm honest with myself, Michael hasn't been on my mind more than a handful of times since Silva came into my life. Am I gay? Is that why I could never hold a relationship with a man? And if I am, why have I not felt this before with women?

Thoughts come and go while I massage her scalp for the second time, and as I gently tilt her head back to rinse it, she opens her eyes and looks at me. She doesn't smile and she doesn't speak, but her gaze says enough. She wants me. The condensation in the bathroom and the dim light of the flickering candles on the vanity fill the space with a sultry vibe, and I'm so close I could lean in and kiss her, but I don't.

When I turn off the water, I can hear our breaths through the silence, and anticipation is hanging between us, thick and heavy. "Do you want some privacy?" I ask, giving her head one last stroke before I wrap her hair in a towel.

"No, please stay. This is nice."

"Okay. I move to the rug on the floor and lean sideways against the tub, facing her. The foam has gone down, giving me a view of her cleavage, and a small smile plays around her lips when she catches me looking. I feel a need to fill the silence, so I point to her leg. "What else are you missing that you can't do with the cast?"

"I might have to think twice about what I say now," she says. "I feel like you're determined to make my dreams come true tonight."

"What's wrong with that?"

"Nothing."

Another silence follows, and gathering all my courage, I ask my next question. "Do you miss sex?"

"Sex..." Silva looks me over. "I don't have a girlfriend."

"Sure. But you meet with women casually, right?"

"No. I mean, sometimes, but I don't do casual very often. It's been at least four months." She shrugs. "It doesn't make me happy."

"Oh..." It's hard to imagine Silva didn't have an army of women at her door when she was still at home.

"But don't forget, I broke my ankle, not my hand." Silva grins. "I can still have sex. With myself and with others." She chuckles at my startled expression. "What? Now you're shy all of a sudden? You started it."

"Started what?" I ask, even though I know exactly what she's referring to.

"With the flirting. Isn't that what we're doing here?"

When I don't answer, she sits up, and her breasts rise above the water, only her nipples covered by the last bit of foam. My heart is beating so fast I can feel it in my throat, and the tightness in my core is killing me.

"I'm starting to get really hot," she says in a husky voice. "Will you help me out?"

40

SILVA

She didn't dare look when she helped me out of the bath, and she doesn't dare look now, but I know she wants to. Maybe this is stupid and maybe we'll regret it, but I already know we won't last another three weeks of holding back on our desires. Our chemistry is strong and constant, no longer limited to brief moments in our training sessions. I sit on the edge of the bath and dry myself while she has her back turned to me, waiting with the robe.

"Are you done?"

"Yes."

Faith turns around and keeps her eyes sternly fixed on mine as she wraps the robe around me and waits for me to tie it. Handing me my crutches, she helps me up, and we're face-to-face. More at ease now that I'm covered, her eyes dart to my mouth and then my cleavage, and there's no doubt she wants me to make a move. I look at her hair; I desperately want to run my hands through it, but I need to steady myself on the crutches. If I could walk, I would push her against the door and kiss her hard while my hands roam under her tank top. Instead, I slowly bring my face closer to hers until we're breathing each other's air. Faith doesn't back away, but she's shaking all over.

"Are you okay?" I tilt my head until my lips are almost on hers and stay there, teasing her while I wait for her to answer. The silence is not uncomfortable; on the contrary. It's filled with lust and longing, and I've never wanted anyone more.

"I'm not sure," she whispers. "But I want you."

Faith's statement makes me light-headed as I inch closer and kiss her pillowy lips. They're heavenly, so soft and welcoming. She takes in a quick breath, as if the light touch shocks her to her core. She moves back, looks at me, then presses her lips firmer against mine and parts them. We deepen the kiss, and as our tongues meet, we both moan softly. It's slow, sensual, so sexy, and my body reacts in crazy ways. Butterflies, intense arousal, and heat spread through me like wildfire, fueling me with passion of the deepest kind.

Faith suddenly pulls away again, and she stares at me as if she can't quite believe what just happened. Bringing her hand to her mouth, she touches her lips, then licks them. "I didn't expect that," she whispers. Her gaze lowers to my mouth, and as we fall into another kiss, her hands slide over my back. Her touch feels amazing, like an angel's caress. The way she scrapes her nails over my spine and squeezes me drives me wild, and I can feel her need in her touch. I wish I could touch her in return, but I can't in an upright position, and I groan as I lift my hand and the crutch drops to the floor, making me lose my balance. Faith catches me and, as if sensing my frustration, smiles against my mouth. "Come to bed with me. You won't need those in bed."

~

"Are you sure?" I ask when she's lying on her bed on top of the covers.

"Yes." Although she sounds determined, I don't want her to do anything she'll regret. "Yes," Faith repeats as she looks at me hungrily.

I take off my robe and let it drop to the floor. Giving her a moment, I enjoy her eyes roaming over me as she takes me in with intense wonderment.

"Fuck... You're beautiful," she whispers.

"*You're* beautiful, Faith." I crawl over her and steady myself above her on my knees.

"Please, kiss me again. I've never felt anything like it."

She probably wouldn't believe me if I said I hadn't either, so I simply smile and run my hands through her hair. It slips through my fingers like satin, and I bring my hand to her cheek, caressing her mouth with my thumb.

Faith's lashes flutter as she folds her lips around the tip of my thumb. She looks incredibly seductive yet so pure with visible nervousness in her expression. Leaning in, I cup her face and brush my lips against hers before I take her mouth and lower myself on top of her. She's shaking all over, but she pulls me in closer and kisses me back fiercely. Her arching back and her hips moving against mine tell me she needs more, so I slide my hand under her top and find her breasts. They're full and soft and perky, and when I run my fingers over her nipple, she gasps against my mouth, then produces a low, drawn-out moan that sends me wild.

"How is this possible?" she whispers. "How can you make me feel this way?"

I know what she means; I've been wondering the same

thing. Faith does things to me I could never have imagined, and arousal is always instant with her. All she needs to do is look at me and I'm a lost cause. I want more of her, all of her. Pushing her top up until her breasts are exposed, I caress them while we kiss and grind into each other, finally releasing all our pent-up sexual frustration. Her hands are in my hair, then on my back before they lower to my behind and squeeze my cheeks. She explores me with her trembling fingertips, and the heavenly aftermath of her touch makes my skin tingle. From the way she moves and moans, I think she's close to climaxing from the friction of my hips alone. Wanting this to last, I raise myself onto my knees again and kiss her neck. Faith welcomes this by tilting her head sideways while I suck at her sensitive skin.

"You're driving me crazy," she murmurs, fisting my hair and guiding my mouth to her breasts. The moment my tongue glides over one of her nipples, her chest shoots up and a deep groan escapes her. "Yes," she says in a ragged voice. "Oh, my God, yes."

Her naked skin feels heavenly, and I tug at her top, eager to see all of her. "Can I take this off?"

Without answering, Faith sits up so I can remove it, then unclips her bra and lets it fall off her. Staring at her shapely shoulders and curvy breasts and belly, I ache for her so much it hurts. She slides down her jersey shorts too, leaving her in a pair of black lace panties.

"Faith..." I'm lost for words as I trace her skin and remind myself to take it slow, because I want this to last, and I want this to be memorable for her. "You are so beautiful." I slide my hand in between us to stroke the inside of her thigh, like I did at the movie theater, only this time there is very little in the way. Moving up to her center, I skim the edge of her panties, and Faith instinctively spreads her legs and lifts her hips to meet my touch. I stroke her softly and marvel at the wetness I feel through the fabric.

"Please take them off," she says. Her eyes are loaded with lust and her chest is heaving fast.

Brushing my mouth over her belly, I pull down her panties and kiss her thighs as I remove them. The thin strip of hair tickles my lips when I kiss her there and breathe warm air over her sensitive skin. She wiggles and grinds against me, her body language urging me to release her. I stay there, making her wait until she sighs in frustration, and then I run my tongue over the length of her center. Faith's reaction is astonishing, like she's never felt anything like it before, and it shakes me. She gasps, elevates off the bed and digs her fingers into my hair so hard it hurts. She tastes divine, and I hungrily repeat the action, savoring her flavor on my tongue while I hold her by her hips. This only happened in my wildest fantasies, and such fire, such passion, is unknown to me. Twirling my tongue around her most sensitive spot, I close my eyes as I feel her explode against my mouth. She shakes and cries out and pulls me tightly against her. Long after she's climaxed, aftershocks still course through her.

"That was..." She lets out a long sigh. "That was incredible."

"Yeah?" I crawl up to bring my face to Faith's, and the sight of her is breathtaking. Her intense eyes, her hand resting on her clammy forehead, her parted lips and her heart that still beats hard against my chest bring a smile to my face, and she shoots me a lazy smile in return.

"Uh-huh." Her eyes flick to the ceiling and she chuckles. "Now I know."

"Know what?" I ask.

"What it's like with you. I've been wondering about that."

"Me too," I admit, stroking her arm. But you'll have to wait with your final verdict because I'm not done with you yet."

41

FAITH

Who knew this could be so good? My face is nuzzled in Silva's neck and my hand is resting on her breast. Basking in a state of extreme relaxation, I inhale deeply against her skin and smile.

Silva takes me in a tighter hold and lets out a sigh of contentment. "How are you feeling?"

"Better than ever." I look up at her and stroke her breast until her nipple rises to attention. Two orgasms later and I'm rosy and glowing. "This is quite a revelation."

"I'm glad you're not disappointed." She kisses my temple and strokes my hair, and I feel so safe and comfortable in her arms that I never want her to leave.

"You know I'm not," I whisper. At least I don't have to ask her if she wants to stay the night. We've been lying like this for the past week, but being naked with her is a different thing altogether. Now that we've crossed the line, I can kiss her whenever I want, and she's constantly searching for my eager lips too. I trace the curve of her hips and her belly, then run my fingers lower, between her legs. My heart starts racing again because this, too, is something I've never done.

"You don't have to—"

"No, I want to," I interrupt her. "Please, let me touch you." I feel her shiver as I shift on top of her and lower my hand farther. She moans softly, and I gasp at her liquid heat against my fingertips. I'm not sure where to go from here, but her expression tells me she likes my touch and that gives me confidence. "Tell me what to do."

"You know what to do." Silva takes my hand and presses it harder against her swollen center, then runs it up and down her hot flesh. I'm not sure why, but it feels so much more intimate than with a man, and feeling her arousal is making me crazy with desire for her. Following her movements, I trace her secret landscape, full of wonder at her reaction. She jerks her hips, sighs, and moans, and all this time, she never takes her eyes off mine.

Roy was right; there is an understanding between two women I never felt with men, an instinctiveness in our interaction that elevates lovemaking to a higher level. Still, the anatomical familiarities feel alien to me. Her body is like mine, but I've never explored my own body like I'm exploring hers. I've never figured out what I like and what I want, and tonight, I'm learning more about myself than I have in the past thirty-three years. Silva likes it slow; she likes it when I kiss her, and she likes it when I move into her with my full bodyweight. She's so sensitive and so receptive to my touch that I feel like we're one tonight. I'm as close as I can get to her, but I still want more, and that's mind-bending. Her skin feels like my own, and there's a comforting familiarity to her curves that puts me at ease. I'm not nervous anymore, I just want to please her. Inching my hand lower, I carefully slide my fingertip inside her, and she moans loudly.

"Yes," she says, lacing her fingers into my hair. I look

down at her small breasts and hard nipples and lean in to close my mouth over one of them. "More."

It's hard to grasp that I'm actually doing this, but I don't want to think; I just want to be in the moment with her. I move deeper and add another finger, sighing at the warmth that welcomes me, and she tenses and lets out a low groan as she throws her head back. Nothing compares to this. Nothing I've experienced in my life, and nothing I will in future. That, I know for sure.

I move into her, slowly, steadily, filling her up over and over like she did to me before. She's the most striking creature in the world, and in this moment, she's mine. Melting into her, I watch her closely as I feel her tensing. I want to remember this moment because I know tonight has already changed my life forever. Nothing will be the same again. Not the way I feel about Silva, not the way I see myself, and not my needs and desires in life.

Her walls clamp around my fingers, and her pleasure is beautiful. She nods and fights to keep her eyes open, but eventually, she loses the battle and falls into ecstasy. I love how she holds on to me, how she becomes a tense ball of fire that ignites in my arms. Something is present that wasn't here before. She's all mine, sating my deep-seated yearning to possess her wholly, emotionally, and calming the choir of voices inside me that calls for her soul.

"Faith..." Silva brushes my hair behind my ears and gives me a look I've never seen before. The frown between her brows is prominent and serious, her eyes are piercing into mine. There's a hint of confusion in her expression but also a sense of wonderment, and it reflects how I feel inside. "You have no idea what you do to me." A tear rolls down her cheek. It's not a tear of sadness, it's a tear of joy.

"I think I do." I cup her cheek, kiss her softly, and smile

against her mouth. "I feel so much." My own eyes well up and my voice trembles. I'm choking up with overwhelming emotions and I feel so alive.

She nods. "Me too." She wraps her arms tighter around me and inhales deeply against my hair. We're breathing in sync, and I genuinely believe our minds are aligned. I close my eyes, cherishing her soothing caresses. So this is what it's all about. This is what makes people get carried away, lose themselves, and do crazy things. This is what inspires poetry, music, art, and other beautiful things in life. I finally understand it now. This is everything.

42

SILVA

"I need to get out for a bit. Will you allow me to take you to dinner?" I ask when Faith comes out of the bathroom. She looks dazzling in black palazzo pants and a black kimono jacket, and her hair is pulled back into a simple braid. "Or are *you* going out? You look fantastic."

"Thank you." She straightens her jacket and gives me a shy smile. "I'm not going out. In fact, I was going to ask you the same."

"As long as you don't mind being seen with me looking like this," I joke, glancing at my wide sweatpants with one cut-off leg and blue shirt tucked in at the front. "It's the best I can do, I'm afraid. It's either this or shorts."

"Don't be silly, you look great." She steps closer and opens the top two buttons of my shirt. "There." We're both silent, contemplating whether to kiss or not. I want to kiss her so badly, and from the look in her eyes, she wants to kiss me too, but then the buzzer goes, and the moment has passed.

"That will be my equipment," Faith says, looking flustered as she heads for the door. We're in a weird space today;

not uncomfortable but definitely a little uncertain, and since I don't know how to handle the situation, I thought dinner might be a good opportunity to talk. I've finished my training sessions, and Faith has been out with Roy most of the day. I suppose she needed to get out for a bit, or perhaps she wanted to discuss what happened last night. I wouldn't blame her for telling him; it must be a lot to process.

"Is there a place you like nearby?" I ask when she comes back and places a large suitcase, a tall box, and a camera stand against the wall.

"You mean hopping distance?" Faith chuckles. "Honestly, I don't go out for dinner much, but there's a Vietnamese place a five-minute walk from here. I've never been, but I've heard it's good."

"Sounds great." I want to help her into her coat, but I can't, and instead, she helps me into mine before handing me back my crutches.

"Thank you. You'd be amazed how many things are a struggle when you can't stand on both legs. My balance is pretty good from all the yoga I've done over the past years, but the weight of the cast messes with my natural balance point."

"How does it feel?" she asks. "Is it painful?"

"No, just itchy. I think it's healing well." We face each other in the elevator on our way down, and the chemistry between us is palpable. So many things have been left unsaid today, and I really want to know how she feels after sleeping with a woman—with me—for the first time.

"Do you regret last night?" she asks, beating me to it.

I smile and shake my head. "No, not at all. Do you?"

"No." She blushes and holds the elevator door while I get out. "I have a lot of stuff to think about, though. Why was I never attracted to women before? And I don't..." Her voice trails away and she hesitates. "I don't really understand these feelings. They're so intense, so physical."

"Do you want to talk about it?" I ask as we head out into the cold night.

Faith shrugs. "Do you think I'm gay?"

"I can't answer that for you. Would it matter if you were?"

"No, I suppose not," she says after a moment's hesitation. "When did you know?"

"That I'm gay? I've always known. Apparently, it was pretty clear because my parents weren't one bit surprised when I came out to them." We cross the street and enter the small restaurant that looks surprisingly basic for someone like Faith.

"How old were you?" she asks.

"Fifteen."

"Fifteen is young." She turns to the waiter and asks for a table by the window so we can look out over the snow-covered street. "How did they react?"

"They were fine, actually," I say as we sit down. "Deep down, they knew, so they'd had years to get used to the idea. It was hard coming out in high school, though. Being the only out lesbian there, I got bullied so bad I had to move schools. The second one was much better. The school was bigger and the environment way more liberal."

"Hmm..." Faith frowns. "That's horrible. It must have been so hard."

"Yeah, kids can be mean. It's probably why I had such low self-esteem for a long time."

"I find it hard to imagine you with low self-esteem," she says, opening the menu. "I mean, not that you're cocky or anything," she hastily adds. "But you seem to know who you are."

"I do, at least now. But it took me a while to get here." I scan the dishes that all sound delicious. "So why is it that you rarely go to restaurants?" Although I think I know the answer, I feel the need to ask the question anyway.

Faith avoids my gaze and pretends to study the menu. "The events I attend are mostly in clubs or bars, and when I have a night off, I tend to stay at home." She pauses. "But that's not the only reason. As you know, I have a twisted relationship with food, and if I can't enjoy it, I don't see the point of eating out."

"I understand. I used to feel that way too."

Faith looks puzzled. "You?"

"Yes." I pause and sit back while the waiter pours us tea. "Are you okay being here?"

"Uh-huh." She smiles. "The food here is healthy, so I don't feel like I have to worry as much. I've been eating very healthily anyway, while you've been living with me, and you were right. It makes me feel good, physically. It's made a big difference."

43

FAITH

"I want to show you something," Silva says, pulling her wallet out of her back pocket. She takes out an old photograph and hands it to me.

I study the picture of a woman who bears some resemblance to Silva, yet she's too fragile to be her. Her cheeks are hollow and so are her eye sockets that have dark circles underneath. She looks starved, skin over bone. "Do you have another sister I don't know about?" I ask, then flinch as a thought strikes me. Maybe she *had* another sister. The girl in the picture certainly doesn't look like she has long to live.

"No, that's me." Silva sits back and regards me while I stare from the picture to her and back. "Ten years ago."

"That's..." I frown and try to imagine Silva really looked like this when she was younger. Her hair is thin, her skin is so pale it's almost translucent, and she looks like she hasn't slept for weeks.

"I always carry it with me, as a reminder," she says. "When I first started dieting, I never thought it would get out of hand. But as the weight fell off me, I realized it was possible for me to be really skinny, and I got carried away, even though my logic told me that kind of skinny wasn't healthy. It became an obsession. I could literally name the number of calories in every single dish put before me, and I strived for calorie deficiency day after day. After a year, I found it hard to eat at all. In my eyes, I was never skinny enough, even at the time when the picture was taken. It was a close call. If I'd lost any more weight, I would have ended up on an IV in the hospital or worse."

"Fuck..." I meet her eyes and for the first time, I see vulnerability in them. "Were you a personal trainer back then?" Remembering the first night she slept at my apartment, mumbling something about calories when she was sleepwalking, everything falls into place.

"No, I was a sports masseuse, but I had to stop working because I became too weak to do my job." She leans in, takes back the picture, and puts it away again. "I never show this to people. It's just for me. But I wanted you to see it because we have something in common—a distorted idea of reality and a whole slew of false beliefs that muddle our perception of ourselves. I used to work with athletes, and being overweight when I was around gymnasts all day, I envied their bodies. You work with size-zero models, and you have a history of mental abuse." She pauses and looks at me pensively. "We don't think this way because it's true, Faith. We think this way because we're a product of our past and present."

I nod. "You're right. But you say 'we.' You talk about yourself as if you're still struggling, but I don't see that when I look at you. You're so perfect and healthy and far from that girl in the picture."

"I was doing great until I broke my ankle," Silva says. "But lately, I've been struggling. That first night when I got home from the hospital, I couldn't sleep. I was terribly worried I'd gain weight if I wasn't able to move because exercise has been what's kept me balanced and sane. The mental benefits of sports are just as important to me. It keeps my anxiety at bay, and it stops me from thinking about calories in an obsessive way. As long as I work out, I can live my life like anyone else and enjoy food. So no, I'm not as stable as you think, and right now, it's not easy, but I'm as good as I can be, and I'm genuinely happy."

Her answer fills me with hope. If she's come this far, then maybe I can too. "How did you get better?"

"I had to reach my lowest point before I finally got a wake-up call." Silva sips her water and hesitates. "That relationship I told you about... Angie and I were together for three years, and we were living together. She was one of the athletes I treated. That's how we met. I was still curvy back then, and she thought I was beautiful, but constantly comparing myself to her, my weight became an obsession.

"As I kept losing more and more weight, I became distant, withdrawn, and detached from her. I didn't want to go for dinner, avoided social situations, and used every excuse to get out of her big Italian family lunches. There was no fun in being with me anymore, and she became incredibly frustrated with her inability to make me see what I was doing to myself. After I had to quit my job because I'd lost the physical strength to function, my mental state became worse, and eventually, she couldn't take it anymore and left. That's when it hit me that I had ruined everything good in my life." She sighs. "Trinny and my parents, who were equally worried about me, checked me into a small, specialist clinic for eating disorders in Fremont, and I was there for three months. I genuinely believe they saved my life by doing that."

"Oh my God..." I feel like getting up and giving her a

hug, but Silva pats my hand, letting me know she's okay. "How was it there?"

"It was incredibly hard at first, but I was determined to get better for my family, who spent a small fortune on the program, and for Angie, as I hoped she might take me back if I managed to get better and back to my previously happy and healthy self. I had both CBT and DBT and talked a lot to the other patients. I was taught about intuitive eating as well as meditation and mindfulness. When I got back into real life, I was able to listen to my body and respect it, so I started working out and eating healthily. That's when I slowly healed my relationship with food and learned to enjoy it rather than avoid it."

"So they *do* work, these places."

"For some, not for everyone," she says. "One young woman—she was eighteen—died after she got out and started starving herself again. I only found out because I tried to contact her to see how she was doing after I got out myself." She gives me a sad smile. "Hearing what had happened to her only made me want to fight harder, so in a way, she saved me too."

"That's so sad." I swallow hard and try to imagine myself in her position, struggling to even swallow a single bite. I'm not too thin; I never will be, and starving myself isn't my thing. My problem is that I've never been able to enjoy food unless I knew I could get it out of my system before it clung to my ass. As I consider this, I realize that I *have* been enjoying food since Silva moved in with me, and I've even enjoyed cooking together. And now I'm sitting here in a restaurant, and I feel calm eating in someone's company. I'm not drinking alcohol and I'm not fidgety or thinking about the next chance to visit the restroom to purge. "Thank you for sharing this with me. I think you living with me has been very good for me."

"It's been good for me too," she says. "It's distracted me from negative thoughts." She smiles. "In fact, I'm really enjoying the roommate situation."

"Me too." I blush, remembering last night. We woke up together after sleeping through her alarm, and Silva had to rush to get ready for her first client. I'm not sure what this means to her, whether it's a one-off thing or something she wants to continue, but it feels deep. We haven't kissed or flirted since last night. Needing to keep busy, I went out to buy lingerie with Roy this afternoon, and I'm wearing my new black set, hoping she'll peel it off me tonight. Feeling brave, I decide to take a risk and lighten the mood with a cheeky comment. "I've been told sex is the best form of exercise."

"That's true." Silva's smile widens, and she gives me a flirty look in return. "In fact, it's my favorite kind of exercise." She chuckles. "I wish I didn't have this damn cast. I promise you, I'm much better in bed if I can move better."

"Oh, are you bragging now?" I tease. "Trust me, I was far from disappointed. Last night was amazing."

"Yeah, it was." She tilts her head, her grin still plastered all over her gorgeous face. "I wouldn't mind continuing what we started."

"I was thinking the same." I lean farther in and continue in a whisper, "By the way, you promised me that photoshoot tonight."

44

SILVA

I enter the bedroom naked. Faith has lit candles on the bedside tables, and she's cleared everything else around the bed. One single spotlight is dimmed to a subtle setting, so the candles still have the desired effect. I expected her to work with a stand and some super-fancy camera, but the Olympus camera around her neck looks dated.

"Is that yours?" I ask, as I can't imagine her shooting covers with such an old device.

"It's not the main one I tend to work with, but it is my favorite," she says. "I told you we were going to do this the old-fashioned way. Pure and simple, with an analog camera." Her eyes linger hungrily on my breasts before they travel lower. "No more filters."

No more filters. I wonder if there's a double meaning to that statement—if she's referring to herself as much as her work.

"It's been years since I've used it," she continues. "I've been too busy shooting size-zero models for evil editors in fake locations and getting worked up over how they've photoshopped my work." She smiles. "I'm excited to go back to basics again, especially with you as a subject."

I'm not normally one to have my picture taken; I've always considered it a vain thing to do, and I only use Instagram because it helps me find clients. But Faith has taken on a different role tonight, and that fascinates me and makes me want to know more. She's assertive, confident, and excited, like she's on the brink of something big. The artist in her has come out to play, and I'm seeing a whole new side to her. "I've never done this before," I say, realizing the roles are reversed now. Naked and vulnerable, I'm a little shy with the spotlight on me.

"Don't worry, you don't have to do anything. It will flow, I promise." She points to the bed. "Will you lie down, please?" She shakes her head when I get under the covers. "Would you mind lying on top? You can cover your private parts with the sheets if you're uncomfortable."

I shift position and drape a little of the white sheets over me, enough to hide what I don't want in the picture. It's silly really; it's just a strip of hair, but I'm not ready for that yet. Not on camera. "Wait. This isn't fair." Raising onto my elbows, I shake my head. "You promised me you'd be naked too."

Faith laughs as she looks at me through the lens, focusing and refocusing. "You're right. I did promise, didn't I?" She places her camera on the bed and starts stripping down before me, her black kimono top first, revealing her black lace bra. Then she slides down her black palazzo pants and steps out of them. Noting my expression at seeing her black lingerie set with hold-ups, she smirks and struts to the foot of the bed in her stiletto heels. "I think I'll keep these on. Are you okay with that?"

"I think I can compromise on you in lace and heels," I

say, squeezing my thighs together. She doesn't just look incredibly sexy; I think she *feels* sexy tonight. She's not trying to cover herself with her hands, and she makes no effort to hold in her belly. I've noticed she does that when we're working out, especially in front of the mirror. "But please be quick. I'm not sure how long I can look at you like that without pulling you onto the bed."

"All in due time," she teases, picking up her camera with a cute wiggle of her hips. "Now lie back and look at me."

I do as she says, but I don't feel at ease. "Like this?"

"Whatever way you would lie if you were waiting for me." She licks her lips as she focuses on me, her elegant hands turning the lens. "Yes, that's perfect," she says when I shift and turn on my side, resting my arm above my head on the pillow.

"This is between you and me, right? I don't want to end up naked on your website."

"Of course." Faith shoots away while she moves around the bed, and my eyes follow her. My mind is spinning with all the things I want to do to her; she's so sexy when she's in artist mode that I can't keep still.

"You're so fucking hot," I say, and when I find myself smiling, she zooms in on my face and takes a couple of close-ups.

"You have no idea how much you're turning me on," Faith shoots back at me. She climbs onto the bed and straddles me so she can shoot me from above. When I reach out to touch her breasts, she playfully slaps them away. "Nuh-uh. No touching, be professional. Hands above your head."

"Oh, and you think you're acting professional by straddling me in suspenders and heels? You're killing me, woman."

"I'm not killing you. I'm eternalizing you." She shrugs.

"But I suppose metaphorically speaking, those two are close enough. Wet your lips for me, will you?"

"Why don't you do it for me?" I say with a grin and squirm when she lowers her camera and leans in to run her tongue over my lips.

"There. A nice bit of shine to capture the light for my final shots." She continues to shoot as if this is totally normal, but I can see a small smile tugging at the corners of her mouth. "Perfect." With that, she takes one last picture and places her camera on the floor next to the bed.

"All done?"

"The shoot, yes." Faith wedges a leg between my thighs and lowers herself on top of me. "But as far as you're concerned, I'm only getting started."

45

FAITH

As I hang the last picture on the clothesline I've spun across the bathroom, I cover them with a piece of cloth for Silva's reveal. I've missed the familiar red glow of the safelight and the calm silence while I wait for my photographs to dry.

"You can come in now," I yell, hoping she can hear me. I've been in here for most of the day and I've totally lost track of time.

"Wow. This is quite the room transformation," she says after closing the door behind her. She curiously glances over the equipment I've set up: a plywood folding table with three tanks for the developer, the stop bath and the fixer stands next to the filled bathtub, in which I've washed my photographs. My enlarger is on the toilet, and I've placed a large chopping board on top of the laundry basket to hold the measuring cylinders, the tongs, the mixing containers, the stirrers, the thermometer, and my timer, as I couldn't use my phone in here in case it lit up.

"It's very DIY, but it works fine. Apart from the guest

bath, this is the only room in the apartment without a window, and it's got a good ventilation system."

"Very clever. What's that?" Silva points to the projector.

"That's the enlarger. It shines light through the negative and transfers the image onto paper. After that, I use the baths to develop the photographs."

"Why the red light?" she asks. "I've always wondered about that, but I never bothered to look it up."

It dawns on me that this process is no longer widely known. With everyone taking pictures on their phone and saving them digitally nowadays, the art of analog photography is slowly drowning in a sea of technology. Endless possibilities in terms of filters and enhancement allow people to create an ideal and slicker self, so no one is interested in a slow process, the outcome of which might disappoint.

"Most darkroom papers are orthochromatic," I say, pointing to the pack of paper on the shelf above the sink. "It means they're blind to red light, so they won't get exposed when it's on. There's nothing mysterious about it. It's purely so I can see what I'm doing. I could turn the lights back on now, but I like it."

"Hmm... me too." Silva's eyes meet mine in the dim light, and she smiles as she inches closer. "It's sexy."

"Uh-huh." I close the distance between us, cup her face, and kiss her. It's been at least eight hours since we last kissed, and it feels like a lifetime. She pulls me closer, and I shiver when she runs her hands underneath my T-shirt. Her closeness feels both soothing and arousing, a glowing cocoon that warms me from the inside out. It's peculiar that I don't even think about the fact that I'm kissing a woman. It's Silva, and she's delicious. I'm close to bursting, but before we get too carried away, I pull out of the kiss and step back. "Not in here. We might knock over the chemicals."

Silva nods and shoots me a grin, her chest rising and falling fast as she licks her lips. "I can wait. Are you going to show me the pictures?"

"Yes. They're beautiful—and I haven't even seen them in the light yet." My pulse still racing from our heated make-out session, I remove the cover from the clothesline and turn on the light. It takes my eyes a while to adjust after hours in the dark, but once the bright-green blobs stop dancing before me, my face pulls into a huge smile.

"Oh my God..." Silva stares up at the eight 8.5x11 photographs and studies them one by one. "It's so strange to see myself like that."

"That's what everyone says after their first shoot." The first is a shot from the foot of the bed. Silva is grinning cheekily after telling me I should take my clothes off. She's resting on her elbows, and she's got one leg pulled up while her casted leg is stretched in front of her, bringing great depth into the image. She had no idea I took this shot, and it shows. Perhaps that's why I love it so much. In the second and third photographs, she's lying on her side and her eyes are fixed lower than the camera. It's clear to the viewer that she's looking at the photographer, and that her mind is on anything but the shoot. It's wonderfully sensual and cool, like having her picture taken is a game to her, which it was, I suppose. The fourth and fifth are taken from the side, capturing the curves of her breasts and her hips with the sensual play of light from the candles. She clearly has sex on her mind here too; her eyes are sparkling with curious flirtation and one hand rests above her head, playing with her hair.

"They're beautiful," she says, frowning as if she's surprised that they've come out so well.

"Of course they're beautiful. It's you." I point to the final two. "Those are my favorites, especially the last one." They're bird's-eye shots from when I was straddling her. Her hard nipples, wet lips slightly parted, and hazy eyes that look into the camera with burning desire would cause a stir in any viewer.

"I look like I want to eat you alive," Silva says with a chuckle. "Which I did. Don't get me wrong, but you've captured how I felt so perfectly it's almost scary. It's like you eternalized my thoughts."

"Does it feel intrusive?" I ask.

"A little."

"That's good. A portrait should feel intrusive in my opinion."

She nods. "You're very good. Can I have these?"

"Yes. I've already printed another set. I'd like to use some of them for my portfolio, but I get it if you're not comfortable with that."

"No, it's fine," Silva says. "I know I said I didn't want to end up on your website, but I don't mind people seeing these at all." She turns to me and looks at me pensively as if she's seeing a whole new side to me. "I love how simple and unstaged they are."

"Thank you." I couldn't be happier that she likes them as much as I do. "There's something unique about using film versus digital. It's the surprise element, the anticipation while I watch the image manifest that excites me."

"Do you prefer to do it this way?" she asks.

"Yeah. I love the connection with the tangible process and the feeling I get from that. This probably sounds weird, but I also find it romantic, in a way. Instead of discussing what you're going to manipulate in an image, you simply accept the work for what it is. You accept the beauty of reality and people either like it or not." I spread my arms as I look up at the photographs again. "It is what it is."

46

SILVA

"Fuck me, this is weird." Trinny narrows her eyes as she stares at the pictures. "You're my sister and these are so..." She pauses. "So sensual and so personal."

"Yeah. I wasn't sure if I should show them to you, but they're beautiful so I'm hoping you can see past the fact that we're family and—"

"And not think of what happened after the shoot?" Trinny interrupts me. "Trust me, I'm trying my hardest not to picture you like that. But you're right. They're amazing. Faith is so talented." She returns to the last picture and then looks at me. "Don't tell me you haven't had sex because these photographs say more than words ever could."

"We have," I admit, taking the pictures and sliding them back into the envelope, as it's busy in the coffee shop today.

"See? I knew it!" Trinny slams a hand on the table. "I knew it would happen and I'm no oracle. It was blatantly clear from the first time I saw you together." She looks around when she realizes heads are turning and lowers her voice. "And? How was it? And what's the deal now?"

"It's great," I say, attempting to suppress the big grin that's plastered all over my face. "I don't know what we are but it's great."

"What?" She gasps. "So it wasn't a one-off thing?"

"No, it's pretty much constant," I say with a chuckle. "We're unable to keep our hands off each other. That's why I thought it might be good to meet you here instead, to give her some space. She's prepping for another shoot this afternoon, with her friend Roy."

"Oh. So is this like some newfound passion or something? I thought she only did fashion."

"She's had a few cancellations this month, and she wants to take her mind off that by focusing on something she loves to do. I don't know if you heard, but she walked out on a shoot the other day."

"I didn't. What happened?"

I show Trinny the video on my phone and she watches it four times before I get it back. "It's crazy, right?"

"It's criminal." Trinny shakes her head. "I had no idea it was so bad. Poor girl. It was brave of Faith to do that, and it's so wrong that she's losing work over doing the right thing."

"I know. But she's positive and she doesn't regret it." I smile. "We're both so happy at the moment that anything could go wrong and we'd still be smiling."

"Aww..." Trinny sits back and tilts her head as she regards me. "I've never seen you like this before."

"I've never felt like this," I say. "I loved Angie, but it wasn't as intense as with Faith. I'm completely consumed by her, and the best thing is, I think it's entirely mutual. I trust her too. I told her about my anorexia."

"You told her..." Trinny pauses. "No one knows apart from me and Mom and Dad, right? That's a big thing."

"Yeah. It felt right, and since I'm living with her, I want

her to understand why I can be a bit obsessive sometimes. I was saying something about calories when I was sleepwalking, so I thought it might be best to get it out in the open. It's good that she knows. She keeps me from falling into bad behaviors." I put a hand on Trinny's when I notice the hint of emotion in her eyes. "What's wrong?"

"Nothing. I'm just so happy that you've found someone who's genuinely good for you. I wanted you to meet someone special more than I wanted it for myself, I never thought it would be Faith Astor of all people." She chuckles. "I imagined a fellow trainer, or someone a bit more low-profile, at least."

"Faith isn't exactly in the public eye. She's behind the camera, not in front of it."

"Most people know who she is, though," Trinny says. "I told my colleagues you were living with her and that I'd met her, and they were totally intrigued." She shrugs. "I said she was lovely and very down-to-earth but they didn't believe me."

"People tend to believe what they see online," I say. "It's rarely a reflection of the truth."

"Of course. But be careful, okay?"

"About what?"

"You know what I mean, Sil. If you have such strong feelings for her and this doesn't work out, you might relapse." She winces. "Sorry, I don't mean to be negative. I adore her and I want this for you, but I'm not going to lie. I am a little worried too. Even if it's all great and it works out, will you be able to deal with the attention you'll get when you're with her? You hate being the center of attention."

"Don't underestimate me. I can handle it."

Trinny nods, but she doesn't look convinced. "Just be careful, okay? I'm looking out for you. I've never seen you appreciate pictures of yourself before or light up the way you do when you talk about her. But you're my sister and I need to look out for you."

I'm a little irritated by her cautiousness, but at the same time, I also know what she's been through with me, and she wants to put the years of worrying behind her. Change is tricky for anyone with my condition. What she doesn't know, though, is that Faith and I can share our struggles, and that makes us stronger. I can't tell her that; it wouldn't be right. If Faith wants to tell her, that's up to her, but unless she does, Trinny will never know.

47

FAITH

Another cancellation. I'm not surprised, but reading the email still unsettles me. *They could have at least called.* The New York fashion scene has officially written me off, or canceled me, as they call it, and I'm losing runway jobs, spread shoots, and even covers. The latter are often booked four months in advance, and as these are very hard for the editors to rebook, it's a true testament to how desperate they are to get rid of me.

I was hoping I might come back from this. Not that I'd apologize to Valerie; I never want to work with her again. But I thought there might be at least a few people who would take a firm stance on the matter and show some support. Truth be told, there's a lot of support out there. The video has already reached over a million views, and I've had countless wonderful messages from ex-models, fashion students, and even some celebrities. But not one significant person from the fashion industry has spoken up about this on social media. Everyone who matters is pretending it never happened, as they have no idea how to deal with the situation. If they side with me, they'll be canceled by Valerie.

If they side with her, their followers may turn on them, so everyone's keeping quiet. I can't blame them; in all these years I've never taken action, so I'm no better myself.

Another email comes in as I close this one, and it's from Anthony's PA telling me they've decided to go with another photographer for his upcoming campaign. *He doesn't even have the courage to contact me himself.* It's too much for me in one day, and as if on cue, thoughts of doom start sneaking into my brain and clouding my logic. *I'm done. Valerie was right; I'll never work again. No one wants me. I'm useless. I'm a failure.* Knowing what these thoughts lead to, I already notice I'm getting restless. I promised Silva I would let her know when I got to this point, but she's having coffee with her sister, and I don't want to disturb her. She might be happy to finally get a moment away from me; I certainly want to get away from me right now. I can feel myself falling into a downward spiral. I still have two hours to kill before Roy comes, and I know there's only one thing that would make me feel better, even if it's just for twenty-three minutes. *Don't do it*, the little voice in the back of my mind tells me. *It's not worth it, you're doing so well.* I already have my finger on the food delivery app, but I stop myself as another thought hits me. *What if Silva comes back early? What if she sees me like that again? I can't risk it; she might stop liking me. Who wouldn't?* In a reflex, I throw my phone across the room, and it lands on the rug with a thud.

Slumping down in a chair, I hold my chest and try to steady my breathing. The dread of not being able to deal with my emotional state in my usual way is killing me, and I need an outlet. Something. Anything. It feels like a panic attack but it's so much more than that. Like an overflowing sink, the hole inside of me fills with self-loathing and expands until my stomach hurts. *I need to get out of here.* I'm barely able to find my shoes and coordinate my coat and scarf as I'm struggling to function through the panic. My therapist told me bulimic people are addicted to their rituals in the same way some are addicted to alcohol or drugs. My therapist is right; I'm acting like a junkie, like I'm going to die if I don't eat and purge.

Rushing out of my building, I'm hoping Silva will be at her usual place, and I'm relieved to find her there. She and her sister are sitting at a window table, and before I have the chance to change my mind, they spot me and wave me in. It's busy in there, and I have no idea what I'm going to say. When I approach their table, Silva senses something is wrong, but Trinny doesn't, and she gets up to give me a cheerful hug.

"Faith, it's so nice to see you again. We were just talking about you. Are you joining us for a coffee?"

Stupidly, I hadn't anticipated this scenario, and I must look like a deer in headlights because I'm staring at her with no idea how to reply.

"Babe, are you okay?" Silva asks, getting up too. "You look shaken."

My bottom lip starts trembling and I bite it hard and hold in my breath for a few seconds before I reply. "I'm sorry to interrupt you," I say, trying my best to keep my composure. My shaking hands are buried deep in my coat pockets, and I force a smile that I suspect must look painful. "I know you're having a private moment and I didn't want to do this..."

"Do what?" Silva wraps an arm around me while she holds on to the back of the chair with the other. "Hey, it's okay, you can tell me," she whispers in my ear.

At that, tears start running again and I lower my voice.

"I'm so sorry, but I need you." It's the first time I've said that to someone. The first time I've admitted I need help.

She knows what I'm trying to tell her; I can feel it when she tightens her grip on me. "Okay, let's go," she says, then turns to Trinny. "Can I call you later?"

"Of course. Do what you need to do." Trinny glances at me for a split second, but thankfully, she doesn't ask any questions. "You go, I'll pick up the bill."

As I head outside with Silva behind me on her crutches, I already feel guilty for dragging her out of here. What is she going to think of me? That I'm needy? Unstable? Crazy? Currently, I feel like I'm all of those, but her presence is helping.

"I don't know what to do," I say, wishing I could hold her hand.

"That's why you've got me. I'm glad you came." Silva's voice is calm and soothing. "We're going to go home, get into bed, and I'm going to hold you while we talk. I promise you'll be okay, even if it doesn't feel like that right now."

48

SILVA

"Sometimes I have no choice," Faith whispers when she's lying in my arms. "Sometimes there's no other way out. I guess feeling extremely overwhelmed with self-loathing is the only way to describe it. Eating and purging provide instant relief. It replaces all other thoughts, actions, and emotions, and everything pauses." She sighs. "Afterward, there's this moment of euphoria because I've regained control, and when my anxiety takes over, it's my only coping mechanism. It's always been that way."

"I understand that, but you have two coping mechanisms now," I say. "You have me, and I'm the healthy option. I'm glad you came to me."

"I know. Me too." She presses her forehead against mine. "I'm sorry I interrupted your time with Trinny."

"Please, don't ever apologize for that. I told you, I'm here for you, and I want you to lean on me. How do you feel now?"

"A little better." Faith has calmed down, and her smile is genuine when she runs her fingers through my hair. "Talking to you helps. It puts everything into perspective, and I don't criticize myself when I'm with you. You see the best in me, and you make me see that too, so thank you. I don't think you know how much that helps me."

"You don't need to thank me, and I'm glad I can make a difference. I'm here for you for as long as you'll let me."

Faith's smile widens. "What does that mean? For as long as you'll let me?"

I don't know how to answer that because truthfully, I'm not sure where we're heading. We've developed an emotional and physical connection that feels almost seamless, and I care deeply about her, yet I have no idea how Faith sees our future. "What is this to you?" I ask, deciding to answer her question with a question. "We haven't talked much about it, and I feel like we need to. Is this experimenting? Is it more?" I pause. "Because to me, it's meaningful, and I feel a genuine connection, but I'm also aware that being with a woman might not be for you long term."

"It's meaningful to me too. More than you know." Faith scoots closer and buries her face in my neck. "You're not an experiment. You're the best thing that ever happened to me and I want to be with you." She inches back and smiles. "I want to be with you and only you. For as long as you'll let me and forever if it's up to me. I can promise you that."

Swallowing hard, I let her words sink in. "Do you mean that? Because I want that too." Nothing she said could have made me happier. I've dreamed of a future with her; I can almost see it before me; a full life with all its ups and downs, lived together.

"Yes. You're the only person who knows me with all my baggage and insecurities, and you accept me as I am. I'm not even talking about the insane attraction and the amazing sex. That's just a huge cherry on top." She sighs deeply. "I'm head over heels for you, Silva."

I pull her tightly against me and kiss her temple. "Does it not bother you that I'm a woman?"

"I don't think I'm that straight after all." She looks up at me and arches a brow. "Do you?"

"No," I say with a chuckle. "My educated guess would be that you're most definitely into women."

"Only one woman." Faith kisses me, and my head swims with desire for her. "Look, I'll probably need some time to get used to the idea that I'm gay, but it's not a big deal in the grand scheme of things. All that matters is that I found you, and you found me." She gives me a shy smile. "So... can we call this a relationship?"

"I'd love that." I smile against her lips. "Can I call you my girl?"

"Yes." Faith chuckles. "That's very, very cute."

My grin is so wide I'm afraid my lips will crack, and my heart is overflowing with warmth for her. "Good. Because I want you all to myself."

"I don't want to share you either." Faith tugs at my sweatshirt and takes it off when I sit up. She straddles me and runs her hand over my belly and ribcage and slides it into my sports bra. My nipples harden and rise to attention, and a stir of arousal courses through me. She makes me crazy, delirious with everything she does, and shivering at her touch, I fall back and sigh in delight as she kisses me passionately. She moans as she moves into me, her arousal potent in her ragged breathing. I run my hands under her silk blouse to caress her breasts in return. Our need is deep, perhaps deeper now than ever. I feel it in her kiss, in the way she moves, and I see it in the way she looks at me. She wants me to take her away.

"I want you," I whisper. I'm suddenly feeling impatient to possess her and swiftly pull her blouse over her head.

She's wearing a navy lace balcony bra that holds her full breasts. She pulls out her barrette, releasing her long, dark locks, and they cascade over her shoulders in waves, framing her beautiful face. Sometimes when I look at her, I'm paralyzed, too stunned to move, or speak, or even think. She's the most stunning woman I've ever known, and she's mine; she's seducing me.

"Have me," she says and unclips her bra to free her breasts. "I want you to do anything you want to me. Anything."

49

FAITH

The doorbell rings as we're right in the middle of our training session, and I mutter a curse as I get up. Normally I'd welcome a break from the exercise, but lately, our workouts have taken a sensual turn with a lot of body contact and a lot of wandering hands.

"Come in," I say, buzzing open the door when I see it's Roy.

"You need to see this," he says, holding up his phone as he barges in.

"Okay, but can we finish first, please? Grab yourself a drink. We still have a way to go."

"No, you'll want to see this now." Roy sits on the couch and opens a message from one of his friends. "Elsie McCarthy—that young and upcoming photographer—walked out on a shoot with Valerie." He looks up at us excitedly. "For the very same reason you did."

"What?" My heart races as I read the message over and over. *Someone's on my side. Someone who matters.*

"Crazy, right? She's like the new girl on the block. I'm surprised she took a stand." He holds up a hand. "I mean no offense to you, but she really is popular at the moment."

"I know." I hand the phone to Silva, who has scooted over on the floor to join us by the couch. "Why would she of all people risk her career like that?" I don't know Elsie personally. We've said hello a few times, but it never went any further than that, as stylists were crowded around her, waiting for a chance to speak to her. She seemed nice, though, albeit a bit reserved. I guess it's quite intimidating when you suddenly find you're the center of attention, or perhaps the reserve I sensed was the same type of cautious skepticism I feel when I'm in the middle of the madness.

"Why?" Because she's got integrity like you," Roy says. "You're not on your own anymore, and wait, there's more." He opens Elsie's Instagram account and plays a video with a short statement from her, explaining why she can no longer be a part of the "circus," as she calls it.

"The fashion industry is a circus, and the circus trains its animals to obey, to follow, and to jump at every command," she says, looking confidently into the camera. *"Models are not supposed to think for themselves. They play an essential role, yet they're never rewarded with praise because there's always room for improvement. No one is ever perfect. Today, I witnessed a young woman being put down for having a little bit of extra flesh. She was told her collarbones weren't visible enough. This is wrong, and something needs to change. Faith Astor was the first to make a statement by walking out on a job, and I'm proud to say I'm the second."* Elsie sighs. *"I'm also ashamed I didn't do it sooner, but hopefully, many more will follow. I will no longer be a part of this circus. I will not participate in an industry that encourages young women to starve themselves. Faith, if you see this, I'm with you."* Elsie shrugs and smiles into the camera. *"I guess I'll start looking for a nine-to-five job now. Wish me luck."*

"Brave, right?" Roy cuts through the silence after the video ends. "She's only twenty-nine, in the prime of her career."

"Very brave," I say, and sit next to Silva. "And very, very unexpected. I can't believe it…" I look her up on my phone and see that she's following me on Instagram, so I follow her back. "I should send her a message, right?"

"Absolutely. Get together." Silva puts an arm around me and kisses my cheek. "This is great, babe. Imagine the aftermath. Something is happening here. Something big. One person is a start, but two is a team, and people want to join teams."

"Wait! '*Babe*'?" Roy asks, making quote marks in the air. "What's going on here?" He points a finger between us and frowns. "I was actually joking about your training last time I was here, but the way you're all snuggled up together doesn't seem like a joke to me."

"Yes, about this…" Both Silva and I attempt to wipe the goofy grins off our faces as I sink back against her and pull her arm farther over my shoulder. I've been so incredibly happy since our talk. I'm not stressing about anything anymore, and I've decided to take every day as it comes. I'm still getting used to the idea of having a girlfriend, but I love knowing where she stands and that she's equally crazy about me. "It's—"

Roy gasps, cutting me off. "Why am I not the first to hear about this? I'm your bestie, for God's sake." He's all drama, but I can see from his expression that he's very happy for me.

"You *are* the first. It's very early days, and I wouldn't have admitted it if you hadn't guessed."

"Seriously? You don't need to admit to anything. It's

blatantly obvious. So, you're together? As in together-together?"

I turn to Silva, and we exchange a knowing look that's probably bordering on lusty.

"Jesus." Roy fans his face. "What's that in your eyes? I definitely never saw *that* when I was with you. You look like you're about to combust."

"But you were gay," I say in defense. "We didn't have the... the thing, you know?" I'm surprised how easy it is to talk to Roy about my current situation, as it's quite a big deal. But it doesn't feel like a big deal.

"You're right. We didn't, and I'm eternally grateful we've both found our path in life." Roy gets down on his knees and joins us on the floor, then gives Silva a long hug. "Honey, I'm delighted to welcome you into our little family of two, but I'm warning you. It's going to be crowded in the bed on Netflix nights because I'm not moving over."

"Thank you, Roy and I'll keep that in mind." Silva laughs and moves the weights and resistance bands away from the mat. "Well, I think we've done enough for today, and I have no more online classes," she says, turning to me. "Want to move to the couch?"

"Good idea. I need to let the news sink in." I'm thoroughly enjoying Roy's reaction. I don't think he expected me to be so relaxed about us, but it feels entirely natural.

"We should celebrate," he says. "Not just the Elsie thing, but also your..." He falls silent as he stares at us again. "Your coming out, I guess."

"Is that what this is?" I ask with a chuckle. I suppose he's right. I did just come out to him.

"Yeah. This is big!" Roy spreads his arms. "Do you have champagne in the house?"

50

SILVA

It's been a month since the accident, and I noticed a clear change in my body as I got dressed yesterday. My reflection wasn't as trim as it used to be, especially my legs since I haven't been able to run or do squats. My shorts are tighter to the point that they're uncomfortable, and I feel like I'm going to burst out of them. Today it seems even worse, or perhaps that's in my head. Rolling to my room on the office chair, I search for a bigger pair, but they're all exactly the same size, and after half an hour of struggling to get in and out of different shorts, I give up and climb back into bed. *It's happened. I've put on weight.* For a moment, I contemplate getting on the scale, but I know that's a bad idea. Being confronted with the number will most likely make me panic, and I can already feel the tightness growing in my chest at the thought. For many years, I've managed to maintain my healthy weight, and that's kept me sane. My weight is still healthy; I know that, but it's not about the number per se. It's about maintaining and control. My injury has caused me to lose control over my body, and it frightens me. *What if my leg doesn't heal prop-*

erly? What if I put on more weight? What if it never comes off again?

"Silva, are you okay?" Faith asks, knocking on the door. "I've made coffee. Do you want a cup?"

Aware I might sound the way I feel, I don't reply.

"Are you there?" She opens the door and lowers her voice. "I'm sorry, were you sleeping?" When she sees my distress, she comes over and gets on the bed with me. "Hey, what's going on?"

"It's..." I take a couple of deep breaths, as it's hard to speak through my anxiety. "Everything is too tight. My clothes don't fit me anymore," I finally say, covering my face with my hands. "I've put on weight."

Faith lies next to me and strokes my hair. "Okay. That must be a hard situation for you to deal with."

I'm glad she doesn't come back with the standard reply. "Don't sweat it, you look great," "I'd kill for a body like yours," or "You look much better with a bit of extra meat on you." She knows that would be pointless, and she understands that, right now, I feel like I've lost a battle.

"You know, sometimes things are out of our control when it comes to our bodies," she continues. "When we're sick, stressed, hormonal, injured, or pregnant. But this isn't forever. Your leg will heal, and you only have two weeks left with your cast on. It will be easier after that. You won't feel so helpless."

I nod and give her a small smile. "Technically, I know that. But it's hard. It's suffocating."

"Why didn't you talk to me sooner?" Faith asks. "You were so quiet yesterday, I could sense something was bothering you."

"You're going through enough as it is." I shrug. "I can deal with this on my own."

"No," Faith says resolutely. "Absolutely not. This is not how it works. You're here for me and I'm here for you. If you're going to help me, you have to let me help you in return, and that is non-negotiable. Our relationship is not one-way traffic. We're together."

I nod and take her hand. "I know. I'm sorry. I should have talked to you."

"Two more weeks," she says. "It might feel like a lifetime, but it's not that long, so whatever you do, please don't stop eating. You've worked too hard to relapse, and you need to remember that just because you've put on some weight, doesn't mean you've lost control. Going back to the way you were would be losing control."

"You're right. I'll keep that in mind."

"I've gained some weight too," she says. "It's probably muscle mass, but it still stung when I saw the number. But then I also remembered that I like the way I look now, at least, more than before. I've been very happy lately, and that might have something to do with it. Happiness is good, right?"

"Yes," I say. "I've been happy too. But my shorts decided to ruin my mojo." I chuckle and realize that if I can laugh about it, I might be okay. I've been through this so many times I always expect myself to react in the same way, but maybe I've changed. Maybe feeling appreciated, accepted, and even adored by Faith has made me stronger.

"I'll get you new shorts and a pair of sweatpants right now." Faith is about to get up, but I pull her back down.

"Don't worry. I'll order some clothes online, express shipping."

"But they won't arrive until tomorrow at the earliest, and I want you to be comfortable and able to go outside now," she argues. "Because it's my turn to distract you. After I get you something to wear for the day," Faith adds. She smiles at me and kisses my forehead, and that alone lifts my mood a little.

"And how are you going to distract me?"

"By taking you somewhere amazing." Faith pauses. "Let me think. Where are we going?" Her eyes light up when an idea hits her. "Ever been to the top of the Empire State Building?"

"No, actually." I pause and laugh at the irony of the situation. "That's terrible since I'm a New Yorker, isn't it?"

"Not at all. I haven't been there either, so let's be tourists in our own city for the day."

"Okay. That sounds fun. I'm not sure if I'll be able to get around that much," I say, imagining the pain of being out and about on crutches for a whole afternoon.

"That's what wheelchairs are for." Faith gets up again, and this time, I do let go of her. "There should be one I can borrow in the building somewhere. I'll check with the concierge after I come back with your clothes." She leans over me and kisses me sweetly. "Stay right here and chill. I won't be long."

51

FAITH

Wheeling Silva toward the Empire State Building, I already spot the line. Manhattan is never quiet, even on a winter weekday, and we seem to be the only locals here among tourists from Europe, Japan, and other states.

"I'm feeling quite excited about this," she says, turning to look at me over her shoulder.

"Me too. I've always lived so close, yet it's never occurred to me to go up there. It's still a bit early, though. The best time for the observatory deck is around six, so we're having a light lunch and cocktails first, and then we're going to watch the sunset together."

Silva's eyes widen. "Really? How on earth did you manage to get a table here at such short notice?"

"I pulled some strings," I say with a wink. In truth, it really wasn't that easy, as I had to make numerous phone calls to valuable contacts while shopping for her sweat-pants, and I even lowered myself to namedropping for the occasion. "Are you comfortable?"

Silva laughs as she gestures to the blanket draped over

her lap. "I'm super comfortable. The question is, are you? This must be quite the workout."

"No, it's fine, actually. The chair is easy to handle." I thank the host, who opens the door of the grill restaurant at street level for us.

"What are you drinking?" she asks, studying the cocktail menu when we're seated.

"How about a Fifth Avenue Old Fashioned? That seems fitting, right?"

"I'm with you," she says with a smile. "Let's celebrate New York."

"Are you okay having lunch?" I ask. I'm aware food is probably not on the top of her list after her minor breakdown this morning, but as far as I can tell she's doing much better.

"Yes, I'm fine. I don't want my life to be overshadowed by my weight. I realized that after I put on my new sweatpants. The world didn't end, I'm still here, and I still look okay."

"You look more than okay. You look smoking hot as always."

Silva shoots me a flirty grin. "You should see me in jeans," she jokes, licking her lips. "Seriously, though, this won't be easy, but I'll try to let go of the reins a little. Not all the way, just a little. I want to try to be less hard on myself."

"You can do it." I reach for her hand over the table and squeeze it. "I'll help you."

"You're already helping me." Her eyes meet mine in a sincere exchange. "Thank you."

After cocktails, white wine, delicious market salads, and grilled shrimp, we admire the beautiful art deco lobby, then head for the eighty-sixth floor, where the outdoor observatory deck is situated. As the elevator doors open, dusk's warm light welcomes us. The golden hue is a stark contrast to the icy winds, but the cold and clear sky also make for a spectacular backdrop, and as we walk around, we can see all the way to New Jersey and Staten Island. Both being New Yorkers, the view feels like a time loop. Silva points out the basketball court in Brooklyn where she used to spend most of her time as a teenager, and I show her the building where I lived with my mother when it was just the two of us and where we moved after she married Andrew. It feels strange, like my life has been reduced to this view one thousand fifty feet above Manhattan, all my memories tangled in the network of streets below.

"Have you ever thought of moving away?" I ask.

"Of course." Silva lets me help her out of the chair and she leans on the ledge so she can see farther. I wrap an arm around her, and she meets my eyes with a smile. "New York can be frustrating. Busy, rude, pompous... I've gone through phases where I've dreamed about tropical destinations or a life working as a PT on a Caribbean cruise ship." She sighs. "But every time I seriously considered it, I got melancholic about leaving and started appreciating New York again. The itch to leave usually manifests in January, but this year it hasn't happened, and I'm pretty sure that's because of you. I wouldn't want to be anywhere but right here with you, Faith."

"Me either," I say, pulling her closer. "I lived in Paris for a couple of months. It seemed like such a romantic idea at the time, so I thought I'd try my luck at photography there."

"And?"

"Career-wise, it was fun, and I'm glad I did it, but I missed home. I missed all this." I marvel at the bird's-eye view of the North-Eastern United States as the sun melts down the horizon and the skyline turns amber. Burnt oranges and reds paint a spectacular picture on the canvas before us, and we watch in silence as darkness falls. The last purple and orange slivers slowly fade away, but when the sky turns dark, the show is far from over, as the city comes to life. Lights spring on everywhere, and as the night closes around us, the Chrysler Building, Lower Manhattan, the Statue of Liberty, and the Flatiron Building are bathed in neon.

"We're lucky to live here, don't you think?" she whispers.

"Yeah." I take the blanket from her wheelchair and wrap it around our shoulders. "I love New York."

52

SILVA

Faith is irresistible. She woke up twice, and each time her eyes fluttered open, we looked at each other for long moments, appreciating what we had before falling into a kiss. Sleeping next to her is bliss and making love in our half-lucid state even more so. She saved me today. She recognized my distress and made it disappear with insight and understanding. I don't know what would have happened if I'd stayed in my apartment all this time; if I'd only had myself and my thoughts to get me through the days without exercise or distraction. She's my angel, and I will do anything in my power to make her happy for the rest of her life.

I'm wide awake, but it's not anxiety or insecurity keeping me up. The reason my mind is churning is that I'm trying to get to grips with my feelings for her. They've changed, deepened, evolved, and I'm starting to realize that what we have is very special. I wanted to be there for her, to help her and support her, but the truth is I need her just as much, and that makes me vulnerable. Watching her sleep makes my heart swell, and Faith's soft heat, rolling curves, and full lips call to me when she stirs awake, so I roll on top of her and sink into her body.

"Mmm..." She wraps her arms around me and smiles, then pulls my face down to kiss me. She lifts her hips underneath me and spreads her legs as she kisses me harder. I instinctively know what she wants and what she craves. Shifting one leg between her thighs, I grind into her until I can feel her wetness against my own, and an explosion of raw and intense reactions unravel in my center, making me throb and swell. She's so aroused; she always is. Being so close to her is overwhelmingly intimate, and we melt together on every level. When she raises her hips, we connect in a way that makes us both moan in delight. I look at her in the dark, and she meets my eyes while I circle against her, mindfully, slowly. It feels amazing; it's so easy to lose myself in her, to lose ourselves in each other.

Stroking her cheek, I kiss her again and drink her in like only she can quench my thirst. I move into her harder but keep my slow pace. It's togetherness of the deepest kind, a dreamy and exhilarating dance of limbs that takes us higher with every thrust. Locking my eyes with Faith's, I pry her legs farther apart with my knees and she cries out, heaving air from her lungs. She's close and so am I, my clit throbbing and my body tense with pent-up sexual energy. Craving as much contact as I possibly can, I take her hands, lace our fingers together, and place them above her head on the pillow. Hungry to possess her wholly, I'd do the same with our feet if I physically could.

"Come with me, baby," she whispers just before she falls, and I push myself over the edge. Faith's expression is glorious, and I keep my gaze locked with hers as we climax together. Her lips pulled into a smile and her eyes hazy, her hands clasp mine tightly until every shudder has left her body. Clammy, tired, and blissfully satisfied, I roll off her and lie on my side to face the wonderful woman who makes my heart sing every day.

"That was amazing," she whispers. "I love being so close to you."

"Me too." I stroke her hair, kiss her softly, and swept away by the moment, I find myself saying something I wasn't planning on voicing yet. "I'd like to tell my parents about you. Maybe you could join me in a video chat?"

Faith's smile widens, and she covers my hand with her own. "Really?"

"Yeah. Would you be okay with that?"

"I'd love to meet them." She studies me curiously. "How do you think they will feel about me?"

"They'll love you. I have no doubt about that," I say, relieved that she's not freaked out. "My mother's been desperate for me to meet someone for years. It will make her so happy." I hesitate a moment before I continue. "And if you want to, and have time this summer, we could go to Hawaii to visit them? I was planning on taking a trip with Trinny. She'd love it if you joined us. It's only a small place, nothing fancy, but—"

"Don't be silly, I don't care about that," Faith says, her face lighting up at the idea. "It sounds wonderful. I had a shoot in Hawaii once. I've always wanted to go back. And I've been so curious about your parents. They must be wonderful since they raised such amazing daughters."

"They're lovely and blissfully old-fashioned," I say with a chuckle. "Honestly, Mom will be over the moon. It will really make her day."

"Then why don't we do it right now?" Faith suggests. "They're six hours behind us—surely they'll still be up?"

"Now?"

“I don’t know about you, but I’m wide awake after this conversation.” Faith shrugs. “Do they know you’re living here?”

“I told them I’d moved in with a friend, which was the truth at the time. But I’ve been avoiding their calls lately, as I knew it would lead to a lot of questions if I spoke to them here and they saw your apartment.”

“Even more reason to do it now.” Faith kisses me and smiles against my mouth. “Unless it’s too soon?”

“No,” I say, charmed by her enthusiasm. “But it might be best if we put some clothes on first.”

53

FAITH

Elsie McCarthy suggested we meet after I reached out to her. The small, low-profile bar hidden away in a mews in Greenwich Village is not somewhere I'd normally go, but it's charming and cozy. She waves at me from a table in the back, and I smile as I greet her. "Hey. Thanks for inviting me."

"Thanks for coming." Elsie holds up her cocktail. "I can recommend the pisco sours in here. They're excellent."

"I guess I'll have that, then," I say and point to her glass when the bartender looks at me from across the bar. I immediately feel at ease with her, now that we're not meeting on fashion territory, and as I take her in, I note she looks entirely different from the few times we've met, dressed down in jeans and a hoodie. Elsie has a fuller figure and tends to rock up in floaty printed kaftans and matching hairbands, but today, she's wearing her blonde hair in a ponytail and her face is free of makeup. I messaged her after she released the video, and we've been in contact since.

"Sorry you had to take a cab here. It's my local and one

of the few places I know I won't bump into anyone from the industry."

"And that's so worth it," I say. "How have you been since your walkout?"

"As expected." Elsie shrugs. "Fashion Week is coming up, and I'm losing jobs left, right, and center but that's okay. My boyfriend owns a gallery and if I'm out of options, I can always work for him." When my cocktail arrives, she holds up her glass in a toast. "Here's to being canceled."

I laugh and take a sip of my drink. "Well said. You know, I was so grateful when I heard what you'd done. I felt like I wasn't alone in this and that there *are* real people out there."

"Honestly, I never saw you as a real person until you walked out on that shoot. You're always so glamorous when I see you. I was too shy to introduce myself."

"I could say the same for you." I smile. "But I think we both know that's just a front."

"Yeah. Anyway, life is more comfortable in jeans." The door opens, and Elsie waves at a man who walks in. "I hope you don't mind, but I've invited a third person to our little meeting."

"Regga Ibrahimovic?" I raise a brow and get up when he comes over because he's not a man to greet sitting down. "I didn't expect to see you here." Regga is in his early sixties, and he's been one of the top fashion photographers for decades. I admired his work when I was younger, and I still do. I've never met him in person; he's very private, and I suppose that air of mystery has always worked for him. He looks older than in the few pictures I've seen of him, but not in a bad way. He looks like a man who's led life to the fullest, a happy and interesting life. Deep crow's feet frame his eyes, and he's got a permanent frown between his brows, but he's very attractive. His silver hair is pulled back into a long ponytail and tied with a black ribbon.

"Well, here I am." He taps his fedora and shoots me a wink before he gives Elsie a hug.

"Regga was my mentor. I did an internship with him," Elsie explains, sensing my confusion. She's in her early twenties, and admittedly, it did seem like an unlikely friendship to me.

"And now she's getting more work than me," he jokes and gestures to the bartender. "I was so proud of her for what she did. The body-shaming has always bothered me, but like everyone in my generation, I accepted the situation for what it was. This kiddo made me realize I can be a part of something positive for once, so here I am. I'm on your side, girls, and I pledge to walk out as soon as I see or hear anything disrespectful."

"I'm sorry, I need to pinch myself," is all I can manage to say because, in all honesty, I'm a little starstruck. I've met many celebrities throughout my career, but it's rare I meet someone I truly admire. If he didn't make such an effort to stay out of the spotlight, we would have probably said hello at some point, but he's been as much a mystery to me as to everyone I know. "You're my hero and you're here."

He laughs and pats my arm. "And you're my hero after what you did. No one has ever stuck it to Valerie. I must have watched that video at least a hundred times."

"Me too," Elsie says. "Nothing has amused me more in my young life than seeing that nervous twitch of her mouth. I wish someone had filmed my walkout because she did it again."

"And she deserved every bit of criticism," Regga says.

"Yeah." I turn to him. "Are you really going to do this?"

"Oh, yes. And there's something I want to discuss with

you. My good friend at the *New York Times* has promised to write a big piece about body-shaming in the fashion industry, and she would love to include the both of you if you're okay with that." He takes off his hat and scratches his long, gray hair. "And before you say anything, no, I am not doing this for attention. I hate being in the spotlight. I always have. But if we want this to blow up, we need the media."

"Boom!" Elsie stares at Regga as if the sun is shining out of his ass, and I can't blame her. This man is seriously charismatic. He seems good-natured too, and I want to be his friend.

"Thank you, so much. You have no idea how much this means to me." I glance from Elsie to Regga and back. "I really thought I was alone, and now Elsie and you... I've always admired your work, by the way. You never lost your edge, even after decades in the business."

"I do try to keep up with the youngsters," Regga says humorously, then thanks the bartender when he brings over his drink—another pisco sour. "And it's an honor for me to be here with you too. Both of you." He holds up his glass in a toast. "So, ladies. What do you say to a collective?"

"A collective?" I ask, my interest piqued.

"Yes," Elsie chips in. "We were talking about this yesterday. A collective of photographers, artists, and models who only produce body-positive work and cut out all poison. Editors or brands who want to work with us have to align with what we stand for. For example, I don't want to work with designers anymore who only sell the smallest size range. I want to work with brands that promote diversity and a realistic representation of the women in this world. That doesn't mean I'm not interested in shooting supermodels as we know them, but the general concept should be diverse." She spreads her arms and looks down at her ample bosom. "Take me, for example. As a voluptuous, plus-size African American woman, I'd love to see someone on a billboard that I can identify with."

"I think it's a great idea," I say. "But what makes you think brands want to hire us? They've already dropped us."

"Because we're three of the most successful photographers in the US. Soon we might be five or six, and if that number continues to grow, the industry will have no choice but to rethink its strategy. Of course, not everyone will jump on board, but it's sure to set off some kind of shift."

"Yes, I suppose you're right," I say. "No brand wants negative publicity. They can't afford to lose their customer loyalty. And if the brands follow, the media will have to start making changes too."

"Exactly." Regga gives me a high five, then downs his drink in one go. "We're stronger together, Faith. And with the media on our side, we can really do some good here."

54

SILVA

New York Fashion Week is something alien to me. I've never been to a show or even watched one online, but here I am, getting ready to go to the opening party on my crutches. It's a shame my cast couldn't come off earlier; I still have to cope with it for another five days, but my suit still looks good on me, even after cutting off the bottom of one pant leg so I could get them on. I've secretly always wanted to wear a suit, but lacking fancy occasions, I never invested in one. The informal black satin fitted jacket and pants are timeless, and the white shirt is just feminine enough, showing a little cleavage. I wouldn't normally be jumping to go to such an event, but Faith is in an awkward position, and she's been indecisive about whether to go or not, so when she asked me to come with her, I couldn't say no.

Trinny is in the guest bathroom, and she's beside herself as she's coming too. Regga, who decided to come out of hiding to stand with Elsie and Faith, offered to bring Trinny as his plus-one, and she's taken the day off to visit the hair stylist and buy a dress.

"You know what day it is, right?" I ask, wheeling myself toward Faith, who is getting dressed in our bedroom.

"What do you mean? Did I forget something?" She frowns, then shoots me a beaming smile. "Oh, wait. I know. It's 'Silva looks super-hot in a suit' day. They should turn that into an official holiday so everyone can appreciate how good you look."

"You're cute, but no." I shake my head and laugh. "It's February nineteenth—the deadline for our workout sessions."

"God, you're right." She chuckles as she fastens a diamond stud in her ear. "I completely forgot about that. So, what do you normally do with clients on a day like this?"

"Well, today is the day you're supposed to officially be in shape and feel good about yourself, so I'd do a physical assessment as well as a mental one. Body-fat percentage, mood, etcetera. And I'd ask you if you've been happy with my services, of course," I add with a grin.

Faith shoots me a flirty look and closes the distance between us, then bends over to kiss me. "As far as your services are concerned," she mumbles against my lips, "they've been exceptional. I'd even go as far as to say you've gone above and beyond. I especially liked all the steamy workouts we've had lately." Stepping back, she reaches for her other earring but never takes her eyes off me. "And when it comes to my physical and mental state..." She pauses to check herself in the standing mirror. She's wearing a spectacular figure-hugging, skin-colored sequined dress that shows off her amazing figure. "I would have never worn this dress six weeks ago, but I feel confident enough to do so now. And above all, I'm happy. Very, very happy."

"I'm happy too." I tilt my head and sigh at the sight of

her. "It should be illegal for you to go out like that. You're going to stab everyone through the heart with your stunning beauty, and they'll all hate me because you're mine."

Faith bites her lip as she looks me over. "I think it might be the other way around. I was apprehensive about going tonight, but I'm so proud to be with you that I can't wait to show you off."

"I can't wait to show you off," Trinny repeats in a teasing tone as she steps into the room. "You too are sickeningly cute together. Please don't make me feel like a third wheel tonight," she jokes. "I've always been the third wheel. It's the story of my life."

"But you have a date," I say, rolling over to her.

"It's a pity date," she corrects me. "I'm only his plus-one on paper, and I'm super grateful obviously, but I don't think big-shot photographer Regga Ibrahimovic will have any interest in me. Besides, he's twenty-five years older. It's not exactly a match made in heaven."

"He's a gentleman," Faith says in all seriousness. "A very intriguing, talented, and good-natured gentleman. If you're his date, he won't leave your side, and who knows? You might like him." She smiles. "But we'll be by your side too, and so will Elsie and her mother. We have to stick together, us outcasts, so I've booked us a VIP table."

"You're hardly an outcast," Trinny argues. "You're Faith Astor."

"I'm canceled Faith Astor, actually. I'm currently old news, someone to avoid. But I've decided I'm not going to stand down or move aside. None of us will."

"That's my girl." I take Faith by her waist and pull her onto my lap. "You're so hot when you're feisty."

Trinny makes a dramatic gagging gesture. "You two..."

"Sorry." My goofy smile must be really silly, but I don't care. "By the way, you look great. You never wear dresses."

"I do sometimes." Trinny shrugs. "Just not at work or at home or..." She hesitates. "Hmm... I guess I'm always either at work or at home, so you may be right. Like it?"

"Love it," Faith says. "Feel free to borrow any jewelry you want. It's all in my dressing table drawer."

"Really?" Trinny's jaw drops, and she makes her way over there, then gasps when she opens the drawer. "Are you serious, Faith? Because I will take you up on the offer." As usual, Trinny doesn't hold back and happily picks a necklace and a pair of earrings that complement her black dress.

"Absolutely. Those look great." Faith looks from me to Trinny and back. "Thank you for coming with me. I really appreciate it."

"Are you kidding me?" Trinny laughs out loud. "You're taking me to the most exciting party I've ever been to, letting me wear your fabulous jewelry, and you're thanking *me*? I'm sorry, but that's too funny."

"No, I mean it." Faith gets up to give her a hug, and I can tell Trinny is taken aback by the intimate gesture. "This is a scary night for me, so I'm glad to be with friends I trust." Putting on a brave face, she steps back and blushes as if she's embarrassed for admitting that.

"You're welcome, and feel free to drag me along anytime," Trinny says, equally enchanted by her new close friend. "By the way, is your sister coming?"

"No, I messaged her, but she's not arriving in New York until tomorrow, and she's fully booked all week, so I don't think we'll manage to meet up. It's a shame, but it is what it is." Faith shrugs it off, but I can tell it's bothering her. "Anyway, let's make a move. Are you guys ready? Regga's limo will be here any minute."

55

FAITH

Regga was right. Together we're stronger, and as we enter the venue I don't feel as nervous as I normally would. It's heaving with photographers, and when they spot Silva and me heading over to our table, followed by Elsie and her mother, and Regga and Trinny, all the attention is on us. I must admit, we're an unusual party, especially with our plus-ones who have nothing to do with the fashion industry, and the other delegates must wonder who they are. I say hello to a few people and receive a polite greeting in return, but no one comes up to me and hugs me like they normally would. That's okay; I can do without the fake cheeriness. In fact, it's quite refreshing for a change.

Roy is here for me, though, and my heart swells when I see him sitting in our booth, holding the fort down with one of his casual flames. He's not scared of being associated with me, and he, too, is on our team.

"Babe. You came." Roy kisses me on both cheeks and gives me a warm hug. "I'm so glad you're here. It's awfully dull without you." When Silva scoots into the booth next to him, he whispers something in her ear that makes her laugh. "And look who you've brought along," he continues, referring to Elsie and Regga. "Isn't this a powerhouse gathering of talented allies?"

I introduce everyone to Roy and order us drinks. Sitting next to Silva, I lace my fingers through hers and kiss her hand. It's blatantly obvious that we're together, and I suspect the curious glances cast in our direction may have something to do with that. That, and the fact that I've walked away from the most powerful woman in fashion and I'm sitting here with another photographer who's done the same. They must wonder why Regga is in our company, as he never shows up at events. We're an unlikely gang, and the general confusion among patrons amuses me.

The screens that cover the whole back wall play advertisements for perfumes and showcase some of the new collections that are yet to be shown on the runway, and everyone who is anyone is here. A woman is watching us from the bar, and I recognize her to be one of the new names showing this week. She's launching her range of ethical couture, which, considering the current climate, is expected to be highly popular with celebrities. When I give her a smile, she hesitates before she comes over, as if she's shy to approach us.

"Hi, I'm Kadi Karesh," she says with a thick Middle Eastern accent, then holds out an elegant hand to shake mine. No air-kissing, no high-pitched screeches. She's refreshing.

"I know who you are. It's very nice to meet you." I scoot over and pat the space next to me. "Would you like to join us?"

"Oh, I don't want to bother you. I just wanted to say that I admire you and Elsie for what you've done." She smiles and gives Elsie a wave.

"Are you here by yourself?" I ask.

"Yes. Well, no. I'm here with my business partner, but she's kind of met someone and she's all loved up. I'm not sure where they went. I only moved to New York last year, and it's my first Fashion Week, so this is all new to me. I'm supposed to network, but I have no idea where to start."

"Then please, sit," I insist. "Unless you think it would be risky for your career? I would understand, no hard feelings."

"Oh, no, not at all." Kadi sits and greets my friends. "It's just that you guys are people I've always wanted to work with. It's a little intimidating." She lowers her voice and leans into me. "Is that *the* Regga? Regga Ibrahimovic?"

"Yes. And he's one of the nice ones."

"Oh my God." Kadi stares at him adoringly. "That's so cool. That man is crazy talented."

I give her a warm smile and nod. "Couldn't agree more. Well, if you're new to this, let me give you some advice. Lesson number one. Never be intimidated. Everyone here is mortal, no one has superpowers. You can be at the top of the scene one day, and the next you're old news. Take me and Elsie for example," I joke. "The most important lesson I've learned is not to care as much about image. It won't make you happy."

"Yeah, I get that. I've been here for an hour, and people are so nice to me, but it's also the most superficial situation I've ever been in. I don't go out much. I work very hard, and when I'm not working, all I want to do is sleep and eat. Add to that, I don't drink, and they never serve tea in these places. How do you do it?"

"I actually don't go out that much anymore," I say, gesturing to Silva. "Since I met my girlfriend, that is."

"Oh. How cute." Kadi's smile widens. "Starting a new

business, I don't have time to date, but hopefully that will change at some point."

"It will come when the time is right." I realize I'm staring at Silva and chuckle as I shake my head. She looks so good in a suit that I have trouble keeping my eyes off her. I was worried she might hate it here, but she's happily chatting with Elsie and her mother, so I decide not to worry about her. "So, your first show?" I ask Kadi. "Exciting. Are you nervous?"

"Yes. I'm so, so nervous."

"Don't be. Word is you're the next big thing, and when that happens, women will be fighting to wear your dresses at the Met."

"That's what my business partner told me, but I still find it hard to believe." Kadi takes a sip of her water and winces. "*Zero* magazine wants to run a feature on me."

"That's great. You're saying it as if it's a bad thing."

"No, it's not. It's just that I'm talking to you, and I know you hate them, and..."

"Hey, you don't have to pick sides," I say. "It's a huge opportunity, and ethical brands like yours are exactly what the world needs, so don't even think twice about the exposure. Besides, I don't hate the magazine, I simply disagree with the culture in general."

Kadi nods. "Valerie wanted to speak to me tonight. That's another reason why I'm hanging around." Her gaze darts to the entrance, where there seems to be some commotion. "Speak of the devil."

Valerie walks in with a whole slew of minions, her black cape flailing behind her. A stressed-looking assistant is carrying a bottle of water and her purse, and the man by her side is showing her something on an iPad, then points to the *Zero* booth.

"Perhaps you shouldn't be sitting here," I say to Kadi. "It might not reflect well on you."

"Nonsense." Kadi shoots me a wink. "You're the nicest person I've met so far, and you said I don't have to pick sides, right?"

As Valerie passes our booth, she spots me first, then Kadi, before she turns to Elsie and Regga. Although she's composed as always, that twitch in the corner of her mouth is back. I can tell she's completely taken aback to see Regga and Kadi with us. Regga the legend and Kadi the newcomer who everyone wants to know more about. I'm not surprised Valerie wants to do a feature on Kadi; the magazine has no choice if they want to stay current.

"Hi, Kadi, dear. How are you? Ready for your big day?"

"Absolutely." Kadi gets up to greet her, and Valerie turns to our party.

"Faith." She gives me a short nod. "Elsie." Then she stares at Regga. "Mr. Ibrahimovic. How lovely to see you here. It's been a while." We all greet her back politely. There's no need for a scene of any kind, and after all, what we want is a dialogue, not a war. "New friends?" she asks Kadi. To an outsider, it would sound like an innocent question, but in truth, it would take an essay to describe the politics behind those two words.

"Yes," Kadi says confidently. "New friends. I heard you wanted to meet with me?"

For a split second, I see a hint of annoyance in Valerie's expression, and I half expect her to make some snarky remark, but she doesn't. Pointing to the *Zero* booth, she nods. "Yes, I have a proposition for you. Shall we?"

56

SILVA

It's been an interesting night so far and the peek I've had into Faith's world has been fascinating. I've rarely seen so much real-life theater and fakeness, but I'm also aware that this is part of a bigger picture and a huge industry upon which many jobs rely. Even after Valerie appeared, Faith has been calm and happy, and therefore so am I. A handful of people have come over to praise her and Elsie for what they've done, and two others have joined us at our table. One of them is a famous model, the other is the creative director of an online brand that promotes a bigger-than-average size range. By doing so, they're making a statement, while Valerie is carefully assessing who is here. I caught her looking a couple of times, and I think she's only now realizing this could lead to trouble, and that not everyone is dancing to her tune. Could she be forced to make a public apology at some point? I don't know the woman, but from what I've seen tonight, I imagine that would be her worst nightmare. By now, everyone here will have seen the videos, and I can't imagine she doesn't feel a tiny bit self-conscious about that.

"Are you okay?" I ask Faith when I see a frown appear between her brows.

"What? Me?" She nods. "Yeah, I'm fine."

"Are you sure?" I study her and decide something is definitely off, as I know her so well. "Because you don't seem fine."

Faith sighs and points to the bar. "My ex just walked in. I kind of expected him to be here tonight, but it's still weird."

I see the man she's talking about and can't deny I'm feeling a stab of insecurity. He's very handsome, tall, dark, and certainly charming from what I can tell, as he's surrounded by numerous beautiful women who are showering him with fake giggles and looks of admiration. He's wearing a tailored, black suit, he's freshly shaven, and one of his sleeves is rolled up, showing off his no doubt expensive watch.

"Is it hard for you to see him?" I ask, not sure if I want to know the answer.

"No." Faith waves a hand and shakes her head vigorously. "I don't mean that I feel anything. It's not that. It's just a shock to my system. I don't understand what I ever saw in him now."

"Oh." Suppressing a sigh of relief, I sit back and put an arm around her. "So there's no attraction whatsoever?"

"Nothing. I feel kind of repulsed, actually." Faith flinches as Michael spots her and comes up to us. He walks with the cocky confidence of someone who's used to getting what he wants and it's easy to dislike him.

"Faith. It's so good to see you again." He looks her up and down like she's dessert. "You look amazing." I'm aware of the irony of the situation. She never told me as much, but I always had a suspicion Faith wanted to shape up before this date because she knew she'd see her ex tonight. But she's moved on, and the hard work she's done has been for no one but herself. I've loved seeing her confidence grow, and although her physique has changed somewhat, to me she was always beautiful, and she always will be.

"Thank you." Faith holds up her hand in a greeting but doesn't bother to get up.

"You've lost weight. It suits you." His comment annoys me. Faith has lost weight and now he likes her? The insinuation is clear: she wasn't good enough before, and it's an insult in my opinion, but I refrain from stepping in, as this is between them.

"I haven't lost weight, actually. I'm just stronger and healthier. There's a difference," she says in a flat tone.

"Sure." Michael clearly doesn't understand what she means by that and keeps staring at her breasts. "How have you been?" he asks, placing a hand on her shoulder as if he's genuinely interested in the answer. "I heard about what went down with you and Valerie. Have you made up yet?"

"I've been really good, actually." Faith forces a smile. "And no, I have no intention of making up with that dreadful woman. At least, not on her terms."

"Right." Michael turns his attention to Regga and gives him a nod, perhaps wondering if he's Faith's date. "Well, I'm sure you know what you're doing." His eyes flick back to Faith's cleavage, and I want to kill him for that alone. "Listen, I'm going to this party later. Would you like to join me as my plus-one?" He shrugs as if there's nothing strange about the proposition. "You know, for old time's sake? It's in the Waldorf. I can get us a room there. It's going to be a late one."

Faith stares at him and grimaces, then leans into me. "Michael, you can't possibly be serious." She waits for an answer, but he just stands there, processing the rejection.

"Okay, let me get one thing straight," she says, tilting her head. "Firstly, you and I will never, ever happen again. It was a huge mistake on my part, and I'll regret it for as long as I live. You have been incredibly disrespectful to me, and I didn't even see it at the time. Not the scope of it anyway. Secondly, this is my girlfriend, Silva, and she's the only one I'll be going home with."

"Very funny." Michael scratches his chin and chuckles, but his face soon pulls into a baffled expression when Faith shows no sign of joking. He hesitates and shuffles on the spot, his mind churning for a reply. "You're serious..."

"Yes. We're together."

"Okay..." he says after a long pause. "Since when are you into women?"

"Since I met Silva." Faith takes my hand and laces her fingers with mine. I can't say I mind the awkward moment; seeing the look on Michael's face is priceless, and I feel pretty smug. "So, no, I don't want to come to the party with you, or anywhere for that matter." Faith clears her throat and gives him a wave. "I'd appreciate it if you left us alone now. Have a good night, Michael."

57

FAITH

Getting ready for my only Fashion Week catwalk shoot, I move my camera stand a little to the left, aligning it perfectly with the center of the stage. Aside from the three designers who replaced me with another photographer this week, I've canceled two shoots myself following my new pact with Elsie and Regga. This particular designer has cast diverse models for their show, and their brand is one I'm proud to work for. The lack of jobs doesn't bother me as much anymore, as I'm really loving all the time I have to spend with Silva, and work is so much more enjoyable now that I'm entirely comfortable with what I take on.

Guests are arriving, filling the seats in the back first. VIPs who sit front row tend to arrive last minute, so I still have time to move around and find the best angle from the end of the catwalk without being in anyone's way. I've been at the walk-through, and I have a copy of the master list for the run of the show, so I'll know when to crank up my stand for the finale. As always, there's tension in the air, but I don't think the guests have any idea of the real chaos that goes on behind the scenes. The event organizer is rushing around with her iPad, instructing her team on who to seat first. Extra chairs are wedged into the rows for VIP arrivals who were unaccounted for, and champagne is handed out by stressed catering staff dressed in black. I too am dressed in black, as I'm not supposed to draw attention to myself. It's an unspoken rule for anyone who is part of a show. All black, no crazy jewelry or accessories, no strong perfume, no phones, and no headphones. Everyone needs to be on full alert after the six months of hard work that has gone into ten minutes of public exposure.

The background music is turned up and the lights are dimmed. Two women behind me are arguing over a seat, and the event manager steps in to clarify their misunderstanding.

"Are you all set?" she asks, briefly tapping my shoulder after resolving the conflict.

"Yes, but it's darker than during the run-through. That might be an issue," I say.

"Don't worry, the technical team is aware of that. As soon as we start, the setting will go back to default." She turns when one of her team members calls for her attention. "Sorry, got to go. Join us for drinks after?"

"Sure. That would be nice." I give her a friendly nod before I turn back to my camera, focusing on the screen from behind which the models will appear. It's been a challenge to concentrate after seeing Michael last night, as I'm still taking great joy from the look on his face when I told him about Silva. It felt liberating to realize he meant nothing to me anymore, and that I was ashamed I was ever with him. Having Silva by my side as my girlfriend in public was even more liberating. Our relationship is no secret anymore, and I was pleasantly surprised by the sweet support from people who were not afraid to be seen with Elsie and me. *My Silva.* Those two words keep playing over and over in my mind, and they make me smile. She really is mine now, and that's a beautiful thought. Her parents were lovely; they made me feel so welcome in the family and I can't wait to meet them in person. If only I could return the favor by introducing her to my family, but that's hard when they don't bother to call me back.

"Hey, hottie."

I jump up and turn around when someone pinches my behind. Ready to dish out a slap, I stop myself when I see Roy sitting there. "Hey, you!" I say, slapping his hand away. "What are you doing here?" I give him a kiss on his cheek and quickly step back, as he's sitting next to the two grumpy-looking women who were arguing over the seats.

"I have an invite." Roy grins. "I always get invites, you know that."

"But you're sitting in the buyers' section." My eyes shift to the lanyard in his hand, and I pull it toward me. "Ben Plastic? Is that your name now?"

Roy hushes me and nervously looks around to make sure no one has heard me. "Ben Plastic is Megadick. We met up last night. Ben was a bit hungover this morning, and gentleman that I am, I offered to come in his place, so he wouldn't get in trouble at work," he says in a whisper.

"Ben Plastic is Megadick?" I ask, raising my hands. "No, wait. Let me rephrase that. You're sleeping with someone called Ben Plastic?" I stare at him incredulously. "You really have a thing for weird names."

"Ben's nickname—which, I'm delighted to report he lived up to—and his last name are not relevant. What matters is that he's super handsome and that I'm front row."

He gladly accepts the glass of champagne handed to him by one of the hostesses.

"Right. Well, you certainly don't look like a buyer," I say, scanning the suit-clad men and women around him. At fashion shows, the crowd is generally divided into four groups of people: the celebrities and industry VIPs who sit at the front along both sides of the catwalk; the buyers, who sit at the end so they have a good front view of the product; the fashion journalists and sponsors, who sit in the second row; and creatives like bloggers and influencers, who fight over the rest of the seats and often cheat by swapping around the allocated name cards so they can sit closer to the catwalk. Roy falls into the last group, and he has made no effort to blend in with the dark suits today. He's wearing a silk tunic with an African print, matching pants, and big, fake glasses with a red rim.

"I don't care, I've got the golden ticket." He dangles the lanyard in front of me and sips his champagne. "Are you coming to the after-party? Buyers get a plus-one, so I've invited Silva."

"Really? That's so sweet of you. But what if Ben Plastic decides he feels better later?" I ask, slowly drawing out the man's second name.

"Don't worry about Ben." Roy laughs. "I wore him out. He won't have the energy."

58

SILVA

I need some time to get used to this new world I've been plunged into, but I'm having fun with Faith, Roy, Elsie, Regga, and a bunch of other people they've introduced me to. Regga has once again decided to come out with us to show his support to Elsie and Faith, and that's incredibly sweet of him since he doesn't like going out.

We're in a private members' club in Manhattan on the top floor of a skyscraper, and the views are incredible. I wondered why Roy was so obsessed with these parties, but I'm starting to see that invites like this make for a lucrative lifestyle for someone who doesn't have the funds to splash out. I suppose free champagne and delicious canapes beat having a microwave meal by himself any day, and the DJ is so good that I wish I could dance. A perk of my cast is that they got us a table, and with the table service, it means we don't have to queue up by the bar. As a result of our table, a lot of people want to sit with us, and with twelve bodies crammed into a booth, I've made some interesting new acquaintances. Most of them engage with extreme enthusiasm but without any real interest in what I have to say, and that amuses me. I know it's nothing personal; everyone is out for themselves, and I suspect what they want tonight is to be seen with the people who have caught the attention of the fashion world more than anyone these past weeks.

Since Faith, Elsie, and Regga were seen together at the opening party, there has been a lot of speculation about who else will side with them, and suddenly people are not so sure which way to bend anymore. Faith has warned me about the fake crowd, and although I can see right through the phony compliments, I'm having a good time and I'm incredibly proud to be by her side. If being with Faith means accompanying her to events like this now and then, I don't mind that at all.

"Would you like another drink?" I ask her, pointing to her empty glass.

Faith shakes her head and shoots me a sweet smile. "No. I'm really tired. It's been a long day. Do you mind if we go?"

"Of course not." I let Faith help me up and pull at Roy's lanyard. "Ben Plastic, we're leaving. It's been a pleasure," I joke. "Thank you."

"Anytime." Roy hugs Faith, and as soon as we've said our goodbyes to the others, he gestures for a handsome man to come and sit next to him.

"I see we're easily replaced," Faith says with a chuckle. "I don't know where you get the energy from, Roy-boy." She hands me my crutches and follows me to the elevator. "Are you sure you don't want to stay?"

"No, babe. I'm here for you, and I can't wait to get into bed with you."

"Good. because neither can I." She sighs. "It's only day three and already I want this week to be over." She points to my leg. "But your cast is coming off soon, so that's great, right?"

"God, yes. The first thing I'm going to do is scratch myself. I've had a terrible itch lately." Relief floods my system at the thought of it. "First, I was excited to run again, but now I can't wait to scratch and have a shower." Faith faces me as we wait for the elevator, and my body immediately reacts to her when she gives me that flirtatious smile. "And other things, of course," I add. "There are a lot of things I want to do to you when the cast comes off and none of them involve running or a shower. Actually, no. I won't dismiss the shower."

Faith laughs. "I doubt there's anything you haven't done to me already," she says in a husky voice.

"Oh, you'll have to see about that. I happen to have a dark side." I have no idea how those words slipped past my tongue, but they were clearly dying to get out.

"Do you now?" Faith's voice goes up a notch, and her breath hitches. "Want to tell me about this dark side?"

"Maybe. If you're a good girl." I can't help but smirk because I've never spoken to Faith like this before. I can tell she likes it, though; the look in her eyes doesn't lie. I've always been dominant with lovers, at least, since I recovered from anorexia and got my life back on track. My therapist tells me it's about control, and I suppose it is. I've had to practice full control over everything I did to recover, and it's no surprise that need manifested in my love life too. But with Faith, it's been the opposite. Breaking my ankle and moving into her home put me in a vulnerable and submissive position, not just because I needed help physically. I also needed her mental support, and that created a whole new and deeper level of relationship that I'm immensely grateful for, which is why it's so curious that now, knowing I'll be independent again after almost six weeks, the itch has returned. The itch to make her surrender.

"And what would you consider me being a good girl?" she asks in a whisper.

"That you think about what I told you. I like to be dominant in bed." I meet her eyes, and she looks startled. I can almost hear her mind churning, and I'm not sure if I regret speaking my mind. Is she scared? I never meant to scare her, and I would never hurt her in a million years, but she seems hesitant. "I'm sorry, I didn't mean to—"

"No, it's fine." She frowns. "You like to be dominant?"

"Yes." I hold her gaze and give her a small smile. "But only if you want me to."

Faith shivers. The elevator door finally opens, but she makes no effort to get in. When it closes again with a *ping*, she looks at it for a moment as if vaguely registering the sound, then turns back to me, raising her chin. "Okay. Show me." She inches closer and her lips linger against mine. "I'm curious."

59

FAITH

"Tell me about your fantasies," I say as we're lying in bed. "Tell me what you want." What she said to me by the elevators keeps lingering in the back of my mind. It's hard to imagine Silva being dominant, but at the same time, I remember that mischievous, almost dangerous twinkle in her eyes when she voiced her desires.

Silva turns on her side and steadies herself on her elbow. "I don't want you to think what we do in bed isn't enough for me. Being with you has been the most beautiful experience of my life, and I love having sex with you. You are what I want, Faith. All the rest is a game."

"Then tell me what games you like to play," I whisper. "This is new to me, and I'm open to experiment in any way because sex has been taken to a whole new level for me, and I love it. I love it with you." There. I've said it. I've been wondering if she's holding back with me, but I never dared to ask. When we're together, it's magical, but Silva never told me what *she* wants.

"Okay." She takes my hands, places them on my pillow above my head, and holds my wrists firmly with one hand.

Then she trails a finger over my breasts and draws lazy circles around my nipples. Her featherlight touch causes goose bumps on my skin, and when she takes one of my nipples between her fingers and squeezes it hard, I gasp. Instinctively, I want to rub the sore, sensitive skin, but she's holding me down and I can't move. She's never done anything like this to me before; she's always so gentle. It hurts a little, but I like the sharp sting that shoots to my center, and I feel wetness pool between my thighs. She studies me, and a small smile plays around her lips. "You like that."

"I do." I hold my breath when her gaze shifts to my other nipple. "Do it again," I whisper, and when she pinches me harder, I moan, lifting my hips off the bed. I'm mildly disappointed when she moves her hand to my face and strokes my cheek. "Please continue."

"Not now," she says, licking her lips in a teasing manner. "When I can walk."

"You're making me wait."

"Uh-huh. It's all part of the fun."

"What's in it for you?" I ask. "How does it work? I may be naïve, but this is not something I've ever read up on or experienced."

Silva takes a moment to think about it before she answers. "To me, it's about control. I've needed full control over every aspect of my life to live with my eating disorder, and I found that I liked to apply that same control in the bedroom with the occasional short-term flings I've had over the years. It started when I came out of the clinic. I learned I could cope as long as I was in control at all times. It's why I don't drink much. It's why I track what I eat and how much I exercise, and why I have fridge OCD. And it's why I like to be dominant in bed. Control makes me feel good and sometimes it turns me on. Your reaction when I did that to you turned me on." She pauses. "But being with you after breaking my ankle taught me, I don't necessarily need that control anymore. Being dependent and letting you help me felt comfortable, and therefore I was comfortable making love to you without being dominant. In a way, you healed that part of me because it's a choice now rather than the only way."

I nod silently as I process what she's told me. It makes sense. "Do you still prefer it that way?"

"No, I don't." Silva pauses and smiles. "But that doesn't mean I don't like playing games now and then, and from your reaction, I think you'll like it too."

"Okay." I stare into her hungry eyes. She's aroused just talking about this, and so am I. "And what would you do to me right now if your leg wasn't in a cast?" I ask, dying to know more.

"Hmm..." Silva's hand returns to my breasts, and she massages them with deliberate, slow motions. "I think I would tie you to the bed frame first." She continues to hold my wrists as she kisses my neck and sucks on it so hard it stings.

Tilting my head away from her to give her better access, I moan when I feel her teeth scrape across my skin. It's exciting to be held down, and although I'm far from helpless, I know she's right. I do like this. "And then what?" I ask, sucking in a quick breath when she nibbles on my earlobe.

"Then, I would touch you and tease you until you're so aroused that you'll beg me for more," she continues, sliding her hand down toward my belly. I hold my breath as she inches toward the strip of hair between my thighs and strokes me with her fingertips. I moan and buck my hips, needing her lower. When she finally slips her fingers over my folds and strokes me, I'm so sensitive that I gasp in surprise. "And then..." She brings her mouth to my ear and her hot breath and sexy voice alone send me to the edge. I spread my legs, and it feels incredible when she enters me.

"Fuck!" My walls clench around her fingers, and I push myself up against her hand. I'm wet and throbbing, and her thumb expertly circles my clit. Before I know it, I'm about to explode.

Silva's breath tickles my ear as her voice trails off to a soft whisper. "Yes, that's right. Then I'm going to fuck you, Faith. Maybe with my fingers, like I'm doing now. Maybe with a toy, or maybe with a strap. It all depends on how I feel." She moves into me, over and over, curling her fingers, and I cry out so loud that my voice echoes off the walls.

"Yes! God, yes!" As I come back to reality and my blurred vision sharpens, she lets go of my wrists and pulls me into a warm hug. Cupping my face, she looks at me, and I see so much in her eyes. Arousal, satisfaction, tenderness, and something much, much deeper, but I'm still dizzy and can't think straight enough to figure her out.

"That, my beautiful Faith," she says, kissing me softly on my forehead, "was just a little taster."

60

SILVA

"I think you're good to go. Let's try and put some weight on that." The doctor steps back and helps me off the examination bed.

I'm half expecting my ankle to break again, and I let out a sigh of relief when I finally stand on my leg, even if it is a little wobbly because I haven't used it in so long. "It feels weak."

"That's normal. You're lucky you're an active person. Your muscle memory will allow your leg to strengthen quickly, but don't overdo it anytime soon. Start with short walks and build it up."

"Sure. And slow jogs?"

"Absolutely not. Maybe in a few weeks." He laughs. "Keen to get going again, are we?"

"Yeah," I say with a chuckle. "But I'll be careful. I don't want anything to get in the way of a good recovery."

"Come here, lean on me," Faith says as she wraps an arm around my back. It's the first time we're able to walk so close together, and it feels wonderful. She's been here for hours while they took off my cast and examined me, and she looks so sexy in her pencil skirt that I've been fantasizing about what I'll do to her when we're finally alone.

"Mmm... I like this 'lean on me' thing."

The doctor seems bemused by our flirtations. "I sense you have a lot of fun to catch up on," he says with a wink when he waves us out. "Enjoy your day."

"Where do you want to go?" I ask as we exit the hospital and hail a cab.

"To my place, of course." Faith frowns. "What? You think I'd send you home right away? I'm not ready for you to leave yet." When a cab comes to a halt, she opens the door for me and helps me in. "I'm happy for you that you have your leg back, but I'll be honest. I was a bit sad this morning, knowing you'd move out soon."

"You were?"

"Yeah." She strokes my thigh and squeezes it. "What about you? Are you dying to go back home? It's okay. You can be honest with me."

Saying I haven't thought about that would be a lie; I've thought of little else in the past week. "Of course I'll miss living with you. It's been nice." I shake my head and sigh. "No, not just nice. It's been totally amazing. Because of you, a difficult situation has turned into something good and healing, and I've loved every second of your company." I shoot her a flirtatious smile. "If I knew breaking my ankle would give me a hot, cute, sweet, and talented girlfriend in return, I would have broken it much sooner."

Faith blushes and shakes her head with a laugh. "Well, you have me, so please don't go breaking any more bones."

"I won't. I'm having too much fun walking again."

The short ride with Faith's hand on my thigh fuel my arousal even more, and as we head into her building, I can barely contain myself. When the elevator doors close, I gently push her back against the wall.

"What are you doing?" Faith asks, her eyes wide as I slide a hand under her top and kiss her neck.

"We've been up and down so many times together and I've never been able to do this," I say, pushing into her.

Faith gasps when I cup her breast and bring my lips to hers. "What about the camera?"

"The security guy is always on his phone. Trust me, he's not watching." I feel like me again, now that I can stand on both legs, and after last night, my libido is through the roof. Pressing my lips firmly against Faith's, I moan at her hungry reaction. She fists my hair and deepens the kiss, and by the time the door pings open, we're both out of breath and out of control.

"Hurry," she says in a ragged voice as she takes my arm and slings it over her shoulder to help me walk faster. "You've made me crazy, woman."

The feeling is mutual, and as we stumble into her apartment, I lose all self-control. "God, I want you, Faith." Finally, my hands are free to pull off her jacket and push up her top, freeing her breasts for my mouth to find. I unclip her bra faster than I've ever managed, tear it off, along with her top, and suck a hard nipple into my mouth as I back her up against the door.

Faith groans in delight, slides her hands over my back, and moves against me. There's no more patience or tenderness, just a carnal need for satisfaction. I know she's loving that we're upright; she's grinding her hips into me with force and arching her back so I can devour her breasts. It's a new experience for her and I'm finally in control again, unapologetically taking what I want.

I hike up her skirt and slide my hand underneath it

while my tongue roams over her breasts and her neck. Faith spreads her legs a little and moans louder, her movements growing frantic and uncontrolled. She's wet and swollen, and it drives me mad with lust. I stroke her until she's squirming against my hand, then slide two fingers deep inside her while I kiss her again.

"Yes..." Faith wraps a leg around my thigh and leans back against the door while I fuck her. She embraces me tightly, and her dark gaze slices through my resolve, making me move faster, harder, deeper.

"Come for me," I whisper against her lips. There's nothing romantic about this rushed encounter, yet it's gloriously intimate. I've pictured this so many times in my mind, and as her moans grow louder, all I want to do is make her explode.

"Fuck, Silva. Don't stop." Faith tenses, and she holds her breath for long moments before she lets out a long, lyrical groan. Her head hits the door with a hard thud and then her walls tighten around my fingers, giving me that addictive hit of euphoria, knowing she's feeling really, really good.

"You're amazing," I say while she rides out her orgasm. Curling my fingers to hit the spot that makes her gasp again, I smile at her startled expression.

"Jesus..." Faith lets out a long breath and bites her lip. "You're..."

"I'm very, very turned on," I say with a grin, pushing into her again. "And I'm not going to stop until you tell me to."

61

FAITH

Silva is insatiable and so am I. Needing a break after hours in bed, we head out for a walk to stretch our legs and get some fresh air. It's still cold, but the days are getting longer, and it's only a matter of weeks before the temperatures will be pleasant. The weeks have flown by, and our time together has been magical. Looking back, I have trouble remembering where it all started, as it's like my overwhelming feelings for her have clouded my memory.

"I'll be very busy after tomorrow," she says. "I still have most of my old clients and I've gained a few new ones, so I'll be out during the days and some nights."

"That's a good thing, though, isn't it?" I ask, noting she looks regretful.

"Yes, but I'll miss being around you so much."

"I'll miss you too." I take her hand and kiss it. "I've got some shoots next week, actually."

"You do? That's great. Before Fashion Week, you were saying most of your gigs got canceled."

"Yeah. But new opportunities have come up. I think I may have survived the Valerie scandal after all."

"You more than survived," Silva says. "I've seen so many articles about body-shaming lately, it seems you and Elsie really have made a difference."

"I hope so." I look up at her and smile. "Let's see what happens with Regga. If he goes public, that will really help too."

"Yes. Let's see." The chill in the air is making me shiver, and Silva wraps an arm around me to keep me warm. She's always so sweet and considerate of my well-being that I can only hope I'm giving her enough in return. Not used to someone who cares so much, it always amazes me, and I'm incredibly grateful to have her in my life. "So, about our busy schedules..." She pauses and grins as if she's embarrassed by what she's about to say. "This might sound cheesy, but how would you feel about setting date nights? You know, two or three nights a week that we keep free for each other. Unless something important comes up, of course," she adds.

"I love that idea." Feeling myself blush, I lean into her. "When can I take you out?"

"Not yet. I'm taking you out first," she says. "The first of many, many dates."

"Mmm..." I point to the Vietnamese restaurant we've been to before. "How about now? I'm feeling hungry." I realize I've just suggested eating without giving it a second thought, and that's progress. There's no anxiety; I'm not subconsciously touching my behind as I say it. With the balanced life I've been leading, it's been weeks since I've felt triggered to binge eat and purge. I'm by no means under the illusion that I'm cured, but I'm better than I've been in years. It's not just the exercise that's made me feel more confident in myself. Sure, my body has changed for the better; I have more muscle definition, and I've learned to embrace my curves. But it's the change within that has made the biggest impact on my mental health. I'm calm, content, and excited about life. I love myself more, and therefore I want to take care of my body. Despite my initial skepticism, Silva's holistic approach is working.

"Are you hungry from all the sex?" Silva asks jokingly. "We can go for dinner, but I can't let this be the first official date. I don't even have flowers for you."

"You don't need to buy me flowers. I just want to spend time with you," I say, pulling her along toward the restaurant.

"I know, but I've been looking forward to doing this the romantic way." Silva's cute smile makes me weak as she continues. "I haven't had the chance to find a florist yet. I have so much to make up for."

"Fine, then it's not a date. We're just going to eat," I say with a wink. "And flirt."

"And flirt." Silva opens the door for me, and we're delighted that our table by the window is free. Now that she's able, she makes a show of pulling out a chair for me, and she's so in her element that I want to hug her. "So, do you have any other plans apart from work this week?" she asks as she studies the menu.

"I'm doing a couple more photoshoots in my bedroom," I say, then slam a hand in front of my mouth and laugh. "That sounded weird, didn't it?"

"A little." Silva grins. "Who?"

"Elsie and Regga. They're both fascinating people, and now that I have good shots of you and Roy, I'd like to expand on those and create a series. For myself," I hastily add. "I don't plan on doing anything with the work. It's for fun, for me."

"Why wouldn't you try to do something with it?" she asks.

"I don't know." I shrug. "I'm a fashion photographer, not an artist. It's refreshing to do something unrelated to a brief, that's all. They won't ever end up on the walls of a gallery."

"I think you're underestimating yourself." Silva sits back and points a finger at me. "You said yourself that you're proud of it, so it must be good. I'm no expert, but Roy was singing your praises too."

"Well, Roy is my best friend, so he's biased, and on top of that, he genuinely loves all pictures of himself," I argue, leaning in over the table.

"You're afraid," she says. "That's the truth. You haven't poured your heart and soul into your work in a long time, so you feel vulnerable, and you're afraid of criticism. It's only natural, but don't let it hold you back."

I'm irritated by her remark, and I'm about to tell her that she doesn't know anything about photography, but I realize that's not the point here. This project is the first thing I've been truly excited about since my portrait series for my graduation, and yes, I am afraid to show it to people. If I'm honest with myself, I do think they're good, but shopping my work around would mean putting myself out there as an artist, and that seems too self-indulgent because I don't feel like an artist.

"You're right," I say after a long pause. "I'm afraid and therefore I'll be keeping the portraits to myself, at least for now. So let me do my thing in private, okay? This is just for me."

"Of course. I'm sorry, I didn't mean to push you." Silva leans in too and covers my hands with her own.

"I know." Meeting her mesmerizing, icy gray eyes, I nod.

"But know one thing," she says. "I believe in you."

62

SILVA

"I thought you hated shopping." Trinny browses the jeans section and pulls out a dark-indigo skinny pair for me.

"I do, but I need some stuff to wear until I'm back to my pre-injury weight." Taking the jeans from her, I study them and sling them over my arm along with a handful of other garments I've chosen.

Trinny nods. "Are you okay? Mentally, I mean, because of the weight gain?"

"Yeah. I think so. Now that I can walk again, I don't feel so out of control. I've been using the gym in Faith's building, and we've gone together a couple of times, so that's been fun."

"Good. Well, for what it's worth, you actually look great with a few extra pounds," she says. "You probably don't believe me, but it's true."

"Thank you. Faith said the same." I smile. "And I believed her, so I suppose that means I believe you too."

"Huh." Trinny walks with me to the dressing room and plonks down on a stool. "Faith is good for you." She raises her voice when I close the dressing room curtain. "So, you're planning on staying there? At her place?"

"For now. I'll move back home soon." I leave it at that because my moving-out date is a subject Faith and I have been avoiding since my cast came off a week ago.

"Do you want to?" she asks. When I don't answer, she fires off the next question. "Does Faith want you to move out?"

"I don't think so." I button up the jeans and open the curtains to get Trinny's opinion. "She suggested I stay a little longer."

"Because it's so nice to wake up together?" Trinny says in a teasing tone. When I turn around, she points to my behind. "Sis, you look amazing in those. Check out your ass. Seriously, look."

As I look myself over, I can't help but agree with her. Yes, my ass and my legs are a little bigger than before, but I still feel attractive, and I know that's because of Faith. She looks at me in a way no one has ever looked at me, and that gives me so much confidence. "Yeah, they're great. I'll take them."

"Wait, try on those shirts." Trinny comes into the dressing room with me and pulls a white one off the hanger. "This will be perfect for your date tonight. Where are you taking her?"

"I made a reservation at that little Italian place you recommended." Buttoning up the shirt, I give myself a nod in the mirror. "Perfect. I'll take this too."

"You don't want to try on the rest?" she asks.

"Nah. I'm done for today. I still need to get flowers."

"Oh my God, you're going all out!" Trinny coos. "You are so cute when you're in love!"

"Hey, I'm not in—" I stop myself there and shake my head with a chuckle. "Okay, I'm totally in love."

"Aww, I love love!" Trinny claps her hands in delight. "Has she told anyone you're together? Or is it too soon? Is she struggling with finding herself attracted to a woman?"

"I don't think that bothers her. It was such a natural process for both of us. She seems entirely at ease. She told her best friend, Roy, a while ago, and she doesn't make a secret of it when we're in public."

"Wow. My little sister is officially dating Faith Astor. For someone who can't even stand being in a store for longer than twenty minutes, dating a famous fashion photographer is quite the leap," Trinny jokes. "What about her family? Have you met any of them while you've been living there?"

"No, she doesn't speak to them very much. From what I gather, they spend birthdays and occasionally the holidays together, but that's about it. I think she misses her half-sister, though."

"Yes, I got that feeling when I mentioned Frankie last time I saw her. It must be difficult. I don't know what I'd do without you." Trinny waits for me to change back into my clothes and follows me to the cashier.

"Yeah, same here," I say and give her a peck on the cheek. We both pause and exchange an uncomfortable glance as that statement suddenly feels loaded. The last time she said that to me was many years ago, but I remember it like it was yesterday. *I don't know what I'd do without you.* It was the day I left for the clinic. If they hadn't sent me there, I may not have been alive today. "Thank you for everything you've done for me. It can't have been easy, constantly worrying about me." Although I've thanked her countless times, I can't say it enough.

"Stop thanking me. You did this. You fought so hard, and I'm proud of you. Ten years ago, it was unimaginable that we'd be shopping for clothes together, and look at you now.

You've tried on a pair of jeans in front of a mirror and admitted that you look good in them."

"Hmm... yes, you're right. I've worried too much about relapsing. I suppose I should have had more trust in my own strength. I'm actually doing really well considering I've had to give up my routine for so long, so I'm really hopeful for the future."

"I'm hopeful too." A flash of emotion crosses Trinny's face, and I know she's relieved. She can take a step back now and stop focusing on me so much. It must have been draining for her, being burdened with such a sense of responsibility, having to check in on me all the time and always cautious, expecting the worst.

"It's my turn," I say, swallowing down the lump in my throat. "I'm going to take care of *you* now, sis."

63

FAITH

"Are those for me?" I take the flowers from Silva and inhale against the long-stemmed white roses. "That's so sweet. Is there a special occasion?"

"No, it's date night, remember?" Silva says, and she chuckles when I blush. I still can't help it; I melt every time she turns up the charm. "You look incredible." She takes in my figure-hugging, knee-length, black dress and black killer heels that bring me to her height, and I'd love to know what's going through her mind. I thought long and hard about what to wear tonight for our first real date. I haven't worn this dress in years, as it made me self-conscious, but tonight I want to look sexy for her and I liked what I saw in the mirror when I put it on. The low cleavage is revealing but not quite low enough to be vulgar, and the wide, leather belt accentuates my waist. My lingerie is not exactly innocent either, and I can't wait to show her what's underneath.

"Thank you. So do you." I wrap my arms around her waist inside her open coat and look her up and down. "Very cute. I see you went shopping. Did you get changed in town?"

"Yeah. I was running a bit late, and I wanted to look nice for you."

"Mmm. Your romantic side is certainly coming out now that you can walk. Are you always this charming on legs?" I joke, taking the flowers to the kitchen to put them in a vase.

"Always." She shoots me a flirty wink. "I'll call for a cab. It's not far, but in those heels..."

"Yes, they're not very practical but I know you like them." As I put on my coat, I try to remember the last time I dressed up like this for a date. It's typical that I've only ever done that for her, a woman. *My woman.*

"I do." Silva puts an arm around me as she leads me out of the door, and I shiver when she lowers her hand to my behind. I love her possessive hold and her assertiveness. It makes me feel giddy and excited, and as we step into the elevator, that dark look in her eyes tells me she wants me.

"Not now," I say when she's swallowing me with her gaze. "We'll never get anywhere if we start now."

"Hey, I'm trying hard not to. Can't you see?" Silva steps away from me and backs herself into a corner, then holds up both hands. "No touching. No kissing. No lifting up that sexy dress to feel your delicious ass or fuck you from behind in those heels until your legs are shaking." She grins. "I'm behaving."

"So am I." Her words make me squirm, and I take a step back too and settle in the other far corner. I like this cat-and-mouse game. It's seriously hot, and I'm not sure how long we'll last without falling into a heady make-out session. "I'm not going to strip for you, or straddle you, or slide my hands into that lovely white shirt of yours," I retort, lowering my eyes to her chest. "I'm also not going to trace your peachy lips with my tongue before I kiss you hard, and last but not least, I'm not—" The door pings open, and I shrug innocently. "Oops. I guess we'll have to save the rest for later."

"Tease. I might have to tease you back after dinner." She wiggles her eyebrows. "Or during dinner."

"Behave." When she lowers her hand to my behind again, I playfully slap it away. My protests are a front because I love the thought of her hand sliding up my thigh under the table. We head outside, and as I get into a cab, I can feel her eyes on my behind. The edges of my hold-ups are visible when I bend over, and knowing she'll appreciate what I'm wearing, I bend a little farther than necessary. Silva has a thing for sexy lingerie; she's made no secret of that. I want her to fantasize about me until we're alone again, and I want her to picture what I'll look like in my black lace set.

"What's on your mind?" she asks, placing a hand on my knee when the cab drives off.

"Wouldn't you like to know?" I say playfully.

"I see." Silva leans in close to whisper in my ear. "I saw what you're wearing." She hooks a finger under the hem of my dress and raises it until she can see the lace. "How do you expect me to behave now?" Licking her lips, she stares at me hungrily. "Want to skip dinner and go back home?"

I throw my head back and laugh. "No chance. You promised me a date."

"I know. I'm only joking. Besides, waiting only makes it more exciting." Silva shoots me a mischievous look. "I went home to pick up some stuff this morning."

"Oh? Are you moving in with me?" I ask. "I'd be delighted if you did." We've had this joking conversation before, but we haven't dared touch the subject in a serious way because it's probably too soon for that. Not for me; I'd love to have her around forever, but I don't want to scare her by bringing it up.

"Very funny," she says. "No, it's just some stuff for tonight."

"Oh. Do tell me." Anticipation balls inside me, as I have an idea of what she's referring to. "What kind of stuff?"

Silva shakes her head slowly and waves a finger at me. "Nuh-uh. You'll have to wait and see."

64

SILVA

Faith's angelic face is glowing in the candlelight, and she looks happy. Trinny was right; this is a very romantic place and I'm glad we came here. The service is impeccable, and the vibe is authentic Italian in its simplicity and charm, which is reflected in their amazing food and the décor. We're surrounded by a huge wine collection displayed on the wall racks, pretty antiques, the owner's family photos, and old maps of Sicily. Faith's leg is resting between mine, her ankle occasionally rubbing my shin. It sends me flying every time she does this, and I'm so aroused that I crave every bit of contact she can give me in this public place. We're eating burrata on toast, grilled artichokes, and swordfish with a puttanesca sauce. It's delicious, but tonight is not about the food. It's about us, having our first official date as a couple.

"You did well," she says with a cheeky smile before taking a bite of her fish. "Best date ever."

"Really?" I try to wipe the wide grin off my face, but it's impossible to keep my cool. I'm so proud to be with her and

I swoon at everything she says or does. I think the feeling is mutual, as Faith is blushing an awful lot tonight.

"Yeah. Amazing. It will be hard to beat this when it's my turn." She smiles. "But I've got some tricks up my sleeve too."

"Do you now?"

"Uh-huh." She bites her lip, and it makes me crazy. "So, how was your day, other than the shopping and picking up naughty stuff from your apartment? Did you have any clients?"

"No. I kept today free for shopping, and I visited a gym not too far from you. It's called Elite. Have you heard of it?"

"Yes. It's for professional athletes, right? Why were you there?" Faith asks.

"I wanted to get a feel for the place. They're looking for staff and I wouldn't mind having an in-house job again. It would save me from traveling so much and I miss being part of a team."

"Oh. How exciting. So they're looking for personal trainers?"

"No, they're recruiting for a sports masseur." I hesitate as I haven't really thought this through until now. "I saw the advertisement online and thought I'd check it out. The general manager was there, and I had a chat with him. He seemed like a good guy and told me I should apply since I have years of experience working with athletes."

"That's so cool. So you're going to do it?"

"I think so. I still love training people, but it seems a waste not to do anything with my qualifications. If they want me and they can't give me enough hours, I'd be happy to work as a PT for them part-time. That way, I'll have the best of both worlds. If they'll have me, of course," I add.

"They'd be crazy not to hire you," Faith says, reaching

for my hand over the table. "You worked with Olympians, didn't you?"

"Yeah. And I loved my job. I gave up because it wasn't good for me mentally at the time, and because I lacked the physical strength due to extreme weight loss, not because I didn't enjoy it. I'm not that young woman anymore, though, and I feel like it's time for a change. I'm older, wiser, stronger. I can handle it this time. I think I'm ready."

"I know you're ready."

I smile, happy Faith is so enthusiastic about the idea. "I don't get this job, it's no big deal. I'll see what else is around and I'll find something eventually. Now that I'm discussing it with you, I'm really warming to the idea of a career change."

"I think it's admirable that you're getting back on the horse," she says.

"Thank you. Your support means a lot to me." I sit back when the waiter leans in to pour us more wine. "I might need to massage you an awful lot in the coming days so I can get back into it," I add jokingly.

"Hey, you know I have no problem with that." Faith laughs. "Hot oil and your hands on me? Anytime, babe. You can start tonight."

"Hmm... maybe I will." I lower my gaze to her cleavage that looks so appetizing in the tight, black dress that I've barely been able to keep my eyes off it. "Looks like it's going to be a memorable night."

"It already is." Her eyes twinkle with flirtation, and she lifts her foot to stroke the inside of my thigh. "I'm so turned on."

"Same. I want you, Faith. I always want you, but right now I can barely wait."

She wiggles in her chair and pushes her breasts forward

as she leans in. "Are you finally going to tell me what you picked up from home?"

Falling into silence, I remember how I used to please women. Always fueled by the need to be in control, it was never about me, and so I had my preferences when it came to sex. I kept my clothes on because I didn't want them to see me naked. I tied them up so they couldn't touch me, I teased them relentlessly until they begged me for release, and I never stayed the night. With Faith, it's different. I've been so comfortable with her that I forgot all about my controlling impulses. I let her have me and I loved every second of her hungry mouth and exploring hands moving over me until I burst. The need to dominate is purely a desire now, and I squeeze my thighs together, imagining Faith tied to the bed with her heels and hold-ups on. I hesitate as I feed her a piece of burrata from my fork. "Do you really want me to tell you right now? In here?"

"Yes." Faith's eyes are intensely focused on me as she twirls the wine around in her glass. "I need to know what to expect."

"Okay..." I watch her chest rise in anticipation. She's pretending to be calm, but I know her well and she's far from it. Perhaps not uncomfortable, but certainly a little nervous. I like that I already have the upper hand, and making her wait gives me a thrill. "Then let me tell you," I say, reaching under the table to stroke her thigh.

65

FAITH

Silva is someone else tonight. From the moment we started discussing this, her demeanor changed the way it did when we were waiting for the elevator after the party. She's in charge, moving around the bed to secure my wrists to the bedframe. My arms are stretched wide, as are my legs, and although I'm still covered by the bedsheets, I suspect that's about to change. It equally excites me and frightens me, but I'm so intrigued and aroused by discovering this new side to her that I have no intention of breaking the ritual-like game by calling the safe word she made me repeat twice.

She told me to strip for her, and I did. Silva has never demanded anything from me until tonight. She's always carefully considered my desires and acted in line with my expectations of her, or with what I thought was within her character, but right now she's circling me like I'm her prey, taking me in with intensity, and I'm aware she's seeing another side of me too. She knows that I want this and that I trust her, otherwise I wouldn't have allowed her to tie me up. I must admit that I've had fantasies along this line, but I always thought they would remain just that. I wasn't an experimental kind of woman before. Sex was just sex to me, and there was nothing particularly mind-blowing about it. In fact, I always considered it quite underwhelming, and I didn't get why people were making such a fuss about it. Since my first night with Silva, my opinion of sex has changed dramatically. I simply can't get enough of her, and I'm eager to learn more about her hidden desires and my own in the process. Being tied up alone has caused an immense physical reaction; just the thought that I'm unable to escape is turning me on and I know my expression reflects how I feel.

"Are you okay?" she asks, placing a warm hand on my wrist. "Is it too tight?"

"No. I'm comfortable," I say, ignoring my racing heart. "What are you going to do to me?" The question is redundant. She told me about her toys in detail over dinner, so I most certainly have an idea, but feeling as helpless as I do now is frustrating. The aching need between my thighs is getting too intense to ignore and I need her to touch me.

Silva shoots me a mischievous grin and avoids the question. "I can promise you one thing. I won't do anything you're uncomfortable with." She runs her thumb over my lips and smiles. "And if you want me to stop at any point, you say the safe word, okay?"

I nod and try to relax as she dims the lights to a low setting. When she walks toward the foot of the bed, my heart is pounding hard, and instinctively, I pull at the restraints. I'm helpless; she could do anything to me now. Anything she wants. Silva watches me for a while without speaking, and my anticipation grows. Her smile is gone, replaced by a thoughtful stare while she takes her time to decide what she'll do to me first. If she's trying to scare me, she's succeeding, but I remind myself that I trust her and that she's not going to hurt me.

Without warning, she grabs hold of the bedsheets, pulls them down, and drops them to the floor. I gasp at the unexpected action and try to close my legs, but I can't. Although I feel vulnerable, anxious, and exposed, wetness pools between my thighs. I'm still in my heels and my lingerie, but she told me to take off my panties and I know she can see how aroused I am.

"Are you still okay?" Silva tilts her head as she regards me, then lowers her gaze to my throbbing, swollen center.

"Uh-huh," I say in a strangled, high-pitched voice. "Yes, I'm okay."

"Good." She inches closer to take in my most private parts, and I hold my breath when she leans in to kiss me there. My hips shoot up and a strangled moan escapes me. Being restrained has caused me to be hypersensitive, and I can barely handle the delicious rush that shoots between my legs. She traces her tongue over the entire length of my center, immediately sending me to the edge. Straightening herself, Silva closes her eyes as she licks my juices from her lips and I'm positive I've never seen anything so sexy. She takes off her clothes in a teasingly slow manner but leaves her boxers and sports bra on. She won't get naked, at least not yet. She's the one in charge and she wants me to know that. Crawling onto the bed in between my legs and raising herself above me on her hands and knees, she stares into my eyes as if searching for unspoken permission to do whatever it is she wants to do to me. When I nod, she smiles and leans in so close I can feel her heat on my face. Her breath is tickling my skin, seducing me, and I want all of her. I raise my head to kiss her, but she pulls back with a smirk and shakes her head. This will happen on her terms, in her time. She's so self-assured, even a bit cocky. I'm desperate to run my hands over her curves, and I'm not sure what's stronger; my need for release or my desire to touch her in return because now that I can't, I want it more than ever. Her mouth touches mine in a featherlight caress, and when she deepens the kiss and parts her lips, a ripple effect of spasms course through my entire body, and I can taste myself on her tongue.

"I've been wanting this for a very long time," she says, moving a hand in between us to trace my hips. "You, like this, all to myself... You taste delicious." I'm hoping she'll kiss me again, but she crawls back and gets off the bed to find something in a bag on the floor.

"What's that?" I ask when she takes out a short, whip-like tool with tassels at the end. It's black and made of leather, and that doesn't surprise me.

"It's a flogger. Don't worry, I won't do anything scary. I just want to test what you like."

66

SILVA

The tension in the bedroom is almost palpable as I approach Faith with the flogger, and I'm in my element. I'm aware I need to tread carefully as I want to make her feel good, not terrified. There's no space for real fear here, only anticipation and trust. She's nervous, but that only heightens the sensation when I drag it over her breasts to caress her nipples. They're already hard as rocks and the flogger leaves a trail of goose bumps on her skin. The soft strokes of the leather make her moan, and when I drag it lower, she wiggles her hips.

"Is that okay?" I ask.

"Mmm yes, that feels good." She knows where I'm going with this, and she can't wait. I linger on her belly, tickling and teasing her. Her chest rises and falls fast, and although her eyes are still fixed on me, her lashes are fluttering and threatening to close.

"Please," she says through heavy breaths. "Lower."

"Lower?" I drag the flogger down a little, but instead of stroking her, I pull it back and give her a quick, firm slap on her left thigh.

"Ah!" Faith's eyes shut tight, she bites her lip, and a frown appears between her eyes.

"Too hard?"

"No." Her eyes meet mine and she gives me a nod. I've seen this look before with other women, but never as intense as with Faith. She wants more. Much more.

Repeating the action, but a little harder this time, I watch her as she tries to squeeze her thighs together.

"More," she whispers, her gaze pleading.

"Are you sure?" Without waiting for an answer, as it's already written all over her face, I strike her again with more force. Her glistening center tells me she's desperate for release, but I want to take my time with her. Having planned this since the moment I told her about my fantasies, I'm craving to own her completely and wholly. Five more strikes and she's tilting her head from side to side, clamoring to free her wrists from the restraints. I aim my last strike between her legs, and she cries out while she rolls her hips. Her eyes shut tight and her jaw clenched, Faith needs a moment before she opens them again to look at me. "Do it again."

Shaking my head with a teasing smile I step back, and she looks disappointed when I drop the flogger to the floor. I massage her thighs, tracing the red marks the flogger has left. Placing soft kisses on her belly, I inhale the intoxicating scent of her skin. God, I worship her. Her mind, her body, her soul... Faith is moaning and twisting while she tugs at the restraints, and I know she'll like my next toy even more. The vibrator buzzes softly as I turn it on and bring it between her thighs. Her lips part, and she sucks in a breath when I hold it just above her center. She desperately wants it, but each time she raises herself, I pull it away, making her wait.

"Please," she whispers, restlessly moving as much as she can. "Please, do it."

I wait for at least thirty seconds before I move the vibrator to her clit, touching her so lightly that I'm surprised at her reaction. She gasps and shakes, then lifts her hips as I withdraw it and give her a slap on her thigh. The sensation of almost climaxing followed by the sting of my hand is effective; I love her hungry eyes and her loud moans and repeat the action over and over until she's heaving and pleading.

"I need you to make me come," Faith murmurs in frustration as she tries to close her legs to no avail. Her eyes follow me as I kneel next to my bag again and pull out a harness. She stares at it, wide-eyed.

"Have you seen one of these before?" I ask.

"Yes. But never in real life."

"Would you like me to use it?"

"Yes," she says as I step into it and fasten it around my thighs. Securing the shaft to the harness, I take great pleasure in seeing the change in her expression. She's not only curious; she looks like she longs for me to fuck her with it. "Come here." She lifts her head but is unable to move anything else. "I want you on top of me. I want to feel your body."

I get on the bed and take my time caressing her gorgeous curves. Letting my fingers slide over her breasts and her stomach, I can hardly wait to make her come harder than ever before. Hovering over her, I lean in to kiss her, and she welcomes my mouth with a hungry moan. Kissing Faith feels heavenly as always, but tonight there's an urgency in her kiss that sets me on fire. I move back and pull at the ties to free her legs, then move up to undo her wrists. She immediately wraps her arms about my neck and kisses me fiercely. The rubbing of the harness against my sensitive flesh brings me close as I lower myself on top of her and grind against her.

The moment I slide into her carefully and slowly, she welcomes me with a deep moan against my lips, and we start moving together. Faith wraps her legs around me and we're so in sync that it feels like we're flying higher and higher with each thrust as we hold each other tight. I lift my head to look at her. She's all ecstasy; her hazy gaze, her furrowed brows, her glistening lips, and the tiny drops of sweat that pearl on her forehead. Clawing my neck, she tenses up and releases a carnal noise that cuts right through me. It's loud and deep and long, and it doesn't stop after she gasps for air. I suspected it would be intense for her, but I've never seen her like this. I don't have time to process it as my own orgasm rushes over me and takes me away. Nothing compares to the two of us together; Faith takes me to places beyond me, and I lose all sense of reality until she wipes a lock of hair away from my forehead and whispers my name.

"Silva," she says, staring up at me with a huge smile on her face. "What have you done to me?"

67

FAITH

"Regga did it. He walked out on a shoot." I hold up my phone to show Silva the tweet Roy sent me the link to. The account belongs to a model, who thanks Regga for standing up for her, and the tweet already has thousands of shares. "And not just any shoot. It was the yearly look book shoot for NY models, a model agency. Apparently, some of the models were scrutinized by their agent when they turned up a pound heavier than the previous year. I wasn't sure if he was serious about quitting, but he went through with it. That was a week's worth of work he threw away."

Silva's smile widens as she reads it. "That's fantastic, babe." She runs a hand through my hair and leans in to kiss my forehead. "Well, not for the model, of course, but for the cause. So, is it time for that big article now?"

"That was the plan. Regga said he would contact me, so I'll wait to hear from him." Before I've even uttered the words, my phone rings, and I'm delighted to hear his cheerful voice as I put him on speaker.

"Faith. Did you see it?"

"I did, just now."

"Good, that means the word is spreading," he says. "Are you busy tomorrow?"

I chuckle when Silva shakes her head vigorously. We were supposed to go to a spa together, but it looks like she won't mind if we postpone it. "I can make time."

"Great. My friend has confirmed the interview for the *New York Times*. Me, you, Elsie, and four models from NY agency. I tried to get more models onboard, but many are not comfortable about speaking up, and a couple of others who were willing initially have changed their minds. I can't blame them. They're young and desperate for their careers to take off, but I'm confident that seven people is enough to cause a significant stir. One of the models is Malay Butomi, by the way, so that should give us even more leverage."

My eyes widen as I turn to Silva for a split second. "Wow. She's huge." Even Silva, who has very little interest in fashion, knows who Malay is. She's been gracing the covers of most fashion magazines lately, and she's just signed a contract with a big network to film a reality series on her life.

"Yup. Between us, we should get quite some traction." Regga clears his throat. "Anyway, tomorrow, two p.m., my place. Bring Silva too. We could have some food and catch up afterward. I'll message you the address."

"Thank you. I'll be there." Even though this is about to cause the biggest shift in my career, all I can think of is that I'll be visiting Regga Ibrahimovic's house, as I still can't help but fangirl a little. When I first became familiar with his work many years ago, I would have never guessed he would be my personal hero one day.

"You go, girl!" After I hang up, Silva lifts me up and spins me around. "This will cause so much upheaval."

"Yeah, it's really good timing, right after the articles that came out during New York Fashion Week. Brands will have to take a stance on the matter, and everyone will be watching them."

"It's excellent timing." Silva pulls me in and kisses me. "I'm so proud of you, babe."

Admittedly, I feel kind of proud of me too. For once, I haven't lost a battle; I've won one, and that feels good. "Will you come with me?" I ask, smiling against her lips.

"I'd love to." She hesitates. "But if it's an in-depth article, they're bound to ask some questions about your personal life too, and what if they ask about me because I'm there? Your family doesn't even know you're with a woman."

"I don't think it's a big deal," I say with a shrug. "I'm not even sure who I'm supposed to come out to except for maybe my mom and my sister. Since Mom's not picking up her phone at the moment and my sister seems too busy for me, they'll have to find out this way." I take her hands and meet her eyes. "Honestly, I hope they'll ask me about you. I'm so proud to have you as my girlfriend and I want the world to know."

"I feel the same," Silva says, then glances at the photograph of my sister in the kitchen. "I'm surprised they haven't contacted you yet. They must have heard about you and Valerie and everything that's been going on."

"Yeah, I'm surprised too, but please don't feel sorry for me. I'm used to not having them around. When Mom feels like herself again, she'll call me, and we'll arrange to get together." I'm hoping my brave smile will disguise the stab of unease I feel because, in truth, I've never gone this long without seeing Frankie. We were never super close. Our age difference was too big for us to be friends when we were younger, but we used to speak regularly after I moved out, and as her older sister, she would often come to me when she needed to talk. I'm starting to wonder if maybe she does know what happened and she's distanced herself from me to stay in Valerie's good books. Shaking it off, I tell myself to stop speculating and focus on the interview instead. Tomorrow is a big day, and the most important thing is that we get our message across; body positivity, diversity, and acceptance above all. "Seriously, it's fine," I continue. "I'll see them when I see them."

68

SILVA

"We want to advocate change in an industry that praises young women for their appearance when they're at their worst," Faith says confidently to the journalist. "But that is only the very beginning. The beauty and fashion industry need to be aware of the ripple effect body-shaming causes in a society where most feel that they're not good enough physically because the standards are so unrealistic. We need more diversity in brand representation, and that includes size, skin color, age, and gender. We need kids to know it's okay to be different, and most of all, that it's okay to be themselves and celebrate what makes them unique." She pauses. "According to the statistics, approximately thirty million Americans currently live with an eating disorder. In reality, that number is likely to be much higher, as eating disorders are more often than not kept hidden. They're the last taboos—diseases of the mind that are regularly dismissed as diets or functional coping mechanisms. But there's nothing functional about starving yourself, throwing up your guts, or working out until you faint, because you're comparing yourself to unrealistic standards. Like so many others, I struggle with this too."

"Thank you, Faith." The journalist makes a note on her iPad. "Would you mind telling me a bit more about that?" When Faith hesitates, she puts a hand on her arm. "I'd like a little bit of backstory. I promise I won't make this about you."

Faith nods and shifts in her seat. "Sure," she says, and takes a deep breath. "I'm bulimic. It's something I've battled for most of my adult life." She shoots me a sweet smile as she leans into me. "I've had ups and downs over the years, but I've learned to love myself more and I'm doing really well. Silva, my girlfriend, has helped me tremendously. Without her, I would have never admitted I had a problem, and it's because of her that I'm able to talk about this."

I smile back at Faith and put an arm around her. We've casually talked about our relationship with the journalist; how we met, how we grew close, and how we fell in love. Her friendly demeanor is reassuring, and her questions don't feel as intrusive as I expected. This isn't easy for Faith, but she's coping well, and she sounds confident with her answers.

"The fashion industry also has decades to make up for the lack of cultural diversity and acceptance," she continues, then turns to Elsie so she can chip in.

"Exactly. Where are all our BIPOC models? Where are the role models we can actually identify with? Where are the ones that *I* can identify with?" Elsie concludes with more statistics on marketing, and Regga finally tells his side of the story. With a long career in fashion photography behind him, he's seen it all, and he's surprised how little has changed in terms of industry culture.

We're sitting around the dining table in his stunning

living room. It's hard to believe he lives here on his own; it seems like too much space for one person. His two-story apartment on the sixteenth floor of a Manhattan high-rise is slick and so minimal and white that it feels like a gallery. When we arrived, he gave us a tour, and we had coffee while we waited for his journalist friend to arrive. His photo studio on the top floor looks out over a private roof terrace with a fabulous entertainment space and three-sixty views. I could tell that even he was a little nervous, but I suppose it's not every day he throws the fashion industry under the bus. The models told their stories first so they could leave early. The four of them were aged between sixteen and eighteen and I was appalled to hear how they'd been treated by their agency. Two requested to stay anonymous, but the youngest model and Malay both felt comfortable being named in the article.

"I think I have enough," the journalist finally says before turning off her recording device. Thank you all for being so open with me. This has been incredibly insightful." She pats Regga's shoulder. "And thank you, my friend, for setting it up."

"Let's hope we all get something out of it," Regga says with a smile. "Join us for a glass of wine, will you?" He gets up when the door buzzes. "Give me a minute. I have another guest joining us for drinks."

When he returns moments later with Trinny by his side, Faith and I exchange a puzzled glance.

"Trinny, what are you doing here?" I ask, getting up to greet her. Trinny is the last person I expected to see here. As far as I'm aware, she and Regga only met once, and I had no idea they'd even exchanged numbers.

"Regga invited me, so I came straight from work, hence the formal attire," she says, removing her suit jacket. The way she forces a smile immediately makes me think she's hiding something. My first observation is that she's not gushing about his décor. Trinny is easily impressed when it comes to interior design, and it would be very out of character for her not to take everything in before asking a million questions about the art on his walls or his original art deco bar. *Has she been here before?* She's also wearing lipstick, which is peculiar, and as she follows Regga to the kitchen, it's like they're not quite sure how to behave around each other.

"Are you thinking what I'm thinking?" Faith asks in a whisper when they're out of sight. "She's wearing lipstick."

"I know." I pause as I hear Trinny and Regga laugh in the open kitchen. "Do you really think they're..."

"Yeah. No doubt about it." Faith chuckles. "Wow... I'd never put the two of them together, but they're both good people and I can actually see it working." She hushes me when Regga comes back with a bottle of wine. "Don't ask. You might embarrass them, and she'll tell you eventually."

69

FAITH

"I bet that's Roy," I say, sighing when the doorbell rings. "Who else would show up unannounced at nine p.m.?" Silva and I were settling into a quiet night with a movie, and I'm not in the mood for Roy taking control of the remote and demanding we watch something with his favorite hunks in the lead.

Tired but satisfied after a long day of shooting and developing, I want to switch off and cuddle up with my girlfriend. I had an early morning shoot for a magazine, and after that, I arranged a private shoot with my assistant Shahari. It's been fun focusing on my own work again and I'm pleased with the results. With his bushy beard and long hair, he was a gloriously rugged subject. Just like with Silva, Roy, and Elsie, I used my bed as the setting and shot him in black and white on film. My four main portraits are now lying side by side on my desk: Silva naked with her cast, Roy looking dapper and handsome in silk pajamas, Elsie flaunting her curves, and Shahari in a robe with his dog beside him. He'd never been to my apartment, and I could tell he was intrigued to learn that I lived with a woman. We talked a lot during the shoot, and when I told him about Silva and me, I managed to capture that ever-present curiosity in his eyes, the eager look of someone who wants to learn and grow in their craft. Shahari is a talented photographer, but like most aspiring fashion photographers, starting as an assistant is often the only way to make contacts and get noticed. He stuck by me when shoot after shoot got canceled, and although the situation was eating into his paycheck, he hasn't gone looking for another employer yet. Whether these photographs will ever be more than my private collection doesn't matter. It's keeping me distracted while we wait for the article to be published tomorrow. "I'm not sure if I can handle Roy right now," I say, deciding to ignore the doorbell.

"Oh, come on. I love Roy." When I make no effort to move, Silva gets up and presses the buzzer on the intercom. "It's not him," she says, glancing at the small screen. "It looks like your sister."

"What?" For a moment, I think she's joking, but a minute later, Frankie's face appears in the doorway. She looks tired and fragile, far from the glowing face I've been seeing on social media. "Frankie, come here." I rush over and she drops her weekend bag and hugs me.

"I'm sorry to bother you," she says in a thin voice.

"You never bother me. I'm so glad you're here." I inch back and cup her face. "Hey, what's wrong?"

"Nothing." She shrugs. "I'm just so tired and I need some rest before LA Fashion Week starts. I'm sick of being on my own in hotel rooms and I don't want to be home either. Mom and Dad are constantly arguing. I think they're going to divorce again. I stayed with a friend for a week, but she keeps throwing parties and there's no privacy. I tried sleeping pills, but they make me so drowsy in the morning that I can't get up."

"Oh God, you shouldn't take that stuff in the first place. Come in and sit down. I'll get you some tea and something to eat."

"I'm fine, I'm not hungry." When she takes off her coat, I notice she looks incredibly frail, and her shoulders are slumped in the oversized sweatshirt she's wearing.

"No discussion, Frankie. You need to eat something."

"But I'm doing the bikini shows next week," she protests. "I'm opening for the McKaren show. Really, I just want to sleep."

"If you don't eat, you'll collapse during the McKaren show," I say and head for the kitchen to get her a plate of leftovers from the fridge. "Here. Silva cooked it. It's all very nutritious and healthy."

"Who's Silva?" As if she's been in her own world, Frankie only then spots Silva, who has been by my side all along. "Oh, I'm so sorry. I'm Frankie." She holds out her boney hand for Silva to shake. "Are you Faith's assistant?"

"No. I'm..."

When Silva hesitates at the question, I step in. "Silva is my girlfriend."

"Your girlfriend?" Frankie frowns as she studies me. She looks Silva up and down, then glances around the living room and notices the burning candles and the blanket on the couch in front of the paused TV. "As in..."

"Yes. We're dating."

"Huh." Frankie stares up at Silva again, her eyes wide in surprise. "I apologize. I didn't mean to be rude, but I didn't know my sister was gay let alone that she had a girlfriend."

"That's okay, she didn't know either," Silva jokes. "And we haven't known each other for that long."

"Sit down and eat up," I say, handing her the plate. "We can talk later, but you look like you're very low on fuel and I'm worried about you."

Frankie props her feet up on the couch, sniffs the vegetable couscous, and takes a careful bite. "Mmm." She takes another bite, then starts wolfing it down. "Jesus, that's good," she mumbles through a mouthful. "Silva, you're a genius."

I make us tea while Frankie eats, and I get her a bottle of sparkling water and an apple. "Have this too," I say, placing it in front of her on the coffee table. I see she's already polished off the plate. "Would you like anything more? I can make you a sandwich or order you something."

"No, thank you, I'm good." Frankie downs her water and sits back. "Wow. I clearly needed that."

"Do you want to go to bed?" I ask.

"I'm too exhausted to get up. Can I stay here with you for a little while?" She curls up in the corner of the couch; she looks tiny with her knees pulled up.

"Of course." I pull the blanket over her and stroke her hair. Her eyelids flutter, and I can tell she's so tired she'll be out within seconds. My heart breaks for her; she's too young to live this life, and I curse my mother for encouraging her into this career.

Frankie smiles at my touch and she looks up at me. "Thank you, Faith. You look happy," she says before she falls into a deep sleep.

70

SILVA

"Faith had a meeting, she won't be long," I say when Frankie comes out of the shower, wrapped in a robe with a towel on her head. "Coffee?"

"Yes, please." She yawns and stretches her arms over her head. "I had the best sleep ever. I don't even remember going to bed."

I don't mention that I carried her to bed and that Faith undressed her and tucked her in. Or that she snored so loudly we could hear her all night. Poor thing. It must be hard to always be on the move, to constantly look your best and smile like you mean it. "You were pretty out of it," I say, pouring her coffee. "Are you feeling better?"

"Much better." Frankie sits at the kitchen table and sips her coffee while she watches me make sourdough toast with sliced avocado. "So how did you and Faith meet?"

"I'm her PT," I say with a chuckle. "I know, it's cliché, but there's more to it than that. I broke my leg and she offered me her guest room while I recovered."

"I take it that guest room wasn't used much," Frankie jokes.

"No, not much." I smile. "I'm moving back to my own place soon, but we keep putting it off because we really enjoy being together. I care about Faith a lot."

"I could see she cares about you too." Frankie returns my smile. "So, do you really think she's gay? Aren't you worried it's a phase?" She bites her lip and winces. "I'm sorry, that came out wrong. I don't want to worry you. She's just never shown any signs of interest in women."

"That's okay. I understand your concern, but I'm not worried," I say. "It's real."

"Good. Because I've never seen her look as relaxed and happy as she did last night." Frankie pauses. "Faith has always been restless and well... a little sad, I suppose. I never understood why she had such bad self-esteem because I've always looked up to her. But with you, I saw a different side to her." She sighs. "I've missed her. I've missed my big sister."

"Then maybe you should tell her that because she's missed you too."

"Yeah." Frankie shakes her head and buries her face in her hands. "I feel bad that I haven't called her back in months. Since my career took off, I've been so absorbed in this whirlwind lifestyle that I completely forgot about everyone important in my life. I've been selfish," she says with regret ringing through her voice.

"Hey, don't beat yourself up about it. You're here now, and she's been worried about you." I observe Frankie as I slide a plate of avocado toast toward her. "*Should* she be worried about you?"

"No..." Frankie eyes the toast and hesitates. I don't think she has an eating disorder, at least, not yet. She looks at food with calculation, not with fear. There's no panic in her eyes when she's presented with calories; she's simply weighing her options. Food versus paycheck. It's ridiculous that hunger equals success in her industry, and it makes me so angry to see a young woman in the prime of her life looking so unhealthy. Not because she chooses to, but because others have decided that for her. And those very people could push her into a lifelong battle with food and a hateful relationship with her body. "No, I'm okay," she says. "But it's good to be here." She waits for a beat, then pulls the plate closer and starts eating.

"I'm glad you're here. It's nice to finally meet you." I eat my own toast and we sit there in silence with the TV on in the background. I've been waiting for the news, as Faith and some others were asked to go to the studio after the article came out this morning. The newspaper with the three-page spread is on the kitchen table, and I'm dying to show Frankie, but I want her to eat first.

"So, what's Faith been up to these days?" she asks after swallowing her last bite. "I heard she walked out of a shoot for *Zero* magazine, and I was meaning to ask her about it, but life got in the way."

"Yeah, about that..." I stop when I hear a reporter say Faith's name and beckon Frankie to follow me into the living room. "Your sister's on the news, let's go watch it."

"What?" Frankie turns the volume up high and gasps when she sees Faith's picture on the news along with six others.

"This courageous collective of photographers and models are boycotting the fashion industry and have vowed to only work on body-positive projects in the future. The movement started when Faith Astor, a thirty-three-year-old fashion photographer and It-girl, got into a disagreement with Valerie Marquez, senior editor of Zero *magazine, over body-shaming behavior toward one of the models. After quitting the job, Miss Astor inspired two other*

photographers to do the same, and four of America's top models have joined them in their quest. Their statement caused immense upheaval throughout the fashion industry when they spoke up in an article published in the New York Times *early this morning,"* the reporter says.

"Jesus." Frankie slams a hand in front of her mouth when the reporter turns to Faith, who is sitting in the studio with four people she clearly recognizes by face. "Why did no one tell me about this?"

"The interview only took place yesterday, and you were in no state to talk last night." I feel myself swell with pride as I watch Faith straighten her back and bravely face the reporter.

"I worry a lot," she says. "I worry about people I care about, I worry for these four young women, and I worry for all those other models out there who lose their periods or grow excess body hair due to malnutrition, not to mention the twisted relationship with food they'll develop for life. Because for most, the downward spiral that has been set in motion never ends. We too have been a part of this, but now is the time we start saying no and acknowledge the huge issue that's been ignored for decades. The industry standard is unrealistic and in no way a representation of the society we live in. Starvation should not be glorified, and diversity should be celebrated."

When the reporter focuses his attention on Elsie, I see Frankie wiping a tear from her cheek.

"Are you okay?" I ask, rubbing her shoulder.

"Yeah." She swallows hard, then quietly watches the rest of the interview.

71

FAITH

I feel strange as I head back to my apartment. It's been a crazy morning with the article coming out, and then being invited for a major live TV interview only two hours later. We barely had time to get ready and make our way there, and it's only now that I can breathe steadily again as the adrenaline that has been pumping through my veins is starting to subside. I'm looking forward to seeing Silva, who has been my rock throughout all of this, and Frankie, who I assume is still there. My phone is constantly pinging with messages, but everything can wait. For now, I'll ignore the storm and focus on my little sister, who is finally back in my life.

Foolishly, I had no idea she was struggling and that her life wasn't as perfect as I envisioned. How naïve. If anyone should know better, it's me, but through her beautiful social media posts and short, happy messages, I failed to see what really was going on. This world is too much for her and she needs to get out, or at least have a sabbatical before she returns, or she'll burn herself out. I curse myself for not trying harder with her, and I curse our mother for being so blinded by her shitty husband that she didn't pay attention to her own daughter. It's no wonder her father didn't pick up on it either; he's been too busy bragging about his daughter being a supermodel to notice her fatigue.

As I let myself in, I wonder if Frankie has seen the interview, but that question is answered when she runs up to me and falls around my neck. I hug her back and pull her against me, and she sniffs and buries her face against my shoulder. I feel her warm tears trickling down my skin and hold her tighter, sensing she needs this. The way she latches on to me makes me wonder if anyone has really looked after her recently. She's only eighteen, practically still a child.

"I'm so proud of you," she whispers, then inches back to look at me through bloodshot eyes. "You're so right. You're so, so right," she says through sobs. "I haven't had my period in months, and I'm worried I'll never be able to have children if I carry on like this. Because I want children, you know? Not right now, but I want a family. A real one, not a dysfunctional one like ours."

"Frankie..." I choke up at hearing this. "I had no idea how bad it was."

"It didn't even click that it had something to do with not eating until I heard you in that interview this morning. I kept thinking I was pregnant because I was seeing this guy, but we used protection and the tests were always negative."

"You have a boyfriend?" I ask.

"No, I was casually seeing someone." Frankie shrugs. "It's over now and that's okay. He was probably a bit old for me anyway. We didn't have much to talk about."

The lump of unease expands in my core, and I feel sick. "How old?" Frankie remains silent. "Seriously, Frankie. How old?"

"Forty-one," she whispers as if deep down, she knows nothing about this is right.

"Who was it?" I'm aware that I have to stop interrogating her as I may push her away, but I can't help myself. My protective instincts have kicked in and I want to kill whoever has been sleeping with my little sister. I mentally scroll through the list of men I've seen her posing in pictures with.

"He didn't want anyone to know we were seeing each other. He said what we had was special, that it was just something between me and him. I promised not to tell anyone."

"Who was it?" I ask again.

"Michael Porter," she finally says. "The art director. We met during a shoot in November."

Holding onto my stomach, I suppress the violent urge to vomit as everything clicks into place. Why he never wanted to be photographed with me. Why he never invited me on work trips and always used the excuse that he would be too busy to spend time with me. Why it was always just him and me, our little secret. God knows how many other women or girls he was seeing. I despise him for preying on Frankie, and I despise myself for ever being involved with him. I can't tell Frankie; she's too fragile and it's best she never finds out.

"What? It's not like it's illegal."

"No, it's not, but it might as well be. He was supposed to look after you, not sleep with you. You're eighteen."

"Why are you yelling at me?" Frankie starts crying again, and I regret raising my voice.

"I'm sorry, honey. I didn't mean to," I say, stroking her hair. "I'm glad you told me." I cup her face and meet her eyes. "Do you promise me it's over? The age difference is not even my biggest issue. You can't trust him."

"Yeah, it's over. I haven't spoken to him in weeks."

Frankie narrows her eyes at me. "You sound like you know him. Personally, I mean."

"I do," I say and leave it at that. "I'm sorry I raised my voice to you. You can stay here as long as you want, and I'm going to look after you, okay? I'll make sure you eat properly and get enough sleep. It's important. You only have one life and one body, and you need to take care of it."

Frankie nods and wipes her tears. "But what about LA Fashion Week? I keep thinking, *one more job, one more shoot, and then I can eat*, but the work never stops. It's so hard because unlike most of my fellow models, I actually *want* to eat. I'm hungry all the time and I don't like feeling light-headed."

"Forget about the shows," I say, furious with everyone who has been controlling Frankie's mind and weight to make money off her back. I could kick myself for assuming she was okay, and all I want to do now is make it better for her. "Cancel them, please."

"That will be throwing away my career," she says.

"What's more important to you? Your current career or your future?" When she doesn't answer, I press on. "Join us. Join me and Regga, Elsie, Malay, and the rest. I promise you, many more will follow. You may not get all the jobs anymore, but you'll get work from brands that have decent values and want to set the right example."

The hopeful look in Frankie's eyes breaks my heart even more. It's her innocence that slays me. Through all of this, at least she hasn't lost her innocence. "Do you really think so?"

"Yes, I do. You'll have friends on your side, people who will care about you and support you." My eyes well up as I pull her into another hug. "I love you, Frankie. Please let me look after you."

72

SILVA

Although I moved to the kitchen to give Faith and Frankie space to talk, I heard everything, and I'm shocked to my core. Poor Faith and poor Frankie. Faith did the right thing by not telling her that they've been dating the same man. Two sisters, fifteen years apart. It's disgusting, and if Faith wants to take him down, I'll be right there with her. I need to get my stuff from the office, as I have a client to visit, and when I cross the living room, they both turn to look at me. Faith has her arm around Frankie and she's stroking her hair in a motherly way.

"Hey," she says. "I was suggesting we'd go out for lunch. Want to join us?"

"I'd love to, but I can't. I'm working." I smile at Frankie. "How are you?"

"A little better," she says in a soft voice. She's much sweeter than I imagined her from the photographs I've seen, where she poses like a pro with huge shades and a pouty mouth. "You're really nice, Silva." She turns to Faith. "You need to hang on to her. She's a keeper."

"I know." Faith's mouth stretches into a huge smile, and

she blows me a kiss. "Frankie will be staying here for a while. You're okay with that, right?"

"Of course. This is your apartment. You don't have to ask me."

"I do, though. You live here."

I'm about to say that I'll be moving out soon, but I know just as well as Faith that she'll bat her long lashes at me and convince me to stay longer in a matter of seconds. I'm totally crazy about her, and every morning I wake up next to her feels like a true blessing. "I suppose I do." I walk over to her and kiss her on the cheek. "We'll have to talk about it, though. Me living here, I mean."

"I know," she agrees. Faith looks tired. It's not just the interviews that have drained her; learning about Michael dating her little sister has clearly added a lot of stress to her agenda. But she's hiding it well with a smile. Either that, or she's so happy to have Frankie here that she's able to ignore the latter for now.

"Oh, come on. Admit it. You don't want to be apart for even a day," Frankie says, nudging Faith. "And the eyes you're giving her? It's teenage style. Even I don't act like that. This seems to work, so why would you go back to living in separate places again? It makes no sense."

Faith and I laugh at her youthful honesty, and I feel my cheeks flush. "Yeah..."

"Yeah..." Frankie repeats, mimicking my voice. "Besides, I want to get to know you better, so stick around, will you?"

"Yes, stick around," Faith chips in as she shoots me a wink over her shoulder.

"I will."

"Promise?" she asks. She makes it sound like a light-hearted comment, but I know it's not.

"I promise, babe," I say and blow her a kiss. I grab my

bag from the office, then stop to turn before I leave. *Why not?* is all I can think as I look into her eyes. *Why the hell not?* I trust in our future, and I don't doubt her feelings for me. "I'll pack my things on the weekend."

"Did you mean what you said about packing your stuff?" Faith asks after Frankie has gone to bed. She props herself against me on the couch and pulls the blanket over us.

"Yes. If it's okay with you."

Faith's eyes well up as she takes my hand. "Yes, yes, of course," she whispers and leans in to kiss me. "You're moving in with me..."

"Are you sure you're comfortable with it?"

"Silva," Faith says. "I want you in my life, always. I want you here, next to me. You complete me."

I kiss her back and smile against her lips. "You complete me too. You're everything to me." Moving in with her after such a short time together is a crazy thought, yet nothing has ever made more sense. "I'll ask Trinny to help me pack."

"I'll help you." Faith sounds so eager it makes me laugh.

"No, you have enough on your plate. Please, let me worry about it," I say, kissing the tip of her nose. "By the way, I heard back from the gym this morning. They've invited me over for an interview."

"Babe, that's amazing. Why didn't you tell me sooner?"

"Well, it's been a hectic day for you," I say with a shrug. "With the article and the interview and Frankie... I overheard your conversation."

Faith flinches. "Yes, that was quite some news." She rubs her temple and shakes her head. "I still can't believe it. Michael is going to pay for what he did."

"What are you going to do?" I ask. "Do you want to talk about it?"

"Not now. I've done enough talking for one day," she says. But I don't want Frankie to know. She'll be furious and hurt, and she might go and see him. I don't want her anywhere near him ever again, but I might pay him a private visit."

73

FAITH

"Faith, what are you doing here?" Michael opens the door a little but doesn't invite me in. "It's super early. I was sleeping."

After lying awake all night and feeling my rage grow to unbearable levels, I couldn't take it any longer and got up at seven a.m. to take a cab to his place. Silva tried to stop me, but by the time she woke up I was already fully dressed and slipped out of the door before she could process what was happening. "You," I say, pushing the door open so hard it slams against the wall. Stepping inside, my eyes spit fire as I look up at him. "You sad, filthy, pathetic excuse for a man." The smell of heavy cologne in his apartment makes me sick, and I try not to think of the many times I've woken up here. It's hard to believe I used to like that smell; that I used to like *him*. That I used to make myself at home here and take long baths while he worked.

"Wait. What the fuck is this about? You can't just come in here and shout at me. Jesus, I'm barely awake." Michael tries to nudge me back out of the door, but I push him away. "Get out, Faith. Whatever this is, we can talk about it later, but this isn't a good time."

"Oh, it's not a good time for you, is it?" I huff. "Finding out you cheated on my sister with me and vice versa wasn't convenient for me either, and I'm sure Frankie would agree if she knew."

"Michael?" A young woman comes out of his bedroom and stands behind him. She's blonde, pretty, in her early twenties, and her young body is wrapped in white sheets. "What's going on?"

"Your boyfriend is a lying piece of scum who sleeps with vulnerable girls and manipulates them into thinking they have something special and secretive, that's what's going on." I turn my attention to the woman but lower my voice, as she has nothing to do with this and it's not fair to yell at her. "Did he tell you to keep your relationship quiet?"

She stares at me wide-eyed but doesn't answer.

"That's what I thought. Be careful with him and consider yourself warned."

"Honey, do you mind if Faith and I talk in private?" he asks in a sickeningly sweet tone. "It's nothing. I'll explain everything later."

The woman shuffles on the spot and hesitates before she shakes her head. She may be young, but she's not naïve. "No. I'd like to hear this."

"Seriously, Bella. This is between me and—"

"Leave her," I interrupt him. I'm sure she'll benefit from what I have to say." I try to calm myself down because I feel an overwhelming urge to punch him. "You stay away from Frankie, do you hear me? If I even so much as suspect you've spoken to her, I will make your life a living hell."

Michael's shoulders drop in defeat, and he remains quiet for long moments before he finally speaks. "I didn't know she was your sister," he says. "Honestly, I had no idea. You don't even have the same last name."

"That's a bullshit excuse, Michael. Everyone knows she's my sister. The whole world knows she's my sister. And even if I gave you the benefit of the doubt, that doesn't take away that you're a lying, cheating, narcissist." I've said what I wanted to say, and I know I should leave now, but it doesn't feel enough. "Was this some kind of game to you? Who's next? My mother?" I poke his forehead and keep my finger there. Lowering my voice, I continue in a hiss. "Listen, you asshole. I don't care if you play games with me, but you don't mess with my little sister. Understood?"

"Understood." Michael nods because there's not much else to say, and apologizing has clearly not occurred to him. Not that I want an apology; it would mean nothing coming from him.

I'm about to walk out, but Bella pushes in between us, grabs my hand, and stops me. "Wait." She frowns as she looks me over. "Do you mind if I ask when you were seeing him?"

"He broke up with me in late December," I say, and a flash of shock crosses her delicate features. I don't want to involve Frankie any more than I have to, so I don't mention he was also seeing her at that time. "You too, huh?" Arching a brow at Michael, I take great pleasure in seeing him go pale.

"Fuck you, Michael," Bella says, and she heads back into the bedroom.

"Yeah. Fuck you, Michael," I repeat, and as I turn my back to him, I feel a little bit lighter. Poor Bella; she'll be so hurt and angry with herself, but she couldn't have known. After all, I fell for it too.

It's rush hour, so getting a cab isn't easy. I wave one

down, but it stops on the other side of the street and someone else gets in. I sigh in frustration as I'm tired and all I want to do is go back to bed. As I'm about to head for the train instead, I hear heels clicking behind me. It's Bella, and she's crying.

"Hey," I say, turning around. "I'm sorry."

"For what? You didn't do anything." She sniffs and wipes her cheeks. "Thank you. At least I know now." Then she burst into tears again and covers her face with her hands. "I thought he loved me."

Being Michael's ex, I don't know if it's inappropriate, but I give her a hug anyway. "You didn't deserve that. No one does."

Bella nods and takes the tissue I hand her. "You're nice."

"And you seem very sweet. I know it's hard, but it's probably best to forget about him." Finally, a cab comes toward us, and I wave it down. "I'm going home. Can I drop you off somewhere?"

74

SILVA

"So, what are you going to do with this lovely apartment?" Trinny asks. She's all ears as I fill her in on Frankie showing up, my upcoming job interview, and the media circus after the article came out. She's helping me sort out my clothes; I'm packing up to take everything over to Faith's place, and Trinny keeps throwing stuff on a charity pile without asking me. "Yuck. This needs to go, by the way." She tosses the old, green T-shirt over her shoulder, and it lands on the couch with dozens of other garments. I haven't done a proper clear-out in years, and I don't mind her decisions, as it feels like a fresh start.

"I haven't decided yet, but I think I might rent it out. Short-term, to tourists or something. It's very soon to move in together, so I'd still like to have my pad as a backup in case things don't work out between us."

"I doubt that will happen." Trinny smiles at me. "Look, I know the last time you lived with someone ended in a painful breakup, but that was mainly because of you and your..." She pauses. "Your disease. But you're so much better now and it's not the same situation. You need to trust that it's going to work out."

"I do. I have faith."

"That's right, you have Faith," she jokes. "And she's amazing, so don't mess it up."

I nod and turn to my last full bottom drawer that I never use. "Why do I have so much stuff? I haven't even worn these since I was—" I stop myself as I look at a top so small I couldn't even fit my arm in it now. It's painfully confronting, and I find it hard to imagine I once wore this.

Trinny stares at it too, then snatches it out of my hand and throws it on the charity pile. "This can go," she says, then goes through the rest of the clothes. "Actually, all of this can go." She pulls out the whole drawer and turns it upside down on the sofa. "There. All one. Now what? Bathroom?"

"Yeah. Bathroom sounds good. That should be a quick one." I smile, relieved she's skimming over the elephant in the room, as I don't want to think about that time in my life anymore. "So, can we talk about Regga? Why didn't you tell me you'd been seeing him?" I ask, opening the vanity drawers. "You always tell me everything."

"We only went on two dates, and we spent one night together before I saw you at his apartment," she says with a shrug. "I didn't know if it would work out, so I didn't mention it."

"But it's working out?"

"Yeah." Trinny grins from ear to ear as she stares into nothing. "He's a good man, and good men are rare in New York." She hesitates. "And it doesn't bother me that he's older. We're on the same wavelength."

I give her a peck on her cheek and rub her shoulder, delighted to see my sister so happy. She deserves love more than anyone, and I really hope it will work out for them. "An age gap doesn't have to be a problem. He's certainly young at heart."

"He's young in bed too," Trinny says, making me laugh. "He has this—"

"Okay, okay. I don't need to know the details." Grabbing a trash bag, I throw in old towels that are too worn to take to charity, then focus on the excessive amount of expired creams and hair products I never use. "I haven't looked at this stuff in a year, so I'm just going to throw all of it."

"Go for it." Trinny holds open the bag and I empty the drawer. "Good girl, you're so efficient." She points to the other drawer with an amused smirk. "Well, well. What have we here?"

My cheeks heat up when I spot a whole bunch of sex toys in the back. I totally forgot I had them, and I've bought new ones over the years, so I don't need them. "Oh, those are old, and I didn't mean for you to see them," I'm quick to say, then empty the second drawer without examining the contents further.

"Hey, you don't need to throw them away." Trinny slams a hand on the vanity and laughs out loud. "You should see your face. You look so embarrassed."

"I'm not embarrassed. I just don't want you seeing my private stuff, and as I said, they're old." I tie the bag and throw it into the hallway. "Don't you have sex toys, Miss Prim?" Shaking my head, I wave a hand at her. "Actually, never mind. I don't want to know."

"You're right. You don't." Trinny winks. "So, what else can we empty? I like how easy this is. It's giving me great satisfaction." She moves on to the hallway and opens the wardrobe that contains my coats, shoes, and some storage boxes. "How about this one?"

I don't even recognize the first box she pulls out, and when she drops it on the floor, the dust that comes off it makes us both sneeze. "I have no idea what this is," I say, wiping my nose before opening it. I immediately recognize the black garments. "They're my old work tunics."

"Wow. You kept them?" Trinny pulls one out and shakes off the dust.

"I didn't know I still had them." The masseuse tunics are still in good condition, but they're way too small for me now. "They can go too. I'll just have to buy new ones."

"Yeah. You won't fit into those," she says. "Are you nervous about the interview?"

"A little, but I'm confident I can do the job. And when it comes to the big gap in my resume, I'll just have to be honest with them." I beckon Trinny to open a new trash bag and empty the box before folding it up. I don't mind throwing them away because there's nothing sentimental about that period in my life. They belong to the old me, and all I want to do now is focus on the future instead of worrying about history repeating itself. "There." Wiping my hands on my sweatshirt, I lift out another box. "What's next?"

75

FAITH

"Miss Astor?"

"Speaking." I don't recognize the voice on the phone, so I hesitate before I continue. My PR agency is supposed to take press calls, as I'm not comfortable with those and my number is private. "Can I help you?"

"Yes, Miss Astor. I'm so glad I managed to get hold of you. I got your number from Roy Bond. He said you two were close and that it would be okay for me to call you."

"Roy, of course." I internally curse Roy; he promised me never to give my number to anyone. *This better be good.* "What is it?"

"I'm Serena, the curator for the Manhattan Gallery. You might have heard about us?"

"Oh. Hi, Serena." I fall silent, suddenly on high alert at the unexpected high-profile caller. Manhattan Gallery is the biggest in New York, an international player. They showcase current works of new artists whose work has been significantly influential in one way or another. "Of course I'm familiar with Manhattan Gallery," I say, leaning on the kitchen counter.

"Great," she says. "Roy showed me the pictures you took of him—the black-and-white shots. Knowing Roy personally, I was touched by them. I loved how you managed to capture his personality in such a timeless and tasteful way. They're truly delightful. He told me there were many more where those came from, and I was wondering if you were willing to share your other work with me? Perhaps consider an exclusive show at our gallery?"

"An exclusive show?" My heart is racing. I'm a commercial photographer, not an artist. At least, I don't see myself that way. "I was having some fun with friends," I say honestly. "I never meant for my private work to be exhibited. I was doing it for me because I enjoy it. Not that I wouldn't be open to a show," I hastily add. "I'm just surprised. It's unheard of for an institution like yours to even consider someone based on one piece of work."

"That is true," Serena says. "As you probably know, we plan our shows a year ahead, but considering the current zeitgeist connected to you and your work, and everything that's happening in your movement, we would love to shift things around and make space for you. Perhaps we could meet up so I can look at your other shots?"

"I've only photographed six people so far, and I don't know how they'd feel about their pictures being on display," I answer, counting my subjects, who now also include Frankie. "And although the style is the same, they're all very different. Some are dressed, or semi-dressed, one is entirely naked. It all depended on their personalities and what they were comfortable with." I think of Silva and wonder if she'd agree to have her picture hanging in a gallery for everyone to see. I wouldn't blame her or anyone else I've shot if they didn't; the images are very intimate. Roy is clearly keen to be up there, though;

he's always loved the attention, and I suspect his reasons for showing Serena the pictures were partially self-motivated. "I have a couple more shoots planned, but that's still not much."

"I understand, but if your subjects agree, eight to ten is a good number. We're keen to do it sooner rather than later, as we want to ride on the wave of your BPFF collective – Body Positivity For Fashion – and all the media attention around it. Pure work is hard to come by these days, and Roy tells me none of your photographs are reworked or manipulated in any way."

"They're not. I'm done with all that." I smile, happy that Serena appreciates what I'm trying to do. "Okay. How about tomorrow? Are you available?" For an opportunity like this, wasting time seems like a crime. "I can come to the gallery."

"Yes, fantastic. That works for me. Oh, and one more thing," Serena says. "How would you feel about a self-portrait? Naked, perhaps?"

Her suggestion causes immediate anxiety, and I tense up. A self-portrait is my worst nightmare, especially a naked one. I've despised my body for as long as I can remember, and although I'm kinder to myself now and don't feel quite as unattractive, it's still not something I'd willingly put on show. I imagine people studying me, pointing out my flaws—the cellulite on my thighs and my behind, and my belly that is far from perfect. It's a terrifying thought.

"I think it would really strengthen the message," Serena continues when I don't answer. "If you're promoting body positivity with your work, it would make sense for you to include yourself."

"Yes, I suppose you're right," is all I can say because she really does have a point. "I'll think about it."

"Excellent." Serena clears her throat. "I'm very much

looking forward to meeting you tomorrow, Miss Astor. Have a great day."

I'm shaking after I've hung up. Contradicting emotions are coursing through me, clashing in my core. I'm so excited that Manhattan Gallery is interested in my work, but including myself in the show is a whole different story. I'm not as brave as people think. All I did was walk out on a shoot on a whim of anger, and anyone can do that. It's not the same as showing oneself to the world in such a vulnerable state. Especially for someone like me. As I head to the living room, Silva walks in with her last suitcases.

"Hey, beautiful. We're done. Trinny just left," she says and kisses me. "Are you okay?"

"Yes." I smile and kiss her back, buzzing with contradicting feelings; anxious from the phone call and overjoyed at the sight of her things piled up in a corner of the room. Silva is here to stay and today is the beginning of the rest of our lives. "Welcome home, babe."

"Thank you. So, we're really doing this, huh?"

"We are. You and me." I glance at her boxes as I wrap my arms around her waist. "Is that all?"

Silva shrugs. "I enjoyed getting rid of stuff. It felt so good to let go of the past that I got carried away, but when it comes down to it, I don't need much apart from you."

"You're sweet." When I bury myself in her embrace, I feel the tension drop from my shoulders. "So you don't feel sad about leaving your apartment?"

"Not at all. It's just a shell." She chuckles. "And your shell is much nicer, so it's a no-brainer."

"I'm glad you like my pad. Our pad," I correct myself. I laugh and look up at her, meeting her twinkling gray eyes. "I'll help you unpack, but first we need to talk. I just got an unexpected phone call, and it concerns you too."

76

SILVA

"How about this?" I say when Faith has updated me on her conversation with the curator. "I'll agree to having my naked portrait on display in the most prominent gallery in the US if you do the same."

She flinches and shuffles on the spot. "I don't know if I can do it."

"If I can do it, so can you. I think it could be cathartic." Brushing her hair behind her ears, I smile and kiss her forehead. "Why don't you try it now? See how you feel? Then at least you can let Serena know tomorrow."

Faith frowns and is lost in thought for a moment, then nods. "Okay, I'll give it a go. It's just..." She swallows hard. "It's the scariest thing I've ever done. I don't even like looking in the mirror, let alone eternalizing myself."

"You're beautiful," I say and take her in my arms. "You're so, so beautiful, Faith."

Faith buries her face in my neck and sighs. "You make me feel beautiful. You make a difference, and I feel better now that I'm working out, but having others see me is not the same." She inches back and looks at me pensively.

"Serena is right, though. I can't go around promoting a realistic portrayal of women if I'm not brave enough to put myself out there."

"She has a point but it's still your choice. You always have a choice."

"I know." She turns and heads for her bedroom. "Okay, I'll give it a go."

"Can I come in?" I ask, knocking on the bedroom door. Faith has been in there for so long that I want to check she's okay.

"Yeah. Come in." She's lying on her bed naked, curled up into a ball. Her camera is on a stand, facing the bed, and the lights are dimmed so low I can barely see her. "This sucks. It doesn't work if I do it myself," she says. "I keep trying to shoot myself from the most flattering angle, and that's not the point. That's cheating. I need to capture the real me, as I am, but I have no idea how to do that."

I lean over her to kiss her temple. "Want me to give it a go?"

She looks up at me and frowns. "You want to take my picture?"

"Yes, I'd like to try. I'm no professional like you, but I see you and I adore you." I walk over to the stand and bring her the camera. "Can you explain how this works?"

Faith gives me a small smile and nods. "I'll set it to auto-zoom. If you stand over there, that should work," she says, pointing to the stand.

"Okay. Can I turn up the lights a little?"

"Yeah. I suppose we should do that. I used the third setting on the lamp for the others and for you. I cheated on the light too," she admits.

"Let's not cheat, shall we?" The room brightens a little as I change the setting on the industrial lamp, and I marvel at her gorgeous body. "It's not that bright. Are you okay with this?"

"I think so." Faith reminds me of myself when I was lying there, waiting to be captured in my most vulnerable state. "What should I do?" she asks.

"Turn on your front with your face by the foot of the bed, then raise yourself onto your elbows and look at me."

"But... then my ass will be in the picture."

"Exactly. And you have a gorgeous ass." It's what she does in the mornings when she's about to get out of bed. We always share one more kiss while she's in this pose, and I feel like it captures Faith when she's with me like nothing else. When it's just her and me, she doesn't worry about what she looks like. She just wants to kiss me, and I love running my hands over her behind. "Please don't cover yourself up," I say when she shifts position and drags the sheets over her. "You don't need those."

Faith flinches as I pull them away, but she doesn't protest and gets into position, raising her upper body and steadying herself on her elbows. Her full breasts look tantalizing. "Try it and see what you think. As I said, you don't have to use these photos. It's your choice."

Faith takes another couple of deep breaths and nods. "Okay. I'm ready."

"You're perfect." I kneel in front of her, and when I kiss her, she moans against my mouth. We haven't kissed in hours, and as always when that happens, we crave each other like nothing else. I pull away and smile as I bring my mouth to her ear. "You look so yummy, I want to get onto that bed and fuck you from behind."

A soft gasp escapes her. She's got that look in her eyes

now. That look that is meant just for me. Getting up and stepping back, I start snapping away. I have no idea what I'm doing, but the way she looks at me is perfect. I can only hope that the pictures are sharp enough, as the zoom keeps changing and I'm not sure if that's a good or a bad thing. I can't stop to ask her about it; I can't interrupt the moment.

After I've taken so many shots that I'm out of film, I put the camera to the side. "Don't move." I get on the bed and lean over her so I can stroke her hair and kiss her neck.

"Mmm..." Faith shivers, and I continue to kiss her shoulders and her spine while I trace her curves with my fingertips. Her hips shift in anticipation and the soft murmurs that escape her don't lie. When I move lower to caress the insides of her thighs, she spreads her legs a little, allowing me access to the pool of wetness that always makes me squirm when I touch her.

"Please tie me up," she says in a whisper. "I want you."

77

FAITH

"Here's what I have so far." I hand Serena the portfolio of 11x17 black-and-white photographs. Sipping the water her assistant brought, I nervously wait as she studies them one by one. Her eyes linger on the first shot of Silva for so long that I'm starting to think she doesn't like it, but then she smiles and turns to the next shot of her.

"Who is this woman? Do you know her well?" she asks, her eyes never leaving the photograph.

"It's Silva, my girlfriend," I say, proudly glancing at the picture of Silva's naked body and the white cast with my doodles all over it.

"Your girlfriend?" Serena looks up at me for a split second, and I wonder what she's thinking. "I love these," she finally says, caressing the photograph with her fingertips. "I can tell that you're lovers. The way she looks into the camera is intensely captivating."

"Thank you." I chew my lip while she studies the other shots, lingering on one of the photographs of my sister.

"Frankie Goldstein," she says. "Your sister."

"Yes. She's living with me at the moment."

Serena's smile widens. "I hardly recognize her. I've only ever seen glamour shots of her. How did she feel about these?"

"A little apprehensive at first." I understand where Serena is coming from. Devoid of makeup, Frankie's hardly recognizable. She's smiling through a mouthful of her burger like she doesn't care what anyone thinks of her. There's a blob of ketchup on her lip, and the Hello Kitty pajamas make her look like a kid. She was so shocked when I asked her last night that I didn't expect her to let me use them, but after I showed her the photographs of the others and myself, she said she was proud to be a part of it. "She's okay with it, though," I say. "Everyone has agreed to be on display."

"Great. Because I love these too." Serena takes her time to study the rest of the portraits, then hands my portfolio back. "Beautiful. Absolutely breathtaking. Imagine the impact when they're enlarged against white walls."

"So, you're happy to go ahead with it?" I ask, trying not to gloat.

"Yes. Just one thing, though. Have you thought about what we discussed on the phone?"

I nod and pull a brown envelope from my purse. "I took these last night. I developed them overnight, so I haven't had time to add them to the file yet. I'm still not sure if I want to include them in the show, but I'd like you to look at them."

Serena opens the envelope and pulls out my self-portraits, or rather the shots Silva took of me. I stared at them for hours before I came here, still deciding whether to bring them or not. Silva thinks they're great, but I'm in two minds because it's hard not to focus on my flaws. I don't look amazing, but I am stripped back to nothing but myself, and the images are pure and haunting. The emotion on my face is a mixture of desire and insecurity; a fascinating story told by the glimmer of fear in my eyes and the flirty smile on my lips.

They're not as sharp as I'd like them to be. Silva didn't get the focus perfect, and therefore they look more like amateur shots. From a creative perspective, however, that makes them all the more interesting, and they still blend in well with the others.

I feel sick when Serena studies my naked body at length; if there was ever a time to feel self-conscious, it's now. The cellulite on my thighs is visible, even in a lying position. "What do you think?" I ask. The devil inside me tricks me into thinking she's disgusted by me, but my creative brain argues there's something special about them.

"They're stunning." Serena lays them out before her and starts swapping them around, changing the order. "This one," she says, pointing to the first picture. "This will be our marketing piece."

"Really?" My stomach drops as I narrow my eyes at the shot I like the least. Lying on my front, my left breast is squashed to the front, its nipple pointing to the camera. The other breast is tucked underneath me, like they're rebelling, blatantly refusing to sit pretty. "I'm not so sure about that one."

"Yet you brought it along." Serena smiles at me. "You know it's good, even if you don't like the way you look."

"Hmm..." I hesitate, realizing she's right. "I'm sure you can tell I didn't take these shots. My girlfriend did."

Serena nods. "That doesn't mean it's not your work. It's your concept. She just pressed the button. This body of work is as much about you as it is about your subjects, and by handing her the reins, you chose to let go of control. You could have used a remote or a timer, but you didn't." She taps the picture confidently. "And now I'd like you to hand over control to me and trust me when I tell you this shot is what we need for our lead image."

Needing a moment to think it over, I sit back and stare at myself. This picture will be on the gallery's website, their social media, advertised throughout the city on billboards and on the front of all the brochures. If anyone is crazy enough to buy it, it will be hanging in someone's home or office. I'm not sure what would be worse: someone buying it or no one buying it because I'm too unattractive to look at. But if I don't take the leap now, why did I do it in the first place?

"I'm afraid," I say honestly. "But yes, go ahead. You can use anything you want."

78

SILVA

Walking at a fast pace, I notice my leg feels much stronger already. It still frustrates me that my abilities are limited, but I'm not in pain and I'm glad that life is returning to normal. The sun feels wonderful on my face, and Central Park is green and filled with spring flowers and cherry blossoms. Stopping for a few push-ups to get our heart rate up, Faith and I watch runners, mothers with strollers, and commuters pass while buskers and food vans set up for the day.

"Spring always reminds me of why I love New York," Faith says, raising her chin skyward to catch the sun on her face. "When the jumble of cultures that live here start spending more time outside and parks become a melting pot of music, food, art, and self-expression." She glances at two men walking hand in hand. "Anyone can be themselves here. There's no judgment on looks, sexual preference, or lifestyle."

She's right; on the streets, diversity and curves are celebrated, and women proudly flaunt their bodies no matter what size. It's behind closed doors where the obsession becomes a problem, in worlds inaccessible to the general public, like fashion and high society. Through Faith, I've had a glimpse of those closed-off worlds, and I don't envy her. "Yeah. We're lucky to live here and I wouldn't want to live anywhere else, but I struggle with the winters. Being outside without a coat again feels so liberating, don't you think?"

"I especially like that I can see your ass in those leggings now that it's not covered by layers," Faith retorts with a flirty look while she breathes through her last push-up.

"Oh, yeah? You like it?" I get up and playfully slap her behind. "Well, I like yours very much too. So much so, I'm a bit nervous about that new dress you're wearing tonight. I might not be able to keep my hands off you." My core flutters as my mind goes back to this morning when Faith tried it on in front of me. The dress was sent to her by the designer she did the runway shoot for during New York Fashion Week. Now that she's become a spokesperson promoting body positivity and diversity, she's getting a lot of praise from the media. Everyone suddenly wants to be her friend, so she's received numerous gift packages from brands that want to start working with the BPFF collective. When I saw her in the silver, backless gown, I had to restrain myself from peeling the delicate fabric from her gorgeous, curvy body. "I still haven't stopped thinking about it."

Faith laughs and shakes her head. "I'm not sure if I'm going to wear it yet. It's a bit too revealing for my liking, but then again, I'll be on display naked soon, so I suppose it doesn't matter all that much."

Heading for our usual workout spot, we start jogging at a slow pace. My ankle can just about handle it, but I'm careful not to put too much pressure on my joints, as I'll have to be on my feet all night. BPFF is throwing a networking event for three hundred people at one of New York's most prominent clubs. With so many wanting to be seen doing the right thing now that the media frenzy has reached its peak, Faith expects a huge turnout with big names and a lot of media attention. *Zero* magazine will have to make a choice: attend and engage in the dialogue or ignore their invite. Either way, everyone will be made to feel welcome if they're willing to talk, no matter what side of the fence they're on.

"You look more than decent in it, babe." Reaching a quiet spot in the park, I take her hand and pull her over the lawn to a cherry blossom tree. When Faith leans against it to catch her breath, light pours through the blossom roof, leaving a leafy pattern on her face. I want to tell her she looks mesmerizing, but her beauty makes me lost for words.

"Do you need a rest?" she asks.

"No. I just wanted some privacy," I say, lowering my gaze to her cleavage, then back up to her angelic face. Cupping her cheeks, I lean in to kiss her.

"Mmm..." Faith embraces me and welcomes my mouth with soft moans. Her hands slowly roam over my back, and she kisses me back like we have all the time in the world. It's crazy how we can kiss until our lips are sore, how we never seem to get enough of each other. The scent of spring is in the air, and I shiver at the breeze on my back as she lifts my T-shirt to run her hand over my skin. The wind picks up, and as we break apart, hundreds of pink petals fall upon us, settling in our hair and on our shoulders. The magical sight of Faith smiling in the blossom rain slays me. She's a delight to look at; so pure and sweet, yet there's the undeniable desire in her eyes that manifests every time we kiss.

"Do you want to go home, petal princess?" I ask, brushing a petal away from her ear. "We could continue this in bed? I have a couple of hours before my interview."

"Yes." Faith bites her lip as she stares at my mouth. "But kiss me again before we go," she whispers. "I have a feeling I'm going to remember this moment forever."

I feel it too; there's something special about today. The sun's warm rays kiss our faces, the wind's gentle arms embrace us, and nature is celebrating our love with petal rain. Although we haven't said those words, I know there's a lot of love between us. The yearning inside me when we're apart, the overwhelming longing to be near her when she's with me, and our deep connection and mutual trust are ever-present. I think we both realize how lucky we are to have found each other, to have recognized such light in another person. Locking my eyes with Faith's, I brush a loose lock of hair away from her face, and as I kiss her tenderly, my heart swells with love for her.

79

FAITH

Shahari, who offered to take care of the organization for us, has done a great job. There's enough space for everyone to sit, and the additional standing tables are placed close enough for people to mingle because that's the point of tonight; people should mingle. Elsie and Malay are the best spokespeople out of all of us, so they'll be giving a speech during the evening. We also have a DJ and a band for entertainment, and there's plenty of finger food and cocktails to go around. The sound of elevated chatter over the music pleases me, the turnout is good, and the general vibe is positive.

Our collective—now twelve-strong—is spread out over the floor so we'll be able to welcome everyone personally and tell them about what we stand for and what we aspire to build: a wider network of artists and models who celebrate and promote diversity, body positivity, and realism in fashion and marketing.

Silva is looking incredibly sexy in her tuxedo, and I have no doubt women envy me for having her by my side. In my circles, many of them swing both ways, but only a few act on their desires openly. Without a shirt or bra underneath, the jacket covers enough of Silva's breasts to pass for decent, leaving me a sensational glimpse of her cleavage. If I wasn't on duty, I'd scan the club for a dark corner because I'm dying to kiss her senseless, but that's out of the question for now.

"There she is," Silva whispers when Valerie walks in. "I'll go get you a drink so you can talk. What do you want?"

"Thank you. Just water would be lovely." I'm craving alcohol to soothe my nerves, but needing to be entirely clearheaded for this, I've refrained from having anything at all. Valerie gives me a nod, then looks to Elsie and Regga as if deciding which one of us to talk to first. Valerie's never been one to shy away, and although I don't like her, I applaud her courage for coming here personally instead of sending one of her editors. Finally, she settles on me and heads my way, her assistant rushing behind her with her purse and the iPad that is permanently glued to his hands.

"I'll have a sparkling water with cucumber," she says to him, waving in the direction of the bar before she turns to me. "Faith."

"Valerie." I paint on a smile. "Thank you for coming, I appreciate it. Would you like to sit?" I ask, gesturing to the booth next to us.

Valerie shakes her head and adjusts her cape, then casually leans on the standing table. "I don't have much time. I have somewhere else I need to be." Dropping a pause, she takes in the crowd, her eyes darting from one table to the next while she assesses the respective rank of each guest. I don't think she'd expected to see so many big names here and to be entirely honest, neither had I. "But there's something I'd like to discuss briefly so if you have time, that would be great."

"I'm all ears," I say, blowing Silva a kiss as she hands me my drink and backs away to give us privacy. Valerie looks like she'd rather chew off her own arm than be here, but she maintains her calm. She must have been pressured by the *Zero* shareholders to come here, and that thought amuses me. She may be the most powerful woman in fashion, but the big guys who pay her salary only care about sales. In our world, being current equals sales, and with all the press here, our collective is as current as it gets.

"We would like to do an edition on body positivity," she says in a robotic tone. "Our personal issues aside, this is something *Zero* magazine would like to champion more in the future, and being positive role models yourselves, we'd love to have you, Elsie, and Regga as our visual guest editors for the July edition." There's a glimmer of frustration in her ever-expressionless glare, and I struggle to force back a chuckle. "We were thinking something along the lines of unretouched celebrity shoots, a vacation special on beach-wear for each body type, and interviews with some of BPFF's members."

"That's fantastic. I'm so honored you thought of us." I pat her arm, and from the way Valerie winces, I sense she hates being touched. "And I'm glad this is a topic you're planning on featuring more. It's important to set the right example for your readers," I add, rubbing salt in her wound.

"Of course," Valerie says. When her assistant arrives with her sparkling water, her eyes shoot poison at him. "What took you so long?" She waves him off. "Never mind, I'm almost done here. Can you get the car ready in five?" The minion shoots off, and she sighs dramatically as she continues. "Where was I? Oh yes, the July issue. So, you'd be interested?"

“I’d have to discuss it with the others, of course, but I’m sure we can make it work.”

“Excellent. I’ll have my assistant call you to set up a brainstorming meeting with my senior team in the coming week. It’s a quick turnaround, so we’ll have to be flexible. Please bring as many ideas to the table as you can.”

“No problem.” I’m surprised when she holds out a perfectly manicured hand to shake mine. I never expected an apology, but by Valerie’s standards, it’s close enough. “Enjoy your night, Faith.”

As soon as she’s out of sight, Elsie comes over to me, her eyes wide with curiosity. “And?” she asks. “What happened just now?”

I smile at my new friend, then pull her in for a hug. “Elsie, it looks like we’re winning.”

80

SILVA

"He's handsome, don't you think?"

"Who? Regga?" I'm glad Trinny is here so I have someone to talk to while Faith is busy with her guests. By now, I know quite a few of them, but they have more important things to do than keep me entertained, so Trinny and I have made ourselves comfortable in a booth with a cocktail apiece. Trinny's glowing face and the sparkle in her eyes are adorable, and she hasn't stopped gushing about Regga for a minute. I finally have a reason to tease her back and I'm embracing every opportunity she hands me.

"Yeah, he's so rough and rugged."

"He's so rough and rugged," I repeat in a mocking tone. "Just kidding, sis. You're cute when you're in love."

"I know. I'm super cute," Trinny says with a wink. Faith is talking to Regga and another man, and she blows me a kiss when we look their way. "How is your lovely girlfriend doing? Is she ready for her exhibition?" she asks.

"She's still got two more shoots planned for her final few images, but her new work looks fantastic." I pull my phone out of my pocket to show Trinny the image of Faith on the gallery's website. "She's the teaser for her own show. Isn't that cool?"

"Wow, I've never seen her without makeup. She looks so natural and pretty."

"That's my girl. She's gorgeous." I lock eyes with Faith and sigh. "God, I love her."

"Then tell her that." Trinny arches a brow. "Seriously, why wouldn't you?"

"I will." I hesitate. "I don't know why it's so scary to say it out loud. I suppose it's just been a long time since I had such strong feelings for someone."

"Love is scary, Sil. But you two are good. There's no doubt about that."

"I know, and I can't imagine not being with her." I pause, considering the idea that's been forming in my head in the past few days. "I want to throw Faith a celebratory dinner after her show opening. Just with her closest friends and some of the new people from BPFF."

"That's a great idea," Trinny says. "Have you discussed it? Can I come?" She presses her palms together in a pleading gesture. "With my plus-one?"

"Of course you're both invited," I say with a chuckle. "But no, I haven't brought it up. Faith is funny about doing things that put her at the center of attention. She's been a ball of nerves about the exhibition, but I think she'd welcome an intimate dinner. She deserves to celebrate after everything she's achieved."

"Totally. She never gives herself enough credit. Can I help?"

"If you have time between your crazy busy job and your new 'young in bed' lover," I say with a smirk. "How do you find the time to meet up with him anyway? You barely have time to have lunch with me once a week."

"We've been seeing each other late at night, mainly." A blush rises to Trinny's cheeks. "But I'm planning on taking it a bit easier soon. I might even turn some cases down so I can actually have a life."

"A life?" I throw my head back and laugh. "I didn't think you were interested in having a life. Does Regga have anything to do with this?"

Trinny rolls her eyes and sighs. "Let's just say I've discovered the joys of simple things. This. A night out with you, new friends, a new man in my life..." She downs the rest of her cocktail and points to Faith. "Now that I come to think of it, I have your lady to thank for all that."

"Are you guys talking about me?" Faith asks as she joins us.

"Yes. But only good things," Trinny says, before giving her a hug. "Aren't you supposed to be out there?"

"I'm taking a break so I can spend some time with my hot girlfriend." Faith smiles. "Did Silva tell you about her interview?"

"Yes, I heard it went well, so I'm keeping my fingers crossed for her." Trinny scoots over so Faith can sit, but she perches on my lap instead.

"Thanks, but I'm going to sit right here. That woman over there by the bar asked me who the handsome woman in the tux was, so I'm making a point." She turns to me, and I feel the heat rise to my cheeks when she kisses me in a way she's never kissed me in public before. "There. Now everyone knows you're mine."

"If that woman's got eyes for anyone, it will be for you," I say, snaking an arm around her waist. "So I guess I'll have to make my point too." I kiss her again until Trinny slams a hand on the table.

"Stop it, you two. I'm right here."

"Sorry." Faith laughs and wipes the lipstick traces from my mouth. "Where were we?" she asks, her expression nothing but mischief. "Oh, the interview. I have a good feeling about it."

"Yeah, me too," Trinny says, rolling her eyes when she sees my hand has slipped into Faith's dress. "She used to practice on me when she was an apprentice."

"I know she's good." Faith says, shooting me a knowing look. "I nearly caught fire when she massaged me the first time."

"Gross. That's my sister, Faith. I obviously wasn't talking about that kind of massage." Trinny gets up and sighs dramatically, but I know she's putting on a show. "Okay. You have your moment. I'm going to get us more drinks. You clearly need some alone time."

81

FAITH

I shiver as I study myself on the tall, white wall at the gallery entrance. The first piece people will see when they walk in is a huge black-and-white photograph of me, naked. Enlarged, the cellulite on my behind is clearly visible, and I still can't look at my breasts at that weird angle without panic threatening to take over. The portrait is called "In the Mirror," which seemed a fitting title considering it's a true reflection of me. The hint of discomfort in my eyes, my flirtatious smile, and the rawness of it all makes it difficult to look at, at least for me.

I'm about to view my work before the show opens tomorrow and I'm shaking with nerves. There's no way of knowing if the selected photographs really work together until I see them all hanging in the large space, and this being my first non-commercial work on display, I'm terrified of the art critics.

"What do you think?" Serena joins me and hands me a takeout coffee.

"It's confronting," I say. "I'm highly uncomfortable."

"It's beautiful." She puts a hand on my lower back and

turns to me. "I know this is hard for you. You're very brave to put yourself out there, but don't linger on it for too long. We'll come back to it." She gestures to the main space. "Let's have a look at the rest together. I'm happy with the arrangement, but if you'd like to swap things around, I have the team here for another few hours."

Turning the corner, I gasp as I look around. The high-gloss black-and-white portraits printed on aluminum are stunning against the white backdrop. Frankie's portrait, titled "I'm Hungry," is the first, and it's shocking to see it so large. Then there's Shahari with his hairy chest and wild hair and beard, hugging his equally rugged dog. This one is called "Best Buds." I walk on to the third picture of Roy in his camp pajamas. He's staring into the lens with a charismatic grin that would make any gay man swoon. He insisted I title it "Mr. Handsome," so I did.

Next is Elsie, sitting on the edge of the bed, naked with her legs crossed, confidently showing off plenty of mahogany skin. Her portrait is called "Proud." Regga's portrait, "Behind the Lens," shows him holding his camera and taking a picture of me while I take a picture of him, my vague reflection visible in his big lens. The deep frown of concentration between his brows looks magnificent close up, and the prominent laughter lines around his eyes make him look all the more charming.

Malay's portrait, titled "This is Me," shows her sitting topless, her lower body covered by the sheets. With one breast significantly smaller than the other, her photographs are always retouched, and on the catwalk, she uses bra fillers. Malay refuses to have surgical work done on her body, and her portrait is a celebration of beautiful imperfection. It's the first time the dark-skinned top model is showing the world what she really looks like, but unlike me, she's not nervous for people to see her, and I admire her for that.

The second to last photograph is one of the three models who were criticized by their agency and editors. Free of makeup in white tank tops and white briefs, they look so young and innocent, and they're lying next to each other like they're watching a movie during a sleepover. It's called "Fired for Being Fat." The title is a shocking contrast to their lean, young bodies, which sums up the fashion industry in a nutshell. With their permission, I printed their names underneath, their body weight, and the institutions that let them go. I suppose this will spark quite some controversy, but I'm ready to defend my work, and the girls are comfortable with it.

Finally, on the sidewall before the exit, is my favorite portrait. The one of Silva. I love her smile, her body, her casted leg that in a way represents our journey, and the intrusively personal look of desire in her eyes... It's called "My Girl," and although I'm not usually one to praise my own work, I do genuinely love her picture. Seeing them all together, I couldn't be more pleased.

"It's good, right?" Serena smiles as she looks at me sideways. "They all work very well together."

"Yeah." I sound surprised, and frankly, I am. "I'm glad I came here today. I wasn't sure if I wanted to see the show before the opening because I was worried I might have a breakdown if I didn't like it. But yeah, it's good." I sigh as I feel my anxiety sliding off me. "The past weeks have been stressful, and I've had sleepless nights over this exhibition."

"Then you'll sleep like a baby tonight." Serena beckons me to follow her. "The flow of the pieces makes total sense aesthetically speaking, and when the viewer leaves—" She turns the corner to the two doors that say "entrance" and "exit." "—this will be the last piece they see for the second time. The first and the last always make a lasting impression. Your photographs are fabulous, but this is what people will be talking about."

Again, I stare up at my own portrait, but this time, it doesn't feel as daunting. Seeing my work has calmed my state of mind and I feel more accepting of myself. Yes, I'm a good photographer. I'm talented and I'm loved and there's nothing more I could wish for. That, up there, is me. I'm not perfect, but it's me, and right now, I'm willing to accept myself. Silva accepts me. She makes me feel beautiful, and now that I look at myself for the second time, I also see my love for her. Silva is the first person I've had such deep feelings for that I feel like I can't live without her. *I love her.* My heart skips a beat at the realization. I love her like I've never loved anyone. I love her wholeheartedly, fully, endlessly. I love her to the end of the world and back.

82

SILVA

I imagined art people to be like the fashion crowd, but I couldn't have been more wrong. They're dressed differently and way more understated. Instead of flaunting wild prints, bold colors, and crazy statement pieces, the men and women here wear suits and simple dresses in muted tones, which makes them look more like wealthy bankers. They don't raise their voices, and no one is drawing attention to themselves. It's not as much of a competition, I suppose, and I like that. It's clear that this is where the real money is; they feel no need to show off, and they have not come with the intention of gaining anything from tonight. They want to view Faith's work and maybe buy one of her pieces. No one is fazed by Malay and Frankie mingling with the crowd. Being world-famous models, they tend to draw a lot of attention at fashion events but here, I'm not even sure anyone knows who they are, or perhaps the people here simply don't care.

The event is elegant in a minimalist way. The vast, white space, the absence of standing tables, the bright, white spotlights, and the clean, almost clinical smell are refreshing. There are no decorations, not even a bar. Caterers in black slacks and white shirts bring flutes with champagne and bottles of water in from the office in the back. The floor is so shiny you could eat from it, and the absence of music or any other distraction ensures all attention is upon Faith's work. It's easy to identify the critics, as they're the only ones carrying notepads, and it's hard to read them. They've mainly kept to themselves, and I haven't overheard them talking to anyone, but Faith told me she's had very good feedback so far.

"How does it feel to be famous?" Trinny asks. "Everyone knows who you are now."

"I'm not famous, I'm just the woman in the cast," I say with a chuckle. "It's weird to be recognized from a naked picture, though, and as proud as I am of Faith, I don't think I'll be hanging around here much over the course of the exhibition. I feel like they're picturing me naked when they're talking to me."

"I get that. But you're okay with it, right?"

"Yes," I say wholeheartedly. "I'm totally okay with it. It's hard to believe that I've gone from a girl who nearly starved herself to death to a woman who posed naked after putting on a few extra pounds." I've come a long way, I realize as I utter the words. I lost control over my obsessive regime, but I got through it, and it's made me see that I'm stronger than I thought I was. The constant fear of falling back into old habits has subsided, and the fact that I'm here now in this bizarre situation is a testament to that. "I actually like myself in that picture," I continue. "It's a timestamp of a very special day, and it expresses perfectly how I felt in that moment."

"You're not the only one who likes it." Trinny lowers her voice. "I spoke to Roy. He told me some woman is buying the whole collection. That includes the one of you."

"Really?"

"Yeah. She's convinced this is the start of a new career for Faith, and she wants to be the first to profit from it. Her name is Celia something. Complicated last name, I don't remember. Anyway, you're sold."

I laugh and curl an arm around Faith's waist as she joins us. "Hello, beautiful girlfriend. I hear I'm sold."

"Almost," Faith says, leaning into me. "Serena is preparing the paperwork as we speak." Her eyes widen in excitement as she continues in a whisper. "Isn't that crazy? I thought I'd be lucky to sell one, but a collector snatched them up before anyone else had the chance to. Not that I'm doing it for the money."

"You always undersell yourself. You're way more talented than you think."

"I agree with that," Roy says, arriving with a bottle of champagne to top us up. Frankie's arm is hooked through his, and she looks so much better than a few weeks ago. Her skin is glowing, her cheeks have filled out, and she looks rested.

"I'm proud of you, sis. The photographs are spectacular. Well, apart from the one of me," she adds jokingly. "I can't believe someone bought a picture of me eating a burger with ketchup dripping down my chin."

Faith laughs. "I disagree. You look adorable." She shakes her head when Roy holds up the bottle. "No, thank you, not for me. I've been talking all night, so I'm too tired for a drink. I'd probably fall asleep standing up and besides, I'm having a drink with Celia Krugerner, the buyer, after she's finalized the sale, which will be any moment. Will you join us?" she asks me.

"Of course, babe. Who is she?" I follow Faith's gaze as she gestures to a dark-haired woman across the room. Everything about her oozes money; her designer heels and purse, her elegant, demure cream-colored dress, the diamond studs in her ears, and the simple, pearl necklace around her neck. She's accompanied by a handsome, exotic-looking woman in a black suit, who looks equally wealthy.

"An American-Swiss art collector. She's quite well-known in her circles apparently." Faith grins sheepishly. "Serena got incredibly excited when Celia walked in, but this whole art world is new to me, so I didn't even know who she was. The other woman is her girlfriend, Erin, and they're both very nice." She turns to Frankie, Trinny, and Roy. "Do you guys mind if I leave you to it for the rest of the night? I'd like to go home as soon as we can."

"Of course not. Regga and I will be leaving soon anyway," Trinny says.

"And Roy is taking me to a secret midnight movie—" Frankie stops herself, and her face pulls into a baffled expression as she glances at the entrance. "Well, well. Look who's decided to grace us with her presence."

"Huh." Faith stares at their mother, who stands at the other end of the gallery, looking up at Faith's work. Although I've never met her in person, I recognize her from the pictures I've seen. She hasn't spotted Faith or Frankie and seems engrossed in the photographs, particularly the one of Frankie. I can't tell whether she's horrified or she likes it.

"I sent her an invite," Faith says, "but she never replied so I didn't think she'd show up tonight."

"She hasn't returned my calls either," Frankie whispers. "I haven't heard from her in weeks."

Faith squeezes my hand and turns to me. "Excuse me for a moment. She doesn't look like she's going to move from her spot anytime soon, so I'd better go and say hi."

83

FAITH

"Mom?" My mother is still fixated on Frankie's photograph, so I tap her shoulder and she snaps out of it.

"Faith..." She blinks a couple of times, then looks at the photograph again and turns back to me. "This is your work," she says, stating the obvious.

"Yes." I'm not sure what else to add. "Thank you for coming." I notice a few subtle glances being cast our way. In the art world, everyone knows who my mother is. She's a big name, and unlike me, I suppose the critics were expecting her tonight.

"You're very good." Mom finally meets my eyes, and I feel a lump form in my throat when I register a glimmer of emotion in her gaze. "You're very, very talented, Faith."

"Thank you. I appreciate that." I point to the photograph of Frankie. "Do you like that one? I noticed you were staring at it."

She remains silent for long moments, looking me over like she's never seen me before. "I've been a terrible mother."

I refrain from answering, as I can't possibly disagree with that. "Frankie hasn't been well," I say instead. "She was weak and exhausted, but she's doing much better now."

Mom nods. "Thank you for taking care of her. I didn't know..." She takes a deep breath. "I wasn't myself. I'm still not myself."

"I know." I give her a small smile, letting her know I understand. My mother has a brilliant mind, but she's always suffered through life, only thriving when her art is thriving. Being a mother always came second to her art.

"It's not just Frankie. I've been a bad mother to you too." Mom pauses. "I know it's too late for an apology, but I want you to know that I've read all about what you've done lately, and I'm so proud of you." Her eyes are glazed, and she seems completely sincere.

"Thank you." I'm dumbfounded by her out-of-character behavior. Mom rarely shows her emotions. She's not cold, but she's one of those people who cry in silence; a woman who hates to display her vulnerability in any way. Yet, she's the most broken and vulnerable person I know, and the sad truth is, I can't fix her.

"You're a good person, Faith. A caring person. God knows you didn't get that from me," she says, her voice breaking.

"That's not true. You're not a bad person," I say in a whisper, not wanting anyone to listen in on our conversation. "I know you struggle, and I knew you'd be back at some point. You always reappear, and I'm okay with that. I don't need to be taken care of. Frankie, on the other hand, she's still young and she needs stability, so it's probably best if she continues to live with me for a while."

"Yes, that's probably for the best," she agrees in a thin voice, then pulls me in for a hug. Tears trickle down her cheeks when Frankie joins us, and she gives her a hug too. "Hi, baby. You look good."

"So do you," Frankie says, even though Mom looks far from good. She's frail and looks visibly older than when I last saw her, five months ago.

Mom manages a small smile and takes both our hands. "Can we have dinner together soon? I'm trying my best to get out of this... this black hole. And I'm getting there. I just need some more time." She hesitates. "I've never told you this, but I tried antidepressants a long time ago. They made me worse because I wasn't able to create when I was on them, and that brought me so much despair, I couldn't function at all. It was like my mind was numb, like the pills absorbed every last ounce of creativity I had in me." She shrugs. "But my doctor has assured me there are plenty of new options on the market now, and I'm willing to try them all, if that means I can be more stable for the both of you."

"Do you mean that?" Frankie hugs her again and holds her tight. My heart cries for my sister because she genuinely needs her mother, and maybe Mom can finally be a semi-stable presence in her life.

"Yes. I promise I will try everything. And your father and I..." Mom looks at Frankie. "We're taking a break. He'll be moving out as soon as he's found a suitable apartment. It's for the best."

I'm not jumping with joy yet, as this has happened numerous times before, but something inside me tells me that maybe, just maybe she's come to her senses about Andrew. That maybe she's finally seen a glimpse of who he truly is, now that she's focusing on getting better. I don't want to comment, as this is Frankie's father we're talking about. Frankie has no idea how he fucked me up and how much I hate him. He's still her father, and she loves him, after all.

Mom looks around, suddenly realizing she's being watched, so she straightens her back and clears her throat. "Anyway, this is not the time for private conversations. You, Faith, have produced truly brave and ground-breaking work, and you sisters should celebrate. I'm going now, but I'll be in touch. Is that okay?"

"Please do," I say, and I mean it.

"Oh, and one more thing." She turns to me. "I learned you have a girlfriend. To be honest with you, it's the last thing I expected, but I'm very happy for you. Is she here?"

"Yes. Her name is Silva, and that's her," I say, waving over the love of my life. "Can I introduce you before you leave?"

84

SILVA

"Your mother seems nice," I say when we close the door behind us.

"I think she's getting a little better." Faith smiles. "She liked you, I could tell. Not that it matters what she thinks," she adds. "But yes, she genuinely liked you."

"Of course it matters." I've been holding back on this subject for far too long, and it's time that I speak my mind. "You always pretend like you don't care when I bring her up, but she's still your mother. And I saw the emotion in your eyes when you talked to her." I pull her in and cup her face. "You don't have to pretend that you're strong for me all the time. It's okay to be vulnerable and to want your mother, no matter how useless she's been. It's okay to love her."

Faith stares at me, but she doesn't answer. She's made up excuses her entire life, telling herself she doesn't need anyone, especially not her mother. But she let me in, and I know she needs me as much as I need her, so that excuse doesn't fly with me anymore. I just hope she knows she can trust me with her feelings when it comes to her family. "Talk to me, babe."

Faith meets my eyes and nods. "Okay," she whispers. "Here's the truth. I'm cautious because I'm scared to be disappointed, mostly for Frankie. It's not the first time Mom's promised to make an effort, but it is the first time she's mentioned getting medical help, and that gives me a tiny spark of hope." Her voice trembles as she continues. "I'll admit that I was happy to see her tonight. It made me feel valued, I suppose. It made me feel like she cared."

"She cares." I kiss Faith's forehead and pull her in. "She may not be the best mother, but she cares, and I believe she loves you both very much, even if she finds it hard to express that love."

Faith nods. "But she always put Andrew first. And a good mother should put her children before anything. She failed me and she failed Frankie, so no matter how hard she tries I won't be singing her praises anytime soon."

"I understand that, but maybe you can try to accept her for who she is. She's not perfect, but she's your mother and —" I bite my tongue because I realize I'm in no state to defend Mary Astor-Goldstein, knowing what Faith's been through. It's easy for me to say all these things; my parents are loving parents in the traditional sense. I may not see them that often because they live in Hawaii, but they'll be here in a heartbeat if I need them. "I'm sorry. I know it's not that simple."

"It isn't." Faith runs a hand through my hair and looks at me pensively. "But maybe you're right. Maybe I should let go of my frustrations and try to accept her. I don't feel anger toward her. It's more disappointment because she's never been there when I needed her. You and Roy are the closest to a real connection I've ever felt and with you, it's..." Her voice trails away and she hesitates. "It's deep."

"It's love," I whisper, sincerely hoping my words won't scare her.

"Yes. It's love." Faith smiles and brushes her lips against mine. "I love you, Silva."

"I love you too." I want to hug her and kiss her and tell her how beautiful she is all at once, but I'm so overwhelmed by my feelings for her that I don't know what to do first.

Faith takes the decision for me and kisses me tenderly. "I know you love me. I can feel it in everything you say and do," she whispers. The featherlight caress of her lips grows more urgent when she pushes her body into mine.

I want her closer and sliding my hands through her hair and down her back, I push her coat off her shoulders, never taking my lips off hers. She's the light inside me; the angel that silences the devil's foul lies. She's the fuel that makes me stronger every day, and the hope that guides me forward. And as we fall into an embrace, our lips locked and our hearts sealed, she pours all her love into me, and I pour all my love into her. Sinking into the bath of her tenderness, I absorb everything she gives me, and it fills me with warmth and joy.

Faith inches away to look at me. Her eyes are filled with promise and glistening with emotion. When a tear rolls down her cheek, I kiss it away and stroke her face. "I love you," I whisper again, and her lips pull into a smile. With every look, every touch, every kiss we've shared, we've moved into a better place together, and I can't wait to see what the future holds for us.

She takes my hand and kisses it, then leads me to our bedroom where she strips, slowly, deliberately. Her suit jacket, her white, satin blouse, her heels, her black slacks, and finally her lingerie, fall to the floor around her. Pulling her hair out of its barrette, she shakes it loose until her dark locks cascade over her shoulders. Faith stands completely naked before me, and all I can do is stare at her. *My Faith.* The sensual action feels almost ritualistic like she's literally giving herself to me, handing me the key to her bare soul because I see her.

When I do nothing, she walks over to the nightstand and takes out the silk ties I've used to tie her to the bed. "Here," she says, placing them in the palm of my hand. "I'm yours."

85

FAITH

I wake up to Silva's beautiful face for the second time this morning when she brings me coffee and scrambled eggs in bed. Neither of us had to get up early, and we made love in the morning light before we fell back asleep. To me, March is a month of hope and light, a gentle ease from the winter darkness. The sunshine streaming through my thin, linen curtains and the sound of the city while I'm lying in Silva's arms makes me feel like I'm part of something bigger, something that makes so much more sense than my old life. She's here to stay; she's not going anywhere, and I haven't felt the urge to abuse my body in weeks. I'm in a place where I can finally be proud of myself. I believe my career is moving in an interesting direction, and the world has taken well to our little collective that is growing by the day. BPFF has had a lot of coverage. It's sparked dialogue and challenged brands and magazines to respond to the issues we've raised, and my exhibition is an extension of that. It's an exciting time, a time of change.

"Good morning, babe." Silva kisses my forehead and

smiles that ridiculously cute smile of hers before getting into bed with me. "How are you feeling?"

"I'm feeling great." Stretching out, I align my body with hers and sigh. I love her body heat, it's so intimate and comforting. "I slept really well, although I woke up once because there was noise coming from the kitchen."

"Noise from what?" she asks, grimacing as she suspects what's coming.

I chuckle and shoot her an adoring look. "You were rearranging the fridge again in your sleep."

"Oh, no. I'm so sorry I woke you up."

"It's okay. You were having a great time, but I still pulled you back to the bedroom eventually and you happily complied."

Silva buries her face in her hands and laughs. "I did think it looked super tidy when I opened it to get the eggs."

"Yeah, I bet that made your day," I tease her. "At least I'll never have a messy fridge with you living here."

"That's for sure." She sits up and sips her coffee. "How do you feel about the show? You must be over the moon that you sold the whole collection."

"Honestly, it couldn't have gone any better, but I'm also glad it's over. Some of the people there were quite intimidating. I'm not used to talking art."

"I would have never guessed. You seemed really confident," Silva says. "I was actually surprised you didn't want to stay longer and celebrate your show. Not that I'm complaining. Last night was special."

"Yeah. It was very special to me too." Remembering our conversation before I surrendered to her, butterflies swarm through my core. "And I was happy to leave early. Celia and Erin were lovely, but I'm not one for celebrating anything personal, especially not with strangers."

"Why not?" Silva asks. "What about birthdays?"

"I don't like birthdays," I say. "My mother used to say it was nonsense, that every day should be celebrated and that there was nothing positive about growing older, so why make a point of it? I never had a birthday party until I was old enough to organize my own. Not because she didn't love me. She just didn't think it was a big deal and always had her head in the clouds. When she felt inspired to paint, mundane things such as birthdays and practical life in general were not high on her list, and when she was down, suffering from an artistic block, she didn't feel like doing anything at all. Frankie always got lavish parties. Her father made sure of that. But me, never. My mother is self-centered. I suspect she may have some serious mental health issues too, but she claims her mood swings are purely connected to her work, so I stopped bringing it up a long time ago."

"I'm so sorry to hear that." Silva's eyes meet mine and she strokes my hair.

"It's okay. Once I met Roy, he always made sure I at least acknowledged my birthdays. He would take me out and get us into the most sought-after parties. It wasn't necessarily what I wanted, but I appreciated his efforts and went along with it. I've never experienced that feeling of excitement, though. Not with birthdays or Christmas or anything for that matter. I just didn't grow up with it." I smile at her. "What about you?"

"Trinny and I are blessed with super devoted and traditional parents who embrace any excuse to celebrate," Silva says, "It was all very wholesome."

"I'm not surprised. They seem so sweet." My phone lights up, and I reply to a message from Roy, confirming I'll be ready to leave at midday. He's taking me to a spa this afternoon. I wanted to spend the day with Silva, as I've been so busy that we haven't seen much of each other, but she insisted that I go with him and enjoy myself. "It's Roy. Are you sure you don't want to come with us?" I ask, already missing her.

"Yes, I'm sure. I'll be here when you come back. You and Roy need some alone time. I'm always around when he comes over, and I'm worried he's holding back because of me."

"Roy? Holding back?" I laugh. "Does he ever sound like he's holding back?"

"No," Silva admits with a chuckle. "I've never met anyone so frank in my life."

"Well, then. He really likes you."

"I like him too, but not today. I'm actually going shopping with Frankie and Trinny." She raises a brow when I laugh even harder. "What's so funny about that?"

"You hate shopping."

"And Frankie hates spas." Silva shrugs. "She suggested we go shopping instead, and it seemed like a fun idea. I want to get to know her better, and Trinny is always up for browsing stores, so I thought why not spend the afternoon with the three of us while you're stewing in your mud bath?"

"Okay." I narrow my eyes at Silva, as something about her story seems a little off. It's the way her voice went up a notch like she's nervous or something. I let it slide because this is not a time for interrogation. Frankie has perked up after staying with us for two weeks, and Silva is a good influence on her. Besides, I really want her to get to know Frankie better too. I never thought I'd be living here with my girlfriend and my sister, but here we are, and it works. I'm so grateful to finally have that sisterly bond, and I'm also incredibly grateful for the woman in my bed—in our bed.

The one who pulled me out of my negativity and made me see that I'm enough.

"What are you thinking?" Silva asks as my mind drifts again.

"I'm thinking that everything is good. I'm so happy." I turn to her and smile. "You make me happy, but above all, I make myself happy too."

"I'm so glad you're feeling better in yourself," she says, taking my hand.

"Me too. Self-loathing is a horrible emotion."

Silva nods. "It may not always be like this. It may become hard to control urges when life gets tough, but I'll be here for you, like I know you'll be here for me." Her fingertips caress my hair as she looks into my eyes. "I meant what I said last night. I love you."

What we have is strong and deep; so strong, it feels like our souls are entwined. We understand each other on every level, from our biggest fears to our greatest desires, and I felt our love before I even realized what it was. "I love you too," I whisper. "And I can't imagine a life without you."

"You don't ever have to be without me." Silva's eyes well up, and so do mine. It's the most beautiful gift I could wish for. The gift of love is everything.

86

SILVA

Frankie is decorating and Trinny is helping me in the kitchen. Four hours isn't much, but we're all hands on deck while we're singing along to Frankie's playlist. Faith has no idea we're throwing her a surprise dinner, and Roy's been instructed to keep her in the spa for as long as he can and message me when they're on their way back.

"What do you think?" Frankie yells over the music as she points to the dining table that we've moved into the living room. She's pulled out the sides and laid it out for twelve, with a brand-new white tablecloth and matching napkins. Candles and white roses grace the center of the table, and she's even gone out of her way to get more wineglasses that match Faith's old ones, as she didn't have enough. She's also secured iridescent helium balloons to the backrests of all chairs, and it looks spectacular.

"So pretty," I say, grinning when I imagine the look on Faith's face when she walks in.

"Good, then that's one thing done." She joins us in the kitchen. "So, what's on the menu? What can I do? I've never cooked Japanese before, so you'll have to guide me through it."

"We're almost done with the sushi," I say, gesturing to the twelve rolls on the counter. "The gyozas need filling and folding, so maybe you can help Trinny with that? And if you don't mind boiling the edamame beans in a pan with salty water, that would be great too. We're also making seaweed salad and okonomiyaki—they're savory pancakes—and we need to grill the rib eye, but we can do that last minute."

"That sounds totally yummy." Frankie steals a piece of sushi and moans as she bites into it. "Delicious."

"Talking about delicious, don't forget about the endless supply of sake!" Trinny chips in. "Nothing better than hot sake to get the party started."

"I don't think I've ever had sake." Frankie picks up one of the bottles and studies it. "Does Faith like this?"

"She does." Trinny takes the bottle from her, fills three ceramic shot glasses, and places them in the microwave to heat up.

"Hmm... I can't believe how little I know about her." Frankie sighs. "At least I have time to make up for that, now that I'm not so busy anymore."

"Sorry you're having trouble getting work," I say. "But you know it's for the best, right? You were close to collapsing when you showed up here."

"I know. And it's okay. I was actually thinking of applying for pilot school. I'm in the lucky position that my father can pay for it, and I've always wanted to learn to fly."

"Frankie, that's amazing. Have you told your parents about it?"

Frankie shakes her head. "Not yet. Mom and Dad are separating again, so I'll wait until I catch Dad on his own.

He's so busy with work." She turns to me. "What did you think of my mother?"

"She was very nice to me. She also seemed a bit out of it, but Faith told me that's nothing out of the ordinary."

"Yeah. She goes through phases where she shuts herself away from the world, both physically and mentally, but she always crawls out eventually. It's something I've learned to live with."

"I'm sorry to hear that." Trinny rubs Frankie's shoulder. "So why flying?"

Frankie watches Trinny make a gyoza, then fiddles with the dough as she tries to replicate it. "It's something practical, and unlike modeling, I could do it for the rest of my life. I'm a little sick of art and fashion. It's too emotional for me, too draining, too fake, and being a pilot seems like a wonderfully straightforward profession. You get people from A to B and make sure they get there safely. Don't get me wrong, I'm under no impression that flying is simple in any way, but it's practical, there's no bullshit involved, and I love being in the air. Just sitting on a plane gives me such a sense of freedom. I can't even begin to imagine how great it must feel to operate an aircraft."

"Silva has a good friend who's a captain. Perhaps you could introduce them, Silva?" Trinny suggests.

Frankie nods eagerly. "That would be great. I'd love to talk to someone about the course and their day-to-day job."

"No problem, I can arrange that. You sound like you've given this a lot of thought," I say, delighted to see the excitement in her eyes.

"Yeah. I've had some time to think here, to clear my mind. It's been good for me." Frankie looks at me intently. "I'm very grateful to you and Faith. Thank you."

"That's sweet, but I didn't do anything."

"You did. You made me feel welcome, and you've been my friend. Like Faith, I didn't have many real friends, but I think that's going to change. And I'm looking forward to tonight."

"So are we. You're a lovely girl, Frankie. You have your whole life ahead of you, and you're going to be an amazing pilot." Trinny takes the shot glasses out of the microwave and hands them out. "Here's one to get us going."

"Oh, God, I feel tipsy smelling it," I say and clink my glass against Trinny's and Frankie's. "Here's to new friends, new opportunities, to the future, and to love."

87

FAITH

"How was that for a pampering session, girl?" Roy rolls his shoulders, then pats his rosy cheeks before we get into the cab.

"That was so good," I say, feeling genuinely rejuvenated after hours of indulgence. We've used the pool, the sauna, and the steam room, and we've had mud baths, facials, and mani-pedis. "We smell amazing, don't we?"

"Fresh as a daisy. We look amazing too. We should do this more often."

"I'm in. I've got plenty of time before I start thinking about my next show," I say. "Want to come to my place for a drink? I've got some champagne cold, and I think I deserve a glass after last night's success."

"Totally. I'm always up for bubbles, and it will be nice to see Silva and Frankie," Roy says as he types a message on his phone. "That is, if they're back from their shopping trip."

I frown and look him over. "I didn't tell you they went shopping."

Roy shrugs and shoots me a grin. "I have Silva's number. We've been messaging."

"Hmm... that's cute. So, what do you guys talk about?" Continuing to stare at him, I wonder what's going on because Silva never mentioned anything about being in contact with Roy.

"Hey, what's that look for?" he asks, pointing to my face with a roaring laugh. "Are you worried we talk about you? Of course we do. We gossip about you all the time." He nudges me as the cab comes to a halt. "Come on, let's have a cold glass of bubbles to end this fabulous day."

I'm surprised at how dark it is when we enter my apartment. I tend to leave the curtains open, and even after dark, the city lights fill the living room with a faint glow. As I'm about to flip the switch, someone beats me to it, and as I blink and let my eyes adjust, I register that not only Silva and Frankie are here, but also Trinny, Shahari, and everyone from BPFF. They're all gathered around the beautifully decorated table in the living room, which is laid out with all my favorite Japanese dishes that Silva often cooks for me. When Roy and I walk in, everyone starts clapping, cheering, and drumming the table. I gasp and slam a hand in front of my mouth, and it takes me a while to find my words.

"Oh my God," I finally say, wiping my eyes when I realize this is a surprise, and that someone has gone through all this trouble for me. "It's so great to see you all. What's going on?"

"We thought it was time that you started celebrating your success," Silva says. She gets up, takes my hand, and leads me to the free chair at the head of the table. "Because you should be so proud of yourself. We're all very proud of you."

"I'm..." The lump in my throat prevents me from answering, so I hug her and hold her tight as tears start flowing. "Thank you."

"I mean it," she whispers in my ear. "You deserve every bit of credit and more. I hope you don't mind we threw a little party for you."

"Not at all, this is so sweet." I inch back, smile at my friends around the table, and laugh through my tears when I see the seven ceramic carafes on the table. "Let me guess. Hot sake?" By the looks of them, they've already had a few glasses; Trinny looks especially chirpy.

"Yes, and only the best of the best," Frankie says with a grin. "This stuff is so good." Hand me your glass, big sis. Let me pour you one."

EPILOGUE

FAITH

It's New Year's Day. While New York is still lying dormant under a thick layer of snow, I smile as I watch Silva sleep. Her steady breathing is soothing, and the way her lashes flutter tells me she's dreaming. She has vivid dreams, and she still sleepwalks, which is adorable. Last week, she got up and mumbled something about finding the right box for my ring. She can't keep surprises from me; she gives them away in her sleep, but I pretend not to know.

One year ago, to the day, Silva came into my life, and I thank my lucky stars and my drunken self for booking her the night before. Even though I was in a foggy state, the memory of our first morning is so vivid. I remember what we talked about, and I remember our walk in the snow. I think I sensed it then, that she was special, as I never open up to strangers like that. After I met her, everything changed for the better, and I know that I've made a positive impact on her life too.

I kiss her forehead, and she instinctively pulls me closer as she wakes.

"Good morning, beautiful." Silva's first words are always

the same, even if we've had one of our rare arguments. In love, everything is forgiven; in love, there's only one way, and that's forward. I love her more than words can describe. "It's a special day," she mumbles and kisses me like she's kissing me for the first time.

"It's a very special day," I whisper, staring into her beautiful, gray eyes. "I know it's not our anniversary, but it does feel like that, don't you think?"

"Yeah. I was thinking about that last night—how I had no idea last year how much my life was going to change on January first."

"Tell me about it. I didn't even know I was gay a year ago, let alone that I'd meet the woman who was the love of my life. I love you, Silva."

"I love you too. So, so much, you have no idea." Silva smiles and kisses me softly, then strokes my hair with a contented sigh. "How are you feeling?" she asks, referring to the champagne we had at Regga's apartment while we watched the fireworks from his rooftop last night. Trinny, who moved in with him a few months ago, threw a spectacular New Year's Eve party and we didn't get back until late. We celebrated a year of change. Our collective is still growing, and although we haven't solved the issues we raised, there's a lot more awareness now and we're proud and comfortable with the job choices we make.

"Not too bad. My head is a little sore."

"Mine too. I might need an aspirin," she says, grimacing as she rubs her temple. "It was a fun night, though. So worth it."

"Trinny and Regga were great hosts," I agree. "But what I loved most was coming home together and starting the new year in bed with you. I'm so glad you don't have to work today." Silva got the job, and she's loving her new life as a sports masseuse and personal trainer at the high-end gym that is only a fifteen-minute walk from here. There are many perks, but the best one for me is that we get to spend more time together.

"Yes, it's so nice to be employed again," she retorts playfully. "And every morning, I get to wake up with you is amazing. I just want you to know that I don't take you for granted."

"I know." Taking in Silva's gorgeous face, I still feel the same insane attraction, only now it's smothered in a thick layer of deep, unconditional love. I know her so well, and although on the surface she seems relaxed, there's also a hint of nervousness in her sleepy gaze and an underlying message in her words that tells me she might pop the question today.

Wanting her to be at ease, I wiggle myself out of her grip and kiss her before I sit up. "How about I make us some breakfast and get you that aspirin? I'll check on Frankie to see if she's hungry." Frankie, who is still living here, is hunting for an apartment, but she's taking her sweet time and that's fine with us. She likes being here, and that makes me a proud sister. "And I was thinking maybe we could go for a walk after breakfast if you're up for it? It's a beautiful, clear day."

"I think we've been rubbing off on each other," Silva jokes. "Me with a hangover and you suggesting an early morning walk in the freezing cold. What happened to us?"

"I think it's called synergy, babe." I cup her face and run my thumb over her cheek. "We've taken over each other's good habits as well as our bad habits, and somewhere, we've found a sweet spot in between."

"I think your spot is slightly sweeter than mine today," she says. Pulling me back down, she silences me with a kiss when I'm about to protest. "Wait. Don't get up yet. There's something I need to tell you."

"Okay..." My pulse starts racing as she reaches over to the nightstand drawer to open it, and before she's even done anything, my excitement takes over and I'm unable to stop myself. "Yes!" I yell with a nervous giggle. "Yes, yes, yes!"

"What?" Silva looks dumbfounded, and she stares at me in disbelief as she takes out a small, black box. "How did you know what I was going to do? Did Frankie tell you?"

"You kind of gave it away," I say with a huge smile. "In your sleep."

"Oh." Silva rolls her eyes and laughs. "I have to admit I was worried about that, but I genuinely thought I'd gotten away with it." Her cheeks are rosy as she hesitates, her eyes lingering on mine. "So... was that a 'yes' I heard?"

"It was, but I got carried away. I still want you to ask me," I say with a goofy smile.

Silva can't stop smiling either. She straddles me in nothing but her underwear, opens the box that contains a beautiful diamond ring, and takes my hand. "Faith Astor, my friend, my love..." Although she already knows my answer, her voice is still unsteady as she continues. "You've always had my commitment and eternal love, but by giving you this ring I want to show you how serious I am about you, and that I'll do anything to make you happy every day for the rest of your life. Will you please marry me?"

"Of course I want to marry you." Failing to swallow down the lump in my throat, I burst out in floods of happy tears. "How could I not?"

Silva's eyes well up too as she slides the ring onto my finger and kisses it. "We're doing this," she says.

"We're really doing this. You and me." I wrap my arms tightly around her and pull her down into a long, tender kiss. A year ago, something very special began, and today is the first day of the rest of our lives. We're happy, secure in ourselves, or as secure as we can be, and we have love. Lots of love. Silva makes me smile every day. She thinks I'm beautiful and I believe her. And that makes all the difference.

AFTERWORD

I hope you've loved reading *In the Mirror* as much as I've loved writing it. If you've enjoyed this book, would you consider rating it and leaving a review? Reviews are very important to authors and I'd be really grateful!

ACKNOWLEDGMENTS

I'm so grateful to everyone who has opened up to me about their struggles with eating disorders. Your stories have given me valuable insights and helped me gain a deeper understanding of the psychology behind, in some cases, a never-ending fight. So thank you for trusting me, I know from experience it's not easy to talk about such incredibly deep-rooted issues. I wish you all the love and strength for the future and hope you remain well.

ABOUT THE AUTHOR

Lise Gold is an author of lesbian romance. Her romantic attitude, enthusiasm for travel and love for feel good stories form the heartland of her writing. Born in London to a Norwegian mother and English father, and growing up between the UK, Norway, Zambia and the Netherlands, she feels at home pretty much everywhere and has an unending curiosity for new destinations. She goes by 'write what you know' and is often found in exotic locations doing research or getting inspired for her next novel.

Working as a designer for fifteen years and singing semi-professionally, Lise has always been a creative at heart. Her novels are the result of a quest for a new passion after resigning from her design job in 2018. Since the launch of Lily's Fire in 2017, she has written several romantic novels and also writes erotica under the pen name Madeleine Taylor.

When not writing from her kitchen table, Lise can be found cooking, at the gym or singing her heart out somewhere, preferably country or blues. She lives in London with her dogs El Comandante and Bubba.

ALSO BY LISE GOLD

Lily's Fire

Beyond the Skyline

The Cruise

French Summer

Fireflies

Northern Lights

Southern Roots

Eastern Nights

Western Shores

Northern Vows

Living

The Scent of Rome

Blue

The Next Life

Welcome to Paradise

After Sunset

Writing as Madeleine Taylor

The Good Girl

Online

Masquerade

Santa's Favorite

Made in the USA
Las Vegas, NV
07 October 2022

56712703R00225